SOUL OF SALVATION

THE DIVIDE
BOOK TWO

ALI STUEBBE

Editor: Stevi Mager (Instagram: @stevimager)

Proofreader: Callista Morgan (Instagram: @callistamorgen)

Cover Designer: Jaqueline Kropmanns (Instagram: @jaquelinekropmanns.coverdesign)

Map Artist: Zoe Holland (Instagram: @artworkbyzoeholland)

Character Art: Marina Ceban (Instagram: @cebanart) / Zoe Holland (Instagram: artworkbyzoeholland)

Unsplash Images: Luca Bravo, Peter Forster, and Lance Reis

TRIGGER WARNINGS

-Violence/Gore/Death
-Grief
-Profanity
-Mention of suicidal intent
-Alcohol use for coping
-Torture
-Overall dark themes

This book is 18+ with explicit language and sexual scenes. SoS is the second book in the duology. You must read book one first, Blood of Desiderium.

If you ever find yourself in need of someone to talk to, there are always people wanting to help when you are ready.

The National Suicide Prevention Lifeline
Call: 1-800-273-8255
Crisis text line: Text "HELLO" to 741741

Mortal Lands

Court of Abhain

Court of Asch

Court of Arbos

Court of Amhall

Court of Asta

Deadrum

PRONUNCIATION GUIDE

Deyadrum - (De-yay-drum)
Helestria - (Hel-es-tree-a)
Asiza - Ah-see-za
Amihan - (Ah-me-han)
Asov - (Ay-sov)
Ahbainn - (Ah-vein)
Tsisana - (Tsee-sah-nah)
Gehendra - (Ge-hen-dra)
Masiren - (Maz-ren)
Zoraida - (Zor-ay-da)
Draven - (Drav-en)
Mauve - (Mohv)
Telion - (Tel-EE-on)
Whiro - (Were-oh)
Ragon - (Ray-gun)

For everyone caught in a silent battle, find your army because there are no rules that say you must fight alone. Together, you can all sharpen your swords.

PROLOGUE

Emma

*E*verything is dark and so fucking cold.

Time is lost here. Each day that passes sharpens me into an indestructible weapon, hardening me from the inside out. I don't know how long it's been since I stepped through the portal. Since the final buzz of life that brushed over my skin as I was simultaneously met with ropes of shadows bound around my wrists. Only to watch the portal close in on itself and disappear from existence, signifying a world left behind while I stood shackled in a new prison I'd have to get accustomed to.

I've grown used to the dark, as I see myself mirrored in it. A sort of kinship recognized within. As for the cold, it's become a comfort, which is expected when nothing here exudes life or light. It's nothing like what was lost beyond the portal that day. The feathering heat of a gentle touch, the warmth of tender words brushing over my skin, and the fire of hope for a free life that I thought would blaze for eternity. All of it...gone. A dream that remains out of reach, and a home that is now lost to me.

But this new prison...it speaks to me and the darkness within. Since coming here, countless Fae have been gifted to me to test my powers on, and the thrill of each kill rushes through my blood. Allowing me to feed off the terror that shines back in their gazes.

When called upon, I'm brought down from my tower and greeted with a new set of eyes that have yet to accept death. Each task has varied from male to female, and old to young. And yet, they look at me like I could be their salvation. Unbeknownst to them, my soul holds no tune. No symphony to play them a final song. Because they don't matter. They are only a means to an end. A showcase of my growth in power for my father. And these tasks are commands to prove that.

The first task, I was told to weave my shadow around a slender female's neck and snap it.

The second task, I had to fill the male's veins until they burst from within.

The third was to lift the Fae as high as I could, only to slam him on the stone before my feet.

With each one, the kill becomes something I crave. To watch as my shadows penetrate their body and claim their life as mine. And if they hope they can sway me to spare them, then they are sorely mistaken.

Because I'm their worst fucking nightmare.

PART I

CHAPTER ONE

Emma

*T*he black ice living in my veins thrums violently with power from the Fae on his knees before me. The whisper's hurried words in my psyche overlap one another in a whirlwind that drones similarly to how someone's heart might race, or how their skin might tingle with quick breaths. All because of the impending death before me.

But…I feel nothing for him, not even the smallest speck of remorse. My pulse ticks in a steady rhythm. Unperturbed. There's no ache in the organ beating quietly in my chest or a frantic pounding racing in my ears, knowing he's slowly dying in this realm as his flesh sinks deeper into his cheekbones. The tone of his skin grows paler by the minute, and his limbs tremble to hold his own weight.

I block the whispers enough to focus as I stare down at the male, showing nothing across my face. Slowly, I tilt my head to the side. Waiting for…something. Knowing deep down the blood on my hands from every kill will never wash away and that it should haunt me. But not even a tinge of regret or burn of pain surfaces as the black pool of my eyes never blinks away from the plea filling his.

What does it matter to him if I kill him now? His heart will stop, and his lungs will cease to fill with air, anyway. His body will continue to suffer the effects of being rejected in Whiro's true home, Gehendra. A realm that is livable to solely gods and the place I have been for who knows how long. The realm where a Fae's body can't handle the atmosphere after a certain period of time.

Time…

No, time does not exist here. There is no light. No way to tell when the day begins or ends. Time simply bleeds together in a disorienting loop, a never-ending fall. Much like the drop off the cliff that lingers a few feet behind the male silently begging me to spare his life. Or how the featherlight specks of ashes hang high in the air. Unmoving. Frozen in the air as if the realm is holding its breath.

The *clicking* of sharp talons on stone breaks my focus on the Fae and I slowly turn my head towards the creature responsible. My chest starts to rise and fall roughly as frustration heats under my skin. I press my lips together, holding back the volcano of annoyance that wants to burst out of me from the interruption.

"Sire, let me have him. Such a pity to waste perfectly good food by having this one let him waste away before she kills him." The ghoul's grated voice causes my jaw to quickly clench right before it spits at my feet. The bluish-grey hue of its skin stretches thinly over its skeletal frame, and its lean muscles twitch when it crouches down like it's ready to pounce on the Fae in front of me.

I tear my eyes off the ghoul and bring them to my father's, expecting him to reprimand his infuriating creature. Except he's not looking at the ghoul. He's looking at me. Watching. Waiting. As if curious to see how I'll handle the situation.

I straighten my spine and shift my body to fully face the hideous ghoul. Whiro is testing me once again to make sure this power has completely consumed me and to prove that I'm capable of being as dark and twisted as him. Whether I'm worth being kept alive in this cursed fate.

But I might as well be a ghost with a beating heart. Death would make no difference.

My eyes stay locked on Whiro as he looms behind the creature. His jet-black arms, which look like they are covered in soot, are crossed over his chest. The rest of his skin is a murky grey with dark blood weaving along his body as if a spider of death rooted itself within. He never wears a shirt, just black pants and shoes that are always decorated with the moving art of his shadows.

I don't waste another moment though as I close my eyes. My own inky veins, crawling under my skin, pulse. Inhaling deeply, I hold my breath and count to three.

One, I let the whispers be free.

Two, my blood begins to vibrate chaotically beneath my skin.

Three, the corner of my mouth tips up wickedly with a twitch.

When the first puff leaves my lungs and touches the air in a freezing kiss, my eyes snap open. Twin orbs of swirling midnight holding a promising threat latch onto the ghoul who shifts on its feet.

I let the coldness of my power radiate outward in a tidal wave, drowning the air with its weight. The freezing touch to my skin drops even more, almost as if one touch will shatter me. My breath plumes in front of my face like a signal of death. A sign that life will never exist here.

The ghoul's enlarged mouth falls open, revealing its narrow, pointed teeth. It inches backward towards Whiro, hoping his master will step in. But my father remains a statue.

The creature's red eyes match those of the Scavengers. Like glowing balls of fire and they flare from the force of my power unleashing around us. Its body tenses and eyes widen the moment black tendrils band around me. Just like its master's.

I should blast a hole through its chest, disintegrating its heart to nothing. But I'd much prefer disgracing it. Proving how *weak* it is. A way to alert the rest of the ghouls that I, too, will be their master. That thought alone blooms the smallest hint of a thrill within; a twisted high of domination, no matter how sick it is.

With a swipe of my hand, a second, stronger wave of power crashes into the ghoul's bony frame. Its bald head slams into the dark stone we stand on as I force my will upon it, commanding my power to pull its lanky arms in front of it to along the sides of its pointed ears. To *bow* for me.

A faint grinding sound snarls through its mangled open nose, even as its body trembles before me. But before it gets a chance to fill the air with its protest, I wrap a silencing shadow around its throat. Muting its feeble retort that I know will come next.

I may not be *the* God of Darkness, but I am his fucking daughter. Therefore, the Goddess of Darkness. These creatures will fear me, serve me, and fucking *bow* to me.

I keep my feet planted and my features placid as my eyes bear down on the restrained ghoul. Reveling in the strength of my power forcing it into submission. But just as quickly, my interest begins to evaporate as a deep huff of air expels from my nose at how pathetically easy that was.

This is just one of the many ghouls dwelling in Gehendra. I've been kept high in the tower with the promise of freedom if I fulfill each task. When I'm ordered down from my room is the only time I cross paths with these creatures as they wander about.

This is a way for Whiro to see my level of strength, but most of all, assess me to see if the light power buried inside from my mother will spring forth. He's been pleased to see no sign of it, hence why this is the longest I've been allowed out of the tower. Lifting my hand, my eyes fall to my wrist donning a bracelet of shadows. A band of his power that still keeps me under Whiro's supervision.

Re-centering my thoughts, I force my mind back to the present. To showing the ghouls that I'm not weak. That I am the player who decides whether these pawns will live or die. A new master to hold the strings of their souls.

I weave a strain of power to grip its jutted chin, lifting it slightly off the ground just enough to force its eyes to connect with mine. "Perhaps you would prefer to die alongside this Fae? It would mean no difference to me."

The coldness of my voice sounds distant to my ears as it causes a more noticeable tremble to rack through its body. I continue to refuse it air by squeezing the collar of my shadow around its throat, watching how its eyes begin to look just like the Fae's. Begging. Pleading with me to not take its life. *Weak*. Because if these creatures fear death, then they would do anything if it meant staying alive. I allow another moment to pass before I call the whispers of my power back to me, letting it disintegrate between us.

Whiro's gaze still never leaves me when I glance up at him. A slight light glints in his corvine eyes, but he speaks before I can figure out what he's thinking. "Why not kill it?"

Such a simple question, and yet…I can tell there is another test underlying his words. Poisonous roots are snaked around each syllable that will bury me six feet under if I say the wrong things. Yet, the numbness of this power, the unfeeling nature of it has me blankly staring at him. Because the outcome of my fate means nothing to me.

I give a half-shrug as he waits for my answer. "It's one of your ghouls, who is now one of mine. I'd rather not kill it when we are on the same side. It would be better to instill fear in it, to make it known that each breath it takes from here on out will be because *I* allowed such a thing. To me, that is far more thrilling than death. Don't you think?"

His charcoal hands rub against the sharp features on his face as his mind seems to turn over my words. Still, he never removes his twin black pits of death from mine. Most would feel fear, maybe shift on their feet, or rub their hands together to be the target of the God of Darkness's gaze. Yet, I remain unnaturally still with no surges of chills or tremors. Only recognition and…a deep-seated desire to take his power like he dared to steal mine before all of this. Only, he doesn't know that.

Aside from the tasks he's given, I've made one of my own. To study *him*, and learn how his mind works, knowing that once my power grows to the level he wishes, my death will soon follow as he reclaims this power. For now, the only thing I can do is to not show the full extent of my power I can feel coursing through my veins, only offering enough to prove it's growing with every task.

A single dip of his chin is the only confirmation I get for passing whatever challenge he secretly created. "You continue to surprise me, *Emmerelda*."

Not even a twitch of a finger is given from me at his words. I let them fade away as I ignore the presence of the ghoul still laying folded on the ground. I face the Fae whose flesh has sunken more under his eyes, darkening like deep craters. His head sways in an attempt to keep his torso upright.

Without looking back at my father, I keep my voice flat as I take a single step towards the male. "May I?"

"He's all yours."

The Fae opens his mouth, but all that escapes his throat is a rough rasp. "No last words?" I taunt in a voice that is less like me and more demonic, as though I'm embodying Death itself. Another straggled rasp coughs up his throat. He's so weak he can't speak.

The energy coursing through my blood grows hungry, getting increasingly colder in anticipation. I raise my hands up in front of me, watching how the black veins swell within me. I don't have to reach far within to grab hold of this power; it's already there on the surface, waiting for me. It reacts to my call as I command it to do what it desires. To take. To deliver death.

Wisps of darkness race out of my hands, slamming into the Fae's chest as I wield it to funnel into his body and wrap around the male's heart. His face morphs with widened eyes and his mouth falls open with a silent gasp. The corner of my eyes lift, relishing in the excitement of fulfilling my power's wants. The beat of his heart grows weaker in my shadowy grasp as I tighten my hold on it. The choice of his life in the palm of my phantom hand.

The icy touch of my power quickly freezes his pulsing heart until it stops. Then, in one swift second, I squeeze. The organ holding his life ceases to exist, shattering in his chest as I watch his body fall back, his knees folding with him. I flex my hand. The sensation of his heart bursting lingers on my skin as if it was my hand in his chest. Yet the skin on my palm is clean, free of blood.

Does it make me a villain to take a life so easily? To take pleasure in the arctic drug that flows through my veins? To wish that my hand was dripping with his life?

I don't waste time on the thoughts as I swipe my hand out, letting my practiced power brush against his lifeless form. It drives him back to the edge of the cliff, making him topple over and fall into the black fog that covers the endless drop.

My eyes are locked on the ledge, waiting to feel something… Nothing but satisfaction comes. Suddenly, my father's voice cuts through the death hanging in the air. "I find much more joy when I can devour their souls and watch their weak vessels turn to ash. But death is death."

When Whiro consumes—feeds from—a Fae, all that is left is a pile of ash at his feet. He doesn't *need* to feed, it's more because he can. If one simply dies with their soul intact, their body remains. Unlike the Corrupted who remain in the Court of Ashes, guarding the court we left from until Whiro needs to use them. They walk amongst the deserted land with souls that are tainted. Poisoned. A stab to the heart will disintegrate them.

A guttural rumble of approval catches in my ears from behind. It draws my gaze to my father—an entity made solely for death and destruction—who turns on his heel before I feel the *pull* of his power.

"Come," he commands as he continues walking along a very narrow path. Both sides are encased by a sea of thick, smothering fog, hiding the never-ending void beneath it.

Turning to follow, I obey.

CHAPTER TWO

Emma

The path we silently walk along looks like it's floating above a forbidding, dusky sea. Gehendra is what most would imagine the deserted depths of death to be like. A vicious misery that clings to the mountains, with a lifeless chill that hums no song of life. Just a broken music box that will never play again. And like the Court of Ashes, there is no stream of air to catch the locks of my hair in its current. The whole realm ceases to breathe.

A skittering echo grates behind me as the ghoul follows from a mindful distance. I keep my steps equal to Whiro's as I swivel my head, noticing how the umbra of the sky matches the deadly hue of the black blood running through my veins. A shadowed moon hangs above, with a dim reddish glow spilling from its edges. It looks like it's breathing fire into the realm, but no warmth is offered. The power slithering within my body masks the chilly air, making me numb to it as white puffs billow out of my nose with every exhale.

There are many jagged stone bridges, all crossing over each other from above and interconnecting with other parts of Whiro's castle. Towering spires rise so high, it looks like they are piercing the moon to make it bleed crimson. Broken mountains are scattered across the distance, suspended on the smog of midnight that swirls along the entire bottom of this realm.

With a subtle breath in, my nose crinkles as a sliver of my curiosity piques. The scent of what I know Death smells like would be that of the Court of Ashes: something foul, or rotten. Even though there is still a constant smell of smoke with ashes dangling in the air, there's also an undertone of something cloying mixed with it. Borderline sweet, with a tinge of bitterness.

"What did you feel when you killed the Fae?" Whiro's voice cuts through my thoughts as if he meant to startle me, but it won't work with this newfound power settled into my soul. I'm too unbothered to be scared. And this power stops him from invading my mind, because it allows me to be strong enough to keep a shield in place that he can't penetrate.

"Nothing," I say without hesitation as I continue to keep pace with him.

My eyes zero in on the back of his head as it slightly nods. "Do you wish to know why he was sentenced to die?"

I keep my feet steady on the deathtrap of a bridge, while specks of stone fall off into the void below with the vibration of each step. "Does it matter? Death is death, after all," I speak calmly to his back, repeating the words he said earlier as we keep trudging forward.

I'm unsure of where he is leading me, but we are approaching the mouth of a mountain brushed with the night sky. The jagged peaks stretch across the land that is attached to the towering castle looming hauntingly above. The same castle I've been kept in, and I am just realizing that if one can't use shadows to travel, the only way in is up the steep, uneven steps. They are chipped so badly that they look one breath away from crumbling to nothing. They have no railing, no wall, and are the same width as these bridges: wide enough for a single body. If you fall and die before you reach the main entrance, then so be it.

Whiro stops abruptly and twists to drag his eyes over me. I halt my steps, keeping my lips sealed together as I wait. He assesses the attire I'm provided here, which is a long, raven-colored dress tunic with dual slits on the sides that kiss my hipbone. Matching black leathers hug my legs with boots to finish it off. My brown hair has been woven into twin braids that fall against the back of my shoulder blades to keep unruly strands from covering my face.

Mostly, it's to keep them from covering the *scars* embedded around my neck. A reminder of a life I lived before, and one that I secretly try to remember more of. The part where my heart found those to cherish. But every time I try to hang onto a memory, the hellish whispers drag me back into the dark. I don't allow my thoughts to convey in my void eyes, shielding myself from my father's critical stare.

Without a word, he spins on his heel and continues taking fluid steps. I've noticed over the time span I have been here that he's softened towards me. Only slightly, because he would still devour my soul without a second thought. But I've pleased him enough to remain breathing for another day. Although, a tinge of acid burns in the back of my throat that there may be a reason for all the tasks he's had me complete. There is something that has burrowed under my skin that makes me question his actions towards me, yet I'm clueless about them.

He guides me through a series of tunnels once we reach the mountain, swallowing us whole as it blocks the semblance of the crimson haze that was given by the devilish moon. Dark, glistening spikes are scattered along the top, like cemented icicles that could kill in one strike if severed. The musty scent of wet, old stone fills the air as I watch a crystal droplet slide off the tip of a spike and splash against the earth.

Various *clicking* sounds merge and echo out from a tunnel to my left. Boisterous grunts funnel out, accompanying the dark silhouettes of hunched ghouls shuffling towards us. Whiro and I keep moving as they become motionless when they notice our presence. One smacks another in the chest before they lower on their haunches as we pass.

Before Whiro brought me out of the tower, he told me about the ghouls, and how there are no secrets between them. The news from another travels at lightning speed as if they share one mind. So, I find my chin raising an inch higher, my shoulders squaring out just slightly, knowing they heard of my shared power with their master. With their *God*. And that they know what I'm capable of.

Whiro pays no mind to them as he takes a right and leads me down a wide staircase. There are no lanterns or torches lit to offer the soft glow that blankets the tunnel, and my curiosity piques again when I notice the source of the light streams from where we are headed. Halfway down the steps, a strong aroma of jasmine washes over me. The floral scent overwhelms my senses to the point of suffocation.

The heel of my boot barely touches the final step and I pause, completely unsure of what my cold eyes are seeing. There's a cadence hovering in the air and it feels like...*life*. Like a distant memory of wind dancing through my hair as I fly under a sea of stars with strong arms wrapped around me. Like the first breath when you break through the water. Of racing hearts and heated skin.

And for the first time since honing this cursed power and becoming this weapon, a tremble skates down my spine. A *feeling* that I'm not used to, that I shouldn't experience anymore. But also *caring* about how it makes me feel, which fucking concerns me.

There are hundreds of wide steps winding around in a circle on the outer edge of a silver pool, spiraling up along the perimeter of the mountain. And in the middle of it all is a waterfall streaming from above in the center.

Craning my head back, I drag my eyes up to towering heights. It's as if the mountain was completely carved out, hollowed to an inch of its life. A shell of monstrosity. The sheer flowing water that moves silently in the middle comes from...nowhere. The peak of the mountain opens to a small circle of light with no connection; it just exists.

There are brushes of little white jasmine flowers wrapping around the cracked pillars that stand tall along the edge of the staircase. Flowers that are in full bloom and thriving in the realm of death. Standing out so brightly against the black, splintered curve of each pillar.

Suddenly, an image flashes of blinding silver eyes looking at me through a midnight sky. There's a dimple attached to a pure smile that causes my breath to hitch as my gaze remains fixed on the flowers. A glimpse of light in a world of darkness.

I shake my head to clear away the memory that felt like lips of warmth that kissed my heart. Whiro stops at the bottom of the platform, right where the stone and water meet. I calmly approach him. He keeps his back to me, staring out at the iridescent liquid filling the entire expanse of the cave.

His shadows dance quietly around his lean frame, giving nothing away for why he brought me here. The moment I reach his side, every muscle locks up. Again, my mind doesn't understand what I'm seeing because this isn't just water. It's something *other*. The pool is not clear, but a shimmery, silver liquid that I can faintly see through if I look hard enough. There are no ripples cascading along the surface, no sound from where the waterfall flows into the center. It's motionless. Mirror-like from the luminescent glow, one that distantly reminds me of a magical light shining in the night that knows my secrets. Another memory from what seems like another life.

But what has me hesitant is the metallic scent that wafts from the water, a smell that is all too similar to blood. And I start to wonder if the flowers hold a purpose, a ploy to mask whatever might lurk beneath the surface.

Because something's *off*.

"You have proven yourself useful to me, Emmerelda." I tear my eyes away from the water and look up at my father, keeping the air still in my lungs.

This is how it has been since he brought me here. He told me that before my mother gave birth to me, my chosen name was Emmerelda. But when she hid me in the Mortal Lands of Helestria, she shortened it to fit it in with my new life. To keep me more protected and not connect me back to the God's daughter. He is constantly calling me by my full name, as if testing out how it sounds. To override the name my mother left behind that I have grown to know. That maybe using the name I was supposed to be given will connect us more. That I am better left alive to be of use by his side.

But even in this state, I much prefer Emma. It's short and sharp, much like my favorite dagger. But deep down, it's because of how it rolled off the tongue of a tattooed winged male, and it ruined all other names for me.

The beat of my poisoned heart is steady and slow as my father waves his hand out to the glistening pool beyond. "This, my daughter, is part of your next task."

16

CHAPTER THREE

Emma

W hiro towers over me so that I have to tip my head back in order to keep my eyes locked on his. To not show fear in the face of death. He clasps his hands together behind his back while his face holds a shred of excitement with the way the corner of his eyes lift.

"I will admit, I was worried you wouldn't accept the darkness when I first brought you here. That you would fight and become more like your mother." He cocks his head to the side as his heartless eyes search mine. "But you seem to revel in the rush of instilling fear. To claim control, since your pathetic life before had you powerless under the guise of a false father." A chilling laugh rumbles from his chest. "You want *power*."

My breath stills in my lungs for a brief moment. He's not asking. He *knows*, since he was able to sink his claws into the deepest, darkest corners of my psyche before all of this. Finding the years of suffering I shoved in a tiny box, hoping to seal away the pain for no one to see. Yet, he brushed away the dust collecting on it and smashed it to bits.

I may have killed King Oren, but the trauma he left me with is still embedded into my soul and the memories are vividly loud. The pain has numbed, but the infliction of every cruel deed is imprinted in my brain, and I don't wish to see it anymore. Unbothered or not, the sight of my blood spilling, of my mother dying, of Cora torn open mid-battle, and the way the Dark Prince looked at me before I stepped through the portal. These are all past reminders I want erased.

The past is a distraction. An annoyance hindering my true goal.

But power…

Power will allow me to make sure none of this happens again. To fully rid myself of who I was and relinquish these memories of loss and torment.

I keep my voice strong when I respond, "Yes. I want power to forget my past self."

That seems to be all he needed to hear because he reaches out, wrapping his long, obsidian fingers around my wrists. He tightens his grip, causing a freezing sting to race around the slender bone. It disintegrates the rope of shadows that have been cuffed around my wrists since I've been here. The rings of power never blocked my own—like the collar King Oren sealed around my neck—but Whiro's cuffs physically kept me in Gehendra and prevented me from leaving this realm. I learned how to portal with my shadows, but these binds confined that ability to only this realm as a way to learn loyalty.

I gently rub my wrist where I can still faintly feel the essence of his power tickling against my skin. Blinking slowly, I drag my eyes to his once more with an unsaid question hanging in the air.

He tucks his arms behind his back again. "I've been in my realm for way too long and have lived more than your young mind can even comprehend, and I'm finding myself growing bored," he says, his eyes narrowing. "You will bring someone to me and if you don't…then I will destroy the lives of everyone in the world you left behind for your failure. So, I suggest you act wisely."

I swallow the unease slithering up my throat. I shouldn't care, but there's this kernel of something building deep within. So much is at stake if I fail. The lives don't matter to me, but failing? That's unacceptable.

"Who?"

The corner of his lips twitches upward before he turns to look back over the water. "The heir to the Court of Asiza. The prince who failed to save you."

Failed? I let myself become this for the battle to end, didn't I? Not giving anyone a choice or even a chance to save me.

For a moment, I want to ask why he wants the prince, but pressure builds behind my skull, blurring memories and muffling truths. The whispers are pounding their fists, demanding the death of Prince Draven. I can feel it in my bones—a sharp ache that desperately wants to drive the sharpest sword through his chest.

I give a sharp nod. "Do you seek revenge?"

He peers at me from the side of his eye. My muscles tense slightly as he fully regards me now. "For once, I don't, but I can see why you would think that." He's silent for a brief moment. "You should have never been able to escape my cells. Only my power was the key that could undo the locks I had in place. So, it seems my power is running through his veins. Then, add that onto the display of shadows he wielded in my library you trespassed in…" He trails off in thought.

The silence grows between us, but I refuse to say a word.

After another minute, he inhales deeply, as if trying to brush away any frustration eating away at him, and then jerks his head to the water before us. "What you see before you is my most cherished love—the Sea of Souls."

My eyes immediately latch back onto the stagnant, polished water, and when I squint my eyes… Bodies. Corpses float beneath in a sterling sea of death. A deep breath fills the air as Whiro's chest expands and deflates. "It's waiting for the next soul I've chosen and the one I must own. You will bring him to me. The moment he is submerged beneath, his soul will be separated from his body and to the world beyond, where even I can't venture."

"The afterlife," I say without taking my gaze off the lifeless eyes watching me below the surface.

"Yes. I may be the God of Darkness, but I cannot go to the afterlife, for I cannot take souls that are already dead."

"Can't the Liminal Stone give you access to the afterlife?"

The muscles in the side of his jaw pop and his nostrils flare when I look at him. "Mm. The Stone I forged that *you* so kindly destroyed. The one that burst with the level of power you created when it amplified two Gods' bloodlines. And now, the crown is not even whole. That Stone is moot." A tendril of his shadow lifts my chin in a firm grip, forcing my eyes to remain on his. "I don't need any souls from the afterlife; there is only one left I need."

"What do I need to do?" The floral scents mix with the metallic and makes the air thick on my tongue, getting lodged in my throat when I swallow.

"Before you go after Prince Draven, you will complete another task to prove to me you can handle capturing the prince." His eyes regard me as I steel my spine. "You must first bring me a male who slipped through the fingers of death and escaped my power. Show me that you are the daughter of darkness, even outside of this realm."

CHAPTER FOUR

Draven

"Try again," Fynn's steady voice of calm is trying to wash away the burning rage igniting inside me.

I close my eyes and concentrate once more. All I see is pure darkness, but my other senses awaken. The chirping of birds can be heard in the distance, the rustling of leaves from the wind, and the gentle creak of branches singing together in a swaying song.

The solid earth beneath my feet grounds me and the scent of pine drifts from the towering trees. I inhale the dense, foggy air and allow it to fill my lungs until it stings.

In one long, drawn-out breath, I reach down to the bond resting in my chest. To penetrate deeper within to break through the barrier and pray I fucking *feel* something. To find the tether that connects to the other end.

To find my heart.

My mate.

Emma.

But all I brush against is a cold, stone wall, shutting me out from her. No sense of where she's at, or what she's feeling. If she's even fucking alive. That thought alone—of the God of Darkness slitting her throat, or consuming her soul, and of her dying all alone—is killing me.

My chest cracks and it snaps that final thread holding back my rage. The growl that erupts from me vibrates the ground beneath my boots, shaking the trees and causing hundreds of wings to beat against the wind. I slam against that impenetrable wall blocking her from me, desperately wanting to crumble it to dust.

I know if we were officially bonded through the ritual, I would feel her ripped from this world with insurmountable pain if her heart stopped beating. For she would take mine with her. Only, we aren't fully bonded. And I'm not sure how it would feel if she were dead right now since I haven't been able to feel her these past months. None of this makes sense to me and it's driving me deeper into madness with the fear that I will never know what happened to her if we can't find her.

I pound against the wall once more, grinding my teeth while infusing my power with it so strongly that the impact makes my head feel light. I snap my eyes open, momentarily blinded by the soft glow reflecting through the clouds as I sway on my feet.

"Whoa there, Drav, take it easy." Fynn's hand clasps my shoulder firmly to help steady me. "You've been at this since dawn and it's already midday. You've barely slept more than a couple hours each day. You need to eat something and take a break."

My hands shove into my hair, clutching the dark strands in a tight grip. "It's been three fucking months, Fynn!" My voice bellows out louder than I intended, but I can't take it back now. So, I try again, speaking more softly. "We should have found her already."

He releases my shoulders and crosses his arms over his chest. "We will find her, but you need to take care of yourself as well, or there won't be a *you* to rescue Emma. You will wither away or fall into a damn coma from exhaustion. Neither of those options include getting Emma back."

He's right. He's so fucking right, and I want to punch him for it. But how can I sit around and *rest* when she's out there somewhere? How am I supposed to sleep when I close my eyes and see her frozen, void eyes staring blankly back at me? The last time I saw her, she was consumed by the dark power. Her blood ran black in her veins. And when I stared deeply into her eyes, I could practically see how it hardened her soul.

My hands begin to shake as I think about every night when sleep evades me. Those nights I spend scouring every court, hunting down every Seer I can find and have them all do the same thing. To try and find her with a fragment of the necklace that blasted off her neck. It holds the final remnants of her essence from the small stain of red that decorates it. Meaning she got hurt when it fell off, and I'm hoping she didn't feel it once her powers surged forth. Because then I imagine her not only leaving but doing so in pain. Yet each Seer I locate comes up with the same outcome...nothing. They can't find a single trace of her anywhere.

Grunts and clashing metal tear through my thoughts. I spin and see Cora and Kye practicing her fighting, which she has been determined to master. She almost didn't make it out alive in the Court of Ashes, but Fynn transported her to our healer, Galeana, who worked all night using her powers to clot and stitch Cora's abdomen back together. Then, she placed Cora into a deep sleep for another two weeks to keep her body still to finish healing on its own. All three of us took turns sitting by her bed, but it was Fynn who took longer shifts and barely rested. Hypocritical bastard.

Cora was distraught when she finally woke up. Frantic to know where Emma was when her eyes bounced around the three of us standing over her bed. Fynn was the one to sit beside her, grab her hand, and break the news. She stayed holed up in her bed and cried for another week.

Then, one day, she stormed out with fists of determination and demanded to be taught how to fight. To help bring Emma home.

Home.

It's funny how this is *home* now for the lot of us. Not my court per se, but us, together. Yet, we all know why it feels broken. Nothing will feel fully complete until her silver eyes are looking into my soul while she spits words that pierce me with her sharp tongue.

I watch Cora spin, then duck under Kye's sword swinging over her head before she kicks up with her boot. The move connects with his chest and knocks him back a couple steps. Beside me, an amused huff leaves Fynn. "She's a natural."

I take a glance at him and see the way his eyes track each precise movement she makes. A small tilt curving his lips, and a look glinting within his stare that I've only seen once before. "She refuses to skip training. She's worked hard, and Emma will be proud to see it."

"Did you see that?!" Cora's voice belts across the forest floor. "I got my blade to his chest before this brute could react!" She shrieks and jumps up and down.

"I offered a small opening to see if you would notice and take the shot," Kye mumbles in defense. "And you did."

Cora rolls her eyes and giggles. "Uh-huh. If you say so, big guy. Didn't know you were such a sore loser." She pats his shoulder with a cackle as Kye whispers something under his breath about not being a sore loser.

She saunters towards us. Fynn claps next to me and pulls her into a squeezing hug that lifts her feet off the ground. "That was damn good, love." He sets her down and winks before slinging an arm around her shoulders.

Her cheeks warm to a light shade of pink as she brings her blue eyes to me, the playfulness falling off her lips. "Anything yet?"

I give a shake of my head, darting my eyes away like a coward because I'm not sure I can handle the look I know will cross her face. A look that grieves her best friend as I continue to fail in reaching her.

"He needs to rest," Fynn cuts in. "We all do, and we can try again tomorrow." Suddenly, Fynn is standing a foot in front of me and clasps my shoulders with both hands. "*Rest.*" His voice holds a cadence of worry as his hazel eyes dart back and forth between mine.

A curt nod is all I can offer because the only thing that will come out of my mouth is that resting is the last thing I fucking want to do. So, I stay quiet.

Later that night, I try to do what Fynn asked of me. I lay down on my bed, fully dressed, knowing sleep will evade me. And I was right, because only a vision of Emma's bare body grips hold of me. Her kissable skin on display and spread out on this very mattress, waiting for me to sink into her. Everything from that one night we shared keeps flashing behind my eyes.

Except now, I don't have her scent clinging to my pillow with the memory. One day, there was a semblance of rose and honey lingering, and the next night, it was gone. Not even fading away to prepare me. It just ceased to exist.

In one breath I sit up straight, swipe the glass off the table next to the bed, and swallow down the rest of the golden liquid in one gulp. It goes down smoothly, and before I know it, I'm on my feet, pouring another glass of bourbon to the rim and chugging it down.

I place my hand over my chest, tracing my fingertips over the raised skin that marks my heart. The permanent declaration for Emma with a slice of my wyvern blade to show how she has buried her way inside my heart, and how I don't ever want her to fucking leave. A daily reminder that everything I feel, everything that happened between us, is real. Because I feel like I'm in my own fucked-up nightmare that I can't escape from.

Every day that goes by feels like my scar has been violently ripped open, causing my crimson pain to flow endlessly until there's nothing left. I may have her chained to my heart, but I feel like I'm trapped under-water and can't reach the surface. No matter how hard I try to swim, I keep sinking deeper. The chain continues to unravel, and I'm losing control of my gods damn sanity.

I pour more bourbon to numb the waves of agony that keep assaulting me. With a strong gulp, I drain the contents in my glass, my grip so tight that my knuckles turn white. My desperation to find her consumes me, leaving me feeling powerless. *Helpless.* I've only felt this way once before, and that was when my father died. There was nothing I could do to bring him back, or to find a way to mend my mother's broken heart.

However, I refuse to surrender. I will never stop searching for her, and I won't hesitate to eliminate anyone who stands in my way. The spiraling of my thoughts causes my hand to shake from the force of my grip, until the glass shatters, sending fragments flying in every direction. My palm is left bleeding, with streams of crimson dripping down my fingers and onto the floor.

I close my eyes, trying to focus on my breathing to ground myself in the present and what I need to do. But I'm finding it more difficult with each passing moment as thoughts and memories of our star-crossed love swirl in my mind. Taunting me and driving me to the brink of madness.

I feel the sadness eating away at me morph into a dark anger. It's starting to take hold as I try to fight it and cling to the last shreds of my sanity. If I lose control completely, there's no telling what kind of destruction I'll wreak.

I grab hold of the amber-filled decanter by the neck, the golden liquid swishing inside with the swift movement. Tipping the mouth of the glass to my lips, I guzzle the rest of it down with hard swallows. The liquid burns my throat, spreading warmth throughout my body. For a moment, the rage inside me subsides and I feel a sense of calm settle over me. A slight loosening in my chest. But it's short-lived. My emotions are too raw, and my powers too close to the surface as my veins are flooded with alcohol.

My chest tightens once again, but this time it takes my breath with it. Rapidly heaving up and down in desperate inhales while my heart pounds loudly in my ears as I fall apart. Imagining never seeing her smile again, hearing her laugh, or feeling the warmth of her skin in my hands is too much to bear.

Suddenly, all I see are shades of red.

A roar rips free from my chest, no doubt vibrating through the castle. Wisps of shadows lash out, striking the books off my shelf, shattering artwork off the walls, and throwing chairs across the room until they smash to pieces. A storm of what feels like our ill-fated love surges in violent gusts of despair and anger. My shadows rage around me with unleashed chaos, snuffing out the fire and casting the room in darkness as I throw my arms back and let free a guttural growl.

I blast my fist into the nearby wall over and over and over again. The sound of my knuckles snapping fills the air before the pain registers. I feel my beast unleash—like a primal, uncontrollable force within myself—but my soul is left behind and my heart is adrift without it. Blood spurts from my injured hand. It stains the wall, creating dents where my fist collides as bits of stone crumble to the floor.

I don't stop even as my mutilated hand swells from the abuse. I keep trying to pound out all the emotions suffocating me. Hoping it will crumble them to nothing but dust and empty pain, and one breath will blow them away forever.

My hand will heal itself, but I don't deserve that. I don't deserve to be freed from pain, just like Emma's not free from the control this power has on her. The power that remained in her soul even when she removed the crown and exploded a piece of it off before walking away from me. And it's why our bond is blocked with utter darkness... She is still lost to it. My hand throbs relentlessly as it hangs limply at my side, causing me to drift back to the present. Bowing my head, fatigue takes hold while beads of sweat glisten on my forehead.

I go to take another swig of bourbon when I realize I already drank the rest of it. The decanter is now nothing but a million shards of diamonds scattered on the floor. With a hiss, I scrunch my face as a drum pounds unforgivingly in my head, my vision doubling. I drank too fucking much. That is proven true when I stumble, needing to brace my hands on the wall. I deeply pull air in and out of my lungs. I want to numb the pain, to not feel it shredding me for just a moment, but I can't. I won't until I have her back.

And with that thought in mind, I leave the broken pieces of my heart on the floor with the mess I made. The power in me slowly curls back into my body, until a deafening silence fills the room. I step forward towards the open wall that leads out to the sleeping forest. My boots crunch the broken glass to dust, along with the part of me I can't piece back together.

The cool breeze warms against the heat radiating from my body as I stare with heavy-lidded eyes to the midnight sky. There are a few stars sprinkled, their light reflecting in the calm pools of water scattered between the trees on the forest floor. But my eyes lock on something else…

I dive out and call on my wings to spring forth, cutting through the night air to land on the roof. The ledge of my castle that holds so many memories. But once my feet touch the surface, I stagger, and it takes a few moments longer than normal to regain my balance before tipping my head back to stare at the moon.

It's not full tonight, but simply a crescent that looks like it's barely holding on. I remain fixated on it as a voice fills my mind with words spoken once before.

"The moon may shine brightly, but it's not always whole."

Something wet trails slowly down my cheek, standing out against the cold. I wipe it away with the back of my hand and stare at the unbidden tear that broke free. I didn't get it before, not fully. But as I stand here, broken without her, trying to keep face in front of everyone…I finally understand.

Without her, I don't feel whole. Everyone around me sees me put together when in truth, my heart keeps bleeding out. My finger mindlessly rubs the tattoo inked on my finger of the image that flashes in my dreams, though I never understood why.

A full moon with a crescent cradled inside. But now, I know it represents us. A sign that I was always meant to find Emma. It's a symbol of our love that we share, a love that shines brighter than any star in the sky. Even brighter than a full moon on a clear night.

It's like my soul is empty inside and hers is broken, but when nothing separates us, time stops and everything fades away. She fills my soul with love, and I shelter hers with mine. Our hearts together will become blinding to all the evil in this world and guide us through the dark.

Love.

I denied the thought for so long, but I knew I loved her before that wretched necklace broke off her neck. My heart has always belonged to her.

Suddenly, everything seems to spin around me. My body sways and feels unsteady as I trip over my own feet, falling backward onto the roof in what feels like slow motion. A long sigh expels from me at the thought of what my father would think if he saw me right now… Wasted and grief-stricken because I failed to save the girl I love. If he can see me from the afterlife, I hope that he turns a blind eye because I don't want him to see what I've become. A disappointing son.

After a moment, my vision clears, and I resituate myself to stay seated, extending my legs out in front of me. My eyes blink slowly as the alcohol continues to override my body. I massage my numb lips together and apply pressure to my eyes with the heel of my hands. Despite my efforts to keep the tears welling up at bay, the attempt is futile, spilling down my cheeks.

Out of nowhere, a clear droplet splashes onto my boot. Confused, my brows furrow as I tip my head back and see the darkening clouds gathering above me. It's almost as if nature can fucking sense the anguish coiling inside me, making the clouds cry a river of grief with me as my heart bleeds.

The rain softly cascades over the fog-tipped trees, creating a serene atmosphere as it drenches my clothing and seeps into my skin. But I can barely feel it—or anything—as my gaze is mesmerized by the forest and how the leaves seem to droop in contentment as the raindrops nourish them.

A slight tingle races up my spine, causing me to bring myself to stand with drunken grace. I tightly squeeze my eyes shut twice to stop my vision from doubling as I become more alert. The wind stills, the temperature slightly drops, and all that can be heard is the patter of rain. My heart thumps loudly, slamming in my chest as a sliver of *something* sparks inside me.

I scan through the trees, back and forth between the falling drops until my lungs convulse. My eyes snag on a blur, unsure if what I'm seeing is real or a figment of my imagination that my drunken state conjured.

The rain starts rushing down, beating harder into the ground, and just on the edge of the tree line…is a figure. With a step forward, it offers just enough for the figure to come out in the open and my eyes flash to silver, zooming in on…*her*.

"Emma," I whisper on a choked breath that is drowned out by the storm.

Shadows dance around her, and my heart feels like it's going to implode within my chest. I press my palm over it and reach for our bond. There. The impenetrable wall that mocks me has weakened. I grab hold of the tether and surge a wave of my love down it, hoping to convey what I never had a chance to tell her with words. But I might be able to let her *feel* it. To let her know that she's not alone and never fucking will be. I'm right here.

With a leap, I launch myself off the roof and swoop down towards her. The rain pelts my face like sharpened arrows. But as soon as my feet hit the ground, she's gone. I frantically dart my eyes around, scanning between every tree. Nothing greets me, proving I'm alone.

Inhaling deeply, I try to grasp her essence. Needing to breathe in her rose and honey fragrance to try and settle the beast thrashing wildly inside me. But the rain obliterated any trace of her scent, washing her away. Pulling at the roots of my hair, I smash my teeth together. *Fuck*!

Am I seeing things now? My eyes drop to where she stood, finding proof of two boot prints that are slowly melting back into the earth.

I collapse to my knees and slam my fists down onto the wet soil. The broken one cries out in agony, but I grit my teeth to suppress it from showing. Squeezing my eyes shut, I dig my fingers beneath the dirt with tight fists, demanding the forest bring her back.

All that answers is a crack of lightning.

I remain there, kneeling under the downpour of grief, with my wings drooping behind me and the bond in my chest growing colder by the second.

CHAPTER FIVE

Emma

A simple mission: grab the male in the woods and bring him here. I've practiced shadowing within Gehendra, but this is my first for traveling outside of the realm. A way to once and for all prove my loyalty before I hunt down the Dark Prince.

The whispers are so loud, snapping and clawing to fulfill this task, that the little grasp of control I've practiced does nothing to quiet them. With one final look at Whiro, I lash my hand out to pour a stream of midnight from it and create a fissure in the air.

"Bring him here alive," Whiro's clipped tone leaves no room for mistakes. He gives a wave with his hand before I can offer a single nod.

Without wasting a second, I slip through the portal, letting the chilling power fizzle over my skin as my foot crosses through and meets damp leaves molded in soil. The moment I fully walk through, I raise my hand out in front of me. Tiny droplets of nature's tears splash in my palm, pooling right in the center. I tip my head back and find I'm standing in a small opening in the forest. In a break between the trees, I see the sliver of a broken moon between dark clouds that cry under the weight of pressure.

A flash of wings jolts into my mind. A memory of another time I was gazing into the sky. My lungs seize momentarily, stealing my next breath. I stagger back a step and shake my head to clear it.

I don't look back up again.

Suddenly, curiosity begins to warm in my chest. It feels like a lone lantern shining in the midst of an icy storm, beckoning me to follow it out of the cold. Without a second thought, I let my shadows swarm around me to follow this feeling. To this heat blooming within the frozen organ residing in my hollow chest.

It only takes a few seconds before my feet hit the earth again, and the rain is still pelting down in a relentless beat. Yet, now there's the solemn castle of Asiza looming just beyond the trees. A shot of heat pumps through my body, and the pull grows stronger. It's as if there's a compass embedded in my chest, a fleeting wisp of an invisible force that binds me to something. My foot moves on its own accord, taking a single step before I force my body to stop.

No, I have a task that takes precedence over everything else. I take a deep breath, expanding my chest to its fullest, and then exhale slowly. Deliberately drawing it out to sharpen my focus and push away any distractions, including this inexplicable pull.

The moment I wrap myself in shadows, I see a dark blur tumbling from the sky. I don't stop to wonder what it could be as I vanish in the blink of an eye, transporting myself closer to my target. The moment my feet touch ground again, I start sprinting through the trees, my boots imprinting the earth with every hurried step. Slicing through the rain that sneaks between the leaves as I pump my arms faster.

I bring the shadows forth to blanket my body into the night, like a hunter surprising its prey. The whispers grow louder the closer I get, helping guide me to my target. Whiro gave me brief details to find him—a male who should not have survived death when it was coming for him.

A cabin with billows of smoke pluming out from the chimney looms between the trees minutes later. An axe is stabbed into a broken stump, with slices of wooden logs piled behind it. The front door creaks open, flooding a stream of bright light with it.

A female steps out, heading towards the discarded wood, and she reaches for the logs. She's not the target, but I don't take another breath of hesitation. I shadow myself right behind her and wrap my arm around her neck. Her body tenses as her hands try to grab hold of me, but my shadows snake around silently to restrain her. I start squeezing and cover her mouth before a yelp leaves her. My grip becomes tighter, until I feel the flutter of her pulse slow.

"Need help carrying the rest in, darling?" a deep voice calls out from inside the cabin.

Her pulse is so faint now that it barely flickers against her neck. The moment her eyes roll back, I let her body slump forward with a *thump* into the muddy soil. She's not dead. I can still hear the blood pumping through her veins.

I should kill her, but there's something prodding deep inside me that's begging to let her keep breathing. It's the faintest voice being drowned by the whispers in my head, yet I can feel the desperation from it. So, I leave her in the pouring rain because my only focus now is the one whose feet are softly padding against the wooden floor inside.

I forgo veiling my body in a shade of night and walk straight to the door. My boots are silent, my breaths are steady, and my eyes are focused. I place my palm on the paneled wood and give a push that elicits a creak to ring in the quiet home.

Trickles of water trail down my body and puddle around my feet. My eyes glance up to take in the room before me. The blankets strewn over a cushioned sofa, the knickknacks lining a shelf on the wall, and a game board set on the table in front of the couch. Chess. The game that resembles far too much of life and the one King Oren taught me before—I dig back to the horrors of another life—*before* he turned into a monster of his own making.

I take in the pieces placed on the squares and swipe my tongue over my teeth. Looks like one of them was three moves away from winning. Unfortunately for them, the game will be left unfinished.

I step over a pair of boots discarded by the door and silently make my way to where the voice came from. The warm glow from the flames dancing in the hearth is inviting, and the heat feels almost soothing against my constantly chilled skin.

"Darling?" he calls out again, but this time, it's higher pitched and louder than the first. *Sorry, but your* darling *is a little tired at the moment.*

I turn the corner and find the Fae crouched down, digging in a cabinet. Busying himself with what looks like preparing some late-night drinks. I stand in the doorway, silently, as I study him. He's acting as if nothing is amiss, but the tension in his shoulders and the stiffness in his movement says otherwise. My head cocks to the side when he stands, his back still facing me as glasses *clink* on the counter.

One of his arms moves to pour something golden in the empty glasses and the other… Half of it is gone, the only piece of limb remaining is from his elbow and up.

I don't bother to worry about any creaks in the floorboards as I walk towards him. The moment the heel of my boot connects with the wood, his spine stiffens. My shadows snake up my arms and behind me, causing the softly lit room to grow darker.

I know he can sense me; he can tell that I'm not his *darling*. Not with the way his bare feet shift on the floor, readying for a fight, or how his fingers grip the bottle harder, and his breaths have become nonexistent. He knows there's a monster in his house.

In a flash, he slams the glass onto the counter with a deafening crash, and dozens of sharp fragments lay broken in his palm. Suddenly, he whirls around, hurling the crystal shards at me with high speeds as they ride on a gust of wind. He's a wind keeper.

I quickly assemble a wall of shadows in front of me, but a few tiny blades slip through before the barrier is fully formed. They hit their mark, slicing into my pale skin, and leaving behind cuts that start bubbling at the seam. The obsidian blood of death starts to flow.

The sting is hardly noticeable, like a ghostly touch, but the sight brings a smirk to my face. He's clever. As we now face each other from across the room, I retract my shadows.

"Is that any way to welcome a guest?" The whispers inside me grow louder, urging me to end him right then and there. That single voice from earlier is gone, lost under the surface. But that's not what Whiro commanded; he wants him alive.

"You are no guest of mine." He scans behind me for a fleeting moment before locking his gaze on my dark pools. "What did you do to Natalia?"

I shrug, closing in on him as I drag my finger over the countertop, leaving a smear of black blood in my wake. "She will be fine, unless you refuse to come with me."

The muscles in his jaw clench and unclench repeatedly, his hand fisting so tightly his knuckles turn white. But he tilts his head near the window, as if straining to hear something. "You're lucky her pulse is still steady."

Ah. He was checking to see the truth of my words, to see if Natalia is fine.

"The moment I felt a surge of panic flow through our bond, I started to go to her. Until I heard your boots step through the door." His lips peel back. "That's when I realized she's not the one you're here to see. So, what business brings you here?" he asks through gritted teeth.

I sigh. "You."

I don't blink or utter another word. I let the silence envelop us, intensifying the tension growing to make him give into me. And it seems sparing the girl's life might be a compelling incentive for him to come willingly, even though I'm itching for a fight. But I will admit, he's not as oblivious to his surroundings as I assumed. And how sickening his love is for his mate, that he would lure a monster to him in order to protect her.

"I didn't know the Corrupted could speak." His hand reaches for the second glass.

"They don't." I slowly tilt my head to the side, curious to see if he plans to throw yet another glass. The smoky scent wafting from the fireplace swirls into the room as the flames continue to pop against the wood.

"Why do you want me?" he rushes out as his eyes stare wildly at mine.

With a sigh, I pinch the bridge of my nose. "I don't ask questions; you are nothing more than a task to complete."

"So, you're what…like, a lapdog who does the dirty work?" The sneer distorting his face is almost amusing.

I must admit that I feel a twinge of admiration for his bravery in confronting someone like me, a monster, so recklessly. Nevertheless, I can't shake the sense of unease that is starting to churn in my stomach. After this, I will never again be anyone's obedient servant, because I now possess my own powers. But until this is over, I have to tread carefully.

Whiro cannot suspect my true intentions—that I hunger to claim his power for myself. He has initiated a new game, and he assumes he's already won. However, what if the opponent has been biding her time? Quietly positioning her pawns until she can revive herself and master her abilities? Becoming a silent killer, but that means no one can know that this game is far from over.

I narrow my eyes at the male before me, taking my time before responding. He has no idea what demon is standing before him, yet I still indulge his question. "For now, but death isn't what I consider dirty work... It's a beautiful form of art, watching what kind of expression will be painted across one's face when their life is moments away from ending."

His brows furrow from my response. I quickly conjure a ball of black, fiery shadows and aim it at his hand, creating a distraction by shattering the glass he's holding into a million pieces. His mouth falls open at the same time I command a tendril of power to snake tightly around his body, while another coils around his mouth to stop him from uttering a sound.

With calm focus, I open a shimmering portal to take us to Gehendra. I drag him towards the opening, and with one final step, we enter the portal and emerge back into Whiro's realm.

CHAPTER SIX

Emma

*I*t's a shock to the system to enter Gehendra from another realm with how deathly still the air feels. But the sense of *wrongness* that slithers over my skin is stronger near the Sea of Souls, with how the scent of jasmine invades my entire body. It's a pretty flower that weeps with grief for every heart silenced in its presence.

I let the Fae male drop and roll along the stone as I unwind my shadows from him. Whiro's back is to us, and the Fae has yet to notice his presence, but I get the sense he can *feel* it. Every muscle in his body tightens when he braces his hand on the ground, curling his fingertips in.

"What is this place?" he grinds out between his teeth, refusing to lift his head to look at me.

"My home." Whiro's voice vibrates through the silence, bouncing off stone and making the Fae's head snap up.

I often wonder what the first thought is in one's mind when they come across Whiro. Do they feel immediate fear to make their lungs lock up?

Do they feel anger and the desire to attack? Or maybe shock of being in the presence of one so powerful. But for this male, he seems to understand the level of danger his life is in without being given any other information.

"Why am I here?" There's a slight shake in his voice even though his face looks unfazed when he finally chooses to tip his head back.

Whiro turns around, walking to stand a foot in front of him. "To appease my interests, for you escaped the fate that comes from my Scavengers." He clicks his tongue. "And I'm not in a forgiving mood."

His words make me wonder if he can sense who his Scavengers spread the curse to, since they are created directly from his power. I refrain from asking and let that thought crumble to dust as if it never existed.

The Fae pushes himself upright to stand, his breathing becoming harsher as he gasps for air. The impact of the realm is already weighing heavily on his weakening body. His chest rises and falls rapidly as he stares at the figure in front of him and asks, "How do you— Wait. Who are you?"

I remain rooted in place, a blank expression on my face as Whiro's grin turns sinister. "I'm the God of Darkness." He takes a gliding step closer and his shadows swirl under his skin. "But I do despise unnecessary chatter." He whips his hand out and latches it around the Fae's throat. "So, enough talking."

Whiro slowly raises the male until his feet hover off the cave's floor. The male's hand grabs hold of Whiro's to try and pry himself free. "I–I —" his words get cut off when Whiro tightens his hold.

A bored sigh leaves my blue-tinted lips. "Maybe we should let him say what he wishes." I gather the ends of my tunic and twist it in my hands and squeeze. Water trickles out and splashes against my boots until a few drops remain, and then I repeat the process on the other side.

"Why is that, *Daughter?*"

The Fae's eyes bulge farther out of his skull than they already are at the realization of our relation. His veins stand out and pulse aggressively from Whiro's grip.

My father only looks at the male with boredom as I speak. "I'm intrigued, and he can't possibly escape. So, his fate will remain the same."

Power vibrates around his body and the blood coursing through Whiro grows darker beneath his skin, seeming to come alive in the silence between us. He drops the male onto the ground. The sound of bones hitting stone is muted with a deep groan as he curls on his side.

"I was *saved*," the Fae grunts out between harsh breaths. "The shadowed male saved me and my mate from a gruesome death. I don't understand why you are targeti—"

A tendril of midnight lashes out and plunges down his throat, silencing him. "Insufferable. You are an example of what happens to those who run from me once they are marked." Whiro turns to face me. His swirling gaze penetrates through skin and bone, piercing straight into my deadened soul. "Throw him in." His head nudges towards the Sea of Souls.

Without a word, I call on my shadows to slither through my veins and expel from my fingertips. Whipping this darkness outward to wrap around the torso of the male who gasps for breath once Whiro releases him. I lift his body off the ground and hover him just above the metallic water shimmering with soul-sucking magic.

"P–please! I'm Vincent! T–tell my mate… I l–love her." The male chokes against my hold, spluttering as he tries to gasp for air when I squeeze tighter.

I'm not sure why I pause, my eyes boring into the male who confesses his final words for another. In half a heartbeat, he tightens his jaw in defiance. A different look infiltrates his features instead of the fear-stricken one that has consumed every Fae I've killed. He is the first who is not showing weakness before death, only a steeled spine of contempt. Refusing to beg to be saved when he understands his fate is already sealed.

But something deep within, that small voice buried beneath the whispers, doesn't want me to let him fall. A cold draft brushes up my spine, leaving chills in its wake. It's almost like my father's power is growing impatient behind me, and that's when I blink away the hesitation.

My power relinquishes, and I watch Vincent's entire body submerge beneath the surface in the span of one steady exhale. He neither makes a sound nor closes his eyes. Instead, they follow me with a look that makes me feel like he might see more than just a she-demon with a corrupt soul. Eyes that infiltrate past the frozen shell encasing my heart, finding a minuscule crack and seeing what might dwell inside.

But I don't tear my gaze away even as his eyes stay glued to mine while he continues to sink. No bubbles rise to the surface from his final breaths, the mirror-like liquid too dense for air to pass through.

My mouth parts when a glow begins to radiate around his body as it becomes still underwater. The light separating from his body detaches completely, becoming blinding before it's snuffed out. Now Vincent looks just like the rest of the corpses that float beside him, colorless and frozen. The white light is nowhere to be seen, and I realize that was his *soul*.

With a quick dart of my eyes, I peer at Whiro before I'm stuck on the reflective pool that drinks away one's life. I notice his gaze is focused on something behind me, but I don't think much of it. Instead, I ask, "Where did it go?"

I feel his presence move to stand beside me, his arm brushing against mine. I can't help but imagine what the sight looks like, just two vessels with the same mutilated soul—death standing next to his executioner.

"The in-between." He pauses for a moment, seeming to think of what he wishes to tell me. "I don't usually trap a soul like his, and I don't truly need it. But I wanted to demonstrate how my treasured pool works. His soul is not alive, nor destroyed. It's simply trapped, existing in the afterlife without the ability to move on. I hold their physical form, and the afterlife holds their soul for eternity."

I stare in bewilderment at the unmoving water, at how something so magical looking can glitter among all the lifeless bodies floating beneath it. Words begin to trickle up my throat, but before they can become sound, Whiro continues to speak.

"Now you see the true beauty this room holds, but the Sea of Souls won't be satisfied until it has the soul chosen for this fate."

I twist my head to look up at him, the braids of my hair falling back behind my shoulders. "The heir of Asiza."

He nods once. "You will return to Deyadrum and continue the act of being betrothed to the new prince of Asov. It will be a sort of peace offering from me and I know his father will eagerly accept now that he is being crowned king. He won't turn away from power joining his side, but this will also provide me some entertainment." A sly smirk spreads maliciously on the one side of his mouth. "Your presence will help draw out the heir of Asiza, and I do love to play with my prey before I trap them."

Silence grows heavy in the stagnant air surrounding us.

"So, hear me now because I won't say it again. Bring. Me. Prince Draven. It's one life, or every soul." Somehow the cold depths of his eyes grow darker, the veins webbing around them swelling. "You have until the next full moon. But understand," he seethes and drops the pitch of his voice, "it won't be my hands that take the souls of every person should you fail."

I head to my chambers shortly after I've been tasked with my next victim, but the thought of luring the Dark Prince here unsettles something inside me. As if my heart is trying to kickstart and thaw the ice clinging onto it.

The narrow spiral staircase dizzily twirls up to the highest peak, spinning my thoughts in a whirl of disarray. Each breath creates a misty fog in front of me, the chilly air heavy on my lungs as I count fifty more steps taken. I could simply shadow myself to my room, but I find comfort in the mindless task of climbing the steps. It soothes the unease in my stomach that has me questioning the lone voice warring against the whispers in my mind. Or the warm feeling that has taken root in my chest ever since I crossed realms.

Another fifty steps left behind, my legs growing weary as I continue the climb. The events of today have taken a toll on me, leaving me desperately wanting to rest before my role as fiancée begins. I try to latch onto that one warning voice fighting against the whispers, but the exhaustion wins, and the voice gets drowned out. The whispers just keep growing more excited with the fun yet to unravel.

I push off the final step and twist the onyx handle to my door, clicking it shut when I cross over the threshold. The only thing I can make out in the dim, flickering light is the small bed in the center of the room, with a candle burning weakly on the ground beside it. The small clusters of wax solidify, barely dripping from the wick as the air freezes them before they can reach the dish below.

The mattress is firm when my body slumps down onto it, my muscles releasing some of the tension as I embrace the silence. I throw up a pathetically weak mental wall to block the whispers, something I've been practicing every day. Steadily weaving a web of power dense enough in my mind, until it separates my psyche from the maddening force.

Pressure builds against my skull as my brows deepen with focus, struggling to hold the shield as a few webs of power snap out of place. A small grunt slips free as I gnash my teeth to stop the shield from weakening so I can let my mind think freely. Trying my best to keep a firm hold as I seek that warmth in my chest again, wanting to brush against something familiar.

A small ember basks in a kernel of hope deep down and I try to grasp it. Light. The part of me that will blind this darkness from keeping its hold on me. It sparks brighter than I've witnessed before as I reach for it, but it fades after every attempt.

Suddenly, my mental barrier comes crashing down and the heat slowly flaring under my skin extinguishes. I blink once, my eyes targeting a piece of ash suspended in the air as I stare blankly at it. The cold settles in once again, icing over the sliver of hope that was pumping into my veins. That shred of longing that makes me believe in something good is gone in a flash. Which is why hope is such a fragile, dangerous thing to try to cling on to.

The darkness swarms around me, hugging close to my body with its voice of temptation filling my skull with thoughts to destroy. To ruin without mercy. My lips twitch with a haunting grin as I take pleasure in the terror others feel towards the dark and the shadows that cling to it. But I am the darkness, and these shadows are mine. If they are scared of the dark, then they will fear me.

Whiro wants me by the side of the male who is weak, but bubbles of excitement rise at how easily I can snap Aiden's neck if he wrongs me. I'll follow along and play the game to lure the Dark Prince to me. I don't know why he's the chosen one for the Sea of Souls if not for some kind of revenge. Even with what he said about his power. But my coal-stained heart doesn't care to know. I'm now the queen on the board who has become the hunter of the king. I am nothing but a weapon: honed to perfection, sharpened, and ready to strike.

CHAPTER SEVEN

Draven

A whistle pierces through the fog in my head as I attempt to peel my eyelids open.

"I told you to get rest, not to pillage your room." *Fynn.* His voice is bright and cheery against the relentless pounding in the front of my skull.

Fuck, even each of my eyes feel like they have their own headache when I try to peel them open. I don't recall returning to my room, only sitting on the roof until… My mind blanks as I try to grasp the events of last night for why I passed out in my bed with soaked clothes.

It started raining on the roof, but then… *Her.*

I blink my eyes open faster, bolting upright in my bed as my destroyed room spins in a vortex of a drunken haze. I must have drank enough to quench the thirst of a whole army to feel this hungover.

Flashes of the moment she took a step out of the forest plague me, but I can't recall if any of it was real. I felt something in our bond ignite, right? But maybe it was all something my mind conjured up and dreamed when the alcohol completely took over, until it made my world go black. Maybe I'm losing my fucking mind.

"You look like shit." Fynn's voice sounds louder, echoing in my ears as

44

I swipe a hand roughly down my face. His light hair is pulled messily in a bun, and he nudges a piece of broken wood with the toe of his boot before shoving his hands in his pockets. His eyes lift to me, then immediately dart to the left. A deep crease pulls between his brows. "Did the wall say some shit to you?"

I turn to follow his gaze and am met with a bloody crater decorating the wall. "Something like that." My crimson-stained hand flexes, the broken bones and torn skin already healed.

He nods in understanding. I have helped repair many holes his fists have blasted through walls when he was drowning in grief. "Get cleaned up and we can try to reach through the bond again." Fynn's eyes set on me with a glassy look of determination. "You won't lose your mate, too. One of us deserves to not feel the pain that follows."

I swallow what feels like sand scratching down my throat as I pull myself out of bed. I step towards Fynn, clasping my hand on his shoulder. "You deserve to have love. She wouldn't want you to remain alone all these years."

The side of his lip curves up. "The pain is still there, but lately, it has lessened." A knowing glint shines in his eyes as I know exactly why the pain may feel lighter these days.

"Hmm. That wouldn't have anything to do with a certain blonde-haired someone who snipes back at everything you say?"

He shoves at my chest with a chuckle. "I don't know what the future holds, but right now, I'd hate to not see her in it." He slightly leans forward, sniffing loudly. "You reek of booze." He laughs again and starts to walk away.

A tap sounds at the door and Emil peeks his head inside. His eyes immediately widen from the tarnish of the room. "Uh..." He opens his mouth to speak but then shakes his head, seeming to hold in whatever was on his mind. "Mother wishes to speak with us."

"I'll be there shortly," I say sluggishly, while I step over shattered glass to go wash up.

"Yeah, I'll leave Drav here to get rid of whatever died on his breath and walk with you to keep Queen Zoraida company," I hear Fynn say as he heads to the door.

I pause and spin around, but too quickly as the room takes a moment longer to stop moving. "She's not calling for your presence, you bastard." My voice is barely restrained with amusement as I watch his jaw drop.

He throws a hand up and walks out the door with final words. "She'd love my company." He bellows a laugh down the hallway, and I can't hold back the dumb smile taking over my face.

"He's one of a kind," Emil quips from the doorway with a light expression on his face. His raven hair falls over the pointed tips of his ears and his deep blue eyes twinkle with laughter. Then, a somber look crosses over his face as his eyes scan the carnage of my room again. "Are you—" He pauses with an inhale and then meets my eyes. "Are you okay?"

"No," I honestly confess in a broken whisper. "But I will be."

He gently gives a slight bob of his head with a small smile. "All right. Well then, I'll see you in a few." Emil takes his leave as I'm left standing in a room as broken as I am.

I step into my mother's parlor, letting the door fall shut behind me. My footsteps falter at the sight of my mother already fully dressed in a deep red gown, her black hair braided and pinned up in a bun, and her hands are hanging down by her side as her fingers play with the satin material of her skirt.

Her back is facing me as she stares out at the misty fog blanketing the forest and the ravens resting in the nearest tree. Emil sits patiently on the ruby velvet chair with his hands tucked under each leg.

The air in the room feels heavy with uncertainty. My boots thud across the polished dark floor as I make my way to stand beside Emil. "You wished to speak with us?" My voice sounds clear in the silent room, but it's as if she is caught in the fog outside, blocking out anything and everything. "Mother?"

Her arms fall to her sides as she turns around to face us, a tight smile stretching across her lips. "Please, sit." She gestures to the chair angled beside Emil's and I step around him before seating myself, my posture stiff with how my mother is acting. Her normal warmth feels like it's wavering.

I watch her slowly make her way to the sofa opposite us, sitting grace-fully and smoothing out the material of her dress that falls over her legs. "Draven, can you please make sure no one hears us beyond these walls?"

I clench my jaw with a quick jerk of my head, stretching my hands out and shrouding the entire perimeter of the room in darkness. I pour as much of my shadows as I can until I'm satisfied the room is soundproof. The candles flicker in the chandelier above, casting us in a soft glow as I bring my eyes back to my mother's and declare, "No one will hear now."

She smiles as she would in front of her people when she has to make a hard decision, the full embodiment of the Queen of Asiza. "Thank you." She clears her throat. "I—" She stops, biting her lips between her teeth in thought. "There's something I must confess."

My heart starts to pound harder in anticipation and I adjust myself in the chair to sit a little straighter, readying for the blow to come. Emil manages to remain perfectly relaxed and unfazed by the bomb of truth I feel will explode on us.

Her deep ocean eyes crash against mine. "Sometimes the stars gift me with a message."

The air in my lungs freezes, and any response I could give lodges in my throat with it.

My brows pinch together, trying to understand what she means by that. I spare a quick glance to Emil, and he seems just as stricken as me. The silence stretches and grows taut like a bow string right before the arrow is released. And currently, I feel like her words are the arrow in this situation. Striking fast and true.

Finally, I manage to let a response roll off my tongue. "I don't under-stand what you mean by that." I see Emil nod in agreement as I lean forward to brace my elbows on my knees.

"It's something I don't fully understand either," she says softly, while fidgeting with her fingers in her lap. "Even when I was a child, it happened without warning. I just know I have to deliver the message." Her brows knit together in thought.

"What kind of messages?" Emil asks the question that was on the tip of my tongue.

She sighs softly, her eyes never leaving ours. "Cryptic ones or ones that are very direct. For instance, when you went away before, and I told you to extinguish the flames..." I give a curt nod. "I was told to relay that to you in that moment."

Blowing out a breath, I shake my head in confusion, wishing I didn't drink an entire ocean of bourbon last night. Because this isn't power, this is something that goes beyond realms and Gods. This is a way for fate to walk among us. Emil sits silently in thought while mindlessly trailing a finger over the designs etched into the velvet material wrapping the cushion.

"Why tell us now?" I ask, because this has been happening since I could remember.

She wrings the extra material of her dress between her hands and locks her deep blue eyes on mine. "I was afraid that the stars or fate would be angry if I gave away this secret." Suddenly, a watery sheen fills her eyes, and she turns her head to look away.

"The night your father passed, I was so—" A small cry tumbles from her lips but she smothers it with her hand. "I begged the stars to exchange me for him, and it—" A flood of tears falls down her cheeks. "It fills me with so much guilt that I could beg for them to take me away from the two of you."

She sucks in a shaky breath as my chest silently cleaves in two while we wait for her to continue. "Then, I begged them to never let either of you feel that pain. To be forgiven for ever thinking that separating from you was an option and that I would do whatever it took, even giving up the ability for them to speak to me."

Grabbing a handkerchief, she presses it to her cheeks. Her chest shakes. Seeing her in this state is like reliving my father's death all over again, and it's tearing my heart to shreds.

When her eyes slowly drag back up to mine, she inhales deeply, holding it and then exhaling slowly. "The stars never punished me with their silence and continue to communicate with me. I'm not shown anything, but I think this is their way of letting me help, but this secret is one I can't hold on to any longer."

Standing up, I walk the two feet and plop down beside her, pulling her in for a hug. "Don't feel guilty for something you aren't alone in doing.

The night he died, I pleaded for him to come back, too. For the stars to take me if it would instantly put that smile back on your face."

She goes to pull out of my arms, but I hold her tighter, needing her to hear this. "He was a better man than I'll ever be. I remember being so angry with fate for ignoring me then. For only responding with silence when I was screaming for them to listen. But all that matters now is that we have each other."

A thump sounds to my right and I find Emil on his knees before our mother. "Mother," his voice cracks. "Please don't cry."

When she pulls back, I let her this time and she cups her hands on both of our cheeks. "What makes you wish to tell us now?" Emil asks after a few beats of silence.

She sniffles and the sound sends a fissure rippling through my chest. "Do you remember when Princess Emma came here for the ball?"

My muscles become tense when I stiffly pull away, my eyes bouncing back and forth between hers. "You know I do."

One tight nod is all she offers to acknowledge that there is no way I could forget the one who swept in like a rising storm and caught me in her path. "The morning she left, I gave her the book she borrowed from the library and in it…" She pauses, nibbling on her lip.

"Was a message?" Emil asks.

My heart jumps, picking up its pace.

"When light and dark collide, your fate will be split in two," she says softly, her eyes pinning mine. "Now we know that was a message for her future and what she was going to face."

Another whip of pain lashes at my heart.

"The reason I bring that up is because I've been sent another message." Every jump to my heart thunders in my chest and I feel the blood drain from my face. Everyone here is fully aware of what Emma means to me, and how thin the bridge I'm standing in the middle of is as I try to make my way to her. The bridge is one snap of a rope away from careening me into the part of myself that will become more beast than sane.

"For her," Emil whispers and she nods. I jump to my feet, scrubbing a hand through my hair as I begin to burn a path back and forth on the floor. "What is it, Mother?" Emil's voice sounds muffled from the pounding filling my ears.

She pushes off the sofa and stands in front of me, halting my movement. Her small hand gently cups the side of my jaw, and a tender smile graces her face. My eyes dart back and forth to her all-knowing ones as she softly swipes a loose strand of hair off my forehead.

A slight shake of her head as her hand drops until her fingers dig into the material of my shirt. "Fate demands the sacrifice of the one who holds the balance of two worlds."

Her cryptic words tidal wave into my chest, flooding my lungs until there's no room for air. I stare at her unblinking as her words replay in my head and my vision starts to blur around the edges.

"Are you saying fate demands Emma's life?" I choke out, my eyes burning with each second that passes when she doesn't respond.

The silence stretches, but her eyes just plead with mine. Her hand falls away when I walk behind my chair, grasping the back of it with both palms and drop my head forward.

I squeeze my eyes shut, grinding my teeth together at the thought of Emma dying. "You can't tell me," I rasp out.

"I'm sorry," she says quietly. "That's all I was told and who it's for. I know nothing else of its meaning."

A long exhale deflates from my lungs. "I know. Gods Mother, I know. This is not your fault." I walk over to her and pull her into me for comfort. A sniffle sounds next to my ear. I pull back to see a sheen coating her eyes, making them look like a midnight ocean glistening under diamonds dripping from the sky. "It's. Not. Your. Fault," I say each word gently. "We will figure it out, okay?"

Another silent nod and then she's reaching back to the sofa for her napkin to dry the tears away.

"Draven," Emil's voice cuts through the ache building in my chest. "You know how my power is growing?"

"It's getting stronger every year." I smile at him.

"Well, now what I see at night is coming together faster once I wake. And everything from last night just…"

"Just snapped into place?" He nods, but his eyes look anything but happy. "What is it?"

A heartbeat later, everything inside me sinks because I have a feeling I know what he's about to say. Then, he gestures with a wave of his hand for me to sit back down.

The moment my weight settles in the chair, he speaks, "I saw Emma in the vision I dreamed last night."

And just like that, the air in my lungs is punched out of me. My grip tightens and the chair creaks beneath my palms. At this point, I'm gasping for air as the room once again becomes a dark blur around the edges. A swell of emotions gets stuck in my throat, but I force my voice to coop-erate no matter how broken it sounds. "Please, tell me everything. I beg of you."

Whether his vision is something that will wreck me, I have to know. She had felt so frozen to the touch before she walked away, and the dead-ened look in her void eyes haunt me every time I close mine. A reminder that she sacrificed herself to end the battle, to give the God of Darkness something he'd want. Her power. And I...failed her.

I want to throw this chair across the room, because Emma has already sacrificed herself and is suffering with a fate I fear is worse than death right now. Trapped alone in a darkened sea, with no signs of light to guide her back to herself. Unable to find the hope that I have been desperately trying to send her with my bleeding heart. She shouldn't have to sacrifice anymore.

Emil stands to face me fully, my muscles tensing for whatever he's about to say.

"I know where she is."

I'm not sure how many times my heart can double over in my chest until it gives out. "Where?" I can barely restrain the plea flooding my voice. He holds up his hands as if warning me I won't like what I'm about to hear, but I don't give a shit. I need to know.

"She was with Whiro in what looked like another realm, because it's nothing I've seen in this world. But as of this morning, she's here. In Deyadrum."

Everything I thought he might say falls to the wind, and I almost get caught in it, too. A million thoughts are running scattered in my mind, wondering if she's okay. Why is she here? Where in Deyadrum?

"Brother..." Emil's voice trails off as he waits for me to come back to the present. My fingers wrap around the beaded embroidery on the arm of the chair. My knuckles turn white as I hold onto it like my life depends on it. I have never felt so lost and on edge.

He inhales deeply, stepping towards me and placing his hand on my head. "Let me *show* you."

The room spins and my mother's parlor disappears. It's replaced by white corridors with seashells embedded in the floor. The sounds of crashing waves and birds chirping echo in the distance. The salty air wraps around me as I squint my eyes from the sudden assault of bright light radiating from outside and reflecting off the stark walls.

Voices travel from the open doorway down the hall, and I waste no time stalking towards it. Whatever Emil wants me to see, it will be through there.

"How do I know you won't go back on your word? That you will keep the Corruption at bay?" *asks a male's voice I don't recognize as I reach the doorway.*

"Because I'm allowing you the courtesy of having your son marry my daughter. To have such power stand on your behalf. But make no mistake, one wrong move against me, and I will rip your soul to shreds."

A tremor skates down my spine. Recognition of this voice has me clenching my fists. It's one I've embedded into my memory, so I know who I'll target with a deadly strike.

Whiro.

I step slowly around the corner and put one foot over the threshold. It's a massive room off the entryway, one where someone could host a gathering or a small ball. There is no furniture placed about, though. It seems to serve as a room to solely connect to other corridors. The shimmering shells continue through the expanse of the room, with a high ceiling that has a mural of a crew at sea on it. White pillars decorate each corner, and even with the lightness the room provides, it feels...cold and unwelcoming.

But only two steps in and the soles of my boots freeze to the ground. My heart pounds rapidly against my ribs with a rough swallow.

Emma. It can't fucking be. But then golden hair flashes beside her. The weasel who disappeared like a coward is still alive with the same arrogance that nauseated me before.

It's the arm Aiden has snaked around her waist that provides all the proof I need.

My stomach churns and my blood boils in my veins with a raging need to cut that arm off his body for ever thinking he could touch *her. For even assuming that she will be anyone's but* mine.

I try my best to control my breathing and calm down the beast thrashing around in me. My eyes drift to her, and even with a frozen heart and eyes the color of death, she still is the most enchanting female I've ever laid my eyes on.

She's not hiding now. Every scar and jagged twist of her skin is on display in the dress she wears. Her back is open to prying eyes, and a slit reaches up to her thigh, allowing a peek at the dagger strapped around it. Her dress is sleeveless, but a small silver cuff bands around her upper arm. The color complements perfectly with the obsidian filling her eyes and veins. She stands tall, with her chin high as her black, vacant gaze stares at the empty space before her while everyone speaks around her. Why isn't she fighting back to put an end to this bullshit?

"Father, let us be grateful he brought her back to me." *Aiden's voice is rough as he grits his teeth. His words sound laced with venom as his arm roughly jerks Emma hard into his side. I take a step forward but pause when I see her turn to look at Aiden, and the anger filling his eyes seems to cower away for a fleeting moment.*

Then, a growl vibrates in my chest, as I now see the resemblance of who created such a travesty of a male.

"Very well," *Aiden's father speaks, a glare shot in Emma's direction before looking back to Whiro.* "I suppose she did do me a favor by taking out the prior king before I had to get my hands dirty. But if one Corrupted is spotted on my land, I will have them killed before you can stop me."

Whiro folds his hands behind his back, walks towards Aiden's father, and leans down to get closer to his face. "The Corrupted will remain with me, but don't think I can't unleash them with a single thought."

"What's in this deal for you?" *Aiden's father asks, causing his son to bristle with a slight widening of his eyes.*

A demonic chuckle powers through the room. "If I tell you, Calloway, then where would the fun be? All that matters is that I don't wish to remain in this realm longer than I already have. Therefore, my daughter will stay in my place. To keep things under control."

Calloway's face grows red. "If she stays, she has no control in my king-dom," *he spits.*

I take a step closer towards Emma, wanting to be near her and still feeling the urge to protect her. Even though I can't within this vision.

"Uh uh," *Whiro tsks.* "It's not your kingdom yet."

"Father, don——"

Aiden gets cut off as his father bellows, spit flying from his mouth with the veins in his neck nearly bursting. "You dare accost me in my own court?!" *He jabs a finger towards Whiro's chest as he stands back to his full height.* "She has no power here, just like before. The only weight she will hold is her blood being tied to yours. She has no control or influence on *my* kingdom." *Calloway is one dumb decision away from Whiro killing him.*

Emma remains silent and unmoving. Whiro stands just as unnaturally still, until he waves his hand and a dozen Corrupted materialize behind him. Tattered clothing hangs off their bodies and black blood oozes from their eyes. The scent of rotten flesh fills my nose, causing the back of my throat to burn.

Calloway goes rigid, not uttering a sound.

"Emmerelda," *Whiro says as he keeps his eyes locked on the soon-to-be king,* "I believe the Court of Asov needs a new ruler."

Emmerelda? Is that her true name or one that he's trying to give? It's beautiful, but it doesn't suit her. Not one fucking bit. She's my little demon, not some trophy to flaunt around. Emma is the name that falls from my lips like a white-hot, soul-binding vow. It's the name I groan in ecstasy. The sound that mixes with her moans and makes her cheeks heat to the prettiest shade of pink.

Calloway's eyes bulge out of his head, raising both arms with shaking hands. "Wait, wait. No need for that. All is fine, just get rid of them." *His eyes dart to the wall of death waiting for a command.*

If this male had a half a brain, he would realize the Corrupted aren't the threat he should be concerned about. It's the cold figure standing before him and the one standing beside his heir. I can't feel her through the bond, but I can feel her power that's stirring within. It seems to only be the surface of what she holds that she's allowing to show.

A smirk plays on Whiro's lips before he looks to Emma. "You can dispose of them for me, Daughter."

A show of power is what he's instilling. I watch Emma carefully as I creep a little closer. Her rose and honey scent is there, but the warmth in her eyes is not. She remains looking bored as her hands come out in front of her, weaving them in one smooth motion that sends shadows flying out to the Corrupted. I expect them to vanish.

54

To be sent back to where they were summoned from, but no… *Her power pierces straight through their chests. Their bodies drop one by one before disintegrating into a pile of ash.*

She lowers her arms as Calloway starts blubbering unintelligible words. Aiden stares at her with his mouth hanging open, but he leaves his arm in place around her midsection. I watch Emma, deeply peering into her eyes in hopes that any sort of emotion will register. But still, nothing. She seems to not feel an ounce of anything, as if ending their lives was a boring task.

"Now, do we have a deal?" *Whiro opens a portal of shadows beside him as he waits for Calloway to regain himself.*

Calloway quickly clears his throat. Tearing his gaze away from the ash on the floor, he looks at Whiro. "Y-yes. We have a deal." *His eyes dart to Emma for the briefest moment, and if I wasn't watching him, I wouldn't have seen it. She instilled fear into him. Good. That's my little demon.*

"Remember what I told you, Emmerelda. Do not think lightly of me." *And with that, Whiro steps into his portal and is gone in an instant. Aiden breathes out a long breath as his father straightens the lapels on his coat.*

"Take her to her room," *Calloway sneers.* "I don't want to see her until my coronation." *He walks towards a set of double doors lining the other side of the main room, before spinning around.* "And someone clean this disgusting filth off my floors! I don't want to see a speck left behind!" *Then, he walks out with a huff.*

Servants rush in to tackle the task of getting rid of the pile of ashes while Aiden and Emma remain standing in place.

I should leave, but the vision still has me caught in its grip. So, I take the final step to close the distance between Emma. Now, I stand less than an inch from her on the side free of Aiden. I slowly trail a finger over her skin without touching her. It follows the sharpness in her face, the slender curve of her neck, and all the way down her toned arms mapped out in black veins.

She remains fixated on where the Corrupted were standing, not a twitch in her body giving away to what she's thinking. Aiden shifts towards her and his eyes trail down her body before lingering on her back. A frown pulls between his eyes and the hand wrapped around her waist lifts, inching it closer to touch the largest mangled scar that follows the length of her spine. One that my lips have kissed.

The moment the tip of his finger makes contact, she flinches and spins around to

55

face him with his wrist already caught in her hand. I can tell her grip hurts with how his fingers are flexing and a sliver of panic fills his widening eyes.

"Don't." *Her voice is harsh, cold.*

"Okay, just—" *He flexes his hand again with a wince.* "Fuck, you're hurting me."

She throws his hand to the side, uncaring of any pain she may have caused him. He tilts his head back, taking her in. "I thought since you have come into this power that you would be more compliant," *he scoffs, then pauses.* "Where are these scars from?" *His eyes scan more of her marked skin.* "Was what your father said in the Court of Ashes true? He…punished you?"

She eerily cocks her head to the side, her eyes narrowing and the corner of her mouth twitching. "Ask your father," *she snarls, and then walks past him to leave the room.*

My arm reaches out to pull her back. To keep her close to me. I don't fucking know what to do, but watching her walk away brings me back in time to the end of battle. The moment she let herself walk away and never look back when she followed Whiro.

The room suddenly begins to blur. The last thing I see is Aiden standing there with a face as pale as the moon and a glare that leaves me uneasy.

My mother's parlor comes back into focus, but it doesn't matter. Everything falls away as my heart stutters and it sounds like water is rushing in my ears. My chest is tight, my teeth threaten to crack as every inch of my body is on the verge of exploding. I can't keep it reined in anymore.

My chest surges to see her so close but so far away and with *him.* I release a roar that shatters the glass on the tray next to me. A roar that shakes the whole damn castle.

Calloway helped make her bleed.

Aiden dared to put his hands on her.

And Whiro is using her for his gain. I just don't know for what. Now that she's been found, there is nothing holding me back from getting to her.

Fate says she must sacrifice something, maybe even sacrifice herself.

"Fate be damned," I say to my mother and Emil.

If she dies, then I'm chaining her to me, and we both will sink to the darkest depths together. Hand in hand.

CHAPTER EIGHT

Emma

My old bed in this palace is more comfortable than the one I'm used to in Gehendra, but the golden light drifting in through the balcony doors is overwhelming compared to the dark hole I've been living in. Small rays of warmth reach the bed and glisten over my pale skin, but I can't feel it. Nothing can rid me from this eternal frozen tundra.

My feet pad across the polished floor as I get ready in a similar fashion from when I first arrived. But I'm missing my leather trousers and long tunic. So, I stick to the task I need to adhere to, which means I must dress the part.

A weapon of ruin wrapped in silk.

I slip on a starless midnight dress, with every mark of victory committed to my body for all to see. A painted canvas of hardened strength.

I feel out of place coming back to this beautiful prison. Only, this time, I secretly hold the key. I finish getting dressed and start twisting the locks of my hair into one braid. I tie off the end and stare at my reflection in the mirror. It would unnerve someone to see the emptiness staring back.

A soft knocking thuds against the door, but I don't bother responding. It's a waste of my breath. The click of the handle turning registers before it creaks open, until it's slightly ajar and carrying the scent of fresh rain and leather.

"May I come in?"

Aiden. I fist my hands tightly before letting out a long breath in an attempt to loosen the tension in my muscles. "You may."

His footsteps grow louder as the door latches shut behind him. Never blinking, my eyes find him through the mirror's reflection. The clothing he's wearing is altered perfectly to his lean frame and is finer than what I remember him wearing back before…everything. My eyes trail down his body, following the gold decorative trim that is pressed intricately along the cream tunic and matching pants.

He pauses and waves his hands down his body when he catches me taking in his clothing. "My father insists on me looking how a prince should. At least until things settle after his coronation tomorrow." He laughs nervously at my scrutiny.

The sight of him causes a roar of power to coil inside, but I've managed to tame the whispers when it comes to setting my eyes on him. Each time he's near, my power wants to know how it will feel to have his heart beat in the palm of my hand, or how his eyes will look if I strip away his air.

But for now, he gets to feel his blood pump through his veins another day.

"How did you sleep?" He walks toward me until he's a foot away and slowly drags his eyes down my body. A look that swirls with desire, fear, and something close to wrath. They retreat up towards my back, where the dress swoops just at the base of my spine, leaving the rest open. His emerald eyes freeze and harden on my shield made from leather lashes. It's then I notice the muscles in his jaw twitch and his nostrils flare.

I shift to face him fully, yet his eyes remain downcast as if he's still staring at my back. "I slept well enough." My voice snaps him back into focus as he brings his gaze to mine.

With a nod of his head and a rough swallow, he clears his throat. "I'm glad to hear that. I've come to see if you'd like to go for a walk with me around the palace." His eyes drift around the room, as if searching to find something that's not there, before landing back on mine. "Like old times, when you used to chase me," he forces out.

His eyes lift on the corners with a tight smile as he waits for me to respond. I'd rather be alone, but for now, I need to play nice and hold up appearances. "I suppose I could use some air."

A satisfied nod and a wave of his hand towards the doorway is all he offers. "After you." I swish my dress to make sure I show the hilt of my dagger peeking through the slit before leading the way.

We've been walking in silence for a while as my slippers sink with each step, becoming full of sand. Birds soar above the sea before diving down to skim just above the water's surface, their talons dipping in.

Aiden's arm casually brushes against mine as we continue to follow the edge, where land and water merge together. "I've insisted the seamstress make a dress for you to wear to my father's celebration tomorrow. It will be delivered to your room in the morning."

"Thank…you," I ground out, not wanting to consider what kind of monstrosity he thought to have created.

"Emma, I—" He sucks in a sharp breath when his hand makes contact with my arm. He doesn't let go. Instead, his fingers grip harder, almost bruising against my skin as he stops and turns me towards him. "You're freezing," he says on a breath.

I watch him for a moment as he takes his other hand to trace the black veins that spiderweb underneath. "Yes, but it has nothing to do with being outside."

I thought I might feel the smallest glimmer of warmth at the touch of another, but I feel nothing. His touch falls numb against my skin. Deep, deep down, that lost sliver of myself—I think—is thankful his touch only repulses me.

He drags his eyes up to mine with a crease between his brows. "You've lost your light, your warmth."

I hold his gaze. "I never truly had my light before, though. Did I?" My words have a hard edge to them that I didn't intend, but the scar around my neck reminds me of the light I could never reach. Aiden notices, too, for his eyes shutter when they take in the raised skin, a mangled remnant that will forever decorate my throat.

His fingers tremble where they remain on my arm as I tip my head to force him to peer into my black orbs. "No." He lets out a deflated sigh. "But I do want to apologize. For the things I said and for all that was done to you. I-I didn't know, Emma."

"He will pay."

Aiden silently nods. "You already made him pay, didn't you? You killed King Oren." The sun suddenly hardens its light, causing his face to scrunch as he looks up to the sky.

"I wasn't talking about King Oren."

His green eyes slam into mine and I cock my head to the side as I wait for his response. "My father?"

Staring blankly at him, I allow my silence to answer for me. And once he understands, he scratches behind his head and looks out to the sea. "You know I can't allow that."

"How would you stop me if I stole your father's still-beating heart from his chest while you were asleep?"

His eyes flare for the briefest moment before he reins it in. "Emma, you must know...I still love you. Even this version of you." His hands gesture down my body and I remain unmoving. "I still want this to work, even if I've had a hard time forgetting your actions towards me before you became this. But my father..." He exhales a long sigh with a swipe of his hand down his face. "He can be unreasonable at times, but don't make me choose who would see the end of my sword."

Those green eyes harden, revealing the core of who Aiden is underneath his manicured mask. "One day, we won't have to worry about him. Once he steps down, it will be you and me who rule as King and Queen of Asov."

Sharp pinpricks of pain break out over my skin for the first time, with unease coiling tightly in my gut at the thought of being crowned next to him. A wave of nausea crashes over me and makes the ground ripple beneath my feet.

"Woah." Smooth hands grab both sides of my waist to keep me upright. "Are you okay?"

I brush a small piece of hair out of my face that became unleashed from its braid by the wind. "Yes." My heart beats faster than it ever has since the darkness claimed me, and I wipe my palms over the front of my dress. "That has never happened before."

The tips of his fingers dig into the silky material of my dress, but I can barely feel it as I grasp hold of myself. "I've got you."

"I'd like to go back to my room and rest for a while."

"Of course, I'll walk you back. Maybe it's the heat from the sun."

He keeps his hand on the small of my back as he leads me to my room, while I rack my mind for what could have caused that reaction. As soon as I see my room, I don't hesitate to curl my fingers around the handle, pushing my door open. I desperately need to be alone to clear my head.

"Emma, wait." I pause in the middle of my threshold and look back at him. He reaches into his pocket and pulls out a white seashell to place in my hand. "It's yours," he says softly. His mouth opens and closes a few times before he speaks again. "Let me know if you need anything, but get plenty of rest before the celebration tomorrow. I'm looking forward to seeing you again."

The obsidian in my eyes begins to swirl and the need to tell him *no* sits on my tongue. But I swallow it down, not sure why I'm getting a rush of unsettling *feelings* when I'm supposed to not to feel a damn thing inside.

Instead, I say, "Tomorrow, then." The door closes behind me without another look at his sea-green eyes that I could easily ruin in my dark storm.

After Aiden brought me back to my room, I drifted off into a deep slumber, only to wake up in complete darkness with no sign of light peeking through the balcony doors. As I lie there, gazing up at the ceiling, the last flicker of the candle's flame illuminates the room with a faint orange glow. I'm not sure how much time passes. Despite my exhaustion, sleep eludes me.

I slip on a pair of boots—not bothering to lace them. I want to go for a walk in the hopes it will tire me into wanting to sleep a few more hours. My shadows wrap around me and take me outside the palace so I can stand at the shoreline.

I mindlessly walk under the starless ebony sky that veils across the sea, mesmerized by the glowing crescent that casts a gentle path of moonlight on the rippling waves that kiss the shore. A subtle reminder that I still have time before the full moon.

Without thought, I step out of my boots and wade into the water, letting it cascade up to my shins. I'm sure it feels refreshing, but it does nothing against my frozen skin. Still…I keep trudging farther until it sloshes around my hips. My fingers skim over the surface as it dances around me.

My head tips back, letting the end of my hair dip into the water as I stare up at the broken moon. I reach deep down within, pommeling my way through the darkness that has sank its claws into my mind, and search for that feeling of warmth that snuck up on me before. The buried piece of my soul that I need to find. The one that's yearning for something beneath the veil of darkness.

My eyes close as I sink deeper into my psyche while the water now crests just below my chin. One deep breath in, and I fall under. Sealing the remaining air in my lungs as I slip farther beneath the surface. Darkness engulfs me but the whispers are the only thing drowning—sounding muffled.

A black abyss swirls around me, but a flash of blue eyes as clear as ice slam into me and my heart lurches in my chest. They gaze at me from between shadowed trees, their cold stare sparking a kernel of warmth I let myself open to it, willing it to spread and burn beneath my skin.

The darkness wavers and I allow my power to wrap around me to follow the pull that feels familiar. My shadows coil around my body, tingling over my skin. Until, one moment, I'm floating beneath the sea, and the next, I'm standing in the midst of a sleeping forest cloaked in a hushed fog.

A hauntingly beautiful castle looms before me and an owl hoots nearby. Droplets of water drip from my body and onto the earth as my toes dig into the soil. I'm in the Court of Asiza. The same place I was drawn to on my last task for my father. That same feeling from before nudges me to want to step closer.

I stand there soaking wet as I let this hum of magnetic energy—this *feeling* I've been numb to—vibrate through my veins. But then, a brush of *heat* trails down my spine. A foreign sensation I haven't felt in months.

Before I comprehend what's happening, a shadow bands around my waist and pulls me back into something hard. But it's not my shadows… Something radiating heat that matches the equivalent of flames feathers over me and threatens to melt away the ice coating the blackened organ in my chest.

Despite my confusion, the pull in my chest grows stronger, tightening even more. My heart pounds loudly in my ears.

"Little demon," a deep voice licks over every inch of my skin. Prince Draven. The one I'm supposed to lure to me by standing beside Aiden, and yet…it seems I'm the one lured to him.

CHAPTER NINE

Draven

*H*er rose and honey scent still lingers even with her cold
exterior.

"Prince Draven." Her tone lacks any emotion despite the electric
sensation of having her back pressed firmly against my chest. I tighten
my hold as I finally exhale the breath that feels like I've been holding for
an eternity. She shivers as I lean closer to the nape of her neck, my
breath tickling the small hairs that are starting to dry quicker than the
rest.

I want to ask her why she's fucking soaked, but I already know she
won't even consider answering. Either way, I'm fucked. Her ivory nightgown is practically see-through as it clings to every inch of her.

I dip down even farther, itching to have my hands grab onto her waist
and never let her go. Instead, I fist them at my side and inhale deeply,
wishing I could breathe her into my soul. "I've been waiting here every
night in hopes you would appear again." She has to know how desperate
I've been for her to come back to me and prove that what I saw on the

roof that one drunken night was not some fucked-up, twisted joke being played on my mind.

Her head tips back, resting against my shoulder. I close my eyes with a sigh, releasing all the agony that has been tearing me to shreds. Her body trembles against mine and I wonder if the dark veil is starting to lift within her as she presses her body further into mine. My fists relax as I go to finally feel her in my embrace again, but before I even lift an arm, her power surges. She cuts it through my power holding her against me, knocking me backward, and I have to hurry to regain my footing.

Drops of water splatter around her like a halo as my heated gaze flickers from blue to silver. The beast in me fights against the surface, wanting nothing more than to claim her.

"Emma," the strength in my voice cracks when I take a step closer to her. She follows suit by taking one back to keep the distance. "Don't do th—"

The swirling black of her eyes locks onto me right before she strikes. A ball of what looks like midnight fire soars directly towards my chest. I crouch down and twist out of its path right before it would have probably blasted a gaping hole through my chest, incinerating my heart with it.

She remains in the same spot, the rest of her unnaturally still as she slowly tilts her head to the side. Her veins seem to move like snakes beneath her skin. It must be a sign of her building more power because the weight of energy drifting from her continues to grow heavier.

I tilt my head to match hers. "Looks like you're making me your villain again."

I want nothing more than to wrap my arms around her and bring her back into the light, but she despised me once before and I managed to get her to warm up to me then. I have no doubt I can do it again. Even though seeing her lost in the darkness—combined with her rejection—is like slowly driving a jagged knife into my heart and twisting it.

We both are alert to the other's movements as we slowly circle one another. I can't help the extra beat in my heart or the small smirk that graces my face knowing that nothing is more powerful than a fated mate bond. Not even Whiro himself.

"I'll be happy to remind you how sinful I can get, little demon," I tease.

This causes her to pause, but only for half a breath before she's throwing another orb of power at me. Without hesitation, I send out my own and watch it collide with hers, disintegrating her attack in a puff of mist between us. She huffs at the same time a crooked tilt lifts the corner of her mouth. Her head shakes as if she's trying to quiet it, but instead starts blasting tendrils of power in the shape of arrows without pause. I meet each one with the same intensity.

Just two cursed souls fighting beneath the stars that fated us.

"So far, you're doing a pathetic job in fighting against me." Her voice scratches against her throat, sounding demonic.

I hold a shadow of power in my palm, prepared for her attack. "I will never strike at you." How could I ever truly fight against the one person who unknowingly holds my heart, my *life*, in her hands? I would forever silence my own heart before ever truly harming her.

Her eyes sharpen on me with a wicked twitch to her lips. "Shall we put it to the test?"

She doesn't miss the deep V that furrows between my brows at her question. All I know is that she wants a challenge. This feisty mate of mine always finds a way to challenge me, even when she is lost within herself.

Her head tips back with outstretched arms, and suddenly, the shadows of the night start swarming around the two of us, stealing my sight. I stay perfectly still in the dark, but even calling on my dragon side, I can't see through this level of power she's wrapping around us. I weave my hand through the air, feeling its caress and the cadence of her power. It's astonishing, but I strain my focus on my other senses and force myself to be alert.

"Time to play a game, *prince*," her taunting voice echoes around me as I stand in the midst of her shadows.

She must remember those very words leaving my lips months ago, when her skin was warm to the touch with a slight pink tint and her needy body arched beneath me. *Fuck*. Not the time to replay the night we shared or my cock's going to swell painfully hard since I haven't been able to give myself any relief since she's been gone. The emptiness I've felt when she became lost to me has consumed every fucking part of me. Numbing me.

Getting lost in my thoughts, I almost miss feeling the strength of power rise to my left. I faintly hear the energy cutting through the air before I twist and jerk my body back in one swift movement. I hiss as a sliver of skin starts burning near my shoulder. I was a second too slow, allowing her attack to cut right through the material of my clothing as a hint of metallic scent wafts in the air.

I hurry and steady my stance as I feel more energy growing for another round of blasts coming my way. My eyes shut, drawing all my other senses to the forefront and begin firing back, knowing each one is hitting with perfect precision. They seem to be coming from every angle as I duck, spin, and sidestep to direct my aim to the closest target. She truly wants me to miss, grow angry, and start targeting *her*. But I never will.

Her attacks are slowing, allowing me to destroy one before spinning around in time to leap in the air and let the final one spear beneath me. She thinks she can hide and fight me blind, but I can physically *feel* her. Completely aware of her and the bond, like a rope pulling me to her.

Midair, I flare my wings out and land right behind her. Snaking my hand around her waist, I jerk her sideways and pin her back against the trunk of a tree. My hand is already holding both of her wrists above her head to prevent her from striking again. With each wild breath, my chest rises and falls quickly from being this close to her. I can't help the small rasp of a chuckle that escapes from how familiar this position is to when we first met in the alley.

"Did I win?" I ask, letting my breath fan across her cheek as I feel her body shiver before me.

"How did you find me when you couldn't see me?" she asks in one solid exhale.

I'm standing so close to her, with only an inch keeping my body from brushing against hers. The sound of her racing heart sounds beautiful to my ears. A drastic change from the hard, cold beats earlier.

Not being able to hold back, I drag my nose up the curve of her neck, inhaling deeply. "I don't need to see in order to find you." Her spine arches towards me and I don't even think she realizes how her body is betraying her.

Her shadows let up slightly, letting me see the damp nightgown that molds perfectly to her curves. A growl vibrates low in my chest. "You could blindfold me, restrain me, or anchor me to the bottom of the fucking ocean. So long as you exist in this realm, you cannot hide from me. Your scent is etched into my being, and the melody of your soul calls to mine no matter what shade of darkness it dances in." My palm engulfing her wrists tightens as I bring the other hand to cradle her jaw, letting the pad of my thumb trace her lower lip. "And in case you require more clarification, my heart desperately yearns to beat in tune with yours."

The shadows of her power slowly lessen even more, allowing me to gaze upon her more clearly. My hand falls from her face and I gently place it over her heart that's beating inside its blackened cage. Her body tenses under my touch, her chest stilling as she holds in a breath. My gaze slams into hers then, the silver in my eyes glowing brighter to crash against the dark abyss flooding in hers. Both of us locked in this moment, unable to look away.

I call on my own shadows to wrap around hers, intertwining as our energies merge together. They caress each other like two lost lovers finally reuniting. Sensing I'm not in harm's way at the moment, I release my grip on her wrists and flatten my palm on the rough bark above her head.

The air in her lungs slowly releases. A small spark warms within the bond and for a moment, the cold gates blocking her from me flood open. Along with a vision sparking of her hand covered in crimson placed directly over my bleeding chest when I freed her from Whiro's cell. Over my scar that is marked solely for her.

Her head shakes, and the memory fades, making me believe that I just saw what she did. The shield to her mind openly connected to mine, pushing that memory through the bond even though she doesn't realize it.

"Emma—" I go to speak, but another memory flashes behind my eyes. The moments the darkness consumed her. When I was running towards her, with her looking down at me and placing a hand over her heart. A meaning, one so clear then. It was a show of *love*.

Now, she mimics the memory. Her hand slowly covers mine on her chest and my eyes follow the movement. "I'm feeling…" she whispers.

My silver eyes cut through the dark as they snap back up to implore hers that are pinned on me.

She gingerly places her other hand on my chest, right where my scar lives beneath my shirt. Feeling both of our organs beat in sync with the other, her fingers dig hard into me. "I'm *feeling.*"

The air around us grows tangible with the rise of our power swirling as one, causing my wings to flare out and cage us in. In one swift movement, I grip her waist and pull her flush against me. "There you are, little demon." My body radiates more heat against her skin that's beginning to warm. The black pools of her eyes start swirling with grey, as if the poisonous fog is trying to clear. And the sight of her in my arms feels like the clouds are finally parting, allowing me to walk under the sun after a storm of desolation.

She tenses against me again before her muscles relax, knowing a sliver of her darkness has cleared and I can see the question she wants to ask that's causing her eyebrows to dip. "Nothing is more powerful than the bond of fated mates."

She sucks in a shaky breath and takes her eyes off my chest, tipping her head back to look up at me. I'm sure she will see the black slits of my pupils slightly larger than before with the beast in me wanting to claim her in every way.

Her eyes dart back and forth between mine. "But you and I aren't—"

I slam my mouth against hers to stop any other words from leaving her. My lips against hers create a spellbinding pulse to build around us that makes me internally groan. I can't get enough, and just as I swipe my tongue against her lips, wanting her to let me in…she does.

That's my good fucking girl.

She doesn't protest as I push my tongue against hers, tasting her with a ferocity that can't be tamed because I'm fucking starving for her. A soft moan comes from her, and I swallow it down, growling into her mouth while roughly sucking and tugging on her bottom lip. The bond tightens between us, buzzing with a mixture of lust and forever.

Need rises inside me, causing my cock to strain against the seam of my pants as I press my hips deeper into her. I let the sigh escape her lips as I trail feverish kisses across her jaw while reaching behind her neck and

69

tipping her head back so I can consume more of her. I eagerly bite and nip. Teeth clashing as I drink her in, never feeling like I will be able to quench my thirst.

Her hands grab hold of my arms, squeezing tightly as she lets me ravish her, wanting me to worship her like the Goddess she is. Even though I know it will never be enough, I need to fucking drown in her.

With every bit of control I can conjure, I pull away, dropping my forehead against hers. The sound of sharp, shallow breaths is all I hear against the rapid pounding of my heart.

"You're mine," I claim against her lips. "Anyone who dares to touch you will meet the end of their fate by my hands, and I'll be happy to paint my promises with their blood."

Her chest rises and falls roughly against mine. The grey in her eyes shines clearer than before, but still not completely. Before I can blink, her head snaps back with a grunt and she slams her hands over her ears. She hunches over, letting out a strangled scream that seems to make the trees wary with the way their branches still against the wind. Pain unleashes in the bond and my eyes widen as her power blasts out, knocking me backward.

I relinquish my wings before my back hits the forest floor. My body skids across it from the force, snapping roots and uprooting plants until my shoulder slams into the base of a tree. I don't bother to brush myself off as I jump back on my feet, noticing the way her eyes resemble death again, dark as night.

She says nothing, the pull to the darkness stealing her away again. But she's a fighter with the strength of all the stars in the sky. She will find her light again, even if I need to start the fire.

In the next breath, she calls on her power to wrap around her, leaving me alone once again in the forest. My eyes change back to blue as the connection to her through the bond drifts farther away. But I won't let her slip through my fingers.

Because I'm under her spell, addicted to her poison, and I will fall into her ruin.

She will forever be my undoing.

CHAPTER TEN

Emma

Ships are scattered near the seaport of Asov, with their anchors released to keep their wooden beauties steady for the celebration. The official crowning of Calloway took place, and now music drifts through the salty air as every court mingles and dances on their ships.

Normally, such an occasion would take place in the throne room, then move to the ballroom for the party to follow. But Calloway is a captain whose sole love will always be on the water with the wind brushing against his sails. If only his greedy love for power wasn't equally matched.

Wooden slabs are strung together to create bridges that are roped to each ship, connecting them for the people to travel easier for conversation and to greet the new king with their congratulations. I currently stand on the main deck, looking out past the fleets of ships and further to the horizon. My hands curl over the side of the ship, the splintered wood scraping the underside of my palm.

Aiden's hand is gently resting on the small of my back that's covered by the design of the gown he had made for me. One that hides every silent

71

scream brutally marked on my skin. The scars of my past which have only strengthened the demon I've become. Scars I now wear proudly, yet Aiden chose to keep them unseen from the public eye. The thought makes me dig my nails into the wood, pressing hard enough to imprint my frustration with small crescent marks.

The dress is gold and catches the light of the sun, shimmering with the smallest movement. Aiden's choice of color is simple; he's showcasing me as if I'm a golden trophy he won. The sleeves cover just below my shoulder, with a flared neckline and the smallest opening that cuts down the front of my chest. A seam cinches around my waist before it drapes down in pleats, and the entire fucking gown is suffocating. I may complement the gold accents that line Aiden's princely outfit as I stand beside him, but that's not why the people stare.

All of them finally feast their eyes on the princess who was hidden away. They try to hide it, but the moment their gazes land on me, they dart them away before the darkness swirling in my eyes locks with theirs. Yet, they can't help but sneak their focus back on me when they think I'm not paying attention. I look like the Corrupted, which makes them wary.

The streams of ebony beneath my skin clash against the bright shine of the gown. Like a war between good and evil.

"I can't believe he's officially king," Aiden says calmly beside me.

I twist my head until my gaze finds Calloway, who is standing at the helm of the ship. His shoulders back and chin jutting out high as if the entire land of Deyadrum is his.

"I'm sure many feel the same."

I can already tell this rank of power is going to go straight to his egotistical head. Everyone in Asov is already suffering under his inevitably harsh rule. For someone so selfish and cruel, he sure isn't hiding it. Already, he shows how little he cares for his people by not providing the necessary goods they need to live without worry, while he refuses to listen to their pleas or answer their questions. The little time I've been back here, I have noticed many leaving to move to another court. His rule has only just begun, and the people are justifiably outraged.

Yet, Aiden acts like his father is doing no harm. Right now, he's wearing a fashionable outfit in the most blinding white that causes my eyes to squint and makes me want to look away. Or maybe it's the simple fact that one look at his face makes me want to smash his head into the wooden boards beneath my feet. A game to see which would crack first, the wood or his skull.

Suddenly, I feel Aiden tense beside me. The hand on my back slides to curl around my waist and draw me into his side. I glance at him out of the corner of my eye as his green orbs harden, glaring. "I'm glad we can put everything behind us and move forward together. You and I, just like we were always meant to be."

My brows pull together. His words are spoken with steel as his eyes stay trained out to sea. For once, I'm not sure how to respond because he and I will never be forever. Just a picture he's painted in his head. Aiden is a means to an end and a ploy to use for the task at hand. He's nothing but a pawn I will have to discard when the time comes.

I follow where his eyes linger and the breath I was about to exhale gets lodged in my throat.

Prince Draven leans against the post of a ship anchored three rows away, arms crossed over his chest and eyes trained solely on me. Couples dance around behind him with the sound of music filtering through the air for everyone to hear. A zap of heat rolls beneath my skin, igniting every nerve ending, threatening them to explode until my heart flutters. I hide everything unfurling inside me while I keep my face blank.

"You are mine," a voice penetrates my thoughts, causing my eyes to widen for a split second. But Prince Draven smirks, not missing my reaction.

Mates. He mentioned fated mates. If the spark in my cold chest isn't enough proof, him speaking into my mind is. I lift my hand, the tips of my fingers absentmindedly tracing the scarred ring around my neck. The reason such a bond could never snap in place. It makes me want to bring King Oren back to life, just so I can kill him again and again.

I almost startle when Aiden speaks, "He needs to learn his place."

My eyes stay locked on Prince Draven. "And what's that?"

Aiden's lips ever so gently kiss the top of my head. When I chance a quick glance up, his eyes look like they are trying to burn a hole into the Dark Prince. "That you were never his."

Bile threatens to burn its way up my throat at the feel of his lips on me and the words that spew from his mouth. Dragging my gaze back to the prince who is making my heart beat irregularly, I keep my shoulders pulled back and breathe slowly through my nose.

Any trace of the smirk on Prince Draven's face has vanished. Hard lines sharpen over his features from the bright rays of the sun, but his shadows seem to darken the air around him. A dark cloud on the verge of a dangerous storm.

"Come." Aiden's fingers press slightly into my side to nudge me in his direction. "Let us join the celebration."

Prince Draven's gaze falls down to where Aiden has his hand placed on me, causing his nostrils to flare. He then snaps those beautiful blues to the side of Aiden's head, narrowing them as something dark seems to pass through his targeted gaze.

I don't pause to get a good read on what that might be as I indulge Aiden, letting him take my hand to guide me into the middle of the ship and dance to a few rounds of songs. We move gracefully with the wind. By the fourth song, a guard interrupts and tells Aiden his father would like to speak with him.

"I'll be back as soon as we're done speaking." A light smile dances over his face. "I suggest you go grab a drink and hydrate because I plan to dance with you until the sun goes down."

My head rears back as my brows come together. "Why all the dancing? Surely it would be more important for you to mingle with the people and other royals of the courts?"

He steps into my space, leaning down until his lips feather against the shell of my ear. "The last ball, I only got one dance with you, and it wasn't enough. I won't make that mistake again and plan to make up for that tenfold." He brings his head back to look down into my lifeless eyes, tucking a loose strand of hair behind my ear. "And there is nothing I want more than to simply enjoy the music and have you in my arms for as long as I can for everyone to see."

"Careful, you're sounding a little possessive."

A telling smirk tips his lips. "Maybe I am, but I won't lose you again."

I hold his gaze, leaning into him until our noses almost touch, his

74

pupils dilating with my nearness. "You can't lose something you never had."

He jerks back as if I slapped him, which probably would have hurt him less than the words I pierced his chest with. But I don't want him to think my heart is warming for *him*. I give him a tight smile to try and bandage the wound my words caused.

"Come find me when you're done speaking with your father." I reach out and give his arm a gentle squeeze before walking towards the back end of the ship, needing to put some space between me and the chaos of festivities.

I lose track of time as I stand at the stern of the ship. The waves crash against the wooden boards, causing the ship to sway back and forth to the rhythm of the sea. The kernel of warmth in my chest has lingered longer than that night I fought Prince Draven in the woods. A small piece of my sanity persists alongside that spark of light, feeling a little more like myself again, even with the darkness still thriving in my veins.

My elbows rest on top of the ledge of the ship as I hold my palms out before me, staring at my fingertips. I reach deep within my core for that small fragment of light that's been trapped and beg for it. Calling it to me with every bit of desperation I feel from losing it.

A tingle spreads through my fingers, heating them until a zap of light pulses from each one. It looks like white stars firing against the night sky. It's a sign of *hope*.

But just as quickly, it's gone. I can feel the well of my light settled deep within me, but it feels like it hides at the bottom of a cliff. Knowing it's there but just out of reach.

A flash of yellow catches my attention in my peripheral, but when I look out to the sea, there is nothing. My gaze scans the waves lapping before me and down along one side of the ship, but still, nothing. It must have been a trick of the sunlight.

"Figured I'd find you away from the crowd," a sultry feminine voice skates over my skin, and I glance at her out of the corner of my eye. Her white hair shines brightly under the sun and her eyes sparkle like two violet gems. Mauve, the sensual Seer, looking like a siren with legs.

"And I figured you would forever stay secluded away in your mountaintop in the Court of Amihan."

She smiles at that as she takes in my appearance, her gaze locking in on the distorted skin around my neck. "You're right. I would have preferred to keep my distance from such an overwhelming celebration." She briefly looks back to the herds of people still spinning to the music. "But then, I had a vision you would be here, looking absolutely deadly since the last time we spoke."

"That should have been your sign to stay away." The coal of my eyes is wanting to dull the vibrant hue of hers. "I will feel nothing if I kill you."

She dips her head with a low, velvety laugh that hums in her chest. "I don't doubt that. I can feel the God of Darkness's power crawling through your veins. But I took my chance because I have a part to play."

My heart sinks to my stomach as I stare at her without blinking. "You know my father?"

She stares out to the sea as if she's searching for something she will never find. "Father," she says softly under her breath. "That explains the level of power I felt in you before, even though it was leashed. But now, the open strength of your power is…immense." She slides her eyes to me before squinting up to the sky. "And to answer your question, I met him once, but it wasn't pleasant."

She breathes in the warm, salty air as if she hasn't felt it in years. And maybe she hasn't, since she lives in the mountains and her skin looks as if it's never been touched by the sun.

"He took the love of my life, Ragon, from me, threatening to devour his soul if I fought him." Her eyes close with a pinched face. "If his soul is destroyed in that way, he wouldn't pass on to the afterlife and be in peace."

My brows furrow together, the edge of my nail tracing the small carvings in the wooden railing, as I listen to her speak. "That's why I live the way I do. I should have fought, but I didn't. The loss of him is a constant ache on my soul. Like a cage of spikes piercing my heart with every beat."

"Why?" I ask the question even though it's one I feel she won't answer. But she surprises me.

"Because I *saw* his soul get consumed by Whiro if I went after him. The vision still haunts me, even when I shut my eyes." She rubs her thumb over her left palm in circles, where a faded black swirl of diamonds marks her skin. Mates.

I let her get lost in her thoughts as I silently watch the haze blur the horizon. Mauve punishes herself by letting her regret and grief eat away at her. She does well to put on a strong face, but deep down, she's tormented from her past and grieving the one she loves.

"Anyway, forget about me. I came because there is something I saw in a vision, and you are the center of it. The last time I saw you, you became a mystery to me, one I can't seem to solve but wish to know the answers to. And it seems I learned one thing that makes sense." She tips her head down an inch to study me. "The Goddess of Darkness, and yet, your black heart still beats to the shade of red." She twists her torso towards me, a gleam twinkling in her eyes.

I raise an eyebrow at her in question even though my face is flat, unenthused.

"Fate requires my assistance to guide it on the right path."

"And what's that?" I ask, blandly, already done with the conversation and wanting to be alone.

It's as if she can read my mind and smirks like she didn't just confess her own haunted past mere moments ago. "Remember, darkness can be broken by the light, but you have to open your eyes." My mouth opens to ask her what she's talking about, but she speaks before I can. "Fight with your heart and hold your breath."

"Wha—"

Her power flows from her hands, paralyzing my body, right before she presses them into my back and shoves me overboard. My voice is silenced in my throat as I fall, slamming into the water with a splash. The moment I hit it, she releases my muscles from her hold. The last thing I see is purple eyes watching me from above as I sink beneath the sea.

CHAPTER ELEVEN

Emma

My dress harmoniously floats with the waves as my eyes are trained up on the diamonds of light reflecting off the surface. The sea continues to pull me down, farther and farther until my lungs are screaming for air. A burning sensation rises up my throat as I'm caught in a current that keeps swallowing me down.

I slice my arms through the water and kick my feet to launch up, but somehow, I don't budge. The current keeps hold of me, forcing me to stay in the sea's embrace. The sting in my chest radiates like a roaring fire, and a black blur starts creeping around the edge of my sight.

Maybe this is what Mauve meant by guiding fate—to end me.

To somehow lock me in this current with no way to swim free. Because ridding this world of me will save Prince Draven. And if I'm gone—by another's hand—then there's a chance Whiro will spare the lives of *everyone*.

You can't threaten someone who is already dead.

And a piece of me has been tormented since last night. My heart unknowingly reached for the prince, and now, I have to sentence my mate to a fate worse than death. That thought twists my stomach into a million knots.

My eyelids fall shut and my arms fall limp as the pain begins to numb. This is it, isn't it? The moments before falling into death's hands?

I've come to realize that someone either fears death—doing everything they can to avoid it until their last breath creeps up from behind—or they accept it and face it head-on with open arms. Knowing that the clock on their life will eventually stop ticking. Death is inevitable. Even for a God. My mother is proof of that.

I've always known there is no in-between. I thought I would feel peace when the moment greets me. Instead my chest cracks, ripping open with the pain of losing something worth cherishing. Of finally finding a reason for hoping my heart will never stop beating. *My mate.*

I don't wish this.

I don't want to die.

I want to fucking *live*.

A tear slips free from my closed eyes, getting lost in the sea to be forgotten.

Right when I'm about to lose consciousness, I'm yanked forward, my body shaken with extreme force. It jolts me awake, causing me to inhale deeply.

Stunned, my wide eyes stare at two that shine like molten gold. My heart pounds roughly in my chest.

I blink once. Twice. My mind slowly comes back into focus, and the air suddenly filling my lungs relieves the tightness. I'm still far below the ship, floating in place, when I notice the air bubble covering my mouth and nose. My chest rises and falls rapidly as I keep greedily filling my lungs until it hurts, thankful for the creature before me.

The Masiren. A creature so deadly it's a haunting nightmare of the sea. And yet, it found me worth saving.

I can't explain it, but there is this connection that gravitates me towards the Masiren. Not even the darkness can steal that from me. It's some deep-rooted piece of my soul that senses something familiar within it, finding comfort.

Slowly, I reach my hand out while I gauge its reaction. It dips its head slightly forward, a silent sign of permission. My palm closes the distance to rest on its head, the grey skin is smooth to the touch. My eyes track the rest of its body, noticing how replenished it looks from when I found it in the well. The red that coated its skin has long been washed away, the singed skin healed. Only bearing a few mangled scars from where it was chained down.

"Thank you," I say through the pocket of air, my voice sounding muffled as it travels through the water.

The moment I remove my hand, the Masiren spins, wrapping its tail around my ankle. It coils tightly to prevent my foot from slipping through right before it starts spearing deeper into the sea. I'm yanked away from the ship to the darkened depths, where the sun can't even reach.

I don't fight, because if it wanted me dead, I already would be. But I can't help but wonder where it's taking me. Is it protecting me from danger above the surface? Is it wanting to show me something? Is the Masiren playing a part in guiding fate, too? A million thoughts race through my mind, but nothing sticks for what the true reason may be.

The Masiren travels deeper and deeper until it dips below into a tunnel submerged with static water. No flow, no current. The only visible movement is caused by our wake.

I'm not sure how far it's taking me away from the ship, but I'm finding I don't care. It's quieter down here, anyway. Drowning out the whispers that scrape along my mind, silencing them.

The end of the tunnel leads us to a massive opening that has intricate designs marked along the stone curving around us. Its tail releases me as I right myself and gradually swim close to the edge, waiting. The Masiren remains still, watching me.

"Why did you bring me here?" I ask, turning so my eyes can scan each carving that has a faint glow emitting from it.

I glance behind me and watch the Masiren's yellow eyes change to white. "To talk to you."

My head tilts to the side as I ponder that, while the tune of its voice causes a warmth to spread throughout my chest. "You've been watching me."

"Since you were born."

Every muscle in my body freezes, as I stare unblinkingly into its eyes. Hesitantly, I ask, "How is that possible?" My question flows through the space with a shaky breath.

Its lethal limbs gracefully sway in the water, and its tail weaves back and forth to keep it steady and in place. "I am a creature of the Gods. Crafted from their power since the beginning. It's why you don't fear me."

I think about how I never met the Masiren until recently. The way it was abused and left to rot in the well... Was that because of me? "Did you get caught by the previous king because of me?"

Its head shakes. "It's my job to watch over you. Getting caught was always a part of my fate. I couldn't tell you when you saved me, because a moment longer would have cost you and your friends freedom." My brows crash together as I bore my eyes into it, and the Masiren's eyes soften to a dimmer glow. "I could hear you...in the beginning."

"The beginning?" I ask.

"When you used to scream."

My lips part with a gasp.

"I am connected to you and can hear you through the link of our consciousness. I could feel your pain. Your fear. Your *hate*. How the loneliness was consuming you more and more each year."

I shake my head, remembering the condition the Masiren was in when I found it, and a small fissure spreads through my chest. "But why couldn't I feel you or the link? I-I would have saved you so much sooner if I knew you were chained in the bottom of some rusted well."

Its tail lashes sharply to one side then the other as if remembering. "Our connection never had a chance to grow for you to feel it. Once the iron was wrapped around your neck, it stunted our bond's growth. Before that tragic day, I was already able to sense you because I was aware of the bond since you were born, opening the link in my mind. But now, in time, you will begin to feel me. To reach out if you need."

My eyes trace over the Masiren in awe, taking in this deadly creature that is so gentle with its kind words. "And those years in the cell were minuscule to my lifespan, but significant for yours." Its eyes flare brighter, but I can't read the emotions swirling in its gaze. "My suffering was nothing to what you endured. I may have burned under the sun, been starved because someone forgot to deliver meals, and cramped in the same hole. But you…"

Its head tenderly nudges mine and it feels like an endearment. "You had to bleed rivers of pain until the king was satisfied. Until death was holding its breath, waiting to open the doorway for you. People were too afraid to come near me, let alone lay a hand on me. But it was the opposite for you, and what I was able to feel through the bond was only a sliver of the agony that you were dealt. You already saved me. It was I who was wishing to save you."

Speechless, I'm unable to find words to give a proper response. All I want to do is pull the Masiren in and hold it. To give it the comfort it never received, to take care of it.

Suddenly, the Masiren reaches out to trail one of its long, pointed claws along the path of a black vein. "And now, this dark power is controlling you. You need to rule over and dominate it."

"There is no need to control it. I already have a handle on it, and this power helps to numb away the painful memories."

The Masiren shakes its head. "No. It may hide the pain, but it twists the emotions from those memories into ones of hate and vengeance. This power is an extension of *you*, but you aren't an extension of it. Force it to your will and find the light within yourself."

"I've tried."

The Masiren hisses and I think it just scoffed at me. "This is why I'm here, to help you open the doors that are locked with shadows. You may be the daughter of the God of Darkness, but you are also the daughter of the Goddess of Light. Both equally exist in you." A flare of glimmering light pulses at the tip of its nail. "To clear the darkness, you just need to shine bright enough."

The tip of its claw connects right where my heart is beating frantically. An explosion of light sends shockwaves through the water that rattles the ocean floor. It surges into my chest, sending heat through my veins that burns like a million suns.

My eyes slam shut with a grunt as it travels into my core of power, slicing through the shadows and opening a path to the part of me that has been locked away. The piece of my soul that has been forced to watch every mind-numbing kill. I follow it, seeing a kernel of pure, white light swirling in the center. My heart beats irregularly as I mentally reach for it. Longing to bring myself out of the dark and live with my own mind intact.

When I go to pull it to me, I hesitate, and the light glimmers just out of my reach. The darkness has been with me for so long… What if this angers it, causing it to lash out? Distantly, the Masiren's voice cuts through my thoughts as if it knows where my mind has headed.

"The darkness *is* you. The shadows are a storm of your creation. They will listen if you accept that they are part of your soul."

Sensing the shadows floating just on the outskirts of my mind, I dive into the memory when the darkness felt like a friend instead of a foe. When it silently held me through the times I thought I would die. A friend that never left.

I reach for the light, clinging onto it as I slowly bring it to the surface. But it's slipping. I can feel myself losing the hold I have on it.

Noo! I cry out in frustration as it falls away, and the shadows start swarming around in a violent chaos.

But the Masiren's sliver of power once again clears a path, pushing the darkness to the side for me to try again.

I must do this. Not only for the Masiren, but for myself. Because I'm worth saving.

With an unsteady inhale, I let my mind drift to try and center my focus. A memory sneaks through, causing my cheeks to raise and my lips to turn upward. It's one of Cora throwing a slipper at Prince Draven, and a small, silent chuckle shakes my chest as it eases the nerves away.

Another memory collides into my psyche. One where I'm held against a warm, strong body, and the steady breaths of the Dark Prince sleeping soundly beside me. A time I felt safe as I was tucked into his arms. My heart swells as a sense of calmness washes over me.

It's then that I find another reason to keep fighting. To not give up. Because *they* are worth it. My friends who have become family to me, and I don't want to lose that.

But I have to break free of Whiro's hold and manipulations. To block the power he holds over me. With that thought in mind, I push the memories away and close the distance to grab hold of the light with all of my will, desperately not wanting to let go.

The darkness behind my eyes disappears as white light detonates with a blinding warmth that spreads through my body. The icy fog in my head clears away and I inhale a deep, calming breath that feels like the first warm ray from the morning light.

My eyes slowly flutter open, connecting with the Masiren as it watches me carefully. "You…" I pause, not sure what to say. For the first time in months, my soul is not divided in two, but instead merged as one. I can feel the two entities of power swirling tighter inside me, balancing each other. "You cleared the darkness," I say softly on shallow breath.

"No, I only guided you to your light."

My mind churns the possibilities of this over in a dizzying vortex, but the truth can't be hidden when it's right in front of me. "Is this truly real?" I ask with a sharp shake of my head. Denial is the first thing I cling on to. "I've tried to rid myself of the darkness and failed every time."

The Masiren tsks. "Lying is not something I'm capable of. I can only speak truths. So, yes, this is real. You are stronger than you realize. And it's not a weakness to need help, quite the opposite. I only cleared a path for you." Its tail swishes through the water before pointing at me. "*You* took hold of your light and pushed the shadows away. *You* are the one who is now balancing the power of two Gods. Not me. I only helped you open your eyes."

I lift my trembling hands radiating with a soft glow from my fingertips in front of my face. Hands that have ended lives who did not deserve such a cruel fate.

I curl my fingers in, fisting them tightly until my nails dig hard enough into my palm to sting. All the feelings that were numb come rushing to the surface. Flashes of that Fae on his knees before me reel in my mind. Of my hand diving into his chest to crush his beating heart. Of the Corrupted I ended without thought, of the male I hunted and stole away from his mate. I can feel myself spiraling, reliving the evil acts that I had relished in.

The tip of the Masiren's tail touches beneath my chin, lifting my head to force my eyes to meet its own. "You can't change what has already passed. Don't fear your darkness, because not all monsters dwell in the shadows. Some have fallen into them, only to rise stronger with the power to command, while keeping their hearts beating with tenderness. The shadows are not your enemy, and *you* are not the enemy. You have only fallen, so it's time to get up."

A burning starts to spill in my eyes, but no tears spring free. I bite my bottom lip to keep it from trembling. The Masiren cocks its head and looks pointedly at my hands. "Show me your powers, because you must control them."

"You mean to hide my light?"

"Only from those who wish to destroy it."

Another game. To pretend that I'm still consumed by the darkness, giving me time to find a way to end another male who calls himself my father. I let my eyes fall shut, reaching deep down to the core of my power. I'm easily mesmerized by the way they both dance together to the beat of my heart. I grapple with both, trying to ignite each power in my hands simultaneously.

Except, as soon as I feel their strength surge through my veins to my fingertips, they spark and then dim out. I huff loudly, clenching my teeth tightly together.

"Try again," the Masiren says patiently.

So, I do. I try repeatedly, to the point that I'm not sure how much time has passed, but most likely enough for my absence to be noted. Exhaustion pulls at me, but I refuse to stop. I will never stop fighting.

The next attempt, I clear my thoughts and push away the frustration. Instead of seeing the power, I only feel for it. Letting it trickle to the surface before pushing each one in a different direction. My heart races as if it will jump out my chest, as one of my hands begins to warm and the other turns freezing.

"The strength lies in you. Open your eyes." The Masiren's voice filters into my mind. I slowly let my eyelids lift, the blurriness clearing away until a gasp escapes me.

Light flares in my left hand, steady and waiting, while shadows play on my right, with black veins that track down that arm. "I did it," I breathe.

"You always could," the Masiren says in a joyous tone.

A question sticks to my mind, and I don't hesitate to ask, "Why are you helping me? You say you are made from the Gods—my parents—but that also includes you being bound to Whiro."

"I may have been created by them, but I was bound to neither. Your mother was unlike any other soul I had met. Your father hated how much she adored the Fae and showered them with kindness and affection. But her gentleness grew on me. So, I chose to remain loyal to her. And when you came into this world, I promised my life to watch over you for her."

"Thank you," I say with all the warmth blooming in my heart.

The Masiren gives a single dip of its head and holds it almost like a bow before wrapping its tail around my ankle and dragging me through the water. "It's time for you to return."

The bottoms of the ships come back into view, where they rock steady on the surface. The Masiren leads me up to the ship I was tossed from, but keeps me a few feet below. "You must embrace your darkness now," it says with glowing white eyes that never leave me. I push my light back into myself, calling solely on the shadows. Letting them wrap around me, to fill my veins and pool in my eyes.

Once again, a monster dressed in finery. However, the fear of losing myself is…gone. I don't feel the tantalizing claws of the whispers trying to take root. It's as if, instead of the storm clouds clearing for me to see the light…I became the storm.

Its tail fully releases me, and then the Masiren takes in my appearance with a curt nod. As if content to see the pale skin with black veins and death-filled eyes. "Remember, you are a fallen, Emma. So, now, it's time to rise."

"Then you must rise, too," I add quickly. "We were separated for so long." I pause, thinking about how the Masiren had fallen into a kind of darkness, too. One of King Oren's making and one it had to become to survive. "Maybe as we rise, we can do so together?" I ask this quietly, but the Masiren hears, pressing the top of its head to my forehead. A silent answer that together, we will embrace who we are and fucking *live*.

And with that, the Masiren pushes a wave towards me that surges me above the water. The moment I break free from the surface, the pocket of air covering my mouth disappears and I feel the sun rain down on my face for a brief moment.

Determination ignites inside me, steeling my spine as a queen on the board who, if given the power, can be a protector or seek to destroy. All I need to do is bide my time and wait to strike.

PART II

CHAPTER TWELVE

Emma

The moment my head breaks free above the surface, an arrow whizzes past my ear, piercing into the water behind me. I snap my attention to the ships scattered across the way as more iron-tipped arrows launch across a hazy orange sky. But I'm not the target; it's the ship that carries the newly crowned king. Thick smoke billows through the air and burns my throat with every inhale.

Screaming and shouting filters over the sea. The waves begin to smash into the wooden vessels with such power, almost like the water is reacting to the war of chaos unleashing above. But it's because those who wield water guide the sea's current to slam into the ship again, disturbing the peace of its beauty.

I glance up the side of the ship, knowing I'm going to need to use my shadows to portal me back aboard because it's too high and unsteady for me to scale up. I close my eyes to focus on the dark power humming within, and I call on it. The moment I feel it surging to my command, a wave crashes into me, pulling me under. I strain my arms and push against the water until I'm back to the surface, my insides constricting like I might cough up a lung from the water that snuck down my throat.

In between hacking up water, I manage to suck in short, deep breaths. Without a second thought, I let my shadows veil over my body right as an arm snakes around my waist. Before I can glance behind me, my power flares to transport me out of the sea, and the soles of my sodden shoes meet a wooden floor deep in the belly of the ship.

I'm immediately pushed against the door that leads to one of the rooms beneath the deck. The bond in my chest begins to hum as pine and maple swirl around me.

"What are you doing?" I sound breathless as he pushes in closer, his hands molding into my body beneath my ribcage. The faintly lit lantern swings above us like a pendulum with every sway of the ship.

His chest rises and falls deeply, brushing against mine as his icy blues frantically scan over every inch of me. "Saving you."

Two words, yet they triple the beat of my heart.

"I had it handled." My molars gnash together as I sharply turn my head away from him, feigning stubbornness even though the firm hold of his fingers digging into me has my knees weakening.

His chest shakes with silent laughter, causing me to snap my gaze back to him. "I can see that. Either way, I told you I will always come for you… and I meant it."

My breath threatens to catch in my throat from his words. With the darkness inside me free from invading my psyche, I can truly look at him. The hard glint of a promise in his eyes. The firm dip of his brows as he stares deeply into my eyes. The way his lips part as if he's holding his breath for my response. My eyes continue to scan over his features, while I can finally allow myself to feel the truth of his words. Even though he still believes I'm lost to the demons inside me.

An explosion blasts somewhere above the ship, vibrating every inch of wood I'm pressed against, and reminding me of what I saw before I brought us here. My head tilts back to look up at the ceiling as if I can see through it to the outside.

Prince Draven turns his head to look out the small circular window that's blocked by the dense smoke. Water drips from the raven strands of hair that have fallen in front of his eyes, and my fingers itch to touch them.

He drops his head back to me, answering an unsought question he seems to think I'm silently asking. "The attack is a rebellion against the new king." His voice is edged with disdain.

I scrunch my face with a nod, not saying a word. If I could, I would join the rebels to end Calloway's rule to the throne in a heartbeat. But if I go after Calloway, then Whiro will know something is amiss. And I can't let that happen, especially being this close to the male who has always seen me to my core. The one who deserves to see the sun rise for centuries to come.

"I should go," I say quickly, pushing against his chest to slip out of the muscular cage he somehow boxed me in. A slight prickle of panic licks down my spine and raises the hair on the back of my neck. I've been missing for too long—long enough for someone to notice and come looking for me.

"Don't." One simple word holds so much desperation that it causes me to halt my movements. The hand along my ribs tightens as his thumb brushes just under the swell of my breast. The warmth of his touch spreads over my skin and goosebumps rise along my body. I lift my gaze to find his blue eyes waiting as they probe mine. "Are you okay?"

His question catches me off guard, and I end up staring wide at him as the tether in my chest intensifies, threatening to make my knees buckle.

But I manage to stay steady and choke out a response. "Why wouldn't I be?"

"Because you were overboard in a sea that's growing angrier by the minute. And I saw you get crushed beneath a massive wave in the midst of a rebellion." Right as the words leave his lips, another explosion hits. It rattles the ship and causes more screams to screech in the distance.

The cries of terror are distant in my ears as I remain fixated on him. His words leave me…speechless. That's what I am right now as my heart hammers against my ribs. I bet if I ripped his chest open to look at his heart, it would shine like pure gold. Dented with imperfections and demons he's defeated, but proof that he would be a fallen just like the Masiren described. And together, we will rise and suffocate our demons on the smoke of the flames they lit to try and burn our hearts to ash.

His calloused palm gently cups my face, tipping his head to touch his forehead to mine. "My heart died a thousand deaths at that moment. Seeing you get sucked under. Watching arrows miss you by a thread." Our breaths mingle together as we share the same air with our lips only an inch apart. "You are mine, Emma." My breath hitches as his thumb traces the curve of my cheek bone. "And I protect what's mine."

My heart is racing, but I remain silent. He hasn't pulled away even though it seems like he's fighting a war within himself as he swallows roughly.

Achingly slow, he slides his hand to the small of my back and pulls me flush against him. Now, our lips are only a hair's breadth away. The hum of the bond inside me sparks every nerve ending in my body. Making me fully aware of every part of me that is touching him and, with it, bringing back everything he has made me feel in the past. Every skip of my heart, moments of overheated skin, and the way my core clenches for him.

"You must know…" He clears his throat, his fingers digging harder into my back while the one still cupping my face is feather soft. A dizzying contrast that has me wetting my lips. "I am not a strong enough male to live in a world where I only get a glimpse of you. To only carry memories of what we shared while watching you from a distance. My heart beats too intensely for you, and you alone." He pauses to take a shaky breath in before releasing it slowly.

He pulls back, just far enough to look down into my blackened eyes.

"I would rather fall prey to your shadows and live each and every day in the darkest hell than live a single day where you're in *his* arms and I have no hope of touching you again. To taste you." His eyelids fall slightly when they drop to my lips, the muscles in his jaw clenches as if all he wants is to kiss me like his life depends on it. Before I can fully finish that thought, his gaze once again claims mine. "To hold you. *Love* you. I may be the chosen one from my bloodline, but you, Emma, are who I choose. Fate aligned us, but without you, I'm as good as gone."

My heart is beating rapidly, and I'm sure with his exceptional hearing that he can hear it's on the brink of exploding right out of my chest. I catch a glimpse of his eyes flaring to silver before he pulls my head to press against his strong chest, cradling it. His heart beats loudly against my ear, calming me from the inside out.

His voice is hoarse when he speaks after a few moments. "I will walk in the darkness with you and destroy all that is good if that's what you wish."

I think I stop breathing as a lump forms in my throat. I bring my hand up to tightly grip his soaked shirt, relishing in the warmth of it against my cheek. "Draven," I whisper.

He draws his head back with wide eyes as they bounce back and forth between mine. I can feel his chest rising and falling in quick, shallow breaths. His thumb sweeps across my bottom lip and I swear I'm a goner.

"Say that again." His voice scratches against his throat as he chokes out the words.

My brows furrow together, not quite understanding. I do what he says, anyway. "Draven," I say softly, with a hint of a question filling my tone.

A small grin breaks across his face when he huffs out a harsh breath. "That's the first time you have called me by my first name since the darkness claimed you." I try to rack my brain to remember our interaction before, and I suppose he's right. Now that I have dug up the lost part of myself that was buried away, my thoughts are once again my own. Which only makes my heart cleave in two at feeling the full force of my love for him—when he's my next task.

Before I can say anything, he places his hand over my chest. My heart speaks for me as it beats roughly against his touch. "I can feel you so strongly," he says.

"Why did I not recognize you as my mate right away?" I can't help but ask. I knew fated mates existed, but no one taught me what happened after. The brief knowledge I have is only from the books I used to read, and those were mostly whimsical stories created from one's imagination.

"I think your heart always knew. It's why we couldn't stay away from each other before. Even after the necklace was gone, I believe the darkness muted the bond, but only to an extent. Because even when you are consumed, you still melt to my touch, your body responds to my words, and you *feel* when we are together." His eyes drop to my lips. "Nothing is more powerful than the mate bond."

The tension between us is all-consuming as my eyes do a quick dip to his lips, too. This bond is growing more intensely every day. It's igniting and pulling us so powerfully together to connect us as one. On pure instinct and need to touch him, I place my palm over his heart. The hum of our powers swirls around us, drowning out the chaos raging above. Making it feel like it's just the two of us concealed in our own bubble as everything else falls away.

"I see that, because…I can feel you strongly, too." His eyes snap back up to mine with such heat, it takes me by surprise.

Suddenly, his mouth slams against mine, stealing my next breath and closing the space between us with a growl vibrating under my hand from his chest. Heat races down to my core as my heartrate kicks up another notch. My fingers curl into his shirt, clinging in desperation to pull him closer, even though I know I should push him away. Anyone could walk down here at any moment, and we are right in the line of sight to the stairs. But given the chaos erupting above, their focus is targeted elsewhere than the two lone souls finding each other beneath their feet.

As if sensing my thoughts, his mouth presses harder to mine. With a swipe of his tongue across the seam of my lips, I open willingly, and all previous thoughts are forgotten. A soft whimper escapes me, and he swallows it down.

My skin buzzes with ecstasy at the feel of him and the way he kisses me like I'm the only thing keeping his heart beating. A kiss that feels like it's pulling us both underneath the water, drowning us together and we are each other's oxygen. Consuming the other like we are our final breath.

Nothing else exists at this moment, only his lips on mine with the ship swaying beneath our feet. All I can hear is the pounding of my heart thumping loudly in my ears and the deep groans eliciting from his throat. I push up on my toes, needing to be closer. Needing *more*.

He growls deeply, grabbing fistfuls of my dress to hike it up before shoving his knee between my legs. A moan rips free from my throat. His strong leg pushes right against my core, putting pressure exactly where I need it. I gasp as my clit pulses, the desperate ache in me starting to build. He rubs his knee back and forth, and I can't help how my hips begin to rock against him.

"That's it," he says between kisses on a hurried breath. "Ride my leg."

He increases the intensity of our kiss with dominance. Demanding me to take all that he is giving and for me to give it right back. So, I do. Teeth clashing. Tongues colliding. Our heavy breaths grow frantic, and with every second that passes, the warmth low in my belly rises, causing me to roll my hips faster.

"*Fuck*," he grinds out.

He stops our kiss to nip and suck a trail down my jaw and neck, causing me to tip my head back as I continue to ride him like I'll die if I don't. Another moan, another rush of heat flooding down my body. Draven's hand skims up my side, over my breast. His fingers graze the tip of my nipple before reaching my collarbone to wrap around my neck. His thumb pulls at my bottom lip as my breathing grows shallow, unable to take in a full breath of air. But that only causes a zap of pleasure to swell.

He forces my head back up to face him, and his darkened gaze holds mine. The pupils in his blinding silver eyes are dilated, dragging down my body to where my hips continue to seek pleasure. He watches intensely, his nostrils flaring, and I know he can smell how aroused I am. My head is growing dizzy, and when I whimper his name, his eyes snap back to mine.

"Take it, little demon," he commands, his voice rough. "Take your pleasure from me. Fucking *use* me."

That only encourages me to do just that. Then, he moves his other hand down my body, sliding it under the skirt of my dress. His thumb presses firmly to my clit and moves in a circular motion, which completely takes my breath away.

"Eyes on me," he grinds out as if he's barely managing to restrain himself.

My mouth falls open, and I shoot my hand up to grab onto his wrist, where he still has his hand wrapped around my neck. I'm holding on for dear life because, at any moment, I'm going to fall over the cliff. The building pressure is too much. My nails claw deep into his arm as my eyes threaten to roll back into my head. But they won't because they are locked on *him*.

"I'm—" I suck in a sharp breath. "I'm going to co—"

"Let go," he demands against my lips. Not kissing me, but just holding my face close enough to his that they brush together with every movement I make.

And so, I do. Those two words, mixed with the desire shining in his eyes and the air thick and palatable with lust…I let go.

And I fall.

My stomach tightens. I stop breathing. And my inner walls clench so hard together, I feel like I might black out. My orgasm rips through my body, tingling over my slick, heated skin and I call out his name. His thumb never relents over my sensitive clit, even as my muscles lock up with the waves of pleasure that overtake my body. My pussy continues to clench on itself as I jerk against his leg.

I briefly hear him groan deep in his chest as he keeps us nose to nose. But it's hard to hear anything as I fall and fall and fall. My body shuddering on a high that only he can get me to. And he's holding me tightly to him, keeping me from crumbling to the floor as I tremble from his sinful manipulations.

Once the final waves of bliss begin to retreat, I am able to suck in a full, shaky breath. Then, he tips his forehead to mine and presses his lips softly to it.

"You are beautiful," he says with so much warmth in his voice.

Heat spreads across my cheeks as I pull back to look at him.

He lifts his hand and grabs the end of a wet strand of hair, letting it twist around his finger. A sly smirk graces his perfectly swollen lips from my kiss. "And always so wet for me."

For the first time in months, a small huff of laughter leaves me. It's so surprising, I immediately cover my mouth in shock because it's a sound that I have forgotten. A weight lifts off my chest from his words and brings a lightness to our predicament because I *have* been dripping wet from head to toe every time.

The silence stretches between us, and the sounds of our heaving breaths fade to the background as clashing metal rings from the battle above. It causes the reality of the past few months to come slamming back into focus. Shame floods my cheeks and burns deep in my chest for indulging in pleasure before checking on my friends. For not remembering their screams and how Cora was limp, left bleeding on the ground when I was lost in the darkness.

A single tear escapes, slowly trailing down my cheek as my chin drops to my chest. "Cora." My voice breaks at just the whisper of her name. "Fynn and Kye?" I add on.

"All of them are well." His hand cups my cheek, tipping my head back and swiping his thumb over my skin to wipe away the evidence of my guilt.

Suddenly, a creak registers in my ear and the raging sounds of battle grow louder, filtering down the steps from the door that just opened above.

"Emma?!" Aiden's frantic voice bellows at the thump of boots hurrying down the wooden steps.

My eyes clash with Draven's, who is still staring at me, not a care in the world of us being seen together.

I give the slightest shake of my head. So small and subtle, but Draven sees it. I know he does. He takes a step back and all I want to do is reach out so I can pull him back in, but I don't. I *can't*. His shadows wrap around him as he presses his body near a darkened corner, concealing all traces of his existence in this room.

My eyes are still frozen to where Draven stands when hands grab my shoulders roughly and twist me. Aiden's eyes are wild, searching every inch of my body as his chest heaves up and down like he can't catch his breath. His golden hair is windblown, and his pristine outfit is stained with soot and splatters of blood.

"I've been searching all over the ship for you," he rushes out.

I stand there, not fully hearing a word he says as my body is buzzing with awareness of the male who's hidden in shadows. I can feel him as if he lives beneath my skin, molded into my bones and wrapping around my soul.

My body shakes and I realize it's Aiden jerking me to focus on him. "Why are you soaking wet?"

Slowly, his question registers as I think of how to respond. "I fell in."

"How?"

I ignore his question in hopes to draw his focus elsewhere. "What is happening above? I came down here to dry off and, suddenly, there was screaming."

Aiden seems to accept the change in conversation as he removes his hands from my shoulders and starts tightening the strap to his blade.

"Rebels from the Court of Abhain. As soon as I was able to sneak away, I came to search for you. To make sure you weren't taken."

Only taken? That's rich. And here I thought he searched to see if I was hurt. I manage to swallow down everything I wish to spew at him and ask, "The court in the east?"

I recall Cora, Kye, and Fynn traveling there. The court with cascading waterfalls that decorate the edge of the crystal-like river that flows through the entire island. A land covered in flowers and grassy rolling hills. But how does he know the attackers are specifically from that court?

"Yes," he hisses through his teeth. "They started firing arrows off their ships to ours. An assassination attempt on my father," he grinds out. "He requests you to stop them."

I walk past him, jabbing my shoulder into his as I do. "You mean he demands that I kill them," I spit with all the venom I have into my voice as I reach the steps. The smells of sulfur and metal creep down here, coating the air from outside the ship. "He does not command me. For all I care, it would be a blessing to end his rotten heart."

Aiden's head jerks back like he's been slapped, but he knows why I have such hatred for him. This shouldn't be a surprise. "He is your king," he says with a trickle of malice.

"I could make him beg me to have mercy on his life while he's on his knees… That is no king of mine." My voice is cold yet weighted with all the power dripping with each word.

A flash of what feels like pride washes through the bond, and it takes every will of strength I have to not dart my gaze over to where Draven resides. Instead, I watch Aiden's knees quiver as I build the darkness up within me, threatening him to buckle with the surge of power I push toward him. The male I once thought was different, who I could change for the better, is nothing but a sad replica of his father. Seeing him almost fall to his knees from the slightest bend of power I let him feel is a sight that has my eyes dancing with venomous amusement.

The darkness in me creeps forward, tauntingly trailing its claws over my psyche. I squeeze my eyes shut in hopes of forcing it away. I know what the Masiren did to help me unlock the light wasn't permanent. It's up to me to completely gain control of both powers living inside of me.

To practice how to wield both. And it seems when my emotions are high with anger, then the darkness heightens to feed off it as it rises to the surface.

Aiden straightens his spine, brushing his hands down the front of his jacket when I rein my power in. "People are being harmed in the crossfire."

I take a step up on the stairs. They creak under my weight, and I squeeze my palm into a tight fist as I look up to the open hatch. "I will help, but only for the sake of the people."

And with that, I hurry up the steps, each one squeaking beneath my shoes. The moment my head springs free from the door, clouds of smoke burn my eyes and I take in the destruction before me. Bodies are scattered on the floor of the ship, some dead, and some injured but will survive.

I curse under my breath when I spot Calloway shielding himself behind his guards. He's willing to sacrifice endless lives in order to save his own.

In one swift movement, I spread my arms wide and surround the ship in a wall of shadows, pouring more power into it so it becomes impenetrable. One by one, each person on board freezes, halting their attack and staring with gaping mouths at the massive shield. Weapons clatter to the wooden boards that slide with each sway of the ship.

Silence engulfs the ship by the time I finish blocking any and all attacks that continue to slam against my power. I can feel every weapon that tries to penetrate my shadows. Right now, I need everyone to work together, and it looks like the new *king* is clueless on how to go about that.

"Wind keepers! I need you to push the ship back towards the palace as quickly as you can!" I scream for every listening ear, drawing wide eyes to land on me. Bodies begin to gravitate towards the tail end of the ship, following my command. "Water wielders! The sea needs to flow with the ship to help guide us back at a faster pace!" Again, some Fae start rushing towards the front of the ship, letting their power stream from their hands.

In a matter of minutes, the ship is sailing across the sea at breakneck speed. Once we are in the clear, I notice Aiden staring at me in awe. His father is behind him, silently seething with a vein pulsing in his forehead. I ignore both as I watch the palace come into focus.

The rush of water casts off the sides of the ship as we speed back to land. The clouds of smoke are left behind, and silence still emits from the ship. Almost as if everyone here is holding their breaths until their feet safely stand on solid ground again. With how fast the dock is approaching, it seems as if the attack never even happened. Except for the noticeable chunks that were blasted into the ship and hundreds of arrows protruding from the wood.

Suddenly, my skin buzzes with heat and it floods my body with want. I follow the feeling by glancing up and scanning the sky. If I blinked, I would have missed the beautiful set of shadowed wings soaring between the clouds. The organ in my chest beats with an ache of wanting to follow. To call him back to me.

But I can't. I've already been commanded to hunt, or every soul will suffer. I can't fall into the depths of emotions that swirl in his eyes and have started to stir in my stomach when he looks at me. I need to keep him at a distance. It's the only thing I can do for now to keep him safe and get my thoughts straight.

CHAPTER THIRTEEN

Emma

$\mathcal{A}$ few days have passed since we returned safely on the evening of the coronation. There have been zero attacks since, and the palace has been eerily quiet. Even the light-colored walls in my room look dim, shadowed with unease of what feels like the countdown to something waiting to explode.

When we had walked through the main doors after the attack, Calloway barely restrained the raw irritation in his voice as he said he would speak with me once everything got back to order. He then turned his back to me and demanded guards to be stationed along every inch of the perimeter surrounding the palace, only for him to remain hunkered safely inside. He seems to forget that a demon lurks within these walls, and she wants nothing more than to end his miserable existence. But if I do, the world will suffer at my hands under my father's command for not playing nice.

Calloway's not the target...for now.

I finish tossing on a backless dress that matches the color of my eyes and the deep-stained blood that runs through my veins. A silver cuff decorates my upper arm and matches the small, sheathed dagger I used to twist and pin all of my hair up. Some might believe this little gem is nothing more than a piece of jewelry to match my outfit. Those who do are gullible, because this dagger is real and can easily slice across a jugular.

I've remained in my room since we returned, and not one soul has delighted me with their presence. Thank whatever divine being steered them away. Even Aiden has been surprisingly absent, and I can only assume he's been holed up with his father.

I've only left to ease my hunger before coming back and continuing to practice controlling my power. It's draining. One night, I broke out in a cold sweat from how hard I was straining my psyche to keep the darkness at bay. It's easier than before, but I want to master this. To know it can never sneak up and steal my sanity again.

There has been a constant pounding in my skull that shoots pain of exhaustion behind my eyes since my first attempt. Despite the throbbing, at least I'm managing to hold control over my power for the longest stretch of time from the help of the Masiren. Each power flares to life in my hands faster and steadier with every time I command it.

I head towards the balcony doors to stare up at the sky in hopes of seeing *him*. With my mind currently clear of the poisoned fog, all I can think of is the betrayal Whiro demands me to commit. I might as well drive the sharpest wyvern sword into his heart and then twist deeper. For that would be a better ending than whatever my father has planned. I'd force myself to watch until the final drop of blood leaves his body as punishment if it came to that. But I can't let that happen. I need to figure out what the fuck to do.

I thought it was a blessing to have a mate, but instead, it feels like a curse; a weakness to be threatened into hurting the one who is bound to your soul. My heart might as well be carved out of my chest and burned to ash because it doesn't deserve to feel his love. I'm exactly what I look like…a monster.

My foot is one step over the threshold to the open balcony when thunderous boots echo outside my room. I spin around right as my door slams open, smashing into the wall, and I'm surprised it doesn't rip off the hinges.

Calloway barrels inside and my defenses instantly rise. His face is flaming, with sharp lines turned inward and his mouth seething with harsh breaths. I suppose he is now ready to *speak* to me, but it feels more like he's looking for a fight and I'm the chosen opponent.

"You," he snarls.

His steps eat up the distance and my eye catches something glinting in his hand when he starts to raise it. Before I realize what he's doing, the hard bottom of his shoe connects with the center of my chest, knocking the wind out of me. The sharp pain that spears through me along my side has my lungs tightening as I fly backward, managing to twist at the last second to try and stop my spine from splintering. Instead, I smack sideways into one of the balcony doors with the handle jabbing in between my ribs. Right in the spot that's already screaming as it starts to burn, and I immediately regret trying to suck in a breath.

My hand clutches my side when I regain balance, wetness seeping through my fingers as I watch Calloway's face morph into one that relishes in the affliction he caused. My eyes drop down to the small dagger dangling from his fingers, and I curse myself for not seeing it.

"You need to remember your place, *Princess*," he spits. "You are only considered one now because of me and my allowance of you being engaged to my son." A scratchy, mirthful laugh leaves him as his eyes flare with what I can only imagine are thoughts of my death.

But in case he forgot to realize, I can heal from his afflictions without that necklace sucking away my powers. Already, I can feel my flesh stitching itself back together.

His arm whips out, throwing the dagger straight towards me. I swiftly duck to the side, letting it land its mark in the door before clattering to the ground. "You are not above me, nor even equal to me and my rule."

The silence throughout the palace these past few days must have been him brewing to reach this point of spilling over and unleashing the monster that lives within. I straighten my spine, ignoring the pang of agony that's still raging along my ribs. My hands fall to my side as I curl my fingers tightly, causing my nails to imprint into my palm—the one hand dripping black with my blood. The repercussion from Calloway's vicious deeds.

"Are you sure about that?" I hedge, the edge of my lip tipping up at the way his eyes widen. The darkness in me that I've been keeping under control is starting to seep in. The darkness used to be a friend that never left and gave me comfort. But maybe if I accept this power and its presence, it will work with me instead of against me.

So, I fall into it. Letting it rise and not holding it back, so that Calloway can see the true monster I can become. Shadows whip out and dance around me, lashing out and causing Calloway to take an unsteady step back. His fingers tremble at his sides as he starts to realize his mistake.

A demonic chuckle grazes up my throat as I follow suit and take a step forward. "You seem frightened, *King*," I mock at his title, while he continues to cower away from me. He's one of the weak ones, fearing death and never accepting that one day his time in this world will come to an end. He will forever cower away from death.

The room grows darker, colder, as I showcase the power I hold as a reminder that he won't ever be able to break me like he thought he could before. I command a tendril of shadows to wrap around his throat, lifting him until his feet dangle in the air. He tries to grab hold of my power, but his hands fall straight through it and I smirk.

"You will do good to remember that I could end you before you have a chance to beg me to stop." His face starts to turn a light shade of red as I squeeze his throat tighter. "You have a truce with my father, but the next time you think you have the right to touch me, I won't hesitate or think twice about snapping your neck."

I release him as he drops to the floor with a loud thud. His hands grapple for his neck as he desperately sucks in the air to the point of wheezing. He tries to speak, but it causes him to cough until he has to gasp for air again. The sight of him struggling on the ground comes nowhere near to what he deserves.

Boots pounding down the hall grow louder before Aiden rushes in and skids to a stop at the scene before him. His green eyes are wild as they dart back and forth between his father and me.

"Emma, what are you doing?" he hurries to ask, kneeling to help Calloway up to his feet.

My eyes pin on him, slowly cocking my head to the side. "Of course, you would assume I'm the one at fault at this moment."

His brows pull together while continuing to assess us both, and that's when his eyes drop to my side. Even though the stab wound from the dagger is already starting to clot and heal, since the pain stings a bit less. Still, the proof is there.

Aiden's eyes stay locked on my side as he speaks so softly, I almost don't hear him. "Father, did you harm my fiancée?"

Calloway shoves his son off him, brushing his hands down the lapels of his ivory tunic as he regains himself. He glares daggers at me, before dragging them to Aiden. "She's lucky that's all I did."

Aiden's face drains of color as he finally rips his eyes away from my ribs to stare at his father's retreating back that's now passing through the doorway.

"Emma…" Aiden's voice is soft, hesitant, matching his body when he steps closer to me.

My shadows are still raging around me, ready to strike if I feel threatened. I keep the darkness close, letting it numb the sliver of throbbing in my side and erase how I might feel with the way Aiden is looking at me, as if I'm weak.

He chances another step closer with his mouth opening to speak, his hands reaching out to me. Before he can get any closer, a roar tears through the sky outside. Aiden's neck twists to look out the open balcony doors, and I reel in my power to unblock the view. The moment my power clears, Draven slams down on the balcony so fiercely, I'm shocked it didn't crumble the siding of the palace.

Draven stands there in all his glory. Silver-slitted eyes are shining brighter than the moon on a clear night. Shadows ripple around him and dance along the reflective silver sheen of scales that cover the areas where his tattoos decorate his skin. And he's shirtless, the perfectly sculpted lines of his muscles straining with every rough inhale he releases. He looks wild and unhinged. But his wings… His wings are flared out in a powerful stance and their silver veining glow starkly against the black.

His metallic eyes never leave mine until his nostrils flare and I watch those black slits blow out wide. A tortured-sounding rumble escapes from his chest as he folds his wings in and eats up the distance between us in two strides.

Before I know it, his arms are wrapped tightly around my waist, and I'm pulled into his large chest. He doesn't judge that I'm taking comfort in this darkness. No fear of walking into the power of my hell. He does so without care if he gets harmed in the process. All that seems to matter is getting to…me.

"You're a——" I hear Aiden's trembling voice before all sounds get cut off when Draven blasts a gust of shadows out, knocking Aiden back on his ass.

A dragon, I think to myself.

The next thing I know, he steps off the balcony's ledge and we're soaring through the sky under the dying sun.

CHAPTER FOURTEEN

Draven

*P*ain. Hot, scorching agony.

One second, I'm in the training room with Fynn, Cora, Kye, and Emil, and the next, I miss the block of Emil's wooden sword when a blinding pain stabs into my side. Only, nothing touched me there. I pause to look down at the bare skin on display, twisting to see if Emil managed to sneak a strike in, but no mark exists to show proof of what I feel.

"You good?" I look up to find Emil staring at me with a dip in his brows and his sword hanging down by his side.

I hiss with a slight shake to my head. The stinging pain starts racing down the mate bond in waves and the moment it seizes me, I smash my wooden sword into the ground. It shatters as splinters fly up in the air from the impact, and before they can hit the floor, I shift into my dragon form.

This pain can only mean one thing…Emma's hurt.

The impulse to protect and keep her close overpowers any other thought. Sprinting to the nearest window, I smash through it as my mind blacks out, launching myself up as I fly over the sea to reach her. The moment I near her open balcony, the scents of metal and roses flood me. Blinding the beast in me to stop at nothing until I have her. The smell grows stronger when I land. Blood. *Her* fucking blood.

It takes everything in me not to shove my shadows into Aiden's body and twist his limbs from within when I spot him and how close he is to my injured mate. Because, as soon as I see her, every fiber in my body tenses with the primal need to take her away from here.

Her shadows are raging like dark ribbons lashing around her body, and the black veins snaking under her skin pulse with every breath she takes. She may be a Goddess, but she looks like a demon of shadows that I crave to get lost in. I'd willingly surrender to her sharp tongue and eyes that still see past skin and bone. Eyes that, no matter how soulless they look, can still see and touch every part of mine.

Nothing will ever keep me from her.

In the next breath, I snatch her into my arms and feed the urge to take her away. I barely register Aiden's irritating voice as I blast him away from us. Wishing to do more damage, but the only thing that will calm me is getting Emma away from here. She doesn't fight and stays silent as I step off the balcony, my wings catching us on a current and gliding us with the wind. The sun has slipped under the horizon, welcoming the twilight of blues and purples to tint the sky.

I pull her closer to me, savoring the way she curls into my body as I hold her in my arms. It has taken every ounce of my strength to keep my distance from her. And by distance, I mean flying above her palace every night to sit on the roof and peer down at her balcony once the moon is high in the sky. I should have barged in the first time I watched from above and claimed her because I know her body craves me, even if her mind fights the thought of letting go. But I won't. Not until she's ready.

The look she gave me on the ship after she rode my leg—like she couldn't fucking stop—keeps flashing in my mind. The subtle shake of her head to stay hidden, and I did, only for her. Even though my bones ached with desperation to close the distance between us. To snap every finger attached to Aiden that touched her when he wanted to take her above the ship. But I gritted my teeth, silently imagining it instead.

My wings beat powerfully beneath the stars, racing against their prying eyes. When we finally make it to my Court of Asiza, I zero in on my castle and tuck in my wings to dive down to my open room. The moment my boots touch the stone flooring, Emma jerks out of my arms, pushing against my chest and clambering out of my grasp.

"*Who?*" my voice grates deeply in my throat as I stalk towards her.

"What?" she whispers vehemently, but it doesn't hold nearly as much venom as she believes. The biting tone still makes my dick hard.

"Who. Fucking. Touched. You?" I growl each word as I close the space between us, towering above and looking down into her blackened eyes.

She remains silent, glaring at me as tension pulls her lips in a tight line with harsh, rapid breaths. So, I try a different approach to ease the beat of her heart to calm down. I lift my hand towards her face, pausing before I close the distance in case she doesn't want to be touched. Except, she doesn't flinch away from my hand or say a word, only keeps her stony eyes on me. Gingerly, I catch the loose strand of hair and tuck it behind the shell of her ear, leaving it there as I stroke the pad of my thumb along the angle of her jaw.

"Who hurt you, little demon?" I softly ask, seeing something flash in her eyes before I can register what it was.

She shakes her head and pushes my hand away. The rejection stings, but I mask it before she can see it take root.

"Why did you come to me?" she asks, evading an answer to my question. Which drives me closer to the edge of completely losing control.

I grind out a response for her in hopes it will encourage her to give me an answer. "Because of our bond—even though it's not completed in becoming one—is strong enough on its own for me to feel you. And that includes your pain, Emma." Her eyes narrow, studying me as she scans over every inch of my body.

I notice her chest hitching slightly when I lean forward and place my mouth beside her ear. "I'm not going to ask again. Tell me, or I'll fly right back to that damn palace and torture everyone in it until I learn the truth." My hand reaches for her waist, barely grazing the blood that soaked through from her wound.

She huffs, letting her stiff shoulders fall an inch as she rears her head back to glare at me. "The new fucking king, who had a bruised ego." Her glower never falters. It's hard and unmoving as she holds my eyes. Still, she continues to challenge me, and it makes my cock swell even more. "But I handled it. Let's just say, he will be sleeping with one eye open."

I don't know whether to spank her or kiss her. Right now, I wish to do both. My eyes drag down to her ribs, staring at the blood matted to her gown. It's healed, and that truth alone has my hackles lowering as I finally draw in the first deep breath since I left to go after her. Still, I silently promise to make Calloway bleed for daring to touch what's mine.

Once the protective fog clears, I finally notice what she is actually wearing. Fuck. I slowly prowl around her as her eyes continue to glare daggers into my soul, following my every move. So much creamy skin on display and my eyes eat it up. They roam over every inch, tracking every scar freely showing for anyone to see. She's wearing her shield of strength —showcasing every battle won—and it's the most bewitching fucking sight I've ever seen. She should know I would willingly fall to my knees for her.

A light chuckle rumbles through my chest at picturing Calloway's face when she turned the tables on him. "You truly are a vicious, little demon." Her black scrap of a dress that clings perfectly to her slender frame matches the ink of death that flows through her veins. I once told her she was a princess of the night, but now, she's a goddess of the night. One who doesn't hide in the shadows, but rather has them under her spell and brings them to her to do as she wishes.

"You'd do good to remember that the next time you think you can steal me away," she snipes back. It only makes me chuckle more as I stand in front of her again.

"I will steal you away again, but the question is… What would you do about it?" I say teasingly as my lips slyly tip up on one side.

Her eyes don't lift in the corners to show any signs of amusement, but instead, they darken more, if that's even possible.

In the span of half a breath, coils of her shadows dart out to drag one of the cushioned chairs in my room front and center. My brows furrow together as I watch her, and only then do I finally catch the finest glimpse of a toying smirk.

I open my mouth to ask what the hell is going on in her pretty, little head, but before I get the words out, she slams her power into me. Not enough to hurt me, but enough to force me back into the seat, expelling a huff from me. The chair tips backward, but I manage to lean forward to bring it back on its front two legs. Thankful it didn't snap from the force of my weight.

"You really think you can whisk me away again?" she asks as she stands unnaturally still at the base of my bed before me. With a nod of her head to me, she says, "Try."

A full smile stretches across my face at the fucking dare because it's too easy.

But when I go to move towards her, nothing happens. I pause. The smile on my face falls as I look down, and that's when I finally notice tendrils of her shadows wrapped around my limbs. I didn't even fucking *feel* them, but there they are, keeping me locked in place. Keeping me from getting to her.

A demonic laugh scratches up her throat. "Something wrong?"

Every muscle, every tendon tenses under the strain I force upon them to free me from her hold. But it's fruitless. Even my shadows can't undo her power as I try to pry hers off me with them.

My head hangs in defeat as my chest threatens to rattle with raw amusement. She fucking has me seated to her will and there's nothing I can do about it.

"All right, little demon. I'll play." My eyes slowly lift to meet hers. "Your move."

CHAPTER FIFTEEN

Emma

*D*raven sits there, bound, shirtless, and completely at my mercy.
        I may be swimming in the depths of this darkness, but I'm not drowning in it. It seems the Masiren was right; I needed to embrace this part of me. The harder I try to fight it and feel disgusted by this power, the more it seeks to claim control. This power fed on my fear, but once the Masiren guided a path for me and I accepted the shadows as mine, there now is no fear for it to feed from.

Draven thinks I'm lost to it, and he should. Fate cursed him to have a mate who has been demanded to lead him to his death. I need to taunt him to act like I'm doing my part for my father, but still keep him at a distance to protect his heart because mine is already shattered. Living each day with a cloud of death that hovers above me to take all those I hold dear. No one needed to tell me that life is unfair, it showed me by shoving me on a path that ends with a cliff, leaving me to stand on the edge and become acquainted with the possibility of death. But this is my ledge that I'm trapped on, not Draven's.

He looks so good sitting before me. Even with my shadows shackling him to the chair, he still looks relaxed. His ankles are bound to the chair's legs, but he keeps his knees spread wide as he lounges back. The muscles in his chest and the abs stacked down his stomach ripple with the movement of every breath he takes. Both of his arms are pulled behind him and bound at his wrists, causing the muscles in his arms to involuntarily flex from the lack of mobility.

His eyes remain pinned on me, darkening as they trail a heated gaze down my body. That alone has my thighs squeezing together, along with the palpable blend of pine and maple that is only him swarming around me.

Almost a week has passed since Whiro sent me here, which leaves me at least two more before the full moon to figure out what the hell to do.

A tinge of worry chills down my spine as my thoughts drifting to Aiden possibly opening his mouth and saying what he saw. To speak the secret Draven so carelessly made known—that the dragon bloodline lives on. He seemed speechless in the moment, but once that settles, I don't know what he will do as a male scorned by the Dark Prince he loathes.

"You should stay away from me," I say in a single breath. Needing to say it out loud because being in Draven's court, in his *room*, brings back memories that have forever imprinted on my soul. And it's twisting me up inside.

"Never." He shakes his head with a rough swallow. The cords of his throat that come to a sharp point move in a masculine way that makes me want to lick a path up it.

The warm glow from the fire contrasts the sharp lines of his face, contouring his features to take my breath away. His once-trimmed beard has grown out, and dark circles shadow beneath his eyes. My heart cracks a little more at the sight, as if he's already suffering before he's learned of my task. A pang of guilt squeezes my heart from not noticing his exhaustion when I was with him on the ship. I don't wish this. I want him to flourish, to not worry.

His chest expands fully before he gradually releases it. "I will never stay away from you. From dusk to dawn, from the deepest depths of the sea or the farthest star in the sky, I will be with you, by your side. You will never be alone, not even in death. You have me, always."

The truth ringing in his words blankets the bond we share with warmth. My teeth gnash together, trying to force my heart to stop skipping, as if it will jump right out of my chest. Words get lodged in my throat with a monsoon of emotions that crash against one another.

And they continue to fail me when I go to open my mouth.

I try to recover, but his deep, velvety voice beats me to it. "So, little demon. What's your move?" There's a twinkle in his eyes and I'm thankful for the change in conversation.

My fingers play mindlessly with the fabric of my dress, twirling and dancing along the material as I trace the tips of them up my side. I'm torn between wanting to touch every inch of his skin and forcing myself to restrain this desperate need to put distance between us. But anytime he's near, my body liquefies inside, seeking to feel only what he can give me. Maybe I can find a loophole to ease this magnetic pull without laying a finger on him, or him on me. Just enough to satisfy this hunger that is slowly becoming insatiable.

"You'll see soon enough." My words hold a hint of seductiveness as my fingers finally reach the ribbon tied at the top of my dress. The way I feel for him is erasing all other thoughts, wanting so badly to free him, only to climb his body and let him have his way with me. But I can't; if I touch him, the guilt constricting my heart will only squeeze tighter. I don't deserve to feel his lips on mine again, but I want him to remember me with a memory that's not destroying him.

His heated gaze follows my hand, the muscles in his jaw jumping as he tries to shift in the chair. I twist the tail of the ribbon around one finger before ever so slightly giving it a tug as my lips quirk up on the side. The soft material of the dress parts and I let it slip down my shoulder, exposing the skin there.

Draven's throat bobs, zeroing in on the bare skin exposed and following the line where my collarbone begins. "What are you doing?" His voice is gruff as it rasps up his throat, like it's hard for him to speak.

"Undressing." I give a small shrug.

His nostrils flare and the way his pupils blow out causes a rush of heat to flood my core, making my clit throb with its own heartbeat. Unfortunately, my thighs can't squeeze any tighter to relieve this ache and offer some friction where my body begs for it.

"But why?" he grinds out.

I let the silky material flow down my body so it can pool around my feet, leaving me completely bare before him. A wave of ebony revealing the demon underneath. "Punishment for taking me against my will." And for risking himself by showing Aiden what he truly is.

"I didn't see you fighting very hard to stop me."

"I'm not trying to fall to my death from thousands of feet in the air." I let out a sigh as I sit back on his obsidian bed and leisurely rub my hands back and forth over the plush blanket. The black pools of my eyes never leave his, because if he wants to take me, then I'll take something from him.

One of my hands glides down between my breasts. The tips of my fingers rub over my nipple, pinching it to elicit a gasp from me before trailing lower. The crackling fire fills the silence until Draven's breaths grow harsher. My legs spread willingly, giving him a direct view of how turned on I am. Of how wet and needy my pussy is to be filled, knowing I'm dripping for him.

"Emma…" he growls low and deep, and the sound sends chills racing over my skin.

"Something wrong?" My fingers make contact with my clit, which is pulsing with anticipation. A faint whimper leaves my parted lips, and my head falls back with a sigh. Aside from Draven claiming those two moments with me, intimacy has been nonexistent. My body is starving for the tender touch of another, for some sort of physical contact. As of right now, my own touch will have to do. But now that I'm grasping more control, and Draven has been finding every opportunity to make me *feel*, the need for lust has come slamming into my body with a frightening force.

My fingers move in a circular motion, chasing the pleasure that's quickly growing. I lift my head up, dizzy with the desire coursing through me, and hold Draven's gaze that's now almost a blinding silver. Glowing so brightly, you would think it would extinguish the shadows around us.

His jaw is tense as he lowers his gaze to my neck, then lets it trail slowly to my breasts, and even further until he zeros those eyes between my legs. A deep rumble vibrates from him as his tongue wets his lips before biting on his bottom one. He looks like a beast being deprived of his favorite meal.

My fingers pick up speed and I apply more pressure, but it's not enough. I snake a tendril of shadow out of my free hand and let it swirl down my body until it reaches between my thighs. Each breath I take grows shallower as I watch him, until his gaze snaps up to mine when a needy whimper passes my lips. I keep my eyes locked on his and let my shadows push inside me, filling me up, drawing a long, wanton moan to echo around us.

"*Fuck*," his voice chokes out, ripping his eyes from mine to watch my power thrust in and out of me. His muscles strain and ripple over his chest, threatening to splinter the chair in half. I watch his hips shift, causing his abs to tighten, and see the large bulge of his cock tenting beneath the seams of his pants.

The sight only turns me on more, making my core drip from the desire he's flooding me with.

Those metallic eyes snap back to mine, darkening and half-lidded. "You can bind me as tightly as you want, but it won't stop you from begging me for more."

My brows scrunch together until understanding widens my eyes. He releases his own shadows, wrapping them around my body, twisting over my hardened nipples, and causing me to yelp as my back arches off the bed. So much pleasure all at once.

"Draven," I breathe out on a shaky breath.

"Beg, little demon."

Each breath expands my chest in rough movements. Tilting my head back up, my eyes plead for him to give me what he knows I want, yet I'm not sure how since I have him restrained.

"More." Another whimper escapes me. "Please."

His mouth twitches with a slight smirk before it falters, his own chest rising and falling hard as his jaw ticks. I watch his shadows brush over my skin, working their way lower, almost teasingly. "Do you trust me?" His question holds no amusement this time. It's open, raw, and vulnerable. His words holding more meaning than what one would believe, but for us, it's everything.

Yet I don't hesitate, knowing the answer I would give even in my darkest hell. "Yes."

He releases the breath that he was holding and his eyelids flutter in relief. Draven guides his shadows not to my core but inches closer to my other hole. Grazing over the sensitive flesh with explosive lust filling his eyes.

My mouth falls open as he eases his shadows in, filling up a part of me that has never been touched. It feels dirty and wrong, but so fucking right at the same time. Air gets lodged in my throat as the pressure increases with every inch he takes, and once he's deep enough in, he starts to build the same momentum as mine. The invasion of both holes being consumed causes my legs to shake. My vision turns blurry, on the brink of blacking out. It's too much, but I also don't want him to stop.

I hear his breathing grow rougher as mine gets faster. Moans expel ruthlessly from me, unsure if I can handle what is to come. His grunts sound as if this is physically painful for him to keep his hands off me. But that doesn't stop him as the pleasure deep inside me climbs higher and higher, causing my toes to curl and my head to press into the bed.

His speed picks up, so I do the same. My fingers are relentless over my swollen clit. Everything tightens. My stomach pulls taut, my legs tense up, and my breathing ceases to exist.

"*Fuck*, look at you." His shadows thrust harder. "I wish that was my tongue inside you, tasting what's mine."

His filthy words push me over the edge. My orgasm crashes into me, causing me to fall. My inner walls tighten, and the feeling of being filled completely makes stars dance behind my eyes. Wave after wave of ecstasy rolls through me, and only when it starts to fade am I able to breathe. Our shadows recede, and the emptiness only makes me crave more. This need for him only grows stronger, and I don't know how to sate it.

Only our heavy breathing fills the space, drowning out any other sound. I keep my eyes closed and my head resting back on the bed, trying hard to catch my breath and slow the beat of my heart.

"You going to set me free now, little demon?" Draven's voice licks across my skin and pulls me back from this high, making me remember where I am and why I'm doing this.

Pulling up on my elbows, my eyes open to connect with his. "I rather like you tied up."

I don't miss the flare of heat that brightens his irises, or the way his shadows grow larger behind him. "Only for you."

The silence that follows weighs heavy as I consider him. Shit, his eyes burn against my skin and feel like sparks wherever they land. I'm so screwed when it comes to him. Taking a good look at every inch of his body, and how fate thought I deserved someone so sinfully pure to be my mate. A male who would destroy anything that got in his way to me and leave ashes in his wake. A heart beating so strongly that I'm scared mine will only poison it.

It's not fair, to have the one thing I've always longed for be smeared with death's mark before I got a chance to experience it—to experience *love*. How one day I wished I'd find a king if I was ever passed down the crown. It was a distant dream that I knew would never arise. But still, just like the pawns on the board, it is the queen's job to protect the king.

I grab my dress off the floor and slip it back on as steadily as I can, feeling the spot where I bled stick to my skin. It's still wet to the touch, even though the wound has since healed. "You aren't safe with me," I say, peering over my shoulder to meet his eyes as I finish tying the strings of my dress together.

The least I can do is give a warning. Whiro hasn't invaded my mind since before my power was freed, and thankfully, the strength I hold on my power is enough to block him from intruding. For Whiro must never find out that I'm not succumbed to the darkness like before. Since I've come back, my heart has begun to beat on its own. The stone encasing the black organ is chipping away.

Draven continues to look at me, staring into my soul and not just seeing what's on the surface. His hair is messy with a single strand falling in front of his eyes, and my fingers flex with the urge to brush it back. The orange glow still enhances his handsome features as it flickers against his skin.

"Why?" he asks softly, but I hear the desperation in his tone as he attempts to sit forward, causing the chair to creak beneath him.

I pause my movements, my eyes bouncing back and forth between his. "Because the darkness is something you should fear."

His head shakes roughly. "I've lived in the dark for as long as I can remember. Your darkness, your *demons*, don't scare mine. Our souls are meant to walk in the shadows together."

My heart splinters so painfully, I wonder if he can feel it. He doesn't understand. My eyes swirl like a darkened storm. "Not my darkness."

I watch his forehead crease as I take a step towards the open wall that leads outside. He grunts and huffs with aggravation, jerking against my power. "Emma—" Another grunt. "Goddamn it. Emma, wait." My foot takes another step away from him. "What the fuck do you mean?" he growls so deeply that I can feel it vibrate the floor beneath my feet and rattle the walls.

My chest pulls tight while I tell myself this is the right thing. I need to keep my distance, protect him, and then figure out what to do once the full moon rises. The thought of betrayal is driving a sword too deeply into my heart; it's unbearable.

"I'm sorry." Not a second after the words leave my lips, I wrap my shadows around me to transport myself back to my room at the palace.

This is for his safety, even if he hates me for it. Even if I have to sell my soul in exchange for Draven's if I can't figure out how to stop my father by the full moon. Maybe that will be enough for whatever Whiro has planned. But right now, I need to handle Aiden and make sure he fucking keeps his mouth shut about what he witnessed.

While I know I'm doing what needs to be done, my heart doesn't seem to understand as it screams at me to go back to my mate.

CHAPTER SIXTEEN

Draven

*H*ow I'm still fucking strapped to this chair, I have no damn clue.

She left only moments ago, yet her power remains. It's like she's taunting the beast, letting me know she has me in the palm of her hands until she's ready to release me. I've never felt a well of power as dominating as hers, but that's what happens when you are the daughter of two gods.

My head falls forward until my chin hits my chest. The only choice I have is to wait until she calls her power back. But she must be fucking joking if she thinks I'll ever stay away from her. My hands had itched to throw her over my knee until she told me what she's hiding.

Her apology felt like a blade carving out my heart so she could take it with her. Like a *Goodbye* instead of a *See you later*. Not. Fucking. Happening.

My door blasts open a minute later, making my eyes peer up to see Fynn storming into my room, his eyes searching. Until...they land on me. They widen for a moment and then slam shut. He bites his lips together, his chest silently shaking as he fights to stop the edges of his mouth from turning up. Shaking my head, I let my eyes fall to the small scuff mark on the floor, focusing on it as I wait for whatever he plans to say.

"I think…this is the first time I have ever been at a loss for words."

With my neck still bent, I sigh, then glare at him from across the room. "Go on, let it out. You and I both know you can't hold it in much longer."

Next, his shoulders start shaking and before he can stop it, Fynn grasps his knees as he doubles over in laughter. All I can do is shake my fucking head again because I'm still bound to this chair and all I want to do is smash it to pieces. He regains himself, standing tall while wiping the back of his hands over the corner of his eyes.

"Shit, Drav. I knew you were into kinky shit, but…not with yourself." He starts chuckling until he can't catch his breath. "Wait—" Laughter once again fills the room. "I have to grab the others. This is too good."

What did he— Wait. Oh, fucking hell. He thinks *I* tied myself up with my own damn shadows *and* he's getting Cora and Kye. Just perfect. And there's nothing I can do.

Suddenly, multiple footsteps echo from the corridor, and I brace myself for being the center of amusement.

"I think you're lying," I hear Cora say as their voices grow louder.

"It wouldn't be the first time Fynn's tried to pull a prank on us." Kye's voice sounds exhausted because, just like me, he can't sleep. I've shared what I know or have seen when it comes to Emma, but I make sure to pull Kye aside and let him know she's unharmed. Until tonight, when I physically fucking *felt* her pain radiate down the bond and lash at my body as if it were my own.

"Which is *why* I grabbed you, so you both know I'm telling the truth," Fynn's chipper voice sounds just outside the door. "Just go see for yourself."

All three of them step into my room. Fynn's cocky smirk screams *I told you so.* Cora's hand flies over her mouth to hide her amusement, and Kye just tips his head down, doing a shit job of hiding the small smile he's sporting.

"I heard his growl vibrate through the wall," Fynn starts to explain.

"So, I stormed in here as fast as I could to see what was wrong. But… apparently, *nothing* is wrong." Fynn winks. He fucking *winks* at me.

I let out an annoyed groan as I wait for him to stop talking. "These aren't my shadows, you insufferable bastard."

That gets him to shut his mouth and silence the laugh that started to bubble up his throat. He walks to me, letting his fingers grace the edge of Emma's shadows. Cora gasps as she inches closer and Kye remains rooted to the spot.

Fynn's eyes widen and meet mine, already knowing he can sense the signature of the power constricted around me. "This is Emma's doing."

"Emma was here?" Kye rushes to ask, finally showing interest in his expression.

I go on to explain what happened—leaving out the sordid details—and how I stole her away because the beast in me overrode all thoughts of my sanity. The only thing on my mind was to protect her.

"Fynn," Cora's feather-soft voice pauses. Her sad blue eyes turn hopeful with raised brows as she clasps her hands together. "Are you able to use the part of your power to see her?"

With a silent nod, he brushes the tips of his fingers over Emma's shadows once more and closes his eyes with furrowed brows in concentration. After two breaths pass, he draws his hands up, those hazel eyes glinting, and waves his palms in a circular motion.

An outline of gold reflects in the air, and I hold my breath. He's searching for her, using her power signature to see what she's doing at this very moment. Not a second later, a blurry image in the center slowly becomes clear, and inside is the female who will never fear the storm, because she *is* the storm. One that I would gladly get swept away in.

Kye steps beside Fynn and Cora follows suit. All zeroed in on Emma, who is standing on her balcony, looking out at the dark sea. I can't help the rapid beat of my heart in my chest at just the sight of her. The way her hair dances in the wind, and the slight tint of pink that still flushes her cheeks from my *punishment* minutes ago.

It was painful and addicting all at the same time. I wanted to rip myself free from her power only to pounce on her and devour every delectable inch of her body. But then, the other part of me wanted to sit back and watch the raised bumps chill her flesh, the hardening of her nipples waiting to be sucked on, and her arousal dripping from her center, glistening for me.

This chokehold she has on me will only grow tighter.

"You said she was here. So, why did she leave?" Kye's question hangs in the air, heavy and pained.

My jaw ticks and I swallow down the flurry of emotions. "She said for me to stay away. That it wasn't safe to be near her."

Kye keeps his amber eyes locked on mine, trying to read between the lines. But there's nothing; she was vague and spoke with zero explanations.

"She's sacrificing herself to whatever she's protecting you from," Cora says almost on a whisper, causing my gaze to shift to her. A watery sheen brightens her eyes as she studies Emma, and slowly softens the longer she stares at her friend. I know that look. It's one of relief coated with sadness. To see her and feel so close yet so far away.

Cora's lip slightly trembles as her hands mindlessly fidget together in front of her. "Look at her," she tells us as we all drag our eyes to the window of power hovering in the air. "The darkness has rooted itself in her, but I don't believe she's completely lost to it. Not anymore. If she was, she wouldn't be staring off her balcony like she used to do before you ever laid eyes on her."

On a shaky inhale, she releases a long breath before she speaks again. "Her mind is sane. She's plotting like I've seen her do almost every time she had an interaction with King Oren." Cora's voice is stronger, sounding more confident in her assessment of Emma.

In my peripheral, I see Cora's hand gesture to Emma. "Look at how still her body is, how even though her eyes are void, they are consumed with thoughts that are weighing on her."

I watch, tracing every curve of her frame, every slant of her face. The look in her eyes, as I dissect her tells. Cora's right, and then the words my mother spoke registers.

Fate demands the sacrifice of the one who holds the balance of two worlds.

. . .

No, she will never sacrifice herself again. For I will rip my beating heart from my chest and shove it into hers. The light in her eyes must never fade for eternity.

"Cora's right," Kye adds. "She will do anything to protect those she loves, and secluding herself to bear the torment alone is all she knows."

Our breathing is hushed until Fynn jumps back, startling Cora with a gasp. "She——" His voice freezes.

We all watch Emma's head slowly twist until her eyes stare directly at us, making us all tense and hold our breaths. We wait as statues, and her gaze never falters.

"Can she see us?" Cora asks.

"N-no," Fynn stutters. "But no one has ever sensed my power like this, which is what I believe is happening. She can't see us, but more so *feel* us."

"What does that mean?" Kye rushes to ask.

"It means…" Fynn slides his eyes to Kye, then to me. "That she is fucking powerful."

We all stare back at her, until her hand whips out, slamming her shadows in the space beside her that is aimed directly at Fynn's power. In the span of a second, his small opening of gold-rimmed power falls away and the vicelike tendrils securing me to this chair extinguish.

We remain silent. Stunned.

I stand, stretching out the kinks knotted in my muscles.

"What now?" Cora cuts through the quiet tension.

I open my mouth to speak, but pause, my eyes still rooted to the spot where we watched her. How the hell am I supposed to answer a question I don't have the answer to? All I know is that we will make sure she doesn't fight whatever she's hiding alone.

CHAPTER SEVENTEEN

Emma

The sun is just beginning to wake, and I sit on the edge of my bed, fixated on the drop of blood on the floor that dried since last night. My teeth grind together, and I can't stop the rush of blood aiming for my head or the increasing pace of my heart. Hunger ceased to exist the rest of the night and sleep never accompanied me. All I know is that it physically hurts to stay away from Draven, and to know of the betrayal Whiro asks of me. The weight of it presses on my chest as if there is a boulder on me. The pain of it feeling like a jagged blade repeatedly stabbing me as it tears me to shreds and flays me open.

If I was still completely succumbed to the darkness, I would feel nothing. Every part of me would be numb and none the wiser. But instead, I can feel this bond like it's a living thing. Pulsing with life, consuming every molecule in my body to burn within my blood and reach for the one it's tethered to.

Just how, not long after I returned from Draven's, I felt a presence near me but couldn't see. I can't explain it, but somehow, I could sense a

129

fizzling sort of energy beside me. Awareness had licked up my spine, causing the hair on the back of my neck to stand at attention. It felt like there were eyes on me, but not the cold and calculating kind like my father. It felt warm and curious. But instead of trying to understand something I couldn't see, I chose to send my power in that direction in hopes it would dissolve that odd sensation. To my surprise, it did.

Waking today, my heart feels chained down in my chest. Slowly bleeding through a wound that was stitched with a dull needle and thread, gradually ripping at the seams. Often questioning how I'm going to survive this. I suppose it doesn't matter; I will do what needs to be done to protect my mate. His family needs him, the *world* needs him. Hell, I need him, but if I can't have my happily ever after, then I need to know he gets his. The people in Deyadrum are blind to how he places himself in death's way for them every single day, protecting each court from as many Corrupted as he can.

He's the villainous hero.

One who just gave his biggest secret away. One that will cause an uproar and for him to be hunted down. He will be feared instead of being accepted and given trust for his actions.

Blood pumps loudly in my ears and I push off the balcony rail with urgency, needing to find Aiden. I have to make sure he doesn't tell the secret that must never be spoken. Ironic, though, that I keep trying to protect the same person I'm supposed to ruin.

Fuck Draven for being so careless and blindsided to get to me. Even if it makes my body heat at the thought. I'm trying so hard to mask this desperate pull to say *fuck everything* and leap into his arms, but he's making it so damn difficult. Everything he says, and everything he doesn't say because he shows me instead. He's denting the shield I'm wielding, and I'm seconds away from dropping it to wave the white flag.

With the new day now greeting the palace, Aiden should be awake. Without hesitation, I hurry with quick steps, making my way to Aiden's room and hoping that he will be in there still. I have to convince him to stay quiet.

Rays of sunlight splinter through the open windows, draping the corridors in a fiery hue. The shells embedded in the floor glisten like a million tiny specks of diamonds. Almost like a trick to the eyes, reflecting light to blind every one of the cruelties stained underneath. I double my steps while keeping my breathing composed. Before I know it, I'm rounding the corner to where dual white doors come into view. I tap my knuckles against the wood and wait, straining my hearing for any movement inside.

When I hear the padding of feet against the floor, I lift my chin up and square my shoulders. The door handle turns, and I swallow down every angry thought I want to shout at him. To choke him with my words and keep screaming every emotion that strangles me until his ears bleed. Instead, I lace my hands together in front of me and relax every muscle in my face.

The door shifts inward to reveal Aiden, whose sandy hair is styled over to the side with small waves curling near the ends and over his ears. He dons a cream tunic, untied at the center that opens to reveal his bare chest. Brown breeches conform to his legs, with his shirt partially tucked in the waistband.

When I bring my eyes back up to his, a smirk plays on his lips, and I decide to use that to my advantage.

"May I come in?"

His eyebrows raise while he lets his gaze drag down my body and back up, until his green eyes connect with mine. "That depends."

"On what?" My eyes never waver from his stony gaze.

"Did he touch you in places you have yet to give?"

I clench my teeth so tightly I fear they might crack. With every ounce of willpower I can conjure, I keep my face bored, never showing the growing rage that is igniting within me.

"Of course not," I say, truthfully. Draven had no chance of touching me once my power wrapped around him. And he doesn't need to know anything that transpired before; he has no right to that knowledge or to try and taint something I hold close to my heart.

After considering my words, he steps back and waves his hand out for me to enter. I hate the sound of the door clicking shut behind me and the twist of the lock that turns my stomach. I glance over my shoulder with furrowed brows.

"So no one disturbs us," he answers the silent question. "My father waltzes in as he pleases. Knocking is beneath him."

All I can do is nod as I make my way farther into his room. At one point, I used to love hanging out here. We'd play chess—even though he's awful at it. Me teaching him as we lazed on the floor with our heads together, making up ridiculous stories.

But now, this room feels…foreign. Unsettling.

The complete opposite of how I feel in Draven's room, which is safe and comforting.

I look around the bland space and I feel like our memories in here have been wiped away. My eyes keep scanning until they freeze on a narrow table decorating a single wall. But that's not what's holding my attention or making my heart drop to my stomach. It's the objects lined up over the top.

Seashells.

White…shells.

"Ahh." Aiden comes to stand beside me, hooking his gaze to the same spot I can't seem to look away from. "I've been collecting them." He walks over and picks one up, tossing it in his hand and turning it over. "Each day I went to find a single shell while you were gone. It made me feel close to you and I wanted it to be a gift for when you came back." With a final look, he gently places it back down. "Now, it sounds a bit silly." He lifts his arm to scratch behind his neck.

Without taking my eye off the shells, I ask, "Did you ever try to find me?"

His eyes never meet mine as they dip to the floor. "I wanted to and regret that I didn't." With his head still bent forward, he lifts his eyes to peek at me. "With each day that passed, the regret grew. But I was angry. After the rejection before the battle—you choosing *him*—and how you disappeared so willingly to the monster who was massacring everyone, the thought of you had made me sick."

The blackened blood in my veins starts pumping harder from his words, but I keep my composure.

He finally lifts his head to look directly at me, taking a small step closer. "But I realized that you weren't yourself. That your rejection and leaving was because of the madness placed in your head. The manipulation of that *prince* and the God of Darkness's power." He comes to stand before me, taking both my hands in his as his thumbs rub over the dark veins threading over them. "The three months felt long and excruciating without you, but you came back to me. Even if you aren't the same Emma, it's still you."

I want to sever his hands and pour my shadows down his throat. Whether he searched for me or not, it doesn't matter. I just wanted to see if there was a decent bone in his body after he let himself fall under the same skewed moral compass as his father and the previous king.

Taking a moment to replay his words, I snag on the two that have my heart sinking to my stomach. Three months. About three full moon cycles. That is how long I was gone. The dose of harsh reality tastes bitter as I try to swallow down the lump in my throat. How did I not manage to break through the black hole that was consuming me?

Realizing my thoughts are drifting, I give a jerk of my head in acknowledgment to Aiden and quickly look away, not being able to stand the sight of his face when all I want to do is take the hilt of my dagger and slam it into his skull. Instead, I take a calming breath to swallow down the lump in my throat. I must have him believe the words that I'm about to say when all my body wants to do is vomit.

"Thank you." Another steady breath. "They are the perfect gifts to come home to, aside from you." Bile threatens to surge upward, but I manage to keep it down, burning my throat in the process. Aiden seems oblivious, beaming at me with a look that seems like he won the golden prize.

Once the churning of my stomach settles again, I continue, "You don't need to worry about Prince Draven." He tips his head in question. "I took care of him, so he won't bother us anymore." The question lining his brows clears as his eyes once again look like they are skipping across a finish line. "But please," I turn his hands over so I can grab onto them, "don't mention what you saw of *what* he is, for I wish to use that secret against him when the time comes."

"I thought you said he won't be a bother?"

"He won't be. This is the information I will use against him shall he dare to do so anyway," I reply quickly, letting the lie roll off my tongue with ease.

Aiden looks down at our intertwined hands, tightening his fingers around mine. "This is the first time you have initiated touching me." He pauses, and I take that moment to keep my features lax to hide the disgust begging me to rip my hands away. "But okay. So long as you let me know if he dares to come near you again, because I will happily tear his world apart alongside you."

My heart jumps but I force my lungs to keep working. "That seems fair." *Lie*. He has no idea what happens when he makes a deal with a demon. So, I smile, making it seem like there are hearts floating in the black sea of my eyes while cursing him in the recess of my mind. And in hopes of keeping up the act, I ask, "Will you join me for dinner tonight?"

"I'd be delighted."

———

Dinner is uneventful. I listen to him go on and on about what he did when I was away, all the while completely ignoring the fact that his father drove a blade between my ribs the night before. He leans back in his chair with ease, folding his arms behind his head with a huge grin stretching across his face. His voice is light and airy as he rambles on, speaking as if we are on a relaxing trip to the springs beneath the waterfalls in the Court of Abhain, with a glass filled to the brim with wine.

It's strange, sitting here, just the two of us. And the seat he takes residence in is the one I used when King Oren announced I would be attending the masquerade ball to Draven's court. A night that has altered the path of my life in unforeseen instances. From meeting the Dark Prince, to finding Aiden—the male whom I believed to be kindhearted—groping a random female in the same evening we were showcasing our engagement.

The contents of my stomach churn at what would have been if I never attended that ball. If I would have never met Draven, and instead, be permanently locked in place beside Aiden while living in this hell of a palace. I refuse to go there as I push all those unbidden thoughts away and continue to watch Aiden talk animatedly.

My tongue swipes over my teeth beneath my lips as I give a listening nod. I'm surprised the glass of water in my hand doesn't shatter, or that the silver utensil never bends between my fingers when he starts voicing his father's plans to take more coin from the people in order to repair his damn ships. The water in my glass vibrates as I feel the hold on my power grow unstable from the instant surge of anger. But I hold my breath and count to three, reassuring myself to accept my power's presence, which seems to calm it down.

Not long after, I fake a yawn with a mumbled apology to Aiden for my sudden exhaustion. It seems letting him speak and feel as if I chose him does the trick, as he brushes me off by saying no worries and that he has to speak with his father, anyway.

When I return to my room, my back rests on the solid door when it closes as I let my eyes fall shut. Pretending to be fine is one of the fastest ways to exhaust myself. Forcing a smile to my lips that want to peel back and bare my teeth. Or to widen my eyes to make it look like I'm hanging onto every word when my eyelids want to narrow to the sharpest slits that hold nothing but hatred. To physically restrain every fiber in my body from acting out. To bite my tongue from words I want to spew. All while trying not to reach a breaking point with the whirlwind of thoughts screaming in my mind.

Letting out a long sigh, I push off the door and walk to the center of my room, sitting down on the floor and crossing my legs. This is where I've been growing my hold on the darkness while bringing light to the palm of my hand.

And that's what I do. I stay sitting here and practice controlling the strength of my power until the sky bleeds with daylight again. At some point, though, my eyes must have grown heavy, because I wake to find myself curled up on the ground at the end of my bed.

This happens for the next three nights. My days consist of remaining cooped up in my room or secluding myself in the cave near the shore when I need fresh air. And occasionally, sparing a meal with Aiden, but only to keep this charade up. But every evening when I return to my room, I continue to better hone my control of my powers, preparing myself for the day I go against Whiro.

Each night has only solidified that joining forces with my friends is the right choice. Because it will also allow them to *have* a choice, and I know all too well how it feels to be told instead of asked. They deserve to know the dangers ahead and I can't stand to see them try to help by going in blind. That will be a sure and quick death sentence.

Tonight, I do the same as every other night: fucking practice. But this time, I think I've got it as both light and dark balance in the palms of my hands. A hum that syncs to my pulse. It's strange. In my life, I have seen more evil in the light—my body carrying the horrors of my past with me so I never forget. It was then that I had found a friend in the dark.

Now, the light swelling around my heart makes me feel closer to my mother. But the darkness—where I used to find comfort—I unconsciously began to hate. It was linked to my father and consumed me to the point of making me a shell of who I am. Empty and washed of any shred of good that existed inside myself. The worst part is that I kept wanting to feel more of the dark when I was lost to it. Desperate for a stronger dose of wickedness to feed into my immoral compass.

But no more. Never again will I fall prey to my father, and in order to fight the monster he is, I must unleash my own. To once and for all accept my darkness like a long-lost friend and welcome it home.

With that in mind, I practice all through the night. Not even a few hours of rest spring forth as sleep evades me. At some point in the night, I ended up sitting on the floor in front of the full-length mirror, watching the color of my eyes change with the more control I gain. With the darkness, my eyes bleed black. With the light, my eyes radiate white. And somehow, I found a way to bring the grey color of my irises back when I'm not using any power. But for the time being, I need to keep the mask of hell veiled over me.

No one can know.

Whiro can never learn I took the rein of his power and plan to use it against him. Someway, somehow.

From the lack of sleep, I can feel the weight of exhaustion pulling on my eyes. There is a war going on in my mind, refusing to quiet because, when my eyes try to close, my psyche shouts louder. A part of me is screaming at myself, demanding to tell Draven everything right this moment. To close the distance between us and give in. And the other part of me is telling me to wait until I have more of a plan. That I still have time before I set off the truth bomb that will explode his life.

I walk back and forth, pacing the polished floor that feels like it's mocking me. So bright and cheery without a worry in the world.

I do that often the rest of the day. Staying hidden away in my room, I only leave to force myself to swallow down some morsels of food that I end up chucking up not long after. The persistent ache in my stomach and the unease that keeps swirling makes the room double. On shaky legs, I let my body fall on top of my bed, the slight bouncing makes me groan from the wave of nausea it creates.

Once it subsides, I focus to keep my body still, closing my eyes and taking long, drawn-out breaths. I feel the beat of my heart slow, the sound of the outside world quieting, and the muscles in my body rid themselves from the tension that holds them.

When my eyes peel open, I can't see well. I blink a few times, trying to get my sight to adjust faster to the darkness smothering every corner of the room. Lifting my head an inch off the mattress, I look out the balcony window to find the sun has once again left, welcoming the moon to take its place as it glows majestically over the sea. Shimmers of light speckle over the quiet waves, while my body feels like it's caught in a riptide as I struggle to push myself up.

In some books I've read, the fated mates struggled to be separated, affecting their bodies in different ways. But that was when the mates were fully bonded, and yet, I feel as if my bond to Draven is anything but normal. So, I have to wonder if it's the distance I've forced upon me and Draven making me feel this way? Will fate punish us for not completing the bond? For fighting the stars' selection of the other half of my soul?

I don't even understand how one would complete a bond, though I've heard it mentioned. All of my books had a happily ever after, an ending I cherished because I knew I could never obtain such a thing. In these stories, they brushed over what took place during the official bonding, because it was a private moment.

And I've never read a story where the characters had to travel separately from their mate, because once they found out, that was it for them. Distance between them did not exist. Nothing else mattered except living each day with their mate.

Maybe I'm causing this suffering to myself. Overthinking and chasing the racing thoughts I can't seem to catch. As I lean against my bedpost and look around me, I realize I truly am missing those who care about me. Before, I tried to fight my battles alone, yet they stood beside me no matter the danger.

My brain churns everything over, and knowing them, they won't let me be. But this time, I can tell them, explain what happened. They don't need to know the shame I feel for the innocent lives I've taken, which has rooted inside of me no matter how many times I try to scrub my hands clean. That's my own misery I silently let myself drown in. Not sleeping helps to keep the visual memory of each kill away, but I will never be rid of what I did. My hands will never be clean of the lives I stole.

This time…it will be in all our favor to go into this together, stronger, and with a plan. To stay a step ahead of Whiro and beat him for his own gain. Because a queen can win the game, only with the help of her knight, rook, and bishop. As I once saw Draven as my knight, I know now, he was always the king I'm supposed to protect.

The clarity of it all is striking, along with the fight I'm losing against this bond straining between us. It physically hurts, and I can't stay away from him anymore. I need him more than my next breath.

The moment realization hits, I grab the black cloak hanging in my closet. The hem brushes the back of my ankles while I toss the hood over my head. The tail end of my braid peeks out as it rests over my shoulder.

I pause a moment when my hand traces over the dagger hugging my thigh, knowing this will officially start a war that holds the future of the world. My fingertips dance over the blade as I get lost in thought, unsure of my fate.

I may find comfort in a sword. Safety. With how its balanced weight and silver-edged beauty molds perfectly in my hands. But I know life is just as sharp, declaring war. It can cut so deeply, forcing someone to live with the pain of a scar that haunts them. Or life can plunge past skin and bone, spilling every ounce of light until there is nothing left but emptiness gazing back. And yet, one still never knows what end of the sword they will fall on until it's too late. So, I wonder, will it be the hilt or the blade for me?

Before I contemplate more on what awaits me, I tightly lace my boots with swift movements, and call my shadows to swarm around me. A sight to behold, and one that I hope the Dark Prince, my mate—or I should say, the one known as *Shade*—will appreciate.

CHAPTER EIGHTEEN

Emma

I let my shadows deposit me outside Draven's castle. Blending in with the night as I stand between the pines, but I can feel *him*. The way the bond between us flares stronger, pulsing with a spellbinding need to erase the distance between us.

The scent that is only him comforts me and soothes the nerves that have been growing from the thought of confessing my secret. Admitting the betrayal I would have committed if I was still lost in the sea of my darkness.

As soon as I go to cloak myself once more and follow his scent, I suddenly feel warmth searing through my clothes behind me. Cedar and maple wrap around me, flooding my senses so strongly that my eyes want to roll in the back of my head.

His hand reaches for mine that's hanging near my hip, intertwining one of his fingers with mine. "Little demon." His velvety voice sends tingles down my body. "You came back to me."

"I can't seem to stay away," I say, my voice thready.

A chuckle rumbles from his chest, and I can't help the small smile that lifts on my face.

"We are all in the library. The others are waiting since I told them I felt your presence." He fully grabs hold of my hand now, spinning me around to press our fronts together, and only then do I retract my shadows from my hood. A smirk settles on his lips. "There you are." A whisper on the wind.

I lift my eyes to him, letting them change to grey, only a second long enough for him to see it. The sight has his eyes flaring from blue to silver, darting back and forth between mine. His large palm grabs the back of my neck, pulling me closer until we are nose to nose. He goes to speak but I coil my shadows around us before he can and pull us into the dark.

A heartbeat later, we're standing in the library with three sets of wide eyes staring back at us. Kye halts his pacing, Fynn smiles kindly, and Cora leaps from her seat in front of the fireplace, sprinting towards me. Only to halt a foot away, her blue eyes scanning me and looking deep into my eyes. She's unsure of how to proceed, and I can see the question filling her eyes, wondering if I'm *me* at the moment. I don't blame her. To ease her worry, I open my arms and spread them wide, a wobbly smile breaking free.

"Cora," I say with all the warmth I can put into my voice.

She chokes on a sob and crashes into me, causing me to stumble a few steps back. Her arms squeeze tightly around me to the point of not being able to breathe. But I do the same to her, thankful she's here, alive, and breathing.

"Fuck, Em," she cries into my shoulder. "Don't you dare scare me like that again."

I can feel her tears soaking into my clothes, but I don't care. I just hold on tighter. "I can't promise that," I huff out as she playfully smacks me. "But I will do my best."

She continues to hold me as each minute ticks by, the room otherwise silent as she sniffles. Eventually, Cora pulls back to wipe her face clean with the back of her hand and takes a deep breath. "We've been so worried about you."

Guilt eats away at me like it's starving, and I drop my gaze down to my boots.

"Princess." The deep voice caresses the organ racing in my chest, gently urging it to slow down.

I peer up to amber eyes that are glowing golden from the flames of the fire reflecting off them. Relief takes over Kye's features as he takes in every inch of me, checking for injuries no doubt. Always the protector.

A long, shaky breath helps hold back the tears burning behind my eyes. "I'm not a princess anymore," I muse.

He smirks, causing the scar on the side of his face to curve with the movement. His cheeks lift, and the corner of his eyes crinkle. The long, wild hair of his has been left down, just grazing his shoulders.

"You will always be a princess to me." His steps eat up the distance before he pulls me in, smashing my face into his firm chest and all I can do is giggle as I hug him back. I can hear the rough pounding of his heart against my ear, and the rush of air filling his lungs as he holds me. "Glad to have you back."

A sigh leaves me as I bury my head further into his chest. Then, I suddenly feel the air softly ripple near my leg and I kick out my foot on instinct, abruptly blocking Kye's leg. I pull back with my hands clutching his arms as I look up at him to find he's grinning.

"Had to make sure you still got it and haven't forgotten all our train-ing." He winks, and this lighter side of Kye, a more carefree version, is causing my heart to swell.

I huff annoyingly even though I can't stop the stupid grin that stretches across my face. "Your training is so engraved into my mind, I could recite every move, every defensive position in my sleep." He laughs right alongside me, and it feels like no time has passed between us. As if I haven't been lost in hell for three months.

"Miss me, darling?" A chipper voice snags my attention.

I snap my neck around to find Fynn standing behind the sofa, leaning back with his elbows bent and his hands firmly gripping the frame to hold him upright.

"Oh, hey. I didn't see you there," I tease.

He pushes off the sofa with fluid grace and saunters towards me with arms wide open. "Ha-ha. So, in other words, I was the first one you saw because of how infatuated you are with me, but you didn't want to make the others feel bad about it. I can understand that." One of his eyebrows raises as he wraps me in a welcoming embrace.

All I can do is shake my head and muffle into his shirt. "You're unbelievable."

The small scar on his lip stretches with his wide smile. "Actually, that would be your broody dragon over there." He jerks his head towards Draven. "He's been a drunken mess that I have had to help clean up every day with you gone. Such a sensitive dragon."

I hear Draven curse under his breath.

"Too soon?" Fynn asks.

Even though Fynn is messing around, my heart twists at the image of Draven suffering on my account. Drinking through his pain in an attempt to not feel it…to not feel *me*. I turn on my heels and grab Draven's hand, squeezing it. Reassuring him I'm here and that I won't… I *refuse* to fight this between us because that won't make him safer like I thought it would.

I may have an idea, but I'd need help.

Draven watches my hand link with his, making his chest rise and fall in two long breaths. I turn back to face everyone, as I try to mentally prepare myself for what's to come.

"I need to speak with you all." My voice is steady, but I can feel the slight dip to it as I face them. They all silently nod their heads as if they have been waiting for this moment. As if they have been *ready*.

We are all sitting on the chairs and sofas that curve in front of the fireplace. Glasses filled with wine and bourbon decorate the table in the center.

I begin speaking but leave out the villainous tasks that will haunt me until my blood bleeds dry. I explain where I've been since the battle, and they tell me it's been three months. It's the second time to hear it out loud and, once again, that piece of information feels like another blow to the chest.

I steel my spine and pin my gaze on Draven's. "Whiro told me I have until the full moon to bring you to Gehendra, or else the entire world will fall prey to his whims. I don't know what he plans, but I know it involves the Sea of Souls and that nothing good will come from it. He said you have his power running through your veins, because no one can unlock the chains in his cells—only *his* power can."

The tension in the air could be cut with a knife, but I don't waver. I watch as Draven turns my words over, giving nothing away as he remains calm.

He takes a generous sip of the golden liquid swirling in his glass, and I watch his throat move as he swallows it down. "Is that all?" he asks.

My mouth opens and closes multiple times with no words. Then I give my head a small shake to clear it. "What do you mean, *is that all?* He wants me to betray you and to play you right into his hands. Aren't you even curious what the Sea of Souls is?" How can he act like Whiro targeting him is not a big deal? I just dropped a huge boulder on him, and he's not fazed. Not even a little bit.

Draven shrugs, choosing not to answer, and my jaw drops. As always, Fynn finds the right moment to lighten the situation. "Told you. If you thought he was broody before, it's nothing compared to now." I look to Fynn and catch him winking to Draven as he reclines back, his arms resting behind his head, and props one leg up on his knee.

I stifle my smile as Cora, who is sitting next to Fynn, smacks him lightly on the leg. "Not the time," she whispers sternly, but there's a twinkle in her eyes that gives away her amusement. "Do you think that is the only reason?"

"I doubt it," Kye pipes in. His large frame consumes the entire chair he's sitting in. "But this also means he likely knows Draven is part dragon."

Draven nods solemnly. "Remember when I told you that the God of Darkness miscalculated his power when creating the first Fae?"

His crystal-blue eyes meet mine as I recall the conversation we had the first time he took me to the Caves of Tsisana. "Yes."

He looks down at the bourbon in his glass and tips it back and forth in thought. "He didn't have to see my true form to know I was a descendant from his creation. He just needed to see the shadows." Once again, his eyes pierce into mine. "Having the ability to wield shadows is rare. So, unless you are an heir of his—which was never heard of until you—the only other way to have them is to be one of the chosen in the dragon bloodline. And, like I said before, my father said it was a gift, but it just keeps proving to be a curse."

"So, what is your idea?" Cora adds in after we all fall quiet.

"When the Masiren spoke to me, it said something about me hiding my light from only those who wish to destroy it. So, I think… I think I need to let Whiro keep believing that I am consumed. Sticking to his task of standing beside Aiden and Calloway, to lure out Draven." A growl vibrates low and deep from his direction, but I keep my gaze fixed in the direction of Cora, Kye, and Fynn.

"I have until the full moon before I'm supposed to drag Draven to Gehendra. So, maybe if I push this as long as possible, it will give us enough time to figure out how to destroy him. That is…if you are with me?"

Multiple scoffs fill the room, followed by Kye's masculine chuckle. "You don't ever have to ask, Princess. Even if you said you didn't want us to help, we would have forced it upon you."

"He's right," Cora chimes in with a gentle smile. "You are stuck with all of us. I'm just proud that you are asking us instead of trying to protect us by putting yourself in danger and doing it alone." She shoots me a raised eyebrow.

Heat scorches my cheeks as I glance away for a second since that is exactly what I was going to do at first.

"We know," Fynn says with tender amusement, seeming to sense where my thoughts were headed. "Cora read you like a book when we were spying on you a few days ago after you tied Draven up like your own personal sex toy."

If my cheeks could turn any brighter, then they do from that comment alone. So, that must have been the presence I felt.

I tilt my head as I look at Fynn.

"You spied on me?" I ask.

Fynn scratches the back of his neck with a scrunch of his face. "Maybe I should have left that part out," he huffs with a hesitant chuckle.

"My mistake, but you only proved how powerful you are by sensing my power and eliminating it. Fucking badass."

"Do you think the wyvern weapons will hurt him?" Kye asks, switching the conversation as if he's been thinking about this idea for a while.

"There's a chance they could," Draven muses. "Wyvern iron can kill Scavengers that are created from his power, and it prevented Emma from using hers—being his daughter. At the same time, it only subdued her power. The touch of the wyvern iron never burned her like it did me."

I ponder that for a moment before speaking. "It only burned me as a reaction to when I attempted to use my power, but a normal blade can also harm me."

Draven nods while taking another swig of bourbon that works his throat in such a delicious way. "Then I think wyvern iron is more fatal to dragon shifters. My bloodline might have a trace of his power that holds enough of his signature to free you from his cell, but there is not enough for me to be immune to the iron."

"So, any weapon will do?" Cora chimes in.

Kye grunts in agreement. "It seems so, but it will take a lot of damage to injure him with his level of power." He slides his hips back, adjusting himself in his seat to sit up more. "Princess, how well are you able to control your powers?"

"Not completely—"

"How so?" Draven interrupts, rushing in with concern.

I sigh, deflating my stiff shoulders. "Sometimes the pressure of keeping the darkness at bay for long periods of time causes my head to feel like someone is slicing an axe through it. Once I accepted this power and stopped fighting it, it eased. I've been practicing, but both powers raging inside me wish to take the lead at times. I have the control, but I'm not sure I've tapped into the full strength of what I can do. That part is still unknown to me."

"Do you have a headache now?" Draven's brows are furrowed together, his body inching closer to the edge of his seat.

"No." I give a soft shake of my head. "The span of control is growing and becoming easier." I look to Kye, directing my next words to him.

"The control of my powers shouldn't be a problem. I will keep practicing them in the meantime, too."

"How will we get there?" Cora asks.

"I can only portal myself and one other until I learn the strength needed for more," I say, and then, an idea forms. "I could take each one of you at a time. Just bounce back and forth between realms?"

We all sit there thinking about how to reach Gehendra, with me being the only one who has ever been. And then, it dawns on me; the biggest hurdle of all once we arrive. "Oh, I may have forgotten to mention that Fae can't survive in Whiro's realm for long. They slowly…die."

More silence follows.

Until Fynn snaps his fingers. "Shush, we can deal with a little Fae-killing air. We just need to be quick enough. So, don't worry, it won't stop us from helping. *But* I've never used my power to go beyond Deyadrum… I think I could with practice, by focusing more on technique and use of my power. It's worth a shot."

An empty glass *clinks* on the table, and I find Draven's hands empty. He folds them together. Leaning forward, he rests his elbows on his knees, which causes the outlines of his muscles to ripple through his shirt. My eyes greedily take him in, thinking of how his fingers feel against my skin. How his lips take hold of me until he's all that I breathe. How the feel of his cock—

"Little demon," Draven's voice is strained and guttural. My eyes tear off his body and meet his, which are half-lidded and darkening with blown pupils as his nostrils flare.

Shit.

He knows what I was just fantasizing about, from where my eyes were drinking him in. And I have no doubt he was smelling my arousal that's dampening the inside of my undergarments.

His hips shift in an uncomfortable-looking way, wiping one of his hands down his face roughly with a deep breath before he clears his throat. "I think Emma should take me to Whiro first. To make him believe that she's doing as he asked. She can even shadow-bind me again to make it believable."

I wince at that, but catch Fynn's snicker, which makes me bite my lips.

147

Draven scratches along his jawline. "Fynn, if you can master how to portal into another realm, then I think you, Cora, and Kye could follow a little bit after us. We will be the distraction. You guys will bring the weapons."

"That's smart," Kye adds. "We can follow your scent to know which direction you have taken. And if Fae can't survive long in his realm, then it would be best if we trailed in later. I think there is a good chance you won't be affected by that since you do hold some of his power." Kye nods to Draven and they both ponder that possibility.

I shake my head. "I'll sketch a map that will lead you to where we will be heading in case the realm's scent throws off ours."

As soon as that comes out of my mouth, I realize it may not be the best idea. "Wait." I hold up my hand as my mind tries to process all I know from being in Gehendra. "Whiro can sense if another is in his realm." Sucking on my bottom lip, my eyes drop to the floor with furrowed brows as I try to think of how to keep them safe. Then, it clicks.

"I'll leave a mist of my shadows where you will portal in at, and then keep a trail of it visible for you to stay in. That way, it should hide your signature, making him only feel mine." It has to work. My energy is more potent to him and sensing me won't cause him to be alarmed.

They all nod in agreement.

But we won't know what will happen until we step foot in a hell they have never seen.

All I know is I need to be the weapon I was born to be.

The one I have carefully crafted and sharpened throughout the years.

CHAPTER NINETEEN

Draven

We continue to discuss various plans for the next hour, even going as far as searching through books dated back to the beginning. No new information was found and none of the plans seems to stick. Only one book mentioned the gods and how they are the reason Deyadrum exists. But nothing notes of a way to kill them or if they have a weakness. All we know is that Whiro killed Emma's mother, therefore, a god *can* be killed.

And every idea we think of seems to be too risky or falls through, especially given that only Emma knows the layout of Gehendra. The only plan that will give us the best chance is the one everyone agrees on: Emma takes me in as her prisoner ahead of time, bound by her shadows.

"All right. So, it's settled then." Fynn stretches with a yawn and pushes himself up to stand. "I'll see if I can tap into the other realm and will keep practicing until I do." He brushes back some strands of hair that fell loose from his bun as he grabs Cora's hand to help her to her feet. "Let me walk you?"

Her cheeks scorch a deep shade of pink as she looks up at him with big eyes. "Okay," she says softly. Cora's head shakes as if she's just now remembered they aren't alone, releasing Fynn's hand to turn to and walk towards Emma.

Standing up, Emma opens her arms as Cora dives in for the hug. "Don't run off," Cora teases.

Emma pulls back to look at her. "I won't. Not anymore. I'm done running." And I can tell she means it. The girl who was waiting for death to claim her seems to have found the strength that has always lived in her to fight back.

To claim death's hand before it has a chance to touch her.

Emma raises an eyebrow at Cora, her eyes drifting to the blonde flirt behind Cora that has yet to take his eyes off her. Cora looks over her shoulder to see what Emma is looking at. She rolls her eyes playfully and the purest smile I've ever seen on her graces her face. "I accidently saw him naked." She leans in, her mouth so close to Emma's ear. The whisper won't stop anyone from hearing, but I really don't think she cares. "He's pierced," I hear her say.

She winks at Emma, who is wide-eyed and silent. Emma starts biting those plump lips I love, her attempt to hold in her laugh. I glance at Fynn, and the fucking bastard is smirking. He heard exactly what she fucking said, and I can practically taste the sense of pride rolling off him.

Kye stands up next, pulling Emma in and squeezing her like he's afraid she will disappear. It's a feeling I think all of us are struggling with. A fear that if we will do something as simple as blink, we're unsure if Emma will vanish before our eyes open again.

The beast in me stirs. It's not happy that we haven't completed the mating bond, and sees Kye and any other male as a threat. Again, I have to remind myself that I know how he's feeling. We both lost her, and it made us get lost in a vortex of endless grief.

Kye is a good friend. Knowing he will always protect her just shows what kind of person Emma is. That underneath the darkness that coats her heart is the deepest shade of red that beats for everyone she cares for.

Fynn throws his hand up with a two-finger salute as he makes his way out of the library with Cora following behind. I stand, grabbing the empty glasses with one hand to give Emma and Kye a little bit of privacy, purposefully trying to listen to any other sound but their voices. And I keep reminding myself I get her as soon as he leaves. Even if my fingers are trembling with the need to touch her skin, causing the glasses to rattle against each other.

A few moments pass before boots thudding on the floor cut through my hearing. When I snag on the sound, I realize they are growing fainter. The truth of that solidifies when the next thing I hear is the door clicking shut. I press the cork in the half-filled bottles with the pad of my thumb as silence hangs in the air, but I know she's still here. I can fucking feel her as if she was stitched into every layer of my skin.

A wave of desire floods my system, causing me to white-knuckle the cart I placed the empty glasses on. It takes me a few minutes to realize the heady weight of lust is coming through the bond and not solely my own. I almost don't believe it until I smell her arousal and it's a drug to my veins. A kickstart to my heart. My dick already painfully hard.

Light footsteps tap along the floor, alerting me to her movement. Instead of coming closer to me, I hear her feet pad towards the rows of shelves housing various books my family has collected. And like the stalker I am, I follow.

The beast in me stalks closer to the surface. When I round the corner of one of the shelves towards the back, the moon casts an ethereal glow that causes the light to reflect off her pools of black. The moonlight hugs every angle of her face, every curve of her body, and displays her hidden desire she can't hide by the subtle shiver cascading over her skin.

Her back is pressed against the books with her head turned in my direction, locking on me the moment I'm in view. "You know I have to go back to him until we move forward with the plan."

She doesn't even need to specify who *him* is. The wince on her face when she says it makes it clear as day. But I know she has to go back, and every fucking bone in my body protests at the thought. The dragon in me wants to rear its ugly head and strangle Aiden to death, slowly, before finishing off Calloway.

I can't restrain the growl that vibrates deep and low in my chest, hating that I have to hold back pinning her beneath me and never letting her go. That I have to allow her to go back to the one place that holds so much pain and stole her life from her.

I close the distance and step into her, towering above her lithe frame and forcing her head to tilt back. Every time she breathes in, her breasts brush against me and it causes sparks to sear into my body.

"I know," I choke out between clenched teeth. "Doesn't lessen the way I want to lock you away in my room and tie you to my bed."

Her breath hitches and it makes my cock twitch. My hand trails up her side, following the curve of her body before cupping her jaw, letting my thumb brush over her bottom lip. The tip of her tongue peeks out to follow the movement, wetting her lip, and it makes me lick my own. I swallow roughly with the intense need to taste her. I'm dying to have her lips on mine again.

After having her ripped away from me, I'm never hesitating on showing her how I feel. Never again will I not take a chance.

So, I let instinct drive all other thoughts as I slam my mouth to hers, eliciting a gasp that I steal. I don't wait to swipe my tongue against her lips, and she doesn't hold off on letting me in. It's like our minds are one, our needs are in sync, and she is just as desperate to taste me as I am her.

She kisses me like a sinful promise that I never want to break. Her hands grip both sides of my collar where it's unbuttoned and then pulls me in, eliminating the small bit of space that was between us. I press my hips in, wanting her to feel how hard I am for her as I ravish her mouth with reckless abandon.

Her pelvis rocks against me, trying to feel me where she needs it. My hands slide behind her, gripping her backside as I haul her up. My weight falls into her, letting the ridge of my cock press hard against her needy clit. I swallow the moan that spills from her throat, our hips grinding into one another relentlessly. And I have no doubt that if I slip my fingers in her cunt that she will be soaking wet for me.

We seem to be locked in the same lust-filled spell because neither one of us can stop. It's not enough, yet everything all at the same time. Teeth clashing. Tongues dancing. Lips swelling. I never want it to end.

I push my hips into her even more, her legs tightening around my waist. I slide one of my hands between us until the pad of my thumb finds her clit and I start moving it in circles. Rubbing over the swollen bud at a quick pace, never giving her a chance to ease into it because I can tell she's already close. And *fuck*…so am I.

"Oh gods…" she whimpers as her head falls back against the books.

"I'm not a god, like you, but I will show you how one should be worshipped." My lips greedily suck along her slender neck, nipping and licking everywhere I can touch. She rolls her hips faster, almost jerking against me, and fuck is that hot. Chasing after her pleasure, riding the solid tip of my dick to make her feel good.

Every ridge of my stomach tenses to hold back the pleasure she's spurring in me. I refuse to let go until she does, fighting against the tingles that start to build in the base of my spine. My balls begin to tighten, pulling up with the impending release that's rapidly climbing. My breathing grows heavy, and hers grows shallow. I lift my head to watch her and how her mouth falls open as her body moves up and down.

"Give me your eyes," I manage to huff out, my voice husky and broken with blinding lust.

She brings her head forward, with eyes of the night staring back into mine. But that's not what sets me over the edge. It's when her eyes change to grey, looking like a calm storm swallowing me whole. *Her* eyes. The ones that I know all too well.

"Emma," I whisper with a groan as my dick swells.

I know the walls of her pussy are tightening with the way her muscles tense up. She'd be gripping me so hard if I was in her. The orgasm rising finally crests for us at the same time. My thumb still draws out her pleasure over her clothing as my eyes fall closed when my release surges through.

Wave after wave of ecstasy tingle through my body, picturing her walls pulsing around my cock, but instead, it's jerking inside of my pants. I can't help it. I have never come this way before, but only she holds the power for me to come undone.

Before she has a chance to take a full breath as her orgasm ceases, I set her on her feet and drop to my knees. In one swift movement, my fingers curl into the waistband of her pants and pull them down.

She gasps. "Draven wha——"

Her words die on her tongue when I lift her up, forcing her legs to hook over my shoulders while keeping her ankles restrained by her pants. My mouth immediately finds her dripping sex, begging me to taste her. To lick every drop of pleasure she made for me. A beautiful fucking mess.

My tongue flattens, licking her from hole to hole until it finds its way to her clit. I nip and suck until she's squirming against me, and her moans are echoing off the library walls.

One of her hands grips my hair, and the other flattens against the books, knocking them down as she tries to get ready for another orgasm that's fast approaching. I swear I hear her curse to herself between panting breaths every time a new book falls.

I remove the clothing trapped around her ankles in one quick motion before pulling her to me as I lay down until my back hits the floor, loving the feel of her weight on me.

"Draven, I'm going to suffocate you."

She lifts her hips just slightly to hover above my face and her glistening pussy is too far for my liking. "Sit. The fuck. Down. Little demon," I growl low and rough. "I don't want to breathe until you come. So, sit on my fucking face before I make you."

She gasps, but willingly complies. Her legs already trembling on both sides of my head. She lowers herself, but not fast enough. I grip her hips, dig my fingers into her skin, and slam her pussy down to my mouth. And I suck. Hard.

She squeals, but I don't stop, never relenting as her thighs start to squeeze around me.

With one hand now gripping her thigh, I slide the other until it reaches her soaking center. I ease two fingers in, knuckle deep, and curl them. She screams. I pump them up into her with rough strokes, making her thighs constrict tighter around my head and her pussy clench my fingers unforgivingly.

I can feel her orgasm building as she grips my digits, her inner walls fluttering. A second round of ecstasy causes her to pulse around me, and her hips begin to slow and do quick, little jerks. Only then do I slowly pull my fingers out of her, bringing them to my mouth and sucking them clean. Then, I flatten my tongue and lick every inch of her that's dripping from the pleasure I gave her. Drinking up every bit she made for me.

She sighs, her muscles going lax. I slowly lift her hips as I sit up and settle her on my lap, knowing her legs won't hold her up if she tries to stand.

Her grey eyes flutter open, a serene smile on her face. Then she's pulling me in, kissing me deeply and tasting herself on my tongue. She moans into my mouth, tilting her head to kiss me deeper. After a few minutes, we pull back with harsh breaths, and drop our foreheads together.

She inhales, long and slow. "I don't want to, but I have to go."

"I know," I say, my voice barely a whisper.

"If my absence is noticed too much, they will grow suspicious."

Again, I say, "I know." Because she's right. If we want to beat Whiro at whatever game he's playing, she needs to act like his puppet. And that means keeping Aiden and Calloway believing nothing is amiss. "There is something you need to know."

She rears her head back slightly as she brushes her fingers through my hair. The feeling makes me bite back a groan. "What is it?"

"My mother said she passed along a message to you before."

Emma doesn't look confused in the slightest, but instead, brings her fingers to her lips when her eyes widen. "I had a feeling it was her who wrote it, but I wasn't certain."

I nod. "And she has another." Emma waits silently for me to continue as I work my jaw and dig my fingers into her waist. "Fate demands the sacrifice of the one who holds the balance of two worlds."

Her face scrunches as she purses her lips and I suck mine between my teeth to stop myself from tasting her again.

"Sacrifice of what?" she asks.

"Fuck if I know. I'm on my knees hoping it's not sacrificing yourself. But I've been racking my mind trying to figure it out."

She bites her bottom lip as she thinks. When those grey eyes meet mine, I find myself completely lost in her. "Let's not worry about it tonight, but I will try to turn everything I know over to see if I can decipher the meaning." She dips her head into my neck, placing tender kisses in a path up to my jaw. "Thank you for telling me."

"Always," I say easily. I won't ever hide anything from her.

She looks towards the window. "I have to go——"

"I know," I say quickly. "You have to go." And I can't even hide the way her leaving makes me feel. Like my heart is cleaving in two as I tighten my hold on her.

Her eyes cast over in a cloudy haze with a slight watery sheen. "It's not safe for you near the palace," she says softly. "If Aiden sees, it's all over. I'll come to you."

All I can do is nod against her because I can't fight her on this.

"Hey." Her voice is so tender as she cups my jaw to lift my face, forcing my eyes to meet hers. "I don't know when, but I *will* be back."

"It's killing me inside to send you back to that hellish place, ruled by yet another monster who only wishes to see you bleed. The only way I will feel better about this is if you stay or I snap their necks. There is no in-between."

She shakes her head in amusement, grabbing my hand and placing it over her heart. The strong beats thump under my palm, calming something inside of me.

"This time, I'm strong enough to deal with them and fight. They will never hurt me again. I won't let them because I need to protect this heart." Her eyes close and I can not only hear the organ in her chest grow frantic but feel it beneath my palm.

"My heart is yours, Draven. It always has been. There are no words powerful enough to truly encompass what I feel for you. I——" Her voice catches before she breathes in, opening her eyes until they stare all the way into my soul. "I love you."

My own heart skips a few beats, pounding ruthlessly in my chest. This is the girl who has suffered at the hand of so many males in her life. The girl who still has a good heart after all the abuse that paints her body. The girl who was simply waiting to die, never afraid to toe the edge of death, while actively hoping for it to end her suffering. And despite all that, she is letting me into her heart. Trusting me to not destroy the last thread of hope that is barely hanging on.

I grab both sides of her face and press my forehead to hers, letting our lips brush in a featherlight touch. "You stole my heart from the moment those beautiful lips cursed me with a dagger to my throat in the alley. I fell for you then. I just didn't realize it yet. But know, I love you endlessly, little demon. And I will shatter the world for you."

Her soft smile lifts her cheeks with a sniffle. She bites her bottom lip to stop it from trembling. So, I help her out as I press my lips to hers in a final kiss for the night. No more words need to be spoken because everything is said in this single kiss.

As soon as we pull apart and make ourselves look more presentable, she gives me a final heartwarming glance before she cloaks herself in shadows and disappears into the night.

CHAPTER TWENTY

Fynn

Energy builds at the palms of my hands, vibrating with tension as I center my mind. I just need to open a door to another realm, no big deal. My breath is thready as I grit my teeth. Carefully balancing this much power just beneath the surface is risky. Every strand of energy tangles with another, and it's up to me to find the right one without snapping any of the others.

Cora and Kye spar on the other side of the room, and Draven stands nearby with his arms crossed for support. I drown them all out. Only focusing on the steady hum of my power. On my exhale, I free it. It beams into the air until it creates a tear, opening wider and wider.

Grunting, my feet slide back, and I press them harder into the ground to keep my body firmly in place. The portal continues to expand, and I ever so slowly shift my hands to help guide it. But in the next breath, it snaps. Fizzling out into nothing, and the ricochet of power shoves me back a step.

"Argh!" With a pounding heart and heaving chest, I roar with every ounce of frustration. I've been trying to tap into the other realm for two days straight with hardly any sleep, and I have had zero luck. Yes, there has been progress, but not nearly enough.

The strain of power to another realm is buried beneath all the others, but that's not the hard part. It's keeping my hold on it—to guide it free from the web of energy that all leads to other places in the world for me to manipulate. But this one fights back. Similarly to how one may catch fish for dinner, once it's hooked, it tries it's best to pull away. Each time I try, I bring the strand of the portal closer and closer, but every failed attempt just pushes me dangerously near the edge of losing my mind.

"You held it longer that time." Draven's voice registers through my thoughts.

"Didn't feel like it," I respond before inhaling deeply and blowing out of my mouth.

"Don't be so hard on yourself." His hand grips the back of my neck. "You are doing something that is thought to be impossible. I have no doubt you will get it, but I suggest you get some rest." He smiles as he steps back. "As some bastard once told me, you won't be any good to anyone if you don't take care of yourself."

The fucker winks as he tries to imitate me. I stop my eyes from rolling when he spins on his heel and waves to Cora and Kye as he exits the room.

The clapping of leather smacking against leather stops as footsteps head my way. I pace back and forth as my hands pull roughly at the roots of my hair with my chin tucked to my chest. I'm spiraling. Losing myself to the self-destructive thoughts that always sneak their way in, to grab hold of me until I believe it.

I'm not good enough. I will never amount to anything. The stars found me unworthy of love the day they stole my mate. I'm a fuck-up who hides behind jokes and smiles.

Shaking my head, I slam my eyes close to draw all my focus on evening out my breathing. Suddenly, the scent of the sea's mist on a cold morning has my eyes opening. A glass of water is being held up towards my chest, which causes me to halt my feet to one spot.

"Here." Cora's sweet voice cuts through the insistent pounding in my ears. The rush of boiling blood raging in my skull begins to simmer at the sound of her lyrical voice.

Lifting my head, I meet her shining blue eyes, so full of wonder and possibilities. The tips of my fingers brush against hers as I take the water from her waiting hand, smiling to myself when I see her cheeks bloom to the softest pink.

"Thank you." Bringing the cup to my lips, I chug it down in two swallows. I find her staring at my lips when I swipe my tongue over them to catch the lingering drops of water.

She clears her throat and opens her mouth to say something. Kye comes up behind her, messing her hair up on her head as she hurries to pat it back down.

"You did good, Cor. Blocked almost all of my advances." He yawns before waving his hand up to me as he turns for the door. "It's late. I'm going to go turn in and get some rest. You two should as well," he says over his shoulder before disappearing from the room.

Leaving just me and *her*. And I gulp.

She's still fixing her hair with her head turned to where Kye walked out. Huffing with frustration and mumbling creative curses under her breath as she keeps finding more strands sticking out.

But I'm lost in the curve of her mouth. The small pout of her bottom lip, and how she's angrily biting it. It's cute, but my cock thickening in my pants thinks otherwise. Watching her has almost made me forget that I was seconds away from breaking my fist against the floor.

She turns back to catch me staring, and then rolls her eyes. Wait a minute. What did I do to earn that reaction instead of that damn charming blush? I swear, this girl gives me whiplash, but that only excites me. It stirs something deep inside of me, making it feel alive when it has been stagnant all these years.

"Why do you keep looking at me like that?" If she thinks her question will unnerve me, she will have to do better.

"Because I'm fascinated by you." That gives her pause with two raised brows. "And I think you might feel the same way about me."

Taking one step closer, I watch a shiver work its way down her body and fail desperately at hiding the smirk that graces my lips.

"What I feel is concern." She wipes a bead of sweat off her forehead with the back of her hand before gesturing a waving palm to me. "You are pushing yourself too hard, and I fear it's going to hurt you. That's all."

Closing the distance, I fix a single blonde strand that she missed. "You worried about me, love?"

The thought of her worrying about me does something funny to my heart. It skips, only to trip over itself while feeling like it's wrapped in a warm blanket. Something I haven't felt since my mate was alive. Nothing can compare to a fated bond, but some love can grow so strong that it's close. And what I've been feeling for Cora has me wanting to constantly find a way to be near her.

To have her eyes always on me.

A subtle nod is her answer, and I can't help but grip her chin between my fingers until she has nowhere else to look but at me. "I need to hear you say it."

"Yes," she breathes out. "I'm worried about you." She holds my gaze, never shying away as she surprises me by reaching up, rubbing her thumb over the lines creasing between my brows, smoothing them out. "You barely sleep, and the last time I saw you eat something was yesterday morning." Those diamond blues bounce back and forth between my hazel ones.

"And I—" Her eyes drop down to my lips. Her fingers follow the movement to gently touch the scar there before her gaze springs back up. "And I feel such a strong pull to take care of you."

To. Take. Care. Of. Me.

Five words that have my knees growing weak, threatening to buckle right before her. Aside from Draven's family, I have been alone for so long. I learned at a young age how to provide for myself because if I didn't, I would not have survived. I didn't have the best childhood growing up, needing to shed the coat of being a boy to a male before the pitch of my voice deepened.

Hearing those words, it tugs at something deep inside me. Once again, sparking something to live inside me that has only felt stiff and murky. I want to wrap her in my arms and breathe her in, thanking the stars that

161

maybe, just maybe they may have aligned our paths to collide. That although not fated, we are destined.

The pad of my thumb softly brushes over the porcelain skin on her cheek. "You promise?"

She leans her head into my touch, seeming to get lost in the feeling before realizing I spoke. "Huh?"

"You promise to take care of me?" I ask again, desperate to hear her answer.

"In every way I can."

Suddenly, my chest tightens, and I feel like I can't breathe if I don't kiss her. Every nerve in my body is screaming to close the distance, brush my lips against hers and show her how badly I wish to take care of her, too.

Those delicate pink lips of hers part as if she wants the same.

I swallow roughly. "I'd very much like to kiss you," I hoarsely force out. Never giving myself a moment to change my mind.

Ever so softly, she smiles, and it draws me in. "And I'd be upset if you didn't."

I groan at her admission, and don't hesitate to press my lips to hers. The moment our mouths touch, it doesn't just feel like a breath of fresh air, but more of a gust of wind that carries us to the clouds. Wrapping around us to keep us close.

My hand slides to the back of her neck, pulling her in so I can kiss her deeper. To feel her tongue dance with mine. She opens willingly and my body shudders. There may have been other females who I've been intimate with since losing my mate, but only to try and feel something. To find a way to stop the emptiness from being so fucking painful. But nothing happened. Most of the time, I couldn't even make it to the finish line.

And I never kissed them. I've never touched another's lips since I lost my mate.

Until her. Until Cora swooped in that training room with Emma with a lightness to her step. It was refreshing.

Everything about Cora makes me want more. She's been a beacon of light in a life so dark and hollow. Like the morning rain that nourishes the earth to grow.

I devour her. Quickly becoming addicted, and I'm not sure if I'll be able to stop. Especially when she moans into my mouth and grabs at my shirt to get closer. My free hand drops the empty glass to the floor to slide down her side and grip her hip tightly, pulling her body more firmly into mine. Luckily, the glass doesn't shatter to disrupt this moment, but instead clanks loudly to the ground.

I have no doubt she can feel how she affects me as she rolls her hips into mine, seeking friction. I tip her head farther back, laying claim to her. Angling my mouth so I can selfishly taste more. I nip at her bottom lip, and I feel her smile against my mouth on a gasp. But I can't fucking stop.

Now that I know what she tastes like, *feels* like, I am fully coming undone. Her lips are so soft and now swollen because of me. Heat tingles down my spine and sparks lick beneath my skin. Her fingers clutch harder at my shirt before sliding up into my hair and gripping at the strands at the root.

She's like putty in my arms, melting under my touch and so damn responsive with every little whimper she gifts me. Moving my palm from her hip, I skate it up her spine underneath the material of her shirt, her silky skin against my fingertips.

She bites my tongue and holds it hostage as she trails her hands down the line of my jaw. When she frees it, she kisses me with fervor, desperately opening her mouth for me to ravage and sink into. She teasingly slides her palms over my chest until she reaches my stomach, inching lower until her fingers curl over my waistband and tug.

I groan into her mouth, my movements growing rough as I hold her more firmly to me. Her tongue twirls around mine and the act puts me in a trance of pure, undiluted desire. Our hips grind into the other at the same time, causing my cock to twitch.

I swallow down another small cry of pleasure that escapes her and find all the strength I can, managing to seek that last shred of control I hold and pull back. Our breaths mingle in sync, but my hands feel like they are shaking, struggling to not dig into her creamy skin and explore every inch of her.

"You have no idea what you do to me." My lips press against her forehead, whispering my confession. The only sounds are our breaths rushing out in heavy exhales.

A small, amused huff leaves her used lips as she pulls back so she can look at me. "I think I have a clue."

I want to leave a handprint on her ass if she's teasing me about how hard my cock is straining against the seam to get to her. But there is a softness in her gaze which makes me wonder if instead, it's because she feels the same.

Something in my chest seems to settle, and I have the urge to try to use my powers one more time tonight before I force myself to sleep. Because she's right, my body needs it and the circles beneath my eyes just keep getting darker. With her here in my arms, it's giving me a different kind of calming strength that makes me feel steadier than before.

Once my heart calms to a normal beat, I say, "I need to try one more time." And I wait for her to demand I just sleep instead.

Instead, she asks, "To try to kiss me again?"

I can't stop the chuckle that tumbles free. "Your mind still stuck in your desire for me, love?" Finally, I get her cheeks to tint the warmest shade of pink, but I continue so she doesn't have to answer. "I want to try to reach Gehendra again. Just one more time. Then, I promise I'll stop for the night."

She studies me, her eyes holding mine as she digs deeper, trying to see if I will go too far. "Once more." Her fingers release from the band of my pants as she begins to turn and walk away, but I grab her around the waist and pull her back into me. The fronts of our bodies perfectly aligned with no space between us.

Her face is in my chest as I hold her tighter, pressing my lips to the top of her head. "Please stay right here. I need you because something about you gives me strength and settles the madness in my heart."

A shaky breath fans over my shirt and I feel her head shift up and down. "Okay." So soft, I almost don't hear her.

Holding my hands out ahead of me, with her safely pressed into my chest, my eyes fall close. I reach for my well of power, centering myself and allowing my head to drop slightly to breathe her in, inhaling deeply.

To feel her essence wrap around me in a comforting hold as I bring my power to the surface. Gripping hold of that one stubborn strand and pulling it to me. The energy hums through my veins and on my exhale, I let it flow free. Golden light ripples in a circle until the golden rings start slowly pulling away from each other.

Cora stays still between my arms, snuggling closer to my chest and circling her arms around my waist, securing herself to me. The feel of her has me opening my eyes when I start moving my hands to direct my power to open the portal. To reach past land and sea. Past time and space.

My breath hitches in my throat at the darkness swirling in the center, sending a frosty chill to cascade towards me. An eerie sensation creeps up my spine at whatever lurks on the other side. The small opening looks like an eye of darkness, evil and waiting.

My arms begin to tremble from the exertion, and I grit my teeth to draw up more energy. When I try to open it up more, my power snaps once again and it all falls away. Only this time, I don't want to slam my fist into the floor. This time, I wrap my arms tightly around Cora, resting my head in the crook of her neck.

"Thank you," I breathe out harshly as the rush of my power comes down. "I *felt* it. Somehow, I managed to touch the realm. It's like a living thing, even though it was as cold as death. But that's the farthest I've managed to surge my power."

She pulls back, bright eyes holding mine. "Whatever is in that realm, I felt it, too." A shiver jolts up her spine, but she brushes it off, reaching for my hand and linking our fingers together. "And Fynn?"

"Yeah?"

She smiles, cupping my jaw within her palm. Her fingers feel so delicate against my skin. "I never doubted you. So, it's not *somehow* you tapped into the realm. It's because of your strength and control of your ability. It's all you."

She has to hear it. The intense pounding of my heart that is trying to jump out of my chest and go to her. And I can't hide the damn hearts in my eyes that have her name written on them. Her words, the things she says, just mend another piece of me that I didn't know was torn. My mouth opens to speak, but she holds up a hand to stop me.

"Time for me to make sure you sleep." She spins and starts walking, pulling me along with her.

A dirty comeback rests on my tongue, but for once, I let it stay silent. Because I'm entranced with the way her hair dances over her back and the sway of her hips with every step she takes. I'd rather take in this moment than cover it up with some sexy joke. Right now, I don't feel like I need to hide. I can simply be quiet and let her take care of me.

When we reach the doors, my heart starts racing at the thought of her separating from me. I need her close right now. Every part of me feels slightly exposed to her—raw and open. And a part of me knows I won't be able to sleep unless I feel her warmth and can smell her sweet, ocean scent.

Squeezing her hand, I ask, "Will you stay with me tonight?"

Her feet pause as she turns slightly, looking over her shoulder at me with one raised brow. Shit.

"Only to sleep," I rush out. "I just—" Fuck, I've never in my life felt so unsure. Dragging a hand through my hair, I continue. "I just…need you close. I can't explain it. You make me feel like the male I want to be."

Turning back on her heel, she starts pulling me again in a steady walk towards where we are staying in the castle. My feet almost trip over each other when I hear her answer, "Okay."

Okay, I think to myself as my heart kicks an extra beat in my chest.

CHAPTER TWENTY-ONE

Emma

A few days pass, and I manage to stay by Aiden's side without emptying my stomach every time he finds a way to touch me. His hands resting on my lower back, or grabbing my elbow to pull me closer. His lips skimming the shell of my ear to whisper something he doesn't wish for anyone to hear.

I'm currently sitting at the table across from Aiden, with Calloway sitting at the head as if it was always his seat to claim. Any time I was told to dine here with King Oren and Calloway accompanied us, I always thought he looked too *at home* at this table. Behaving as if he was the ruler back then with no common courtesy.

Now he's chomping on his peppered chicken with loud smacks of his lips, causing small sprays of spit to fly out between bites. The way he eats crawls under my skin, making my eye twitch as my knuckles beneath the table turn white from clenching my silverware with thoughts of shanking him with it.

"Have you heard the news?" Calloway says with a mouth full of food.

167

"Heard what?" Aiden asks, and I thank the stars he waits to speak once he swallows down some of his dinner.

"The rebels!" Calloway shouts with glee as he bounces once in his seat before shoving another forkful of potatoes between his vile lips. "Seems they realized who they are up against. No sightings to be seen. And you know what's even better about no rebels?" He nudges his head towards his son with a sort of joyful craziness twinkling in his eyes.

"I don't," Aiden says blandly, slowly dragging his eyes from me to his father. "But I assume you are going to enlighten me?"

Calloway bellows with a furious laugh, slamming his hand on the table and almost knocking his goblet of wine off in the process. "Right you are, my boy! No Corrupted sightings either! At least, not on our land. Can't say the same for the other courts."

"From my knowledge, you have not been in touch with the other courts since the rebellion. So, is this confirmed that there have been sightings there?" Aiden tacks on nonchalantly, which causes his father to pause mid-chew.

Calloway collects himself and slashes his hand through the air, brushing off Aiden's words. "Nonsense. Makes no difference to me so long as I'm safe."

"Don't you mean so long as the court and people are safe?" Aiden says against the rim of his glass before taking a swig of wine.

"If that is the answer that will make you sleep at night, Son."

Rage. Pure, hot fire sears down every track in my veins. I knew Calloway was a self-centered bastard, but this is a whole new level. And Whiro seemed to hold his promise to keep the Corrupted free of Asov, but the rest of the lands might still be suffering. The Corrupted will only keep spreading and more Fae will die. I hoped going with my father would end it all, but now I can see that it doesn't matter. They are left to roam and keep fear lurking around every corner, solely for *entertainment*.

My fork slams harder than I intend when I set it down and find two pairs of eyes on me. "My apologies, it slipped."

Calloway narrows his beady eyes before gulping down the rest of his drink. "You seem tired. Why don't you retire to your room and let us discuss such important matters that would bore your female mind."

My toes curl in my flats until I'm sure they'll crack. The power in me begins to pulse, but I push it down, demanding it to settle.

His time will come, I repeat in my head.

I keep my tone light, even though I'm on the verge of destruction. "My eyes do feel heavy." I push my chair back to stand and straighten my spine, refusing to bow. "I'll take my leave, then."

Wooden legs scrape against stone. "I'll walk you," Aiden rushes to say.

"Nonsense! The girl can walk herself. She's capable enough for that." Calloway starts refilling his golden goblet as Aiden remains frozen in place. "Sit!" his father bellows harshly.

Without a word or sparing a final glance, I whisk around and steadily take my leave. I keep my footsteps light and sure. Once I make my way through the hallways to my room, I let the door fall shut and just stand there. My mind racing, knowing there has to be something I can do to help.

I can't do nothing. Not anymore.

Without another thought, I make quick work to change into a black tunic with matching leather pants, tossing on a cloak that will also blend into the night.

With my dagger strapped to my thigh and boots laced, I throw my shadows out, guiding them to take me to the Court of Abhain. The sun is just beginning to roll beneath the horizon as red, orange, and yellow hues smear across the sky, fading into a deep blue. The wind whistles over the rolling hills, the long blades of grass swaying to its tune. There is the rush of a waterfall crashing into the river beside me, and a bird chirping in the distance.

I slowly glance around and let the darkness of my power surge forth, hoping it will let me track the Corrupted. I briefly wonder if Draven still hunts them or if my disappearance has truly consumed him in a dark cloud he can't clear.

But I can't let my thoughts drift. I need to center my energy to see if I can sense where the Corrupted may be lurking. I let my shadows fill my hood, masking my face in case I run into anyone. People will recognize me now, and I can't let that happen.

My eyes fall closed, delving into my power until I feel a glimmer of familiarity a little farther away. The same recognition I felt in Whiro's presence. Except, this isn't as potent. In quick strides, my boots pound on the cushioned ground of thick greenery. I race towards this connection, driving my legs faster as I ignore the burn that begins to tighten in my muscles.

When I reach a small path leading into a village, I slow my pace. The grass fades into dirt that starts crunching under my boots with each step. It should be here. I take a deep inhale, inflating my lungs until it hurts, and immediately smell the rotten scent that lingers on the Corrupted. My body instinctively bends into a crouch as I round the nearest corner, peering around the building until my eyes lock on my target.

I have no idea if anything I do will work, but I have to try.

Whiro continues to steal the lives of innocents, to manipulate, while threatening me with ending the entire world. No. I refuse to let that continue. For him to destroy this land that holds so many families and beautiful lives. I have to do something to save them, to protect them.

I stand and step out in the open, walking right into the path of the Corrupted searching for something to tear into. My heart cracks at the sight—so loudly that I don't know how this Corrupted doesn't hear.

It's a young girl, maybe about to hit puberty. Her light blonde hair a tangled mess, her pale blue dress torn and covered in dirt and blood. The skin under her eyes has sunken in, black veins scattering her whole body and eyes that match mine. Eyes that look dead inside.

She spins, noticing me as I approach. A faint shriek spills from her small mouth.

I gingerly walk closer as she hunches forward, spreading the spear-like claws to push through her fingertips. Her chest is heaving in deep, quick breaths as her lips peel back to show her teeth.

I inch closer, not daring to hold my breath. For this to possibly work, I need to make contact. Every cell in my body is urging me to do so.

One slow breath out and I push all my weight into the soles of my feet as I take off. Charging her with quick steps, arms pumping, and my shadows swarming around us, blocking her from escaping. Even though now, her only focus is to rip me to pieces.

The moment I'm in front of her, I spin to the left before her claws can sink into my stomach. My hands land on her shoulders as I focus on my well of power. Drawing more shadows to the surface, wanting to pull out the darkness in her. Hoping my own calls to hers, commanding it as a way to lure it out of her petite frame. *Needing* to free her from this curse my father has created. Desperately wanting to save this girl who is lost to the dark because I know all too well what it feels like to walk in the shadows alone.

I can feel the cursed power dwelling inside her. How it has burrowed itself into the marrow of her bones, tainting her blood cells and rooting itself into her heart. Yet…her darkness doesn't obey mine. I try again with more grit as I scream in frustration, but the strain on my mind causes spots to dance before my vision. Still, nothing happens.

She screeches, shaking beneath my palms, and drops her body out of my grasp while I'm still trying to clear the spots floating around us. She rams her shoulders into my legs, knocking me back until I slam into the ground with a grunt.

Shit.

Something cracks in my side, and with the way the air leaves my lungs, I'm sure that earned me a broken rib. That's what I get for leaving an open window for an attack. An attack I wasn't fully expecting, considering who I am. But it seems she's more unhinged, more lost to this curse. It makes me wonder if Whiro is lessening his hold on them to do whatever their feral minds wish. Not caring what happens to them or others.

My palms scrape over the loose pebbles scattered in the dirt and they bite into my skin as I force myself back to my feet and away from her. But I'm not fast enough.

Her hand wraps tightly around my calf as she sinks her talons into the muscle, causing me to grind my back teeth together. A blast of shadows spears from my hand, nailing her in the chest to throw her backward, but her talons take bits of my skin with her.

I jump to my feet, pain immediately stabbing my leg as I shift my weight to the other. Wetness soaks the material of my pants around the wound, but I know it will heal soon. Same for why the bruising pain in my rib cage is dulling. A benefit of not being restrained by a necklace that steals my power and something I'm still trying to get used to, considering I still keep a stash of healing salve for comfort.

My chest heaves through the stinging gnawing on my calf as I limp towards her. The girl's body unnaturally pushes off the ground to stand, those bleeding black orbs locked on me. Out of reflex, my hand itches to pull my dagger from its sheath, but I don't want to hurt her. There has to be a way.

Suddenly, Mauve's words come surging forth. *Remember, darkness can be broken by the light, but you have to open your eyes.*

The Masiren said the same thing, to open my eyes, but to the light. It helped clear the darkness in me once I was able to grasp it.

I don't have time to change my mind because the girl is charging at me. Her shrilling screeches bleed in the midnight air. I brace myself, ready for the impact.

One deep breath in.

A steady exhale…

Hmph. Her body collides with mine, the tips of her nails slicing into my stomach as I wrap my arms around her. Blinding pain seizes me, causing stars to dance before me, my vision doubling as we smack into the ground. I hold her tightly, locking her arms between us even if it means keeping her claws buried inside of me. I ignore the burning that begins to spread as I constrict my hold and a fuzzy warmth shoots through my veins. My eyes threaten to roll back the moment my light plunges into her.

I hear her suck in a breath, her shrieks dying in her throat. White blindly glows around us like an explosion in the dark. I don't dare squeeze my eyes shut. I push my power into her, letting it pulse around us in waves. I'm panting from the force of it, unsure of how much power to drive into her small body, but I don't want to take a chance. I've never done this, and I refuse to let her live another day with the savage intent to kill.

The vigor in her attack falls away, her muscles loosening as I shift her to lay flat on the ground. The claws in my stomach rip free, and her eyes are wide, radiating light. She begins to tremble in my arms, but I realize it's not her body doing it, it's mine. My arms shake uncontrollably as my power starts to recede, coming down from the high. It snakes back into my veins, settling once again and welcoming the undisturbed dark of night.

The black tracks that webbed over her body are gone, and those once obsidian eyes are a pale green that reflects off the moonlight. She blinks a few times before a tear slips from the corner of her eye. I watch it follow the small curve of her cheek as she sits up until it drips down over her chin and disappears.

"Who are you?" she whispers hoarsely.

I almost forget she can't see me, for my face is lost in the shadows. "Someone who only wishes to right her wrongs."

She wipes the next wave of tears away with the back of her hand, her movement steady and calm compared to me. Her skin is filling with the color again, and the dark circles sunken beneath her eyes are brightening.

"No." Her small voice sounds stronger. "You are my savior."

My body stiffens, yet my heart beats wildly in my chest. My eyes still not believing what I'm seeing and that no more Corrupted have to die. I help her stand once my body lets me take back control and stop the tremor in my muscles. She brushes herself off to the best of her ability before looking at me with a twinkle in her eye.

"Do you have a name?" she asks.

I'm quiet for a moment, knowing she can feel my gaze upon her. "If I tell you, you have to promise to keep it a secret."

Her teeth glow white with the wide smile she throws my way, along with an enthusiastic nod. "I promise."

Cupping my hand close to my mouth, I lean down to speak near her ear. "It's Emma."

She repeats my name on her small lips, and then throws her arms around me in a firm hug. My muscles tense with my arms frozen above her. But then, she tightens her hold, burrowing her face into my chest and my heart thumps roughly in my rib cage. Hesitantly, I lower my arms, letting them fall around her, welcoming this feeling. To make her feel safe. To save her from the monster that took over her little body. And to know she will get to live out her life.

I make sure she gets home safely after that and watch in wonder as her parents fall to their knees and smother her with love. The sight causes me to draw in a shaky breath, but I don't let myself dwell on the lack of love from a parent that was never gifted to me growing up. Seeing this girl have those who miss her and will cherish her fills that hole in my heart.

I slowly retreat to the rooftop, but pause to peer down at the one who makes my heart jump in my chest. I sensed Draven the moment I held that little girl in my arms, but he remained shrouded in his shadows. When I left tonight, a small part of me knew he would find me. Someway, somehow. And it makes me wonder if it's like before, that he felt my pain from the wound she inflicted on me that alerted him.

My gaze drops, never wavering from where he stays hidden, but I know his shadows and the way they dance around him.

The heat from his eyes burns along my skin, warming me up from the inside out. But I shake it off, this need to climb him and take what my body craves. Yet, underneath all that, there is a sense of comfort and safety that his presence brings. Something I'm still trying to understand and become used to. All I know is that I very much like how he watches me, and how he doesn't stop me.

Closing my eyes, I reach my shadows around until I sense another Corrupted nearby. I leap from the rooftop, letting the reunion of the little girl's family slowly fade from my view. But as I latch onto my new target, it's then I realize…I never learned her name to remember her by, and a sharp pang stabs my heart.

So, from here on out, I will keep track of every Fae I save, knowing them by name so they will never be forgotten again. And it's with that silent promise under the stars that I vanish, disappearing into the night with the Dark Prince on my heels.

But I don't miss the irony: where the Corrupted were once hunting me, it is I now doing the hunting.

CHAPTER TWENTY-TWO

Draven

Falling asleep has been nearly impossible, but I manage an hour or two each night, though my soul needs the comfort of Emma to truly rest. To feel the steady beat of her heart near mine. To pull her body against mine and nuzzle into her neck to breathe her in. But instead, I lay here, with my arms tossed over my head, fighting the urge to go against Emma's wishes. To storm into her palace and bring her here no matter the consequences. Every part of me hates that she's alone right now.

But then sharp, searing pain jolts me upright as I grab my side.

The feeling takes my breath away, but this pain is not my own… It's Emma's. She's fucking hurt. The shred of control I held snaps, throwing my blankets off without bothering to get fully dressed.

My mind plummets to the vilest thoughts as I call on my wings. Limbs will start being torn from bodies if it was Aiden or his father, and I don't care if he's the fucking king. Because tearing limbs wouldn't be enough. I'd then keep an iron blade pierced through their stomachs while hanging them upside down, to make them bleed slowly without ever being able to heal. Making their blood drip, drip, drip, and leaving them in agony as I watch.

Reaching deep within me, I grasp onto the bond and follow the pull that will lead me to her. In the blink of an eye, I leap from the opening in my room and soar across the sea as I feel her presence grow stronger, my beast pressing on the walls of my psyche for me to close the distance.

As I near, I can't help but question why my little demon would be in the Court of Abhain. A million other thoughts race through my mind for what would bring her so far from her bed where she should be sleeping.

My wings beat brutally against the wind, flying faster than ever before. I touch down, skidding to a stop on the outskirts of a village I've only been to when hunting the Corrupted. It's just as run-down and deserted as I remember.

Immediately, her rose and honey scent invades my senses, driving the beast in me to pound against my bones to find her and claim her. Having her near me without our bond snapping into place has been fucking diffi-cult. Every instinct inside of me wants to complete the mating ritual, to be buried deep inside her and have our marks imprinted on our hands.

But I've been restraining myself because I just got her back. I will only mate with her when she is ready, and I can tell she's not there yet. Not completely. She just found her way out of the dark, and I will be patient for however long she needs until she wants me to join her in the light.

I know she doesn't understand the full extent of what completing a bond entails, and when the time is right, I will tell her. I don't want it to sway her to choose to complete the bond because we'd be able to speak to each other in our minds. Even though it would settle something in me if I could reach out to her to check in, making sure she is okay.

Like now, for instance. Instead, I'm raging inside to get to her. Even being able to feel her pain shouldn't happen until the bond is complete. Since this is not the first time, I'm thinking the reason is because she's so powerful that it's enhancing our connection. But even without all the extra bits that come with a mate bond, all that matters is her and I.

And that thought stays with me as I cast my shadows around my frame, staying unseen as I make my way down an empty path. Then, a shriek fills the air from the direction the bond is calling me to. My legs pump hard, my bare feet pounding on the ground as I round the corner of a building, only to halt my movements.

Emma, face shrouded in shadows, is on the ground with a young Corrupted in her arms. I can smell the metallic scent of blood before I see it seeping between them. The moment my feet go to move, blinding white light makes me cover my eyes.

It flares and pulses around them and when it starts to fade, I slowly remove my arm from in front of my face. My eyes widen and my jaw gapes because when the light fully dies down, I no longer see a Corrupted, but just…a little girl who is trembling in Emma's arms.

I stay hidden, watching the girl sit up, slowly looking healthier and more alive by the minute. My little demon can cure the Corrupted, bringing them back to life as if there was never a trace of darkness in them.

I continue to watch, following my mate as she safely takes the girl home, but I don't miss the subtle shift of her brows or how her eyes linger on the family. My chest aches to go to her, to wrap her up in my arms and never let go.

I know she can sense me near her. When she makes it to the roof, her hooded face shifts to my direction, and I can feel the weight of her eyes on me. Seeing through my shadows as if they don't exist.

And if I wasn't sure just a moment ago, the warmth that liquiefies through the bond gives her away. It feels like a sense of comfort with a sprinkle of lust because we are a fated pair that is still unmated. This desire will only intensify.

The way she looks, cloaked in shadows, has me grinding my molars, the sight causing my throat to dry. She's everything, made from wisps of beautiful chaos that holds a heart of all that is good. But she manages to mask it as she leaps from the roof, with me following a good distance behind.

The rest of the night I watch over her as she finds a handful of Corrupted. Guilt weighs heavily. I stopped being Shade when my entire world was taken from me. But it seems more lives can now be saved, when all I could offer was a quick and sure death to end their misery.

177

Right now, stalking her is all I can do so I don't disturb what she's doing. Deep down, I feel that this is something she needs to do on her own. To heal a small piece of herself.

She looks to the horizon, gauging something before vanishing, and I follow the pull to her once again. This time, it leads me to the sea off the coast of Abhain. Cautiously, I stay high in the sky, blending into the dark as I beat my wings to keep me hovering far enough away above a lone ship.

A group of males and females are on board, keeping their voices low. I catch something said by one of the males who steps up and seems to be the leader of this group.

"How much longer do we have to hold back?" There is a desperation to his harsh voice. But my little demon is unfazed.

She doesn't answer right away, but tips her head up, looking straight into my mist of shadows. I hold my breath as I watch, needing to understand what's happening.

Her gaze drops back to the male questioning her. "Not much longer. He believes you all have given up. The coronation was executed perfectly, and he doesn't suspect a thing. But I will give you the vengeance you seek." She places her hand over her heart. "You have my word."

"Then we will remain hidden," the male says with a firm nod. "And we will be ready."

"I'll meet with you as soon as I can," Emma says before meeting the eyes of each member with a final farewell. Her shadows then swallow her whole.

I remain floating above the rocking ship anchored in the sea, studying those on board and thinking on what I heard. She could have blocked me with her power to not be able to hear the conversation. But Emma wanted me to hear, to not hide whatever this is.

They mentioned the coronation…the execution of it…

My eyes widen, looking closely at the small group on board. The rough clothing, and the weapons hanging on their bodies ready at a moment's notice. This group is only a handful of them, and it seems to be the head ones who lead something much bigger. Something that would sentence them all to a quick execution if known.

They are the rebellion, and my little demon is working with them. Even though I could see the sliver of fear glinting in their eyes when Emma was before them, they still have respect for her to listen. Respect for their princess they always wished to meet, who is helping them rid Asov of a careless king.

Seems she doesn't just have plans to take Whiro down. A wicked smirk tips my lips, forcing my wings to beat hard with a loud gust. I brush deep down in our bond, reaching for the thrumming pull that will lead me to her.

Pride swells in my chest as I glide above the sleeping clouds. Once upon a time I thought the Princess of Asov was an ignorant, selfish female who didn't give a damn about the world and the people who lived in it. But I learned quickly how fucking wrong I was. I judged her by the cover of what I saw, before taking my time to read her. To understand her. The deeper I sink into who she is, the more I truly see her. And she only keeps surprising me. She is so much more than anything I could ever imagine.

I dive down to a forest near the edge of a village, sensing her presence as if I've known it my whole life. I thought maybe she would head back to Asov and get some rest, but I realize that's far from what she's doing as she nears another Corrupted in the night. She's already got her hands on the cursed male, using her energy to save him. But her faint, white glow begins to lose its flare in the distance.

I stalk closer, seeing how her body starts to waver. Her movements slow. The light of her power flickers as she grunts, pushing another wave of light into the vessel that has been consumed by the evil of her father.

Defining my sight to zoom in on her, I see her eyes flutter and the muscles in her body begin to quiver as she stumbles slightly. She's exerting herself past her limits. She'll black out if she keeps going because her body can't handle the amount of power she's using in so little time.

Not even a heartbeat later, her eyes roll back right before her body drops to the ground. The Fae in her arms is staring at her in panic, and I can feel his heart beating twice as fast. Without a thought, I rush to her, letting this Fae figure out his way home as I swoop her limp frame in my arms, pulling her in close.

I'll drop her off in her room without being seen, even though I hate to leave her side again. Fynn is so close to tapping his power into the other realm. Another day or two should be all he needs, and then we can fight together to rid the world of Whiro so she can live her life how she wishes. To be free.

I push open her patio doors when I land, and carefully lay her on her bed. Her breaths are deep, and I slowly brush the hair that fell on her face behind her ear. My fingers can't resist tracing the bridge of her nose, following the curve of her jaw, before feathering over her pouty lips.

I lower myself, pressing my lips to her forehead, before dropping my head to hers. "Stop fighting your demons alone," I whisper. The tightness in my chest lessens with the contact of her skin on mine. "You have me."

It takes every bit of willpower to remove myself from her side to fly home. My wings beat slowly as I war with myself in wanting to turn around and take her with me. To kidnap her while she's unconscious. And I tell myself it's only for her safety, but that would be a fucking lie. I can be a selfish bastard when it comes to what I want.

I've never wanted something or someone as badly as I do her. Even with how I hold my breath until she looks at me. Or how her saying my name makes me want to drop to my knees and bury my face between her thighs until she screams it. She's it for me.

And as I fly closer to my home, it gets harder to take a full breath. My lungs constrict and my chest feels tight. The distance is causing the ache in my chest to feel like an anchor pulling tauter with every mile I put between us.

But one day, it will be her and I putting distance between us and the world.

CHAPTER TWENTY-THREE

Emma

Screams rip free from my throat. "Tell me, Daughter, who do you obey?

Another whip cuts through another layer of skin, fueling fire to a wound already blazing. I scream again, my cries falling on deaf ears.

"Your screams aren't an answer, Emma."

He's dead.

He's dead.

He's dead.

I chant in my head, yet the vision before me has me reliving the horrors King Oren inflicted. Another lash of the whip flays my skin, and the blinding pain and blood trailing down my back feels too real.

This is the day that I remember the most. The one that took a piece of me I never got back. The day I became mute to his torment and stopped letting my pain be heard as I bit back every scream.

Suddenly, I'm ripped to another memory of what I endured by his hands and how much he loved slowly carving a knife into every layer of skin. Like I was his very own canvas and my blood was his paint. But I never screamed.

The dream twists and blurs until it brings me to Gehendra. I'm standing there, facing the Fae Whiro told me to kill, who is on his knees before me. The one who already kisses the doorstep to death as his eyes plead with me to save him, but I don't. And I can't stop this assault of my past. I'm prey to these memories, a puppet to the truth that this is what I've done. The monster I've become.

My hands move on their own, following the memory of what I did, killing the Fae by piercing his chest with a shadow hand and holding his heart with it. Crushing it to dust before pushing him off the ledge and into the endless void. I can still feel it. Every beat of his life. The way it swelled as I squeezed tighter before bursting.

Only, this time, I don't feel the adrenaline I did before. Now my heart sinks, splintered with a million shards of guilt. Innocent lives have been taken by my bare hands, but what's worse… I had enjoyed it.

My stomach twists as the Fae disappears and I'm pulled into another memory when all I want is to wake from this nightmare.

I jerk upright, gasping with uneven breaths. One moment I was throwing Vincent into the Sea of Souls with his eyes holding mine. When he hit the water, I felt myself falling, and I woke before my body could hit the ground.

My eyes blink rapidly as they try to fully open from waking up so abruptly, but the room around me is a blur. Fisting my hands to rub my eyes, trying to bring myself to focus, but the exhaustion pulling at me is making my eyelids heavy, even though my heart is racing. The sheets are damp and tangled around my legs, and there seems to be a black hole in my mind because I don't remember returning to my room.

I squint, trying to look out the balcony windows, but only able to note that the sun is setting. Meaning, I slept the whole day away. Scrubbing my hands down my face, I reach around to pull my hair over my shoulder and fix the braid that has become undone.

My head snaps to the soft knock that fills the silence before my door creaks open.

"Just checking in. I haven't seen you all day." Aiden. His sandy hair looks windblown as if he's been out at sea.

I pull up the lingering strength I have left to look at him. "I'm good. Just tired."

His brows crease but he doesn't question me. "Okay, just making sure you aren't avoiding me."

I can't tell him that I would if I could. So, instead, I shake my head. "Of course not. I just had a rough sleep last night and it caught up to me."

He nods, strands of his hair shifting in front of his eyes from the movement. "Okay, well, get some rest. Once you feel better, maybe we can have a meal outside by the sea tomorrow. Like we used to when we were kids."

My heart clenches at the vibrant memory, but it's now stained a murky grey with how the male before me is no longer that little boy. "That would be nice."

A small grin spreads on his face before he dips his head and takes his leave. Just in time before the room starts to spin, dragging me into its vortex. I try to fight it by widening my eyes and straightening my spine to remain sitting. I'm terrified to fall back to sleep. To become weak and defenseless against my past.

Even as I try to muster up the strength to hold my body upright, I can feel my arms giving out as I fall back onto the mattress. I must have used too much power when healing the Corrupted because now my body is facing the aftermath. Needing sleep to restore itself.

Black creeps along the edge of my vision as I shake my head in protest. But the next thing I know, I'm sucked back into sleep with my memories chasing after me.

CHAPTER TWENTY-FOUR

Draven

"Almost," Fynn grunts between clenched teeth.

After I returned Emma to her room, I came back to mine as the moon was welcoming the sun. I paced aimlessly for a while, battling every wild thought to go back to her. But I need to keep busy so that I don't go against her wishes to stay away… For now.

Fynn was awake—probably never went to sleep—before I came to join him, as he continues to practice reaching Gehendra. He's been attempting this for the past few hours, inching closer little by little.

"You've got this. I can feel it. This is it," Cora cheers him on as she stays near his side in case he blacks out from the amount of power he's exerting, like he did the other day.

The air in the room starts to feel heavy, his power radiating waves of energy. I can only imagine how his body feels trying to control it. In the next breath, a golden portal fizzles and tears a seam in the center of the room. Slowly, it expands. Fynn's hands shake as he spreads the edges wider, guiding the opening to follow.

"Fuckkk!" he roars, sweat beading down his forehead.

Kye steps up behind him, holding his hands up. "Keep going. I'm going to try something."

All Fynn can do is grunt a response with a jerk of his head. His eyes are hard as he focuses on the portal that's wavering, but it's almost there.

Kye's palms flatten on the back of Fynn's shoulders, closing his eyes until a flash of blue pulses from his hands. Cora gasps from the side, covering her mouth with her hand and watching in what looks like fear and amazement.

The rush of Kye's power infuses with Fynn's, and it's genius. Kye's power *is* strength. So, adding his will only help boost Fynn's and give him the push he needs. Then, Kye releases his hands from Fynn's shoulders and steps back, as Fynn continues to keep the portal open.

Darkness creeps from the center of the portal, and we all watch it expand to its full size. Our breaths plume out in front of us as a coldness creeps into the room. Taking a step forward, I call on my dragon half to try and see deeper into the realm, but still, only a dark hole greets me. But there is no mistaking the eerie sensation that prickles down my spine.

Fynn's chest is heaving in deep pulls as he manages to keep the portal open, then smirks at me. "Part one of the plan is a go."

I nod, relief flooding my system as Kye's eyes glint with what looks like excitement. Another step closer to seeking revenge for Emma and saving her from the deathly grip she's in.

"You only needed a little push of my power," Kye says to Fynn. "I think you can just as well do this yourself when you are fully rested again and fuel your body with food."

Cora watches Fynn lower his hands to let the portal fall away before nodding with a wide smile. "I think he can, too," she adds. Then, she turns her head to look directly at me. "But did you feel the same uneasiness I felt from what lurks beyond in that realm?"

My eyes still stare off into the space where the opening to Gehendra was, and how it seemed almost too quiet, leaving me slightly on edge. I tear my gaze away to look at Cora with a troubled nod. "I did. Whatever waits for us in that realm is not for the faint of heart. We can never drop our guard from the moment we step foot in there."

"Emma said that the air is toxic to Fae," Kye adds in.

Fynn rubs his neck as he turns to Kye. "My throat started to burn, but I wasn't sure if I just needed something to drink."

Cora shakes her head. "Not just you; I felt the same."

I scrape my palm over my jaw. The coldness that slithered in the room felt off to me, but not in a way that made my throat burn. It just felt clammy on my skin.

Kye blows out a long breath, looking at me. "You, too?"

"No," I say as my eyes shift back to where the portal was.

"Maybe you won't be affected from the realm as quickly, if at all, since you hold part of Whiro's power," Kye thinks out loud.

I grunt in thought. "True. Either way, we will have to work fast to make sure you guys stay safe."

Cora claps while jumping in the middle of our little group, darting her eyes animatedly to each of us. "Some poisonous air is not going to stop us from helping, right?" Her smile stretches as she spins, clasping her hands on her hips and looking pointedly at me. "When do we implement the next part of the plan?"

She means, when do we travel to this other realm and attempt to take down the God of Darkness, who has never been touched, in an act of war. I have already gathered the weapons and stored them in my room until we are ready.

Four days have passed since Emma was here, telling us everything she knows. Each day that goes by brings us closer to the full moon, putting her and the world in danger.

I look to Fynn and then out the window of the tower we are in, knowing Fynn will need more than just a short night of sleep. He will need to rest most of the day as well so he can portal back out when all is done.

"Fynn needs to rest. The soonest can be at nightfall tomorrow, but even that could be rushing it." I twist to meet Fynn's gaze and he nods in understanding. This is the time he needs to truly save his energy. No more practicing if we are doing this.

Fynn turns to pat Kye on the shoulder, then squeezes. "Thanks for the push. It was like I could *feel* the weight of your power and how strong it is." He steps towards Cora and drapes an arm over her shoulders as he smirks to Kye. "Let me know if you want me to return the favor." He winks at Kye, who stares at him blankly before shaking his head and muttering a curse under his breath.

"How will we let Emma know?" Cora asks, pushing Fynn's slumped body up a little while walking towards the doorway.

"Leave that task up to me." I keep it simple and leave it at that because I have no idea what my little demon is up to today. I would assume she is still resting after overdoing herself with the level of power she used for all those Corrupted. She may be the sweetest poison to me, but to the Corrupted, she is their antidote.

I haven't even told the others that she was out all last night, saving one life at a time. That is something they need to hear from her when she's ready, because right now, that information won't make a difference in our plan.

I feel Kye standing beside me before I notice his bulky frame in my periphery. "Do you think that Whiro knows what we're up to?" He keeps his eyes staring straight ahead out the window as his question hangs in the air.

I sigh, letting my head drop forward. "I'm not sure. I fucking hope not, but it's now or never." I remain silent for a moment before peering at him. "Promise me something?" I ask.

He blows out a steady breath. "Depends," Kye says hesitantly, dragging his amber eyes to meet mine.

I chew the inside of my lip for a moment before I lay it out for him. "I might not make it back." His brows immediately crash together. "If it's me he wants, I will do fucking anything to protect her, and that means if I have to stay behind and fight Whiro alone, I will."

I release a heavy sigh. "We don't know what to expect there and the plan might work how we wish it. But the unknown is a sneaky bastard. So, if shit gets out of hand, drag her back here with Fynn and Cora. I don't care if she screams, begs, or tries to claw your skin off. I need to know she will be safe."

The silence that follows is deafening. He brings one of his meaty palms up to his face and pinches the bridge of his nose. "Fuck, you know I will lay my life down for her. But knowing how important you are to her, that means I will do the same for you."

"That's very honorable of you, but this is a choice I'm making for you. Please give me this reassurance so I can rest a little easier."

Kye roughly nods. "And if shit goes south, I know you will do the same."

"You have my word."

CHAPTER TWENTY-FIVE

Draven

We all parted ways to rest for the remainder of the day, but sleep has yet to make an appearance. The hole in my wall stares back at me as I lay on my bed. Taunting me with my failures. Bringing back memories of a time I didn't recognize myself. The lows I faced when Emma vanished were restrained…because there was still a sliver of hope of her being alive.

But when my father died…

When he died, I became the beast I always knew lurked within if pushed.

Sure, I may embody and look like a "Dark Prince," as some call me, but that's not the true reason why. And it's a part of my past I'm not proud of and don't ever talk about because, for years, I never smiled. I spilled more blood than I'm capable of giving back. I searched for reasons to fight, to feel my fist slam into the bone of a person until I heard that satisfying crack. I was possessed by grief. There was no hope. My father was dead.

The one that I remember the most was when a male laid a hand on a child for knocking his drink over and spilling it. Everything became a blur for me. The crowd faded as I dragged him back to the alley and landed blows on him until he reached an inch of his life. A small cry had cut through the haze of red I was caught in, looking up to find the small child huddled near the back door of the tavern.

The look in her frightened eyes caused me to pause and back away from the male who dared to harm someone so young and innocent. And when I had taken a step towards the little girl to reassure her, she stepped away from me, which caused something sharp to twist inside my chest.

She was just as scared of me as the one who hurt her. That was the night I began taking my grief out on the Corrupted. To channel my anger and keep the fear out of the eyes of my people.

I promised myself to never return to who I was then. I need to be someone Emma deserves. I need to be worthy of her.

During the months she was gone, I never allowed myself to think too long or fantasize about her. Now that I know where she is and that she's *safe*, I let myself have that comfort.

There have been more times than I can count when thinking of her, picturing her pleasuring herself right here in this spot, which made my cock harden in seconds. Making me fist it tightly and jerk to the image of her until I roar out another orgasm.

But today, I just want to picture her lying beside me, curled up in my arms. The way her hair looks fanned out over my pillow, our legs tangled together, and her chest rising and falling softly against mine. She would look so magical right now in that position, with how the sunlight drifts over the bed. With that painted in my head, I let my eyes fall shut, imagining her.

I can feel my breathing slow down, my body melting further into the blankets as the mate bond in my chest warms and stirs. Suddenly, my eyelids grow heavy, refusing to open, and the next thing I know, I fall asleep.

. . .

Darkness steals my sight until my surroundings come into focus. My nose burns from the heavy scent of metal and something musky, as if where I'm at has been rotting away. The single lantern dangling in the room finally becomes clear, but that's not what steals the breath straight from my lungs.

It's the girl beneath it, tied to wooden posts with her body slack. A shadow hovers over her body that's slick with blood, and I find King Oren standing above her with a long whip in his hand.

My heart hammers in my chest and my throat goes dry at the sight. How am I dreaming this? How am I seeing…

Emma. Fuck. She must be sleeping, having opened her end of the bond. Screening her dreams to me and pulling me into it without knowing.

I watch in horror as he raises his hand and slashes his arm down with a flick of his wrist, causing the skin on her back to split in half with streams of crimson. Her jaw falls open, a scream tearing from her throat that bleeds into the walls.

I can't tear my eyes away from her face, noticing how those pupils that were wide with fear have now shrunk as if she's closing her mind to what's happening. Allowing herself to disconnect because the look in her eyes now seems hollow. As if I'm witnessing the fight in her die, making the organ in my chest bleed right alongside her.

"Tell me, Daughter, who do you obey?" He whips her again when she doesn't answer, forcing another piercing cry to fall from her lips. "Your screams aren't an answer, Emma."

Blood rushes to my head. I wish I could bring King Oren back to life just so I could kill him again, but slowly, until he bleeds the same amount of infliction he caused her.

I flinch when there's another crack of the whip, her back bowing when it lands its strike as she pulls against her restraints. My gaze follows the trail of her blood that's creating a river to the drain near her bare feet, the drops dripping with every ragged breath I exhale. This time, she doesn't scream. Only silence follows. The lash of the whip ricochets louder in the room, causing King Oren to seethe at the mouth.

Suddenly, the room spirals until I'm looking at a new memory. The same disgusting room that I now know is painted with layers of Emma's blood. But this time, she's strapped to a table—a little older in age than the last one—and stares hard at the ceiling that is starting to peel above her. Deep cuts mark her skin as King Oren holds a knife over her, spewing nonsense to her about being seen by one of his visitors.

I take a step towards her, knowing damn well they can't see me and that I can't do anything. I clutch at my chest as my heart feels like someone is digging nails into it,

191

shredding it apart. A choked sob breaks free at seeing the fucking torment she was forced to endure alone. That she suffered for so many years while fate decided to have us meet when it was too late for me to truly save her from this.

The look I'm seeing in her glazed-over eyes is something fierce. As if she locked herself away into a dark corner of her mind to hide from the pain, to block out the harsh words and blood that threaten her life. To become numb to it. But there is also something different in the look in her eyes from the last vision. Because now, she is holding a glint of that little demon I met the first time. The part of her that promises violence.

Again, I'm sucked away from the room, clenching my teeth tighter to prepare for what I might see next. The ground sways beneath my feet until everything evens out. I'm standing somewhere I don't recognize. The air is freezing, darkness claims the sky, and specks of grey float in the air.

But then, her voice fills the eerie silence. "No last words?" *The tone is almost demonic and sinister.*

I slowly spin around until I see Emma standing before a Fae who is on his knees, already looking moments away from his last breath. Whiro stands and watches his daughter with his arms crossed and a wicked tip to his lips.

The frosty stillness of the air and unease that accompanies it feels similar to what seeped from the portal Fynn opened... So, this must be Gehendra, the realm where she was taken to for three excruciatingly long months. The place where I couldn't reach her, feel her. This dark and lonely place, with no light in sight except for the bleeding moon. My mate was all alone, and that would make anyone go mad.

Everything happens so fast. Emma throws her shadows straight into the Fae's chest until I see the moment she crushes his heart by the way his jaw falls open on a silent gasp. But I watch her. Studying her face for any emotion as she ends his life and pushes him over the ledge. Nothing registers in her eyes. No twitch of sorrow, no crease of guilt.

Yet, the way she inhales slowly is as if she relishes in the kill. High on the adrenaline from holding such power.

Clenching my jaw, I swallow roughly. Knowing these actions will slowly eat away at her now, just like my past did to me. A part of me wonders if that's why she went to save the Corrupted the other night. To make up for the ones who are too late to save by her hands. Just how the Corrupted was a way for me to try and quiet the demons that lurked in my psyche.

I fear this darkness she was lost to took more than she was ready to give.

Before I can blink, I'm pulled into another flashback, but am still in Gehendra.

Nothing will make me forget the smell of this place now that I've been here. It smells like burning bones, but with a dose of floral sprinkled in. And when my vision clears, I understand why. Thousands of flowers decorate the pillars that wrap around some kind of pool.

My eyes frantically dart around until I spot Emma beside another Fae male, yet this one…

My breath stalls in my lungs. Vincent. The male I saved with his mate in the woods. His one arm still the only limb missing, which makes me thankful he hasn't gone and cut any other part of himself, and that the infection stayed clear from him. They have stayed safe. So, why is he here?

I don't get an answer, though. Instead, I watch Emma toss him in the metallic water as Vincent stays calm, staring at her. When he falls beneath the surface, a white light glows around his body, slowly getting brighter until it gives a final flare and dies away.

My eyes are locked on where Vincent was just moments ago. Heart racing to see if he will resurface, but nothing happens as the water evens out and the ripples fade away. Only Whiro and Emma remain, both just as transfixed on the spot as I am. Except, Whiro seems gleeful in his dark gaze and Emma… She looks lost, making me wonder what transpired before she threw him in. Because her brows dip just a hair, and a small glimpse of questioning thoughts shine through that brief look.

My eyes rake back to Whiro, but this time, his gaze is targeted at me.

I jerk upright with a gasp as if I was holding my breath for too long. My eyes wildly scan my surroundings to find I'm in my room. The sun is fading from the sky as the shadows of night start to cover the lands. Panic still seizes me once my pulse settles, only to realize it's not my own.

Emma.

I don't fucking think when I tear out of bed and force my wings free.

CHAPTER TWENTY-SIX

Draven

*H*er balcony doors are exactly how I left them. So, I slide my shadows underneath the small seam on the floor to sense for anyone else in the room to prevent another slipup. Her whimpers carry through the pitch black when I nudge her door open and slip inside. No fire crackling. No lanterns lit. Nothing.

I dissolve my wings but keep my dragon half present. The sight I get from this half of me is sharper, allowing me to see more clearly in the dark. I spot her sleeping, petite body thrashing in the bed. Her blankets get twisted between her legs as she shakes her head back and forth, muttering under her breath.

"I'm sorry. I'm sorry. I'm sorry," her broken whispers plead.

Tears stream down her cheeks as wavy strands of her hair get caught in them. Her fingers clutch her sheets, pulling them as she starts to sob. "F-forgive me."

She may be whimpering on the outside, but her pain, her guilt is screaming through the bond, clawing to get free. Seeing her like this impales my heart with a million needles. Her eyes are squeezed shut, panting out more frantic pleas.

I don't fucking hesitate, I scoop her body up into my arms as the mattress dips beneath my weight, cradling her tightly to me. "Little demon," I say against her hair, then start peppering kisses over her tear-stricken face. She starts to stir but is still gripped by her nightmare. "Emma." I wipe away the wetness on her cheeks with the pads of my thumbs. "Wake up. You're safe."

I rock back and forth, sliding my hand into her hair and pressing her head closer to the strong drum pounding in my chest. Breathing her in. Her cries start to bleed away, and her heartbeat begins to slow. When I hear her inhale a shaky breath, I look down to find stormy eyes staring back.

She blinks. Her eyes scan her room before meeting mine again. She pushes off me to sit up, and I step away for a moment. Allowing her to collect herself, I place fresh wood in the fireplace and spark a new flame.

"Why are you here?" Her scratchy voice flashes back to what I witnessed in her dream. To how her voice sounded just as raspy when blood-curdling screams tore through her throat.

I keep my back to her, stoking the log in the fire as I answer, "For you."

The sheets rustle, followed by a sigh. "Draven, I told you that it's not safe for you to be here. Did Fynn find a way to reach Gehendra? Is that why you are here? To tell me?"

My molars gnash together. This girl. This infuriatingly sexy little demon just doesn't fucking get it. The beast in me wants to slam her down on the mattress to set her straight, to claim her in the way she needs to be claimed.

I take a long drag of air, stepping away from the crackling fire to face her.

She has the sheets pulled up to her chest, with her knees bent as she sits against the headboard, tracking me.

"Fynn succeeded." I stalk towards her to stand at the side of her bed. "But that's not why I'm fucking here, and you know it." It comes out on a growl because I'm barely able to hold my beast back.

Her eyes widen a fraction as she jerks her head away to face the fire. "Clearly, I don't," she snaps.

I lower myself on the bed to kneel in front of her, grabbing her chin between my finger and thumb to force her to look at me. Her eyes are still slightly pink and puffy from crying in her sleep, and she's trying so hard to hide it.

"Stop hiding." Her eyes flutter with a watery sheen. "I saw what you were dreaming."

She sucks in a gasp and tries to shake her head, but I tighten my grip. Her lips tremble until she bites her bottom one to stop it. "H–how?" she asks on a whisper. "Was it like before?"

I slowly shake my head because this was different. I didn't have to touch her to be sucked into what she was dreaming about. This time, she reeled me in from a much farther distance, and I want to believe it's because she's free from the necklace that was holding her back before.

"I was in my own bed this time, and you reached through the bond to pull me in without even knowing. I don't know how, but I do know you are fucking powerful. So, it doesn't surprise me in the least."

Her eyes bounce back and forth between mine before she slams them shut. "Then you know…" I wait with bated breath for her to finish that sentence, and when she does, it fucking destroys me. "That I am a monster."

I softly shake my head, letting my gaze travel over every inch of her face, completely transfixed. "Far from it," I huff on a breath that is so full of love that I wish she could see herself through my eyes. "You are no monster, because I *watched* you save the Corrupted." I wasn't going to bring it up, but she needs to hear this.

Her eyes widen with what looks like uncertainty.

"Your power beamed in the night. You looked like a blade of lightning amid the darkest storm. Powerful. Bright. And mesmerizing." Her grey eyes swirl with so many emotions that my words almost get lodged in my throat. "I will happily let you strike me down if it means I get to be with you in the end."

She sniffs, parting her lips as she holds back a soft sob. "But I *killed* them. Innocent people! And one who you saved!" Tears well again at the corner of her eyes and I immediately wipe them away, knowing she's letting the guilt eat away at her. That it is dragging her down beneath the sea with a weight tied around her ankles.

"And I—" She rips her face out of my grasp before covering it with her hands. "I enjoyed it when I saw the life leave their eyes. I can *feel* their deaths as if it was a living thing crawling beneath my skin. And their voices…"

I gently brush some of her hair back behind the shell of her ear. "What about their voices?"

Another sniffled sob, her voice becoming muffled in the palm of her hands. "Their final pleas still haunt me. Every. Single. Day."

Her cries fill the room and my fingers twitch to pull her back into my arms, but she needs this moment. To spill free everything she's been holding tightly locked away.

I fold my hands together as I look at the wall above her bed. "When my father died, I lost myself. I didn't care about anything or anyone. I just wanted to feel…something. I was so angry, so lost within myself."

Her sobs soften to little pants as she slowly quiets to listen.

"If you think you are a monster, then you are the most angelic one I've ever seen, and it puts me on a one-way trip to hell." I huff out a laugh to try and lighten the mood. "Maybe that's why Whiro wants me—to make me pay for all the lives I took."

Her hands fall away as she swallows roughly. "How many?"

I let my eyes drop down to her wide ones and my chest fucking hurts as I relive one of the darkest times in my life. "Too many to count, little demon. I went looking for fights. At the first sight of blood, it only fueled me to keep going instead of stopping when I should have. I'm ashamed of what I did, and I have no one to blame but myself."

I inhale deeply, searching her eyes for any fear or disgust, but finding none.

"I never wanted to tell you because I feared you would despise me, leaving me with all of my ghosts and demons you don't deserve." My eyes close as I voice what she needs to understand. "You could never be a monster, Emma. Not in my eyes."

I feel her soft touch blanket my hands before pulling one free to interlock our fingers together. "Our demons are meant to walk in the shadows together, remember? They don't terrify me." Her thumb runs lazy circles over mine.

I cup her cheek and pull her face close, our lips an inch apart. "Then don't fear your grief, but *feel* it. Don't let it consume you until you don't recognize yourself. Instead, live each day doing something to honor them."

She sniffs with a small smile, letting her head lean on my hand. But then, something heavy falls over the look in her eyes and her smile drops. That sight alone makes something splinter in my chest.

"I am not worthy of you."

For her whole life she has been cast aside and ignored. The only attention given to her was when she was abused, and after seeing the extent of it… I can't seem to make the images of her smothered in her own blood leave my mind.

The longer she stares at me, waiting, the more I want that fucking smile back on her face. I want her to know that she is not the one who is unworthy.

In the next breath, I slam my mouth to hers. I put everything I want her to feel into this kiss before I pull back to rest my forehead against hers, breathing heavily. "I want every part of you, Emma. Even the parts you seem to think are unworthy."

I tilt my face just enough to kiss the side of her jaw. "How many times did your screams make your throat raw before you chose silence?" I feather against her skin, moving my lips to kiss the other side of her jaw. "How much blood did you have to lose before you locked yourself far into the recess of your mind to protect yourself?"

My fingers trail down her arms, taking the sheet with it until I find a scar beneath my fingertips when I reach the top of her thighs, caressing the raised skin. "How many scars did it take before you couldn't look in the mirror?"

She sucks in a trembling breath, her body shivering beneath my touch.

"I saw it all, Emma. I fucking hate that you suffered through that, but I am thankful you survived. The silence you chose held power. It was like a sharpened sword in the night, ready and waiting. The cage you locked yourself away in your mind has hardened into a shield, to never let another hurt you again. And your scars…"

I trace soft circles around the one on her leg, exposed by the short-hemmed silver nightgown she wears.

I lean in until my lips brush the shell of her ear. "They tell a story of a girl who survived and not only wears her strength but grew her own wings, woven with bravery to save herself," I whisper.

Chills break out against her skin as she turns her head to face mine, our noses touching and our breaths sharing the same air. Her wide eyes are so open, so fucking raw, it makes the organ in my chest lurch. I'm one weak thread away from tearing at the seams for this girl, to pull her in and force her to see how resilient she is.

CHAPTER TWENTY-SEVEN

Emma

My throat closes up and my pulse skips from his words. How does he always say the right thing that makes my blood rush through my veins and my heart sing? I never wanted him to know details of my past or the sins I committed in Gehendra. I didn't want those to weigh on him like they do for me, or for him to take one look at me and see a ruthless killer.

But I should have known he will see me with eyes that can read every page of my thoughts and look past the smeared ink of my sins. Should have known, that he will never judge me. The bond between us sizzles, causing heat to pool between my thighs. His eyes darken, becoming heavy with lust.

He's so close. If I swipe my tongue between my lips, I could lick his. It's so tempting, and I can't stop my eyes from dropping to his lips that are begging me to taste. My heart is pounding in my ears, drowning out my sanity.

"Show me how to fly then," I breathe against his lips, slowly dragging my eyes up into his that are half-lidded and full of heat.

The air is crackling with desire, growing thicker until I feel I might suffocate. This time, I can claim him as mine. I don't have to pretend.

Draven must see where my thoughts have headed because a deep rumble vibrates from his chest as he crashes his lips to mine. He doesn't just kiss me, he devours me. Stealing the moans that break free from my throat and swallowing them down as he claims them.

He doesn't seek permission for me to open my lips to him; he pushes his tongue through the seam, demanding me to let him in. To let him show me how to fly. My hands come up to grab hold of his raven hair, gripping at the strands to pull him closer.

Teeth clashing. Tongues colliding and swirling together. And our moans mixing into one beautiful symphony.

"No games this time, little demon," he rasps against my lips, throwing a dense wall of shadows to cover the perimeter of the room to block the sounds he's about to conjure from me. "I want to fuck you hard and fast before I take you again and again. Slowly worshipping your body and your heart so I can show you how to fly high and make you fucking feel the depths of my love for you."

His hands travel down my body, skimming down my legs and back up again. Teasing. "This silky little nightgown is going to be the death of me," he says as he plays with the black lacy hem. "But right now, I only want to see it on the floor."

In the next breath, he rips it over my head, my arms following the move-ment to help, eliciting a wave of chills down my spine. I gasp and arch my back off the bed when his mouth lands on my nipple before the fabric even hits the ground, sucking and nipping while his other hand slides to my other breast.

He's anything but gentle and it makes my eyes want to roll to the back of my head in the instant rush of desire he's building in my core.

My hands claw up his back to the nape of his neck. "I need you," I whimper.

He releases my nipple with a wet pop before he sits back on his knees, reaching behind him with one hand to pull his shirt over his head in a smooth motion. Carved skin contours sharply against the warm glow from the fire, and my fingers desperately wish to follow the indents of his muscles from his chest all the way down his abs. To follow the light trail of hair that dips below his waistband.

"You have me," he tells me roughly, knowing he's watching me drink him in. But I don't care. I'm ready for this. To allow myself to open my heart to hopes and possibilities. To love.

With quick movements, I get on all fours and crawl to him. He stands so I can help push his pants off as he kicks them aside before I pull his wrist to sit near the headboard.

I lick my lips at the way his muscles ripple with every move he makes. Once he's situated, he lifts me up onto his lap so I'm straddling him. His hands grab hold of both of my cheeks as he starts to massage them, and I rock my hips as my slick center rubs up and down the hard ridge of his cock. His head tips back with a deep groan as his hips lift with mine.

I bite my lip on a moan and one of his hands slides up my back. Fingertips kiss the surface of every scar before he wraps his hand around the back of my neck.

The feeling of him against my warm heat makes my eyes close without realizing it, and when they flutter open, it's to find him watching every shift of my hips. The way our bodies slowly move together, building up the need of wanting to be filled.

"Fuck, I need to be inside you, feeling you suck my cock deep into your pussy. I'm about to fall off the edge of my control." His fingers dig into my skin as he buries his face in the crook of my neck and breathes deeply. "I desperately need to claim you. To complete the bond. To never lose you again."

The bond. The one that ties me to him.

I've wanted this kind of connection with someone for so long, but it was only lost wishes that never reached the stars. Getting trapped in the dark box with me as they faded away, slowly becoming a distant fantasy, then a dream of what could be.

I'm tired of refusing myself something that will bring me happiness. A part of me wrestles with the thought that I might not make it when it's time to face Whiro, and that wouldn't be fair to Draven. To have him endure that pain. But as of right now, I think I might truly die if I don't bond with him. If I go another day not binding our souls, I feel as if mine will wither away.

So, I'm done holding back. He's mine, just as I am his.

My breathing quickens as he licks and sucks at the curve of my neck. I tilt my head to give him better access. "Mark me as yours."

He growls, teeth biting at my skin as he trails his lips up to my mouth, slanting over mine to consume me again. The way he kisses makes my head buzz and has me dripping my desire onto him.

He bends forward, making me lean with him as I hear a scrape from behind me. I see the glint of my dagger's blade he took from the sheath when he brings it between us.

"I thought you said no games," I say as I watch him slice his left palm.

"I promise you, it's not. Do you trust me?"

I smile, sinking my teeth into my lip to hold back my laugh as I remember the first time he asked me if I trusted him. Back then, a piece of me secretly knew I could.

So, I gently nod, keeping my eyes locked on his. "With every part of me."

He clears his throat with a thick swallow. "Give me your left hand."

I do, and he keeps his eyes on mine as he cuts a line across the meaty flesh. He tosses the blade carefully to the floor before wrapping our arms around each other, holding his bleeding hand in front of my mouth.

"Taste me," he says huskily.

I don't hesitate. I flatten my tongue to lick his blood from his palm, and it sends sparks throughout my body the instant I swallow. His nostrils flare, jaw clenching as he watches me intensely.

"We've never had a good time to talk about this. But to complete a mating bond, the blood of the fated must be shared," he grinds out as I feel his cock twitch beneath me.

Excitement bubbles beneath my skin, as my pulse starts to race. "Then what?" I whisper, still licking the heady taste of his blood on my lips.

"Then, I fill you as I bind our hands together, so they bleed as one."

That causes me to rock my hips on a lust-filled sigh. He brings my hand to his mouth, sensually licking my blood. Then, he's clasping our two bleeding hands together, interlocking our fingers tightly. A gasp leaves me as an unrelenting flood of need surges through me. Every cell in my body is thrumming to life and overheating. Desperate and hungry to ease the ache. I need him. Now.

"Fill me," I gasp as tingles spark against our joined palms. "Please, Draven."

In one swift movement, he uses a hand to lift my hips, and I help to hover above him until he's lined up with my center. Then, he drops me, his dick spearing into me in one full, hard thrust. I cry out, my pussy instantly burning as it stretches around his length. Unforgivably gripping him to keep him deep inside me.

All of my nerve endings ignite at the feel of him buried so far into me with his skin against mine. Our blood runs freely together between our palms, burning so hot it takes my breath away. But he gives me his, slanting his mouth over mine greedily as I clutch his shoulder with my free hand.

I don't start slow; the need is too great. I grind up and down on him, lifting to his tip before slamming back down, and frantically kiss him back with just as much eagerness.

He takes. Dominates me and grunts as he starts thrusting harder, making me lose my rhythm as he moves below me with ease. I pant against his mouth, moaning every time he hits that spot deep within.

"You're going to take every last drop I have to give when I make you soar," he grunts out.

My whimper gets cut off with a sharp inhale as he twists, pinning me on my back. Our joined hands are locked above my head, and pressed into the mattress. His other hand grabs behind my knee, lifting it to hook my leg over his shoulder until he bends forward to press my knee to my chest.

I scream at the intensity of how this position feels as he continues to drive into me with powerful thrusts. My pussy clenches tightly around him, the pleasure in my core rising higher as my stomach begins to tense.

"Ohh…Draven," I groan out before he nips at my lips, pumping faster. His fingers dance down my hip until he reaches between us, pressing the pad of his thumb over my swollen clit.

I yell out in burning ecstasy and my vision starts to blur. It's too much. I can't take it.

"You can and you fucking will, little demon," Draven rasps out between frenzied breaths. I must have said that out loud, but I can't seem to find a reason to care now as my blood warms up. The cut on my palm begins to pulse, matching the beat of my heart.

His thumb quickens as he presses more firmly and that sends me spiraling over the edge. My pussy chokes his cock so tightly as my breath gets lodged in my throat. My head thrashes back and forth right before I fall into a blinding orgasm.

"*Fuck*, so tight," he hisses. "That's it. Squeeze my cock until you feel me swell inside of you."

A silent cry escapes as my inner walls pulse hard around him. Claiming him as mine. Waves and waves of burning pleasure almost makes me black out. I'm lost, drowning in him and him alone. His hips keep driving into me as a glowing light forms between us, like flames feathering against my skin.

My pussy continues to pulse around him as I feel him swell, his grunts growing more clipped, and his hips start to jerk against me. He attacks my lips with a searing kiss as I feel him spill inside of me with a deep groan and his thrusts begin to slow down. The light sparks and flares between our chests, then fizzles away as he pulls back.

"What was that?" I pant against his swollen lips.

"*That was the mate bond binding us together.*"

My eyes widen as his deep, velvety voice speaks into my head, leaving me speechless.

"*We can now mentally communicate to each other, no matter the distance.*"

I can't stop my mouth from falling open in shock as I stare at his silver eyes that have captured my heart. I was sure I've heard his voice before in my head, but I thought it was a figment of my imagination. A trick of hope.

My eyes start to burn as my lips slightly tremble at having him be the only voice speaking into my mind as the rest fade away. It's comforting because he just replaced the voices that used to plague me, and this is something we can share together.

The power in my blood has shifted and I can feel it flowing more strongly. He must hear my thoughts, or I sent them to him down the bond, because he answers, "Completing the mating makes us more powerful. We can't use the other's power, but we can lend the strength of it to each other through the bond."

But that's not the only thing that's different. I can *feel* him. His love for me, the beat of his heart, and how being with me now is soothing something inside of him.

Slowly, he brings our joined hands between us and separates them. My heart beats wildly in my chest as I see our mating mark in place of the cut. It's the same symbol as the tattoo on his finger, the one that he said he would see in his dreams. A full circle with a crescent resting inside, and on our palms, there is a light dusting of swirls that intricately wrap around it.

"It's beautiful," I say with wonder.

He brings my palm to his lips, pressing a tender kiss over the mark. "It's ours." My eyes begin to burn as I watch him rest his cheek in my hand. "Our story of two moons lost in their phase of life, finally finding their home in the arms of the other." He pulls my hand back, tracing the black shimmering swirls with his fingertips. "And this is tying our souls together, so we can never feel lost again."

The tears welling behind my eyelids fall free, leaving a trail of peace in their path. I've never felt so complete, I was always left to wander alone in the dark.

But now, I'm…

"*Home*." The word feels like a cherished forever as I speak it in my mind.

Draven nods, grabbing the nape of my neck to pull me close. "Home." And then, he claims my lips, pouring every emotion he's feeling into it. I link my fingers into his hair, begging him closer, to infuse everything I have to offer back. I want us to burn together.

My hips rock and I gasp between his lips, feeling him deliciously hard within me still. My pussy is already growing slicker with the feel of him teasing me with small nudges. "H–how?" I ask on a breathless moan, not understanding why my body is starting to grow hot again. A roaring heat scorching through my veins as I squeeze his cock deeper into me.

"It's the mating frenzy that makes us unable to stop, only wanting more of each other." He grounds out as he sucks one of my nipples into his mouth, twisting it with his tongue.

The mating frenzy… My mind tries to think of every book I've read, but none had his part written in the story. They had found their love and then the end. But I much prefer how my story is being told as I rotate my hips.

A ragged breath expels from him. "I told you I wanted to take you hard and fast the first time because I couldn't hold back any longer, but now…" He flattens his tongue and licks over my chest, up my throat and jaw until he reaches my swollen lips. "Now, I'm going to take my time. Taste every inch of you and devote my body to your pleasure."

His pupils blow out wide as he drags his body down mine, pulling his length out of me slowly, which causes me to whimper in protest. "Greedy, little demon." His breath teases against my skin.

My body is flaming from within. Everything feels overly sensitive, and needy whines unwillingly escape me from feeling empty without him in me.

Draven tsks, his face between my thighs and only inches from my soaked center. "So needy." He kisses the inner part of my left thigh. "Don't worry. Soon, you will be exploding on my tongue." His nose brushes over my clit before kissing the inside of my right thigh, causing my ache to grow excruciatingly painful.

Panting, I lift my head to watch him, and then cry out when he shoves two fingers inside me, all the way to the knuckle.

"I love seeing my seed fill you." He pulls his fingers out, bringing them up to my lips. "Taste us." It's dirty, but I'm too far gone and do what he says. Wrapping my lips slowly around his fingers before sucking them clean and causing him to groan.

Apparently, that breaks his restraint because he roughly slings my legs over his shoulders, pulling my hips up to his mouth and burying his face in my pussy. My back bows off the bed with a moan as I try to squeeze my thighs together, but he's not having it. He drives his expert tongue into me before swirling it over my clit without pause.

Tingles race down my spine, my mouth falls open, and before I know it, I'm screaming my release with my fingers digging into the sheets. Clutching to it as if it will hold me steady as I fall into utter ecstasy.

Pleasure rushes up my spine and before I can catch my breath, he's thrusting two fingers into my pulsing center, curling them and causing my orgasm to explode into another toe-curling climax. Stars dance in my vision as I start to come back into myself. My heart thunders in my chest and I shiver when he does a final swipe of his tongue to clean my release.

"Your taste is addicting, and I can't live without it; it's a habit I never want to break." His lips glisten with my orgasm as he trails wet kisses up my body, taking his time to nip at my skin before licking the pain away.

"I need to taste you," I say breathlessly.

A low, rumbling laugh vibrates his chest that electrifies the nerves in my body. "Not yet, little demon. There are countless ways to make you come that I've fantasized about, and I can't wait any longer."

His words trigger a plea of want to fall from my lips as I reach between us to wrap my fingers around his hardened length that is leaking with pre-cum. A growl tumbles from him as he attacks my mouth with his. "You make me so painfully hard, and I plan to fuck this pussy until the only thing you can scream is my name. To make sure you know this pussy is mine. That *you* are mine. And I'll keep claiming you until your body physically can't take any more."

I cry out as he thrusts into me so hard that my body already starts to feel like it's shaking. He pumps into me with such a primal force, and I can't stop myself from begging him for more. He moves his hips harder. Faster. Seizing my clit as he nips at my shoulder. It's not long until I'm spasming around him as he continues to drive into me until he roars his release.

But he doesn't stop. He fucks me again and again, making my body fall over the edge, only to have me flying before I hit the bottom. Just like he promised.

CHAPTER TWENTY-EIGHT

Emma

The dusting of morning light wakes me, along with the delicious ache that throbs between my thighs. Draven stayed true to his word and made my body shake with pleasure until I passed out. He must have cleaned me up afterward because I'm in a new nightgown and there is no stickiness coating my center.

The bond nuzzling in my chest practically purrs with the connection of touch we shared last night, and I can't help but raise my hand above my head to stare at the shimmering black mark that now lives on my palm.

From now on, I will have to wear a pair of leather gloves to keep this a secret until we can put an end to everything threatening to tear us apart. The mating mark catches in a yellow ray that faintly bleeds through the shadows Draven kept on guard, and my heart warms at the sight.

Sheets rustle and a delicious scent of cedar and maple swarm around me, making me turn over on my side to find black tousled hair attached to a sleeping Dark Prince. I bite my bottom lip as I drink him in, entranced by how his lips part slightly with every exhale.

Slowly, my fingertips feather over his eyebrow before tracing a path down the straight bridge of his nose, only to curve up and brush along his cheekbone. A lone strand of hair falls over his eye and I softly push it back. His steady breaths bring a sense of peace, making me feel safely tucked away from all the dangers in this world. I wish I could capture this moment and secure it into a bottle so I can hold onto it forever.

I know this moment of luxury is not one I can stay in because we have to walk right into Gehendra soon and face darkness in its most sinister form. Small breaths puff against my fingertips as they dance over his lips, but then they start to curve upward.

Crystal-blue eyes shine so brightly when they catch the morning light that they almost look translucent. My breath hitches. A swarm of emotions swims in his gaze and what feels like a million wings flutter in my stomach.

"I could get used to resting my eyes on you the moment I wake," his morning voice rasps. Here I am thinking that nothing could be sexier, until his smile brightens, and that damn dimple appears.

I chew on my bottom lip for a moment before I speak. "Careful, I may never let you leave my bed."

Suddenly, he digs his fingers into my hips and hauls me to him, closing the small gap between us. I immediately feel the hard ridge of his cock straining in his pants against me. His hands rub over every inch of skin he can reach, sighing as I melt into him. He buries his face into the curve of my neck, inhaling deeply before nipping the sensitive skin there.

"A sacrifice I will gladly accept." His breath tickles against the shell of my ear and I can't stop the giggle that creeps up my throat.

I go to crack a joke, but then Draven snaps his head, his muscles tense as he sits up in one swift motion. "Someone's coming," he rushes out. "As much as I wish to have the world see me by your side and rip the eyes out of those who dare to look at you with carnal thoughts, right now is—"

"Is not the right time," I finish for him, cupping the side of his face in the palm of my hand. "One day, we will get to have our forever."

He grabs both sides of my face, pulling me in as the pounding of boots grows louder. "One day very soon, little demon."

He kisses me, hard. Before I can open my eyes from savoring his lips on mine, he's gone. Wings drifting on the wind right as a tapping comes from my door.

"Emma?" Aiden's chipper voice makes me want to curl into myself. "You awake?"

"Yes!" I put on an act of sounding happy to have him find me so early. "Just a moment, I'm indecent." The moment the words leave my mouth I want to smack my palm to my forehead, but it was the only thing that came to my mind to keep him on the other side of my door.

A throat clears. "Oh, yes, sorry. I'll leave you to it, but I was wondering if you would like to join me for that meal by the sea you promised?"

I may have politely agreed, wishing I could just kick him where it hurts again, but I never promised him shit. "Sounds lovely!" I wrestle with the sheet tangled between my legs, cursing under my breath. "Meet you near the cave once I'm presentable?"

His chuckle irks something inside of me. "See you soon." A final knock to let me know he's leaving. A breath wooshes out of me as I finally manage to win the war against my devilish sheets. I wipe the beads of sweat from my forehead with the back of my hand as I take a second to collect myself.

I hurry to brush my hair with rough strokes as my trembling hands start to calm. That was too close. I hate having to live this lie, but I can't let Whiro suspect anything is off. All will be over if he does.

With a deep breath, I settle the rapid pounding in my chest before I get dressed in my typical long black tunic, pants, and boots combo. Only, this time, as I press the crease out of my tunic and see the black mark on my hand staring blatantly back at me, I remember to toss gloves on.

The toes of my boots almost kiss my door when I pause. Closing my eyes, I reach into my well of power, searching for the whispers of night. In a matter of seconds, I manage to bring the darkness forward, letting it take its form along my skin and behind my eyes. The rush of ice slithers through my veins.

Draven must feel the shift in me because warmth blooms through the bond and I bite back the smile in an attempt to stay in character.

"That's my little demon." His voice is thick and heady, but there is a hard edge to it, knowing I have to go to Aiden. But we both understand this sacrifice I have to make for the time being. I can't let the truth of my control slip free.

I lift my hand to grab the handle to the door but freeze when a rush of liquid heat spreads under my skin, followed by a husky laugh down the bond. *"I can't wait to fuck the darkness out of you with my own shade of shadows."*

My throat bobs, my thighs squeeze together, and my hand's white-knuckling the door handle. I can't respond, not without prolonging the inevitable and causing my body to liquefy more. He knows that as another deep chuckle echoes in my mind. This bond is a dangerous thing if he can get me this wet with words spoken from miles away.

Heat rises to my cheeks, and I have to count to ten to cool my body off and get my thoughts straight. *"Tomorrow,"* I say to him down the bond. *"We will go to Gehendra tomorrow at dawn if everyone feels ready."* I inhale deeply, letting it out in a rush. *"I need this to end once and for all."*

A pleased hum brushes around my heart. *"Then tomorrow, we will end it."* His voice is filled with determination. *"But tonight, you are mine again."*

Sucking a sharp breath, I respond, my voice thready, *"Tonight, and every night after, I am yours."*

Clearing my throat and steeling my spine, I mask the jitters of what awaits tonight as I give the doorknob a sharp twist before stalking my way towards where Aiden awaits.

"How is the food?"

My eyes snap to Aiden, who is sitting beside me with a twinkle in his green eyes. The sun is warm against my icy skin, causing me to squint when I look at him. The water laps up at the shore only feet away from where he placed a blanket and basket to make a little picnic charade for breakfast.

I slowly chew the piece of jelly biscuit in my mouth, now wondering if he poisoned it with the way he's watching me eat. Grabbing my glass of water, I use it to roughly swallow it down.

"Good." I'm not sure how he's expecting me to respond. So, a clipped answer is all I give him.

He nods, before taking a sip of his drink. "I only ask because I helped make it."

I almost choke on the water sliding down my throat. "You cook?"

All he does is shrug. "No, but when I'm bored, I tend to go to the kitchen to help dabble in whatever meal they are scrounging together."

Nothing comes out of my mouth. So, I just stare.

"You seem shocked," he says with amusement.

"I suppose I am." My hand waves in front of him. "I just never pictured you enjoying helping in the kitchen. Especially when you are picky about food." Flashes of us sitting at the table as kids spring forward, him barely eating as he uses his fingers to slide his food around his plate and slumps in his chair.

A hearty laugh bellows from him that makes me raise my eyebrows. "This is why we are such a good match." He leans his elbows on his knees, keeping his head turned to look at me more closely. "You know more about me than anyone else."

I simply let my deadly eyes stay frozen on him as I keep quiet. Bringing another bite of food to my mouth instead.

But he continues on. "I'm glad you are feeling better and got the rest you needed. I came to check on you again before I retired to my room."

My lungs seize as I watch him carefully, noting the way his jaw clenches. Something flashes behind his eyes before it's gone. A gentle smile on his face as he nudges his boot against mine in the sand.

"I didn't hear anything. So, I assumed you were still sleeping, and I didn't want to disturb you."

I keep my features cool as I nod. "Well, I appreciate that. I don't know what came over me, but my body needed the rest."

"I get like that sometimes after a long day of sailing. Sometimes a full day of sleep is still not enough." He chuckles softly, before leaning towards me. "Next time, use my bed to rest so I can take care of you and keep you safe and warm."

I pull away from him, rearing my head back as I go to speak but he beats me to it. "Nothing more than sleep. Cross my heart." He leans back away from me, righting himself as he does the crisscross motion with his hands over his chest.

"I'll think about it," I gingerly say, not quite sure how to respond as my mind is still reeling from him coming to check on me last night. Did he hear anything before Draven tossed up his shadows? Does he know I wasn't alone? Or does he truly believe I was sleeping?

His head tilts to the side, studying me, and every part of me wishes I had the ability to read minds at this moment.

"You still resist me," his voice is soft-spoken as he watches me wash my food down. "Why won't you just let yourself be happy and fully give us another chance? I promise things will be different." His hand lifts to my hair, picking up the ends and twirling them between his fingers. "I can give you everything and more than any other male."

Such pretty words, yet I can't help but wonder if it's to hide the venom that coats them.

I set my glass down hard beside me, water splashing over the lip. I brush the sand off my pants to stand, pinning him with my glare. "I suggest you stop telling me to give you, *us*, a chance when I'm still choking on the blood from the last time you stabbed my heart."

Before I turn to walk away, Aiden's jaw tenses and he drops his gaze to his half-eaten plate. Internally, I shake my head at the sight as my feet move me closer to the palace.

But I pause.

"I wish to be left alone for a while," I say, keeping my back to him. I continue to steadily put more distance between us as I return to my room, preparing for our plans to go against Whiro.

CHAPTER TWENTY-NINE

Draven

"Anything?" I ask Emil as he solemnly shakes his head.

"Maybe this is a good sign then." My little brother is always incredibly optimistic, and I hope nothing steals that from him.

I thought I'd see if he had any visions last night that may help us in this journey. If there are any warnings or insight into what we might face. But, like he said, maybe seeing nothing is a good thing.

"I wish to join you." He lifts his chin and puffs out his chest, and I know how badly he wants to fight, to prove himself.

I reach out to rest my hand on his shoulder with a squeeze. "But I need you here. If I don't make it back or if something happens to me, then the crown will fall to you." Pulling him in, I embrace him in a strong hug. "You staying here is just as important because I'm counting on you to lead in my stead."

A look of determination settles over his face when I pull back to look down at him, my eyes lighting up at the strong boy in front of me who used to whack wooden swords at my shins.

"Plus, your dear, old mother needs company," our mother says as she breezes gracefully in through the doorway, joining us for a small meal in her sitting room.

By small, I mean everything is the size of my left nut. Little snacks of appetizers that can be eaten in one bite. I grab a mini tea sandwich and pop it into my mouth.

Once she joins us, I don't say a word. I don't have to. I just keep my eyes steady on her deep ocean-blue ones. She sighs with a crease in her brows. "I wish I could tell you the answers you seek, but I know nothing else of what the future holds."

The food suddenly turns bitter in my mouth as I clench my fists. I'm not angry with her, but I'm frustrated with walking into the unknown and putting Emma in harm's way when every bone in my body seeks to protect her.

"All you can tell me is that fate demands the sacrifice of the one who holds the balance of two worlds, right?"

She nods. "I'm sorry."

I hunch forward, elbows on my knees as I hold my head in my hands and grip my hair. Even with everything else going on, that one line has been weighing heavily on me.

"Draven, the only other thing I can say is to hurry back. That realm and its air are not safe for Fae."

"I know. Trust me, the last thing we want is to overstay our welcome." I lift my head, finding her gaze. "Do you think it will work?"

She turns her head away to look out the window with a distant look in her eye. "I believe that with magic and the power of love, anything is possible."

I push to my feet. "I never once doubted where Emil gets his optimism from," I say with a small chuckle.

"You should try it sometime," Emil says with restrained laughter. "You do enough brooding for the lot of us."

I turn to raise an eyebrow at him. "Now where would be the fun in that? Someone has to grunt curses down the halls."

A hand squeezes my arm. "Please be careful, my son. I may be told many things by the stars, but nothing is ever certain. I can't control what I cannot see."

"I will do everything I can to make sure I come back to you." She doesn't have to tell me for me to know the fear she has is for where I'm headed. Her petite body slightly trembles, and her eyes are haunted by the memory of my father never returning. I can't promise her I will, but I will fight like hell to do so.

"You must go." She nudges me towards the exit. "I've had lots of food made for you all to eat and fuel your strength. You will need it."

"Thank you," I say as I stand over the threshold. "I'll see you soon."

Her lips quiver, but she simply nods with a tight smile as Emil races towards me to attack me in a hug.

"We'll be waiting."

Gently, I rub the back of his head to ruffle his hair that he refuses to cut and hold him a little tighter. We don't leave until tomorrow at dawn, but I need the rest of the day and night to clear my head with no distractions. I need to make sure I'm alert and on guard.

The moment I release Emil and turn down the corridor to meet the others, my heart aches to leave them. But deep down, to my core, I'm ready to beat Whiro at his own game and free Emma from his threats.

"Are you going to swoop her off her feet and bring her here?" Fynn asks as he clears the rest of the food off his plate.

My expression is blank as I stare at him. "No." I shake my head. "She will be here when she can."

A shriek causes my heart to drop momentarily. "I still can't believe you two are officially mated!" Cora jumps to her feet, swirling around in a circle while she hugs herself. "After all of this, we need to host a celebration."

"Yeah, it's not every day you find your fated mate," Kye adds on with a small smile that has me doing a double take. It's not often you see this burly man softening his features.

"I'll leave it up to Emma when things settle down," I tell them as I continue to sharpen the blades for each of us that I have been storing in my room. I'm seated in the corner of the library, which seems to be our favored space lately.

The room falls silent with a weighted somberness to it. That's when I look up to see Fynn staring off into space, his eyes locked on the empty wall with a crease between his brows. Cora stops dancing when she notices and glides over to him to wrap her arms around his neck. She sits on his knee as she tucks him into her chest in a caring embrace. Dipping her head to kiss the top of his before she rests her cheek on it as he breathes out a heavy sigh and closes his eyes.

Fynn has been through a lot of shit, and losing his mate made him step one foot deeper into the grave. If Cora knows about her, then Fynn's heart is crumbling in her palms, letting her in. She doesn't seem to fret about searching for her mate if the stars gifted her one. She only ever seems to want to live in the moment and focus on the here and now.

When Fynn tips his head back to look up at her, the weight of emotions hanging into that look is one I haven't seen since his mate was alive.

Peace.

The more I watch him look at her, the more I see adoration shining in his eyes. The way his eyes track every part of her face, engraving it into his memory. It's exactly what I do to Emma. And the way his arms wrap around her, his fingers digging in to clutch onto her. How his whole body seems to lose its tension when she's nearby. These are the signs of *love.*

She seems just as enraptured with him. Always making sure he knows that she's there, by his side, offering small touches of comfort when he silently needs it and accepting the past that still haunts him.

"She's falling for him but hasn't told him yet." Kye's voice is low and it still startles me. "I have to listen to her gush about him since Emma's not here because if she holds it all in…I believe she will literally explode." His head shakes and I can't help but smile at the image of him having to spend hours listening to her gossip about a guy.

"She must be rubbing off on you to come to me and gossip about a new love brewing between the two of them." My hand moves mindlessly with another swipe of the sharpening stone over the silver blade, making it spark.

He clears his throat, huffing a curse as he leans back in his seat and spreads his legs out with his arms across his chest. "Cora does that to people. Just wait and see."

I peer over at him as I reach to grab a new sword, noting the way he watches them. "Did you feel something for her?"

His eyes slide to look at me from the corner of them, raising a sharp brow. "She has always found a way to get under my skin, and I her, but we could never be mad at each other." He pauses for a moment.

"Maybe if fate had different plans with my life in the past, but I could never weigh another down when I was under King Oren's command to protect my parents. It wouldn't have been fair. So, I never allowed myself to think of anything more." He sighs. "But now, I only feel protective of her, much like Emma. Finding a companion is the least of my worries, and I wish to only enjoy this freedom while I can for now."

I can't imagine what it was like to live under King Oren's rule and spend each day following his command. But I will forever be thankful that Kye chose Emma. That he risked so much to leave with her and keep her safe. Cora, too. They protected my mate and became her family when she was barely hanging on. And now, they're part of mine.

The fire dwindles to mere embers as the shadows of night begin to blanket the castle. We've waited a couple of hours and Emma has yet to show. Every blade is sharpened and pristine, and each of us is going over the plan again. Emma and I will arrive first, her shadows binding me as her prisoner to trick Whiro into believing she betrayed me and is delivering what she was told.

Fynn will open a window to find Emma's exact location she transports us to so that he, Kye, and Cora can do the same when he portals in a little while after us. They will stay hidden and follow the trail of shadows Emma will leave behind, leading them inside the broken mountain. And just in case, she drew a map of which way to go.

I scrub a hand over my freshly trimmed beard, my foot tapping lightly against the floor.

"Time's ticking, little demon. If you aren't here in five minutes, I will toss you over my shoulder, spank you to leave my handprint, and fly your ass here."

Everything is calm in the bond. Nothing alarming that should worry me, but I speak to her through it because I'm on fucking edge without her. With not seeing her since we completed the bond. My beast is becoming restless without her touch.

My foot taps faster as it now spreads up my leg, until I hear her voice penetrate my mind and I go still. *"If you think that will be a punishment, then you are sorely mistaken."* I hold my breath as I bite my bottom lip to stop the smirk daring to rise. *"Because I will enjoy it."* A fizzle of amusement trickles through the bond from her. *"Be there in five. Needed to tie up some loose ends."*

Loose ends? I'll have to ask her if her loose ends are the same group she met on the boat, but right now is not the time to get into it. The letter I've been clutching in my hand feels heavy. Small creases remain on it that I can't seem to smooth out. Each beat of my heart pounds harder the longer I stare at it, as if it will jinx the journey. But I have to do this, even if this note makes it all feel real.

With a final breath in, I let go of the letter, setting it gently on the table in front of me. In case I don't make it back, I wanted my mother and brother to have final words from me to help give them peace. To remind them of why I love them. A little bit of closure none of us were able to receive when my father died.

I've never left behind a note, but even if we have a goddess on our side, we are still going after a god in his terrain. A prickling sensation skates up my neck as my heart beats in a thunderous beat.

She's here. A misty cloud of black forms in the center of the room, revealing Emma as she walks through it. Even with her eyes as dead as night, I can see the measured look of determination.

CHAPTER THIRTY

Emma

The library is eerily quiet when I step through, looking around the dark space. Four pairs of eyes shine against the dimming fire, locked on me. But mine connect with pale blue pools on instinct. I watch as those icy eyes drop to my gloved hands, eliciting a rumble to roll through the room with a clench of his jaw.

I know Draven understands why the mate mark must be covered, but the primal side of him—his dragon—does not. Before I know it, I'm standing right in front of him, grabbing his left hand, and bringing his inked palm to my lips, causing a tremor to tumble through him.

"Remember, our forever is waiting for us, but right now, we must protect it," I whisper the words against his hand until he pulls away to grab a pair of his own gloves.

The light returns to his eyes with a smirk. "Just like old times." He winks, dipping his head to kiss my cheek.

Smiling, I look about the room to find Cora, Fynn, and Kye frozen in the middle of a three-way sparring match. Chuckling, I wave my hand towards them. "Don't stop on my account."

Cora shrieks as she runs to me, colliding hard into my chest with hers as her arms wrap around me. "You're mated," she breathes emotionally in my ear. "I'm so happy for you." She pulls back, just enough to twist her head and peer at Draven, too. "For both of you."

He gives her a thankful nod as I sniffle to hold back the tears welling behind my eyes. "I'm happy for you, too."

Her brows furrow as she cranes her head to the side in question. She follows where my eyes have landed, on a male who is so completely infatuated with her. His gaze has yet to leave her, and when she notices Fynn watching intently, pink blooms on her cheeks.

She scrunches her nose with a smile. "I'm happy for me, too." She giggles and I nudge her with my elbow.

"Welcome back, Em," Fynn greets me. "Maybe now Drav will stop growling under his breath and burning a hole in the wall with his glare." He nudges his head towards the broody male who proves Fynn's point by growling in a huff as response when he sits down in the cushioned chair.

Fynn laughs before winking to Cora. "C'mon, love. You promised to knock me on my ass, and I'm waiting," he chides as he watches Cora roll her eyes before she skips over to him.

Brushing my hand through Draven's hair, I press a chaste kiss to his temple before leaning down, licking up his throat and nipping at the lobe of his ear. *"I think your growly broodiness is hot."* My breath feathers against his ear as I speak into his mind. Tingle dance along my spine when I pull away and find his eyes staring darkly at my lips, his nostrils flaring.

"Fuck. Hot enough to make you wet for me, little demon?" He inhales deeply and his eyes shutter. *"I can smell how turned on you are for me."*

My lips part and my throat dries. Slowly stepping back and away from him, I bite my bottom lip. "Tonight, I'm yours." I don't speak that through the bond because I want him to hear the huskiness in my voice, how my breath hitches with the words.

His jaw clenches but his expression shifts slightly when laughter bellows behind us. I turn around and find Fynn on his ass, with Cora's boot pressed to his chest. I can't help but smile; this is my family.

I notice Kye standing off to the side with his arms crossed, and I make my way over to stand beside him. "Are you brooding, too?" I ask him, but my eyes are watching how Fynn grabs Cora's ankle and pulls her down on top of him.

A smoky chuckle sounds next to me. "No, Princess. Just…worried."

I twist my neck to look up at him. "About going after Whiro? Because you don't have——"

"No." He cuts me off. "I'm worried about you." Those amber eyes meet mine, and what I see swimming in his gaze feels like a punch to the chest. Always the protector.

"I'll be fine. My powers aren't restrained anymore, and I can take on the strongest soldiers because of you. I honestly wouldn't be able to say that if you never taught me how to fight." Naturally, I place my hand on his forearm, squeezing it. "You gave me that gift… A way to protect myself."

He huffs, but the smile gives away how big of a heart he has. "You just needed a helping hand." The way he says it sounds like he's brushing off my words, as if he's not important.

"No." I move to stand in front of him, staring sternly at his face to make him understand. "I needed you. *Only* you." Now I huff, but this time in aggravation. "So, don't do that. Don't make it seem like it could have been anyone to teach me." My eyes bounce between his shocked, unblinking ones. "No one gave a damn, anyway," I whisper. "But you did." I jab a finger into his chest. "So, accept that you are worthy to worry over, too."

"Princess…"

"I'm worried about you. About all of you." A shaky exhale leaves my lungs voicing it. Bringing reality crashing down on top of me all at once.

Suddenly, my cheek is pressed to his muscular chest, the rough beat of his heart pounding in my ear. "Then worry, but only for a moment. We all are choosing to fight with you, even if you say no. It's our choice to make, and one I would make repeatedly." His voice vibrates against the side of my face as he gently strokes my hair. Then, his stomach shakes with a soft chuckle. "I know one way to make you feel better and ease your thoughts."

I pull my head back to find him smiling wide at me, and the scar on his face stretches with it. "And what's that? A sugary dessert?"

He laughs louder as he lets me go, and the sound makes my heart swell. "Sorry, Princess. No dessert. But maybe a good sparring will help instead?"

My eyes light up with excitement. It feels like forever since he and I have trained together, and I don't hesitate to get into position. I widen my stance, only slightly with a small bend to the knees. Tucking my elbows into my ribs as I raise my fists, tracking Kye's movements as he does the same.

With a smirk, I crook two fingers to egg him on. "I'll go easy on you," I taunt.

That earns me another smile before his features settle on his face. Calm, neutral, unnerving. This is the warrior I know. The one who understands the calm before the storm, focusing on every twitch of my muscles, the direction my eyes wander as his zero in on me, studying my every tell.

A lightness fills my chest as we stealthily walk in a circle, facing each other. And when he darts in to kick out my leg, I realize how much I've missed this.

We trained for the next hour, until beads of sweat trailed down my spine and my muscles felt warm and well-used. All of us were spent and agreed to call it for the night since we would leave bright and early in the morning.

When we all reach the break in the corridor, Draven and I say goodnight to the others as they go their separate ways towards the tower. The moment they are out of sight, Draven swoops me up, eliciting a squeal as he tosses me over his shoulder. Before I even know what's happening, a loud smack echoes in the silent hallway. A sting of pain blooms on my backside until his palm massages the spot, gripping and rubbing the now-tender flesh.

"I need to be deep inside you." His footsteps are quick, thumping on the floor as we make our way to his room. "Watching you fight has made me so painfully hard. I almost spread you out on the floor and took you roughly until you screamed my name in front of everyone. I'm losing my damn mind right now."

I gasp at his admission and wiggle my hips in anticipation. My core already clenching at what's to come and how guttural his voice sounds with sinful promises. Nothing could prepare me for how it feels to be desired in such a desperate, almost primal way. Like he will go insane if he doesn't sink himself inside me.

I only register we made it to his room when he kicks the door shut, his hands still clutching onto me tightly as I get the best view of his perfectly sculpted ass. My brows furrow when I see him walk past his bed.

"Draven, what are you doing?"

I barely finish asking my question when I'm flipped back up and set down on the stone counter near the sink, his lips pressing roughly on mine in a heartbeat as I sigh into his mouth. My hands immediately wrap around his neck, digging my nails into the nape, needing to pull him closer. His hands are everywhere. Digging into my hips, sliding up my side, and cupping my breast before sliding back down again.

I'm lost in him. He's everywhere, all-consuming. And everywhere he touches sparks a bolt of heat over my skin, causing my heart to race.

The bathing room is shadowed with night, while glimmers of moonlight softly blanket us from the window in the ceiling. It's just the two of us, forever finding each other in the dark. He makes the darkness not so lonely like it once was to me. He really is the prince I dreamed of as a young girl. The one who would rescue me, holding out his hand for me to take. A gesture that promised a better future. One where I was *free*.

Except, this Dark Prince is also promising pleasure that only his touch can give.

"*Fuck*," he rumbles against my lips, sliding his hand up my spine to grip my hair. Twisting it around his hand before pulling my head back, forcing me to look into his eyes. "You're greedy for me, aren't you? I bet you're soaked. Your pussy begging for my cock to take away the ache." His voice is nothing but a rasp now.

I try to nod but his grip is tight, restraining my movement.

His tongue licks up my throat before pressing his face as close as he can to mine without our lips meeting. "I need to hear you say it."

The echo of my heart pounds in my ears, his cedar and maple scent swarming around me like a drug I need more of. I never want to smell anything else. The rough swallow of his throat registers, making me realize I never responded. I'm too caught up in how close he is, the painful pleasure of the slight sting on my scalp from his grip, and the way he's prodding my soul with those icy blues.

"Fucking say it, little demon," he grinds out as if he's barely restraining himself and the beast within.

I swallow down the moan wanting to break free, and I sound breathless with need when I speak. "I crave you. Every part of you." Wetting my dry lips, I arch up into him. "I crave to know every part of your heart." My eyes drop to his mouth before slowly dragging back up, demanding his eyes with mine. "And every inch of your cock. I'm fucking greedy for it."

He growls. A warning or a promise of what's to come. I'm not sure but he doesn't give me a moment to think more on it when he crashes his lips into mine. A shocked gasp leaves me before turning into a moan when his hand cups my pussy over my clothes, rubbing me there.

I can feel the slickness of my arousal dripping from me already and when he rips himself from me, I know he can smell it. His pupils are blown out, jaw tense, nostrils flaring.

"Strip," he growls, taking one step back to offer me room to stand.

I make haste in removing every layer of clothing, as he remains stiff, tense. His eyes trail the curve of my body, and that simple look heats my skin like he's caressing me with his tongue. I can feel his want through the bond. It's heady and overwhelming. And that only makes my insides burn hotter.

My eyes wander over his muscular frame, snagging on the bulge tenting in his pants. I lick my lips.

He's right. I truly am greedy for him.

Before he can make another move, I drop to my knees, my fingers making quick work of freeing the hard length of him. His cock springs free, hard and throbbing. Bulging veins trail the length of his smooth skin, and a small bead of pre-cum teases me at the tip. I wrap my fingers around the girth of him, noting the heaviness of how huge he is.

He blows out a long breath with a deep groan when I tighten my grip, slowly sliding up his length.

"Little demon," he chokes out. "You hungry for me?"

My knees shift, pressing my thighs together as his words make my clit flutter.

Instead of speaking, I answer by pinning my eyes on him. I flatten my tongue to steal the small drop that still glistens on the head of his cock, waiting just for me.

He hisses.

Twining my hair in his hand, he grips tightly as his mouth falls open.

Smiling, I drag my tongue down to the base of him, letting my eyes roll back as I do. He tastes so damn good.

The stone floor is cold beneath my bare knees, my nipples are hard, and a shiver races up my spine from the cool air brushing over my skin. But I don't care. I feel like I'm burning up under his gaze. Loving the way he watches me with harsh breaths. The way I hold the control in this moment, giving *him* the pleasure.

I want to tease him more. To drag this out until he's the one begging for me. The only reason I don't is because I'm addicted. It's me who can't wait a moment longer to taste him and have him fill me. To fuck my mouth.

My mouth wraps around him, flattening my tongue as I suck him deep. His breath hitches and that alone makes my pussy clench. Working my mouth over him, hollowing my cheeks as I glide up and down, taking him further and further. His fingers dig into my scalp more firmly, his hips jerking in tune with me.

He grunts, cursing under his breathe, which makes me move faster. I suck him even deeper until I can't breathe, causing me to gag on his cock. Tears brim the corner of my eyes as I twirl my tongue around the tip of him.

"Fuck, not yet," he rasps, wrapping his hand around my throat, guiding me to my feet. "As much as I want to spill myself down your throat, I want to fill your cunt more."

Chills race over my skin, his words making me whimper. His grip tightens around my throat, not enough to block my airway, but enough to feel his dominance. Which only triples when his mouth collides with mine. Ravaging. Savoring. Claiming. Angling my face to stroke his tongue deeper, my toes curl and my knees weaken.

His massive frame is exuding heat as he presses his hips to mine until the swells of my ass hit the smooth edge of the counter. But he leans further into me, kissing me harder so that my back bends over the stone.

He swallows my moan when his teeth nip my lip. The way Draven kisses is better than how it was described in the books I read before.

This is an explosion. A detonating pleasure that makes my bones quiver.

The scruff of his beard deliciously scratches against my skin with every swipe of his tongue. Both of my hands grip onto his wrist, needing more support as my knees weaken and my arousal drips down my inner thigh.

When he breaks the kiss, he spins me. I shriek when he bends me over the counter, his rough exhale feathering over my spine. Using his feet, he spreads my legs wider, and a draft of cool air brushes against my soaked center, making me hyperaware of how wet I am for him.

He growls.

I gasp when he drops to his knees, his tongue licking clean the drops of arousal tailing down my inner thighs, before reaching where it aches the most.

"Draven!" I cry out as he buries his face in my cunt, sucking my clit, and causing my thighs to tremble from the rising pleasure.

Before my climax can crest, he inhales deeply, like he couldn't resist himself from savoring my scent. In the next breath, he's standing, pressing a firm hand on my spine to keep me bent over for him as he lines the tip of his cock to my entrance. My hips wiggle, desperate for him.

"You are making such a beautiful mess for me." His voice sounds deep, more beast than male.

"Yes," I breathe out, panting in anticipation for him to stretch me with the thickness of his length.

"You are mine," he grinds out the moment he slams into me with one hard thrust.

I cry out, my back arching, and my teeth sink into my bottom lip. Enjoying the burn from the way he fills me as I push back against him. His hands move to my hips, digging his fingers into my skin to stop my movements.

A sharp sting has my mouth falling open on a silent cry when he spanks me before clutching my hip again.

"So greedy. This cunt is mine to pleasure," he rumbles. "Mine to take care of."

I can feel his dick twitch inside of me, making a breath woosh out of me with a faint whimper.

Then, he starts thrusting hard and rough, his nails biting into my skin as he uses my hips to fuck me deeper. The peaks of my nipples rub against the cold stone from the buck of his hips.

Already, I feel lightheaded, high on the rising pleasure scorching through my body. My inner walls clench him, urging him to seat himself even deeper. My hands desperately seek for something to hold onto.

But then, his hand curls around my jaw, lifting me, pressing my back to his chest as he continues to fuck me. Hitting that spot inside me that has my body wanting to fall limp in his hold.

"So fucking warm and tight," he rasps in my ear, tightening his grip under my jaw.

The tattoos on his hands are the only necklace I will ever willingly wear again.

"I can feel how close you are. Your pussy is trying to choke my cock with the way it's sucking me deeper."

His thrusts are brutal as he drags the length of himself all the way to the tip before slamming back in. And his rhythm is relentless, never letting up. My inner walls flutter. The muscles in my lower belly begin to tense as my orgasm nears the edge of the cliff.

"Ohhh!" I scream out when his other hand trails down my body until he presses down on my swollen clit. Moving his fingers in a circular motion that has me seeing stars.

"That's it," he encourages. "Come on my cock. Let me feel you spasm around me."

His dirty words do me in. Everything inside me tightens until I can't breathe. Darkness creeps around my vision from the high of my climax. The mark on my palm pulsing and flaring with warmth.

"Draven!" I scream at the top of my lungs, until my orgasm steals the air from my lungs. My back bowing as every muscle in my body stiffens.

It's too much. I don't know whether I want to push him away or pull him closer, but it doesn't matter. He never stops pounding into me, doesn't stop massaging my clit as waves and waves of pleasure roll through my body.

Panting heavily, my vision slowly comes back into focus. His hips start to jerk unevenly as he grunts. Draven's breathing is ragged when he roars, the warmth of his release spilling inside of me, my inner walls still pulsing around him.

He holds me tighter to him as he twists my head, capturing my lips in a searing kiss. The peak of his climax fades, but he continues to slowly drive himself into me. Causing my already oversensitive clit to flutter again.

I feel his teeth against my lips as he smiles against my mouth with a knowing smirk. "I love how greedy your cunt is for me."

"Only for you," I breathlessly say against his lips.

He groans, swallowing roughly as he dips his head to nip at my neck. "Let's get you cleaned up." A soft kiss eases the sting from his teeth. "As much as I'd love to sink my cock into you all night, we have to rest."

The truth of his words hurtles me back to what we have to do. That nagging worry trickling back into my mind.

"I'm scared." Those two words tumble out without thought. But when the two of us are in the dark together, it makes me feel like my secrets are safe. That they won't exist once the sun rises.

He pulls out of me as I turn to face him, placing my hand over the scar on his heart. "I'm scared of losing you," I whisper.

Cupping the nape of my neck, he pulls me in roughly, pressing his forehead to mine. Our eyes close, never wanting this night to end.

"You won't." His voice sounds pained.

When I open my eyes again, his piercing blue ones are already zeroed in on me.

"I'm not going anywhere." His jaw clenches as he exhales a shaky breath. "I could never leave you." But a flash of what looks like anguish shutters in his irises before it's gone. As if it was never there.

No matter how many times I check, I don't find any worry in his eyes the rest of the night. Even when he washes me in the tub, my body seated between his legs as the steam billows around us. The silence is comfortable as he peppers tender kisses to the tops of my shoulders.

Once we're both clean and dry, he tucks me into his body, tangling our legs together in bed. His arm drapes over my waist in a secure hold as his lips press a kiss to the top of my head, inhaling deeply. He whispers how he wants to hold me like this every night in his arms. As he says it, I can feel the love that bleeds into his words through the bond. It makes my eyes start to well with the force of it.

Except, I can't stop the unsettling feeling that has me on edge. And as my eyes close, I begin to drift off to sleep with trepidation trailing my every thought.

CHAPTER THIRTY-ONE

Emma

I wake up feeling like I never slept. As if I shut my eyes only for Draven to gently shake me awake, telling me it's time to get ready. Even now, my eyelids feel heavy as I struggle to keep them fully open, rubbing them with fisted hands while holding back a yawn.

Meanwhile, Fynn is so awake and lively, I almost want to ask if he stole the sleep right from my body.

"All right, let's do this!" Fynn's voice cheers as I turn to see him throw a fist in the air.

While Draven hands out the weapons he sharpened and polished, I make sure to lock eyes with Cora and Kye. Silently asking if they are ready because I will not love them any less if they wish to back out. Though, everyone has made it very clear that they are set on their decision. Both of them give a firm nod with a soft smile, making my heart clench.

"Secure your weapons," Draven tells us all before going over the plan one final time. When we all feel confident in what we have to do, Draven stands directly in front of me. His hands rise up to his chest, placing his palms up and his wrists bared to me.

"Time to make me your prisoner." His voice holds an air of playfulness, but his eyes are hard, focused.

My smile falters as I wind shadows around his wrists. A small trickle of fear skates down my spine as I flick my eyes away from his. I want so badly to protect him because I know how cruel this world can be. I was born with many monsters dwelling in every corner, and the only way I survived was to slay them. But Whiro? I hate to admit that he's the scariest one of all.

The one who stole my mother's life.

The one who killed Draven's father.

And the one who will wipe my friends away without a thought.

But then, there's Draven… the one he truly wants, and it kills me to not know why. To not understand why out of every soul in the realm of Deyadrum, he wants my mate.

There is no doubt that he gladly will rip away my love, taking my heart with him.

I won't survive it. None of it.

So, I straighten my spine, swallow down the lump of remaining doubts, and meet Draven's gaze. "I'm ready."

"You always were." His words take my breath away. Instead of responding, I throw shadows around us to take us where death clings in the air and thrives free from the shadows.

A blur of darkness swarms us until an icy chill dances over my skin, causing my breath to fog in front of me. Draven grunts beside me when our feet touch ground.

"I don't think I'll ever get used to that," he rushes out in a huff.

"Get used to what?" My eyes are scanning the outskirts of the broken mountain.

"Transporting through shadows."

I regard him as a thought crosses my mind. "Have you ever tried?" I ask quietly. My shadows flow across the ground, moving like water to sense if Whiro or any ghouls are nearby. "I mean, you command the shadows too. I just wonder…" I trail off when I retract my power, sensing nothing amiss.

"I've never thought to attempt it. But…" He shrugs. "My beast would feel dormant if I don't stretch my wings, and flying is…"

"It's freeing," I finish for him.

"Very much so." His breath plumes in front of him, but no matter how freezing it is, his body emits heat like a walking fireplace.

The silence is heavy as we regard one another, a single nod to acknowledge it's showtime. I feel down the bond, checking to see if the toxicity in the atmosphere is affecting him, but I don't feel any burning pain. His lungs expand with ease.

I leave a trail of shadows shimmering in our wake as we start our trek. I nudge Draven as one would do to a prisoner. Impatient and annoyed.

He remains silent, but his pride and appreciativeness swell through the bond, caressing the organ in my chest. A comfort to the ache that grows with every rough shove I give him.

Otherwise, we remain silent, not wanting to draw attention and blow our cover. Eventually I move to walk in front of him, pulling him along behind me, and keeping my back to him as if he was a piece of dirt on the bottom of my boot.

There haven't been any sightings of Whiro's ghouls, which I'm grateful for. Though I could easily take them, the question would be if I'm fast enough to silence them before they mind-link the others. This sparks a kernel of hope for the path to be clear for the others as well.

Steady, sure steps keep my balance on the stone bridge as the smoky fog swirls beneath. I almost forgot how stale the air is and how the ashes floating around us part as we continue forward.

I follow the same way Whiro took me the last time he showed me the Sea of Souls. But something burns in my throat in warning as we step into the broken mountain, and the spears made of stone cry as their tears splash on the ground.

Scuffing echoes down a tunnel, revealing a handful of ghouls who pause. Their vile gazes snaring on me as they hunch forward, sniffing the air. Their eyes blow wide before screeching, the piercing sound bounces off the cave walls and sends waves of sharp pain to stab into my eardrum.

This is it; I think. No turning back.

They jump on hobbled feet, following behind us. I refuse to look back, to make them think I care about them or worry about the male tied up behind me. One deep breath in helps loosen some of the tightness building in my chest. And I keep a steady awareness in our bond, making sure Draven is okay and that none of the ghouls dare to touch him.

When we round a corner, the stairs leading to our destination appear. Waves of jasmine crest the moment my boot touches the first step, flooding my senses. Draven coughs behind me, before he clears his throat as we continue our descent.

"Are you okay?" Even my voice in our minds tremble, my worry evident. Though no one would be able to tell with the hard set of my face as we reach the final step.

"Checking up on me?" comes his velvety voice in my head. *"I'm all right. The floral scent caught in my throat for a moment."*

Still, a sense of unease trickles through me.

"No need to worry about me, little demon. I have the most spectacular view." His next words almost hurtle me out of character and have me snapping my head around to him. I manage to refrain, staying ramrod straight and biting my cheek to keep my lips from turning up.

Light glows brightly in contrast to the rest of Gehendra and rushing water fills the silence from the waterfall existing in the middle of the massive silvery pool. My heart threatens to pound like raging fists against my chest, but I focus on my breathing, slowing it down. I can't show any sign of change; I have to be the demon he believes he created.

We scale down towards the water's edge and only then do I turn around to Draven, quickly meeting his gaze before tearing my eyes away. I can't linger on him, even when all I want to do is look at him, to help wash away the chill that's causing the hair on the back of my neck to rise. From what I can see, he is playing the victim perfectly with a broken look glistening in his eyes.

Ghouls gather behind us, lined up and scaling the perimeter of the cave, watching, waiting. Their clicking grates on my nerves, making my power hum in my blood with the need for vengeance.

"On your knees." The tone of my voice holds weight as I ram my elbow into the top of Draven's back, forcing him down. A small fissure in my heart spreads, but then a comforting warmth soothes it. The way for him to let me know it's okay. He may have mentally prepared for this role, but I didn't. Not to this extent.

Even though I have to act like the villain, it still makes me want to curl into myself for letting my mate see this part of me in the flesh. It's one thing for him to see how far gone I was in my dreams, but this is...*different*. Making those brief glimpses he witnessed real.

My thoughts drift to the others, hoping they portal safely here. Crossing my fingers that maybe we are drawing the crowd away so they can sneak in unnoticed. I flare my shadows high above me, making a swirling vortex to call Whiro to me. To signal my father.

"Father," my voice grating demonically to my own ears, "I have returned." I speak directly up to the whirling power of his call as my throat burns with a raging need for revenge.

Every muscle is tense as I wait, my lungs seizing as I hold my breath.

More ghouls line up as the air begins to pulse, his power leaking into the room. Whiro's own shadows snake around the air, revealing his body a heartbeat later. The obsidian skin that has been creeping up his arms has now reached his shoulders. Black veins webbing over his otherwise grey skin swell in a rhythmic pulse.

Those dark eyes narrow, digging past skin and bone to search deep into my soul. I don't react, staying perfectly still, with measured breaths and unblinking eyes that never sway from him. His eyes dip to Draven on his knees behind me, cocking his head slowly to the side.

"Seems you've done well, my daughter." The compliment feels like acid being poured into my ears. "And in a timely manner."

He steps closer and stares down at me, causing my head to tilt back. A way for him to assert dominance and show me my place. A glint of mischief creases his eyes, and if I wasn't so trained on him, I would have missed it. "But you must understand my reluctance of you delivering me your prince without a piece of hair on his head harmed."

Crushing my molars together to stop myself from widening my eyes and showing fear. "That wasn't part of the order." I force my voice low, trying my best to keep it sounding strong and steady.

He shrugs. "Now, it is."

Blood rushes to my head from my heaving breaths. But then, a sudden flutter brushes in my shadows, the ones I left behind for the others. Alerting me that Cora, Fynn, and Kye have arrived, and a silent sigh of relief has me inhaling deeply.

Whiro's footfalls tap tauntingly around me as he circles us, his power scraping over my skin and snaking around my neck in a threat before falling away. When he's before me again, he snaps his fingers, summoning a ghoul to scurry up to him and deliver a dagger.

He takes hold of it, twisting it up in the air to let the light glimmer off the blade before offering it out to me. "Stab him."

Two words.

That's all it takes for my worst nightmare to come alive. For my heart to stop and sink.

Staring at my reflection through the blade, it twists my features into someone I don't recognize. The hands that hang down at my waist tremble, so I fist them to hide it. To demand them to stop. I let my nails dig into the palm of my glove, wishing for the sting that will give me some reprieve.

Every ounce of fear comes surging forward, my eyes burning with unshed tears as I force them back. Whiro notices, never taking his eyes off me. But it's the way his gaze hardens, becoming colder, that has me questioning everything. My lungs refuse to inflate, feeling myself suffocating from within. I want to scream, yell, slam my fists into the ground until the mountain is nothing but dust. Anything to fight back against this.

Draven's silent behind me, but he must sense my panic because there's a gentle nudge in the bond. It has me taking the glove off my right hand to reach up to take the dagger. My fingers curl around the hilt until my entire arm shakes. The weapon weighs heavily as if it holds a million deaths.

I take a shaky breath in, slowly turning to face the one I love who sits proudly on his knees. His back is straight and his crystal eyes are already on me, full of so much peace. I don't see a glimpse of fear, only a hint of sadness that shows from the small crease in his brows and the subtle shift in the bond. It's almost as if he's known and prepared for this.

I try to convey everything I feel for him in my eyes. Letting every ounce of emotion pour through the bond. Of how I love him desperately, and that it should be me in front of the blade, not at the hilt. My knuckles turn white as my grip tightens and I–I *can't.*

This is too much.

I won't survive this.

My spiraling thoughts freeze when a cluster of movement disrupts my shadows where Cora, Kye, and Fynn were following. I strain my energy, hoping to sense what's happening.

The clicking of Whiro's tongue makes my blood freeze. "Something wrong?"

My eyes dart to his, but I bite my tongue.

His displeasure is obvious, but then he rumbles a low, vexing chuckle. "Seems like you are hesitant, but I'm feeling…generous. I suppose I can give you a choice."

His words are like nails digging beneath my skin. I go to respond, but the words get caught in my throat when a scream pierces the air.

"Let me go!"

No.

This time, I can't hide the pure terror widening my eyes, or the racing pulse jumping in my neck. Not when Cora's grunts echo down the steps, until they become muffled. Only a heartbeat later does a group of ghouls drag Kye, Fynn, and Cora roughly down the stairs before throwing them on their knees.

My head shakes. My stance unsteadies as I stumble back a step. This can't be happening.

"You either stab your prince, or I get to kill these three stragglers in any way I choose."

No!

No. No. No. No.

Haven't I suffered enough in this life?! And yet, the only ones who truly mean anything to me are paying the price for the tragedy in my blood I was born with. This is all my fault.

"W–Why?" is all I can ask, my voice wavering. I brought Draven to him. So, why go this far to threaten more lives and cause more pain?

"It's simple, really." Whiro glides leisurely around me in a circle. "A certain someone told me he overheard you with the Dark Prince before the room was muted. His displeasure to know you were lying through your teeth about staying away from the one you told him would never be an issue again. He asked me if I could *handle* the problem, to guarantee you as *his*. It's pathetic really, the lengths he will go to so he can have you." He tsks. "You are nothing special."

I see red.

Damning Aiden to hell while recalling my memories. It must have been the night Draven woke me from my nightmares. We spoke for a long while, even started kissing until the shadows blocked our sounds. My brows furrow. I didn't hear any footsteps, and neither did Draven that night. Unless he used his power to phase himself every ten feet. We wouldn't be able to hear him then. The knowledge of that has my blood boiling hotter.

I knew all his silk-woven words during our lunch were laced with poison. He was just waiting for the right moment to unleash it.

My fist shakes uncontrollably as my nostrils flare.

He. Will. Pay.

"But…" Whiro continues, linking his hands behind his back. "None of that matters."

My breathing picks up as I dare to dart a quick glance around, making sure Draven and the others are still unharmed. Their eyes are focused on Whiro, hard and unyielding.

"You were always a means to an end. I never planned on sparing you. Only an entertaining game to watch you ruin your soul with every kill. To bring me the final piece I need for my power." Whiro tips his head back and laughs.

It's forced due to being unused. Scratching his throat as it bellows through the air, causing me to wince from how *unnatural* it sounds.

"You see, it's just a game that you never had a chance to win. A *trick*. I always knew you would find a way to go against me." He sneers at me then. "I even knew you went after the Corrupted—I could sense the change."

Widening his arms, he gestures to the ones I hold dear to my heart.

"This was always the plan. To destroy your soul while gaining the soul I needed." Towering over me, he inclines his head, looking down as if the sight of me nauseates him. "I never wanted a daughter. Not then and not now."

His words shred my insides, as if he struck with the blade still clutched tightly in my hand. I have no love for Whiro, only wanting to be the one to destroy him. Still, his words still sting, hitting their mark.

I let the silence speak for me. Too angry to say anything that won't come out screaming and full of rage. Nothing that will help save those I love.

I glance at Draven, then at my three friends being pushed to the ground. Suddenly, all goes quiet. The rushing water fades away, the scrapes and clicking from ghouls disappear, and it feels like it's just me, all alone. I drown it all out. Focusing on the steady pounding of my heart as I close my eyes.

Whiro thinks there are only two choices for me at the moment.

Plunge this dagger into my mate or let him do his worst to my friends.

But he forgot a third option…

And one I plan on taking.

Slowly, I inhale deeply, letting my lungs fill to the point of pain before pressing the tip of the blade against my chest. The sharp point pushing past my clothes and digging into my skin, piercing through the first layer. My pulse is steady and rhythmic. But far in the distance, it sounds like yelling.

I go to take one final look, but panic radiates down the bond like a bolt of lightning. My eyes snap open, finding Draven trying to stand. Whiro has wrapped his shadows around Draven, keeping him on one knee. The ache in my heart spreads as Draven's mouth moves roughly. Though, I'm still lost in the rushing haze of contentment, of what I must do.

Then, I slide my gaze to my friends. All three are trying to push against the ghouls as spit flies from their mouths with desperate words I can't make out.

But this has to be the way. I can use the blade on me, enough to distract Whiro. To stab it straight through my body and let my shadows grab hold to send the blade flying through him. He's in the perfect position behind me for the blade to make a direct hit. Giving the rest enough time to escape, because if you cut off the head of the leader, the rest will follow suit.

With one final breath in, I pull the dagger back to give it enough room to force it past skin and bone. But when I do, a rush of air takes hold of me, causing me to stagger as I look to my right. Whiro is there. Shadowing himself beside me and latches his fingers around my wrist, the iciness of them biting into my skin. His hands are unrelenting, restraining me in a hardening grip as he twists my wrist to shift the angle of the blade and then surges us forward.

A grunt registers. Pain charging down the bond like a tsunami of flames, whooshing the breath from my lungs. Warmth seeps through the glove on my hand. I turn my head away from Whiro, paling as all the blood drains from my face.

Finding bright silver eyes staring blankly at mine.

PART III

CHAPTER THIRTY-TWO

Emma

The world stops turning and the ground shifts beneath my feet, choking back the sob threatening to break free. His eyes blow wide, mouth agape, and his breath is getting caught in his lungs as he hunches forward.

My hand is shaking uncontrollably, but Whiro grabs my wrist, pulling the blade out in one quick movement. The dagger slides out too easily, slick with blood. My legs give out, falling to my knees before him.

Rivers of red spill from his stomach, seeping into his shirt. I can't take a full breath in; my lungs are constricting as I watch his body jerk, and his chest shake. He coughs, blood spewing from his mouth. Every ripple of agony coursing through his body flows into mine. First, it burned, scorching and blinding. Now…my head is light, a cold sweat replacing the heat.

A crystal drop drips from the corner of my eyes, tracking down my cheek. The pain in our bond vanishes, making my eyes go wide. Draven's skin is still pale, clammy. It's then I realize he put up a barrier in our bond. Blocking me from his suffering.

"It seems I had to make the choice for you," Whiro's deep voice penetrates through the rushing of blood pounding in my ears. Everything blurs, darkness creeping on the edges of my vision, as I sway on my knees. I can't tear my eyes away. Draven continues to bleed, painting the ground in a pool of crimson. Why is he not starting to heal?

Whiro's hand grabs my shoulder, and the icy touch of it burns through my clothing. "I may despise the Fae, but they did one thing right."

My eyes drag away from Draven, staring down at the now-red dagger in my shaking hand.

Whiro's hand gives a bruising squeeze. "They created a weapon specifically to kill his kind, to help rectify my miscalculations."

My heart drops to my stomach, and the air freezes in my lungs. I don't even realize my head is shaking in disbelief as the pad of my thumb swipes away some of the blood coating the end of the blade. A hiccuped cry escapes me the closer I look at it, and the realization has me slamming my eyes shut. Instantly, the blood in my veins heats, searing the chill of darkness inside me.

"Wyvern iron," I seethe between clenched teeth.

The echo of a slow clap mocks me. "Smart girl," Whiro chuckles with devilish amusement.

Draven's pain sears down the bond again like an arrow on fire. But it's gone just as quickly, as if he's struggling to keep the barrier up.

So much blood. So much *fucking* blood continues to leave his body. I see double as I glance up at Kye, Cora, and Fynn. Their bodies sway in two different directions, but their silence hangs heavy in the air. The shocked grief in their eyes is like a punch to the chest.

Fisting the hilt, trembling from the force of my grip, my gaze drops back to the wetness coating my hand and to the male I love.

Then, I break.

The silence I've trained myself to hone rips away as I scream.

I scream until my lungs burn. Until my throat feels like it's on fire. Until the water vibrates and the stone shakes, causing the ghouls to cower with their clawed hands covering their ears. My shadows rage around me in a flurry of utter chaos.

In the next breath, I spin on my knee and slam the bloody dagger into Whiro's side. He roars. His power blasting out around him sends me flying back. I tuck my body, but my head slams into the side of the mountain, causing stars to dance before my vision. Shaking my head to clear my sight, I watch in horror as Draven slams into the bottom of the steps, leaving a trail of red in his wake. But he still tries to push up on his elbows with a raspy cough.

He's with the others, and they take full advantage of the momentary distraction of the ghouls hindered from my scream.

I push to my feet, ignoring the throbbing in my skull. I throw out a wave of my shadows to slam the ghouls farther away from them, hoping to hold them back.

"Emma!"

My head snaps up as I see Kye sliding a sword to me, scraping across the ground. Without hesitation, I snatch it up, forcing my power to surge in dark and light around me.

Keeping my eyes on Whiro, who is baring his teeth at me, I shout to the others, "Take him back! I'll get myself out of here."

"*No,*" Draven demands roughly through the bond, gripping my heart with one word alone. Opening a plethora of agony that rips my insides in half. But I can't watch him die. I must protect him.

Kye's shout cuts through my thoughts. "Not without you!"

I'm too choked up to respond, the words getting lodged in my throat. Dammit. Damn all of them for not listening. For not saving themselves since this whole thing backfired.

I reach back to Draven through the bond, pushing past the pain. "*I need you to live. I can't survive if you stop breathing. Especially from my hand.*"

Whiro rips the dagger from his body, tossing it to the side where it clangs off the wall and clatters to the ground. My eyes track him, readying for his next move as warmth caresses me down the bond.

"*Then let's end this and go home.*"

A tear springs free. *Home.*

Knowing he won't budge, I reach within, grab all the strength I can muster, and think. Something Draven had said about the mate bond springs forward, almost taking my breath with it. We can't control the other's power, but we can share it. Offering *strength*.

I let my power swarm around me in a storm of my own making. A rush of it pours through the bond, forcing it to break past any remaining barrier Draven has tried to keep in place. I can feel when it absorbs into his body. When alarm blazes through him.

"You dare go against me?!" Whiro bellows loudly enough to cause pebbles to crumble off the walls.

His power rages out of control around him as he slowly rises to hover off the ground with his arms up. Suddenly, the ghouls shriek, crowding us with a war cry.

Cora, Kye, and Fynn don't hesitate. They start fighting against the ghouls, spearing them down one by one. Their blades clash and slice along their grotesque bodies, causing the screeches to die in their throats.

Shock brushes through the bond as Draven manages to stand. *"You gave me some of your power…"* He trails off, disbelieving the effect. Even though he winces, pain etched on his face with the movement, the color on his cheeks has come back. His torso is still wounded, and yet he nods his head at me with a bloody smirk. "I'm with you." The tone of his voice is strained but strong.

My heart pounds wildly in my chest to see him standing. The relief is evident as I finally draw in a full breath. I'm not sure if I've healed him from the inside out, or if I only offered more strength for him to push through the pain.

Cora would know, but she was immediately thrown into battle, and there is no free moment to spare. Yet, I'm in awe of the way she's weaving her weapon in a lethal dance. Her footing is sure and precise as she bends, swerving out of the way before landing her final blow.

A dark blur snags my eyes, only to find Draven running toward Whiro. A faint dripping of blood still seeps from his torso.

I can't let the worry for him fester, and I launch myself in the same direction as Draven. Teeth gritting with every hard thud of my boots on the ground. Whiro laughs manically as Draven and I toss our shadows out, wrapping them around his throat. His laugh gets cut off when he looks down at us, simmering with red-hot anger. The air vibrates the closer I approach Whiro.

He shreds our power off him, but we wrap more tendrils of darkness around his body. Only, this time, I add in a rope of blinding light. Watching it mix with the dark and burn against his skin as he thunders out his pain.

Draven unleashes his wings, letting his dragon side come forward. With a leap in the air, those powerful wings beat to bring him above Whiro. Using the moment of Whiro's suffering to his advantage as he swings his sword along Whiro's side, which causes another roar and wave of power to pulse from him.

Draven launches upward before diving down, looping around the god to avoid the kickback of being caught in his power's current. I push off the ground mid-run and let my shadows swarm around me, portaling me behind Whiro. The moment I appear in the air, the blade of my sword drives into his back.

My body falls, landing just on the pads of my feet before tumbling into a roll. The impact reverberates through my bones as I finally skid to a stop. In that brief moment of Whiro being stunned, Draven rapidly flies around him, leaving dense tendrils of shadows in his wake to constrict him.

I take a quick glance and find the others are holding their own, while bodies of ghouls litter beneath their feet. Kye combines his power into each swing of his sword, painting a streak of blue in the air. Fynn portals quickly to dodge an attack, only to appear behind them. He lands a blow and makes them spew blood on the ground.

And Cora is gracefully holding her own as she spins, jabbing the sword into the stomach of one before twisting the blade behind her back and landing a mark on another. Pride swells in my chest at how strong she has become since the last battle. It still lingers in my mind like a splinter you can't remove because it is embedded too deeply.

Knowing they are okay, I take off again, straining my muscles to move my body faster. Draven's face is set with determination as he swoops out of the way. The sharp movement creases his brows as a jolt of pain fires down the bond before suddenly getting cut off. That nagging worry spirals

249

back to the forefront of my mind as I watch him weave around Whiro's power that has altered to look like arrows.

Everything happens in slow motion.

A slow tip of the corner of Whiro's lips as an orb of fiery shadows form in his hands. Draven continues his path to career around him, readying his weapon to strike through his neck.

"I'll take what is owed to me," Whiro's voice detonates. That growing orb raging in his palm hums like it's magnetic. As if it's trying to draw all signs of life into it.

Chills lick up my spine as I watch in horror, forcing my feet to move faster as the ball of energy gets aimed at Draven.

I don't think, I just act. Shadowing myself in hopes of getting to Draven in order to block it. But Whiro strikes. His power booming in the air, nailing Draven and sending him speeding towards the Sea of Souls. Draven's body slams down hard on the stone, rolling until the momentum dies away and he's laying limply near the edge of the water.

The impact through the bond reverberates through my bones, rattling them. Knocking the air from my lungs.

The aftermath of the orb sends shockwaves of darkness that slam into me midair. Before I know it, my spine slams into the hard ground with the back of my head following suit. Everything hurts. The room spins. My lungs struggle to expand.

Leaning over on my elbow, I cough up blood while something drips down my skull. My fingers touch and feel my hair is damp and matted. Dazed and confused, I lose a sense of reality for a moment. Everything is ringing around me until it slowly starts to fade and screaming blares loudly in my ears.

Then, the blood drains from my face, my pulse kicks into overdrive, and everything in me begins to go cold. Draven. I lose focus on anything else going on around me. Solely focused on him. I have to get to him.

On shaky limbs I scramble up on my feet with a wince, feeling the bond in my chest slowly become dull. Suddenly, another scream tears me from my thoughts and I whip my head around.

"Emma!!!"

Before I can blink, Kye is charging at me, knocking me back right as a rain of dark arrows streak down to where I was just standing. To the place where Kye is now standing…

"Kye!!!" Cora's rippling scream tears through the cave. The air deflates from my lungs. Cora's eyes are panicked as she shoves and thrashes against each ghoul that charges her.

Looking back at Kye, his amber eyes are wide, mouth parted open as he slowly looks at me. His legs give out, slamming his knees to the ground. A dozen arrows had to have pierced straight through his body, all to save *me*.

"Kye," I choke out. Grabbing his head with both hands, my eyes bouncing back and forth on his. His chest hitches in a sharp gasp for air. A strangled sob rips from me as I pull him in, holding him to my chest. His breathing is shallow and strained, raspy and wet as blood starts to trickle from between his lips.

With a jerk of his arm, he uses the strength he can muster to grab hold of me, making me pull back to look at him. "Go. Save. Him."

More tears tidal wave out of me as I sob, my eyes frantically darting all over him. My hands are violently shaking as I press them to his wounds, needing to stop the bleeding. So much blood. It seeps through my fingers as I place my palms over another hole with all my weight, willing the blood to stop, wishing I could save him. But I don't even think Cora's power can heal him back to health after this. Not with all the holes gaping open, streaming with blood.

"I can't leave you," I cry out, tasting the saltiness of my own tears.

"Prin…cess." His breath catches on the word, his face scrunching up in pain. "We will see each other again." A large, calloused palm cups my cheek. "You were the one th- thing that made my life worth living."

I sniff, wiping the wetness trailing down my cheeks with the back of my hand. "You made me strong," I say, chewing on my bottom lip to try to stop it from shaking.

A wobbly smile lifts his mouth as he wheezes to draw in a breath. "Y- you already were. This w-was always how I was m-meant to go. Pro- protecting you." Slowly, his body starts to loosen its tension, the hand on my cheek falling limp. And I watch… I watch the amber hue of his eyes dull, becoming lifeless as one final puff of air leaves his crimson lips.

Tugging his head to my chest, I rock back and forth as guttural sobs tear from my throat. No. This is a dream. A fucking nightmare I need to wake up from.

"No!" I scream, lying him flat on the ground, as I begin to shake him. "Kye!" I shake and shake and shake. Determined to force life back into him. "Wake up! I need you to wake up!" I pound on his chest with tightened fists. "You can't leave me!"

My fists continue to pound unforgivingly, and the tears falling from my eyes soak into his shirt. I pound and pound, demanding air to fill his lungs. But then his head flops to the side, signifying the cold truth.

Kye's dead.

I stare numbly at him, my fists pausing midair, letting them fall to my sides with defeat. Why? Why does he always have to be the protector? Another rack of sobs cripples me. Kye deserved more than anything to be the one protected. I was too blinded by my need to get to Draven that I left myself vulnerable. An easy target. And I hate myself for it. He didn't have to die.

Hunching forward, my head rests on Kye's still chest.

But then, every muscle in my body feels like it's being electrified. I jerk my body up when I realize it's coming from the bond. Draven. The water lingering in my eyes blurs my vision, but I blink it away. Launching to my feet, I sprint until my lungs scream.

Whiro holds Draven in a giant hand made of shadows, hovering him above the Sea of Souls, and it's like my heart is hanging from a noose, waiting for the drop. Draven remains unconscious, his limbs dangling off the darkness cradling him, and my heart lurches in my chest.

"Stop!" My voice shreds the inside of my throat as I fall to my knees, willing to beg Whiro not to harm my mate. "Please," the word breaks on my tongue.

Clashing steel and grunts still rage on behind me, knowing Fynn and Cora must be tiring out from keeping the ghouls away. Whiro's head twists slowly, pinning those deadly eyes on me.

"Take me instead." A broken tear leaves a trail of desperation in its wake.

A rumble echoes from his chest. "You still don't understand,

Emmerelda," he spits with venom. "No one can replace the chosen. Not even you."

With a final, menacing glare, he lets Draven fall.

I'm on my feet in half a heartbeat. Dodging the whips of darkness Whiro throws at me, because nothing…nothing will stop me from getting to my mate. And everything raging inside me that's been slowly building finally explodes. Darkness lashes out in every direction, a storm of my own making. The main force of it drives right into Whiro, stunning him.

Keeping my arms pumping, I leap in the air. Just missing the final blast of power Whiro had sent to the stone beneath my feet, causing the ground to break apart. Grasping hold of my darkness, I shadow jump from one stop to the next until I'm diving into the Sea of Souls headfirst.

The glassy water is neither cold nor warm. It feels like nothing at all, yet I still have to hold my breath. Pumping my arms outward, I swim towards him, letting the bond guide me. Even as I chance to open my eyes, it doesn't burn. Somehow, below the surface, I can see everything.

My hand brushes against something firm and when I turn to look, I startle. Air bubbles escape my lips in a rush.

A body. Floating lifeless. The male's skin looks pristine, as if the bodies don't decay over time. Scanning around, my heart stutters, finding hundreds of bodies suspended in this deadly pool.

I spot Draven, kicking my feet to reach him with my arms stretched out in front of me. The glowing white orb of his soul is rising through his body, and the sight has my heart racing and kicking my feet faster. When I grab hold of him, I place both of my hands on his cheeks, smashing my lips to his.

I call on my light as it races out of me, tingling against our lips in a spark.

In a blinding flash, his eyes snap open, locked on mine. Wide and unblinking. Though they aren't silver at this moment, his dragon dormant. No, these are the colored eyes that took my breath away the very first time I saw him. An icy blue.

I press my lips harder against his, as I see his soul pause its ascent up his throat. As if my small burst of power gave him an extra breath of life.

But I start to feel lethargic. Every muscle slowly smoothing out its tension, my chest rising and falling in a longer rhythm, and a ripple of heaviness pulling at my eyes.

Time is slipping through my fingers. The well of power within me is draining quickly. Like a ship caught in a black vortex at sea, getting sucked beneath the surface. I'm so tired. So very tired. My lungs are burning, and a numbness is beginning to settle over them.

Gripping some of my power, I feel a kernel remaining, just enough to save him. Enough to push into his body and give him strength. And to get him out of this soul-stealing pool.

The pads of my thumbs tenderly brush over his cheeks as I touch my forehead to his. *"Hold on for me."*

I let the words flow through the weakening bond with every ounce of warmth my body can give. And then I slam my hands to his chest, emptying the rest of my power into his body, while blasting him out of the water and back on land. A small wave of my shadows sets him down gently before it vanishes in a misty pop.

The heart in my chest is losing its song, but I will still love him silently with every breath he takes. And that's when I feel it. Nothing. Not life. Not death. But nothing at all.

"I love you," a broken whisper of my voice is all I can conjure, hoping he hears those final three words.

Every cell in my body comes to a stop. The blood in my veins ceases its flow. The hint of warmth beneath my skin fades away until everything feels cold. My eyes register a flash of light around me before they fall closed, and everything goes black.

CHAPTER THIRTY-THREE

Draven

"*H*old on for me.*"

Water launches up my throat. Rolling to my side, I cough until I'm able to suck in a large gulp of air. Everything fucking hurts.

Wyvern iron is my curse. The one thing that is a sure death for me. But somehow…somehow, Emma fucking *saved* me when she forced her power through the bond. I've never heard of a mate being able to heal the other, but she did. Not completely, but enough to rid the effects of the wyvern iron from my flesh, internally healing every organ that was sliced through. All that remains is the outer layers of skin that remain open, but that's not enough to kill me.

My body protests every strain of muscle, every breath, and every thought. I mentally push the haziness away, feeling like all of my blood has drained from my body.

Her voice rings like an echo in my head, fading fast to the barest whisper. *"I love you."*

Emma.

Emma. Emma. Emma.

Saying her name like a prayer in my head.

No!

How dare she risk her life for me! Only to not save herself too! The fucking world can survive without me, but it will all burn to ash without her. She has so much life to live. So much good to offer this world.

But then there's a cracking in my chest, a torrent of pain that shreds my throat with a violent roar.

"Little demon," I whisper, my voice raw. My eyes welling, hobbling over on all fours as I try to heave in air. Try to ease the soul-shredding pain.

I don't believe it. I need to see her.

She's okay. She's okay, I repeat to myself, hoping that it will make it true.

I don't blink as I force my battered body to the edge of the water, feeling panic grip me by the neck. Grinding my teeth against the assault of pain with every movement. But I don't care.

Our bond is weak and distant. The heightened, soul-deep pain can only mean one thing.

Grunting, I scour for my power, feeling it skimming the bottom of its well. I fucking grab hold of it, sending it into the damn water with labored breaths.

My shadows find her, knowing her very essence as if it was my own. Commanding them to wrap around her, I pull. But my power wavers. I grit through clenched teeth, feeling the veins in my neck strain as I try again. Growling in frustration as my hands shake uncontrollably.

My eyes dart to where Whiro is still recovering from an attack, one that Emma must have sent when I was unconscious. When I dig deeper within, I find a kernel of extra strength Emma must have poured into me. With it, I command more shadows to spread around Whiro as he roars, trying to relinquish them.

Focusing again on the Sea of Souls, I band my power around her body. This time, she slowly begins to sail towards me. I'm desperate. I refuse to fucking believe it. But I can't catch my breath. It's like a thousand knives tearing straight down the center of my chest.

But then, my shadows grow, feeling stronger as they pull Emma to shore faster. And that's when I register the warmth on my back. Finding Cora there, her palm is flowing her energy into me, *healing* me. To regenerate my draining power, closing my wounds and helping to free Emma from the water.

Not a breath later, Emma's frail body falls into my waiting arms. "No…" Her skin is freezing against mine. I hold my breath as my eyes scan over her face, my ears straining to hear her pulse. But I know what I'll find because the pain cleaving me in two hasn't let up. All that greets me is silence, making my heart sink.

Frantically, my fingertips hover all over her limp body, trembling. Not sure what to do or where to touch. The entire world feels like it's been tipped on its axis.

The beast in me becomes feral, raging inside with an earth-shattering wail. Everything starts to spin, drowning me in this cruel fate. My fingers brush wet strands of hair off her ghostly white face, tracing over the blue-tinged lips that were the softest pink minutes ago.

Pulling her hard into my chest, I rock back and forth on my knees. Praying to the stars to fix this. To give her back. To take me instead.

"You aren't supposed to leave me," I roughly whisper. My voice breaks, feathering along her hair as I numbly rub my hand over the back of her head. The base of my chest shakes with shock. Grief. Anger. Wetness streaks down my face, but I barely feel it. Everything around me is numb, fading out of focus. Only the violent waves of agony deep within the bond are what consume me.

The pain and torment of what follows when a fated mate dies. An eternal suffering all on its own.

Pounding registers, vibrating the ground beneath me. It's growing louder, until I faintly hear Fynn's voice. "This is our only chance. We have to go!"

A guttural roar shatters the air, bits of stone falling from the sides of the cave.

"Hurry!" Cora's voice sounds panicked. "He's building more power!"

Fynn curses. "He's going to fucking incinerate us." Boots shuffle on stone and then Fynn's laying Kye beside me. "He's not being left behind."

Harsh breathing sounds next to me and a feminine grunt on my other as Cora and Fynn huddle in close to me.

"Thank you. I got him now," Cora croaks as she begins to softly mumble pleas for Kye to wake up. "I got Kye," she whispers more to herself.

Suddenly, hands are gripping onto me and shrieks are raging around us. In a daze, my eyes drag up, noticing a massive torrent of darkness aiming for us, but not before a golden light forces my eyes to slam shut, followed by silence.

More heavy breathing surrounds me as two pairs of hands release me. Peeling my eyes open, I find the portal gone as I kneel on the floor in my library. A room full of life that blooms between pages, but the one I want ran out of ink. Emma's pages are now blank, empty, which is how my heart feels.

Heavy breathing racks the silent room as Fynn and Cora seem to try and catch their breaths, drinking in the clean air. A shuddering sob causes me to drag my eyes to the source, and I find Cora dropped down beside me. She angrily wipes at her tears, before reaching for a lifeless Emma in my arms.

"Don't you dare die on me!" she screams. "I can't lose you, too!"

I distantly realize Cora only helped me pull Emma out of the Sea of Souls but didn't linger. Escaping that realm was hers and Fynn's focus, while I remained a broken statue of despair.

Placing her hands on Emma's chest, she pushes waves and waves of her power. Tears drip off her chin, blending into Emma's soaked tunic. She whispers mumbled words under her breath as she remains transfixed on Emma. Cora's eyes never blink, like she doesn't want to miss the moment Emma's heart will beat with life again.

"Cora," Fynn gently says with a soft touch to her shoulder, crouching down beside her.

But she's lost. Stuck in a trance to bring Emma back. And I selfishly don't want her to stop. To keep going until my mate's calming grey eyes open with life.

"Cora." Fynn tries again as she grunts and her power flares brighter, her head shaking in denial. He looks like he's warring with what to do, but with a final look at Emma's pale body and stiff chest, he gingerly places his hands over Cora's. Curling his fingers over hers before whispering, "Cora, love. I'm so sorry, but she's not coming back."

Thorned vines twist around my heart at those final words. Coiling tighter and tighter. I want to scream. To yell and tell her to never stop. But instead, I watch her power dwindle as she falls back into Fynn's arms, covering her eyes with a shaking chest and a silent cry.

"Draven." I hear Fynn, but everything around me is fading away until she is all I see. Hands shake me, but I can't seem to tear my eyes from hers... Eyes that won't look at me.

Eyes that won't fucking open to let me know everything will be okay.

"Draven!" Louder this time, but I'm trapped in one of my worst nightmares as silent screams rage within my mind while I stare at her frozen chest, hearing a muted heart.

"Fuck," I faintly hear Fynn cursing. "We don't know when Whiro will be back, but it's very fucking clear he's pissed and that this is far from over." His boots shuffle before me, burning a path into the floor. "We need to properly bury them both. Kye and Emma deserve an honorable ceremony."

A sniffle before another soft whimper from Cora. "They would both w–want their ashes out to sea. To be free."

Kye. The one who protected Emma when I couldn't. The one who ended his life to save her. Kye deserves me on my fucking knees before him, every day, to honor him. But I'm caught in a web of all that is her, feeling like my chest can't expand until I hear blood rushing through her veins and air pumping into her lungs.

Warmth rushes into me, only to find Cora healing the rest of my wounded body and hating that it didn't work for Emma. That she's still growing colder as I cling onto her.

Their words register a beat later. A growl spilling from my lips, vibrating my chest.

Pulling Emma closer to me, I hold her tightly. Refusing to let anyone take her.

"No," I grind out roughly, digging my fingers into her hair as I clutch onto her harder. "No one is taking her from me."

Soon, everything drowns out, hours pass, and I never let go.

I never fucking let go.

CHAPTER THIRTY-FOUR

Draven

One day later

*E*verything is dark. The room feels cold. Her lifeless body is clean, lying unnaturally still in my bed as I sit in the chair beside it. Watching. Hoping. But life holds no color anymore; all I see is grey. All I see is *her*. The world is numb to me.

I lost her.

She's gone…

Gone.

Gone.

Gone.

CHAPTER THIRTY-FIVE

Draven

Five Days Later

*W**here are you, little demon? I can't feel you.*
The mark of our bond still remains on my hand, though faint. Barely existing. A dull, colorless connection that only holds pain.

The loss of her is a constant ache on my soul, unrelenting. Like a cage of spikes piercing my heart with every beat. Now, I know what my mother and Fynn suffered through.

I don't want your silent love. I want a love so loud that it can be heard by the stars and pulls me into your chaos. I can't let go of you.

I never fucking will.

CHAPTER THIRTY-SIX

Cora

*L*ight blinds me when I peel my eyes open. For a brief moment, my vision is blurry. All the colors reflecting from the sun blend together as one, but my gaze lands on Fynn beside me in bed. The fractured rays glow against his skin, making him look radiant and otherworldly. He is absolutely stunning. When my vision finally clears and his features sharpen and become more refined, heat blooms in my cheeks.

I wince when a relentless drum beats against my skull. Reminding me of the hours I spent crying until no more tears fell. The puffiness around my eyes ache, and every limb in my body feels weighted when I go to sit up.

A gentle touch helps me upright. Soft lips press a chaste kiss to my forehead, making my heart swell.

"Are you going to Emma?" Fynn asks, trailing his fingers tenderly down my spine.

I nod. "I have to tell her that today is the day."

He smiles softly at me, but I can see the sadness that wants to glisten in his eyes. Events that I never imagined would happen have come true. Emma is dead. Kye is dead.

Every time I wake up, that blaring truth sours my stomach and I want to crawl deeper into a dark hole that I should be digging myself. I'm a *healer*. Lifting my palms in front of me, I stare at them with disgust. How can I call myself a healer when I couldn't save them? I fucking failed them both.

Today is the day we honor Kye and say our farewells. Emma should be honored, too, but Draven refuses to be separated from her. He keeps her in his room, making sure she's cleaned and never alone. We all know he is nowhere near ready to give his final goodbyes. Truthfully, neither am I.

The mattress dips as Fynn shifts to grab both of my hands and bring them to his lips. It's only then that I realize I must have zoned out, staring at my palms for what they failed to do.

"Go have your time with her, and I'll get everything ready for Kye," he reassures me with so much care.

Fynn has been by my side through all of this, even though I know he's hurting, too. He surprises me with how attentive he's been, helping me stay on my feet when all I want to do is fall apart from the grief… From the shame.

I don't bother to brush my hair when I slip on the rose-colored cotton dress strewn over the chair at the foot of the bed. It's the same dress I wore yesterday, but I don't care. It seems like such an inane concern after two lives were lost. And all I did was curl in a ball and weep in it. So, I suppose my tears washed it clean.

Fynn is watching me while sitting on the edge of the bed when I walk over to him. I take his hand in mine and give it a soft squeeze. "Thank you," I whisper, breathing in deeply to keep the fresh tears at bay.

He squeezes back. "I'm here for whatever you need."

Since the world flipped upside down, it's been hard to find a sliver of joy. But Fynn… He knows what to say to earn a smile, no matter how small. It's an odd feeling for my lips to turn upward when my heart is still bleeding with grief.

"I know you are, and I'm here for you in any way I can be," I say, noticing his shoulders drop as his muscles relax.

I've been distant in my mind. Getting lost in my thoughts often, but I want to be there for him, too. It just may take me longer.

I let my hand fall from his as I turn on my heel to go see Emma. When I enter the hallway, it's dark in mourning, filled with the hush of death. The only sound is the pad of my slippers that announce life still exists here, but I feel like I'm disrupting the tribute the silence is offering.

When I reach Draven's door, I stand there with my arms hanging loosely at my sides. I stare at the intricate designs in the wood, building up the courage to go inside again. To face my friend that my powers couldn't save… And to face the male who is broken in more ways I knew was possible. I know he won't register I'm there; he never does. I failed him, too.

I raise my hand to grab the door handle but pause a hair's breadth away. I used to knock, but it makes no difference anymore. Draven never responds. My fingers are trembling as they barely brush the metal and I fist them quickly in hopes for it to stop. After a few heartbeats, I hesitantly curl them around the handle and twist.

The room is silent when I push the door open. Draven is sitting in the chair he's made permanently stay next to the bed. His elbows rest on the mattress as he holds one of Emma's limp hands in his, staring at it as if he can will it to move.

On a shaky inhale, I walk to the other side of the bed, my eyes never leaving Emma. Even though she lies there cold and lifeless, she looks somewhat peaceful. The worry for us that creased her brow is gone. The tension lining her lips is smooth.

My knees brush the plush blankets hanging off the side of the bed as I stare down at her. "Hey, Em," I say, quietly.

Draven doesn't move from the sound of my voice. When I briefly glance up at him, his eyes are still focused on her hand. I don't even think he knows I'm here.

Tears start to leak from the corner of my eyes as I go to speak again. "Today, we are honoring Kye's life." I sniffle and try to swallow down lump of emotions in my throat. "I wish you were here to say your goodbyes…" A soft sob racks through me and I let my head drop forward, squeezing my eyes shut for a second to clear away the tears.

"I promise I will tell him for you: how much you loved him. But he knew—" I shake my head gently with a small smile. "He knew how much you cared for him, and that he had a special place in your heart."

I wipe my eyes with my palms. It offers a little comfort to talk to her, hoping she can hear me. I know she's dead. Anyone would by looking at her, by feeling the lack of her pulse. But when I tried to heal her, I sensed no injuries within her body. Nothing to tell me how she died or why her body remains intact, though it doesn't pump with life.

"I miss you," I say in a broken whisper as more tears flood down my cheeks.

It's not fair. When I was laying on the brink of death after the last battle, I was able to heal. To come back to life and *live*. Except, Emma had gone to the darkness then to save us all. Now, she won't get the chance to wake up, to see that I'm right here. Her and I… We were a team, and I miss my partner in crime of stealing desserts. Of covering for the other to sneak out and gossiping about boys, even though it was mostly me doing the talking.

Glancing up, I take in the circles under Draven's eyes that have grown darker. The slow rise of his shoulders with every inhale, as if he's too tired to breathe. Walking around the bedframe, I stand behind him, gingerly touching my palms to his back. I open the gates to my power and let it pour into him, hoping to ease the ache of exhaustion from his body and cure the hunger pains I'm sure are twisting inside him.

Draven doesn't budge, but his breathing does steady out to a normal pace. Pulling my hands away, I step back. My heart beats painfully at the sight as I give one final glance at the two of them before making my way to find Fynn.

The evening breeze is cool, and the fog is hanging low today when we set sail a little way out to sea. The day passed in a blur with getting everything ready, and Kye's parents—who were a miracle to find—wanted to wait until the sun set. I can see why though; the sky is smeared with soft blues and purples. It's beautiful.

I hold onto Fynn's hand tightly as we stand on the bow of the ship, needing to feel his strength as I watch Kye's father place his son's body on the small boat and lower it down by ropes to the water. A few soldiers help take care of the ship so we can pay our respects.

Queen Zoraida and Emil are also here to honor Kye. They're holding their hands over their hearts as Kye's father—a wind keeper, I found out —uses his power to glide the small boat away from us and towards the horizon. He tosses a flaming torch down onto the boat next, and slowly, the fire starts to catch, spreading along the cloth wrapped around Kye's body. The only part of him visible is his strong face that looks like he's resting.

My eyes snag on Kye's mother, who clutches onto the wooden rail of the ship, crying out as she drops petals down to the water one by one. A mother should never have to experience the loss of their child. A beautiful soul she brought into this world, only to watch it leave. And Kye cared for them deeply, or he wouldn't have offered his life sentence as a guard to protect them.

The boat drifts farther away. Silent sobs tear through my body uncontrollably as I softly choke out my goodbyes to the wind that carries him. "I promised Emma I'd tell you… Though, I know you already know, that she loves you, very much. And I hope you are reunited with her in the afterlife."

The crackling of flames fills with his mother's cry that shrouds around the sea. "Thank you," I continue as Fynn steps closer to hold me. "Thank you for being there for Emma as a friend, and for training her when none of us knew the abuse she was enduring."

A hiccuped cry catches in my throat. Emma never told us about her suffering, but I understand why. She was protecting us in her own way. Making us unaware…kept us safe. Still, imagining her pain makes me want to avenge her in any way I can. And Kye… He offered her a sense of security and protection by training her. Giving her strength back when others wanted to take it away.

I clutch Fynn's hand harder as I watch the flames on the boat grow higher. Clearing the fog that lingers above it as the fire flares brighter against the twilight sky.

"And thank you for believing in me," I whisper, knowing the breeze will deliver it. "When I woke from my injuries and wanted to learn how to fight…you didn't hesitate." My lips tremble and I feel my nose start to run. "You told me that nobody would stand a chance against me when I learn how to use a sword." I pause, remembering this exact moment. "You had said *when*…not *if*."

Fynn kisses the crown of my head, offering comfort as I continue. "You taught me, just like you did Emma. Giving me the strength to help protect those I love, even when I wanted to keep training through the night." I huff out a wobbly laugh. "And I heard every curse you mumbled under your breath, but just so you know, that only spurred me on to fight harder."

Leaning my head back, my cheeks soaked with grief, I rest against Fynn's chest as the boat becomes small the farther away it gets. "You helped me overcome my secret fear of fighting. To take a life when all I've known is to save them. And gods, Kye…" My lungs tighten as another onslaught of tears consume me. "I wish I could have saved you." This time, I break. I can't breathe… I can't speak, as I cry out for his loss.

Fynn releases my hand to wrap his arms around my chest, burying his face into my neck as he holds me. It's then that I realize my legs gave out and he's keeping me upright, letting me breakdown in the protection of his arms. And for the rest of the night, he stays by my side, never letting me fall.

CHAPTER THIRTY-SEVEN

Fynn

*C*ora's hair fans in golden waves over the pillow. Her eyes gently shut as she breathes softly. But even in sleep, she's drowning in grief with the way her brows stay furrowed together and how she tossed and turned through the night.

Four days ago, we set sail just off the coast of Asiza to honor Kye. But it took us a whole day to locate his parents and deliver the news. They weren't easy people to find and said they hadn't seen their son in some time. But I almost broke when his mother fell to her knees, clutching her stomach when I told her their son was dead. And his father bent down with her, keeping her from falling more, holding her tightly as he broke down, too.

They mourned him on the sea with us that day, their hands linked the entire time as they stood at the tip of the ship, shadowed with grief.

I've lost count how many times Cora has thanked me for grabbing hold of him in Gehendra instead of leaving him behind. But Kye is one of us. Even in the afterlife, he will always hold a place in our hearts.

The whole time Cora clutched onto my hand as if her legs would give out if she let go. Tears brimmed in her eyes as Kye's father placed his sons body on the small wooden boat. Then set it aflame to let it drift towards the blue and purple brushed horizon. The fire consuming his body glared brightly against the twilight sky while each of us whispered what we wished we could tell him. Our final goodbyes and our deepest respects. And his parents dropped petals into the sea, letting them float behind their son. An act of hope to have peace in the afterlife.

Every day since, Cora has cried. The pain too much with his loss and Emma's. But with Kye, she got to say her goodbyes, and with Emma, it seems she's not able to. I catch her sometimes, pausing in front of Draven's room where he took her, refusing to let Emma out of his sight. And Cora will take multiple deep breaths before pushing the door open for her daily visit. The moment she leaves, her body crumples right into my waiting arms.

Although, it's strange. Emma's body holds no pulse, no sign of life. Yet, she remains perfectly preserved. Cora said as much the second day she visited, when she flooded her powers into Emma's body to check for any sign of injury but found none.

When I stood at her bedside, Draven was holding her frail hand to his lips. That's when I caught sight of it: the mating mark. Seeing it made my brows crease together because when a mate dies, so does the mark. I had lifted my own hands then, only to stare at unmarked palms. The only sign that I once had a mate is the light scar sealed over the flesh that was cut.

Draven's and Emma's… Although it is faded and nearly nonexistent, the marks still show. Yet, Draven is still experiencing the soul-splitting pain that destroys you from the inside out when you lose a mate. None of it makes sense.

Usually, a body would start to decay, and it's been something I can't seem to figure out. I'm not sure if the water in the Sea of Souls holds something that keeps a body intact, or if maybe…Emma's not dead. What if she's in a deep sleep?

The thought is crazy, but the Sea of Souls is unknown to us, and something we don't understand. There is no history or written knowledge of what it can do.

But Draven… He can't see past her unmoving body and the silence in her chest when I voice my questions. And I don't blame him. I know how consuming the pain is that has taken root.

I've seen him in bad shape twice. When he lost his father and when Emma was missing. But this… This is different. He's not raging. Not seeking violence or speaking to anyone. He has become a shell of himself. Hardly sleeping, and if he does, it's for minutes at most when his body forces him to. Even then, he stays sitting beside his bed, gripping Emma's hand.

Dark crescents bracket under his eyes and his face is looking paler and more gauntly from him refusing to eat anything placed in front of him. And it's like he doesn't even realize if anyone is in the room with him or if we drop food off.

There is no way to free him from the place he's trapped himself in. Not until he's ready. And I would know; it took me years to pull myself out of my self-destruction.

Giving a final glance at a sleeping Cora, I leave her to rest. I need to go check on Draven to see if anything has changed. But when I open his door, the hope vanishes in an instant. Still in the same chair, leaning over the side of the bed, and holding her limp hand to his mouth. His dull, bloodshot eyes never leaving her resting face.

Seeing my friend like this is crippling. And I feel like I'm drowning with him, but he needs me to be strong. He needs me to be his backbone when he's ready to stand on his feet again. Just like he did for me.

The door creaks and I turn to find Queen Zoraida walking in, her eyes holding a watery sheen as she looks at her son. She briefly nods to me before standing beside Draven, placing her hand on his extended arm on the bed. But he doesn't so much as flinch or look at her. He remains a statue.

"Son," she voices softly. "This is not the end."

In a flash, his muscles tense and a heavy cadence of power thickens the air. In the next heartbeat, he shoves himself out of his chair, looking down at his mother.

He lashes his arm out and points towards the door. "Get out!"

With a gaping jaw, my stomach tightens, locking the air inside my lungs. My eyes are not believing that he moved, and my ears are in shock to hear his voice again. Days of no reactions from him, and the first one is blazing red with everything that he's locked inside of himself, tearing out in a wild rush.

He's not himself, because he only has love for his mother and has never once raised his voice at her. Never has he been cruel towards her. This is the immense pain he's lost in that's lashing out. The feeling as if his chest has been pried open and his heart is cleaved in two.

"Drav—" she goes to speak but he cuts her off.

"No!" His chest is rising in harsh movements as he drops his hand in a shaking fist. "Why couldn't the stars tell you the sacrifice would be her life?!" He roughly shakes his head with a deep snarl. "I would have kept her here. Safe. Even if I had to lock her away to do that, she eventually would have understood. But now…" His voice breaks as he shifts from anger to defeat, falling back into his chair. "She's dead." Dropping his head on Emma's shoulder, he breathes in a shaky breath. "My mate is fucking dead."

His head tips towards us, and the next words get lost as he chokes back a wave of tears prickling at his eyes. "And I can't fucking *breathe* without her."

His mother softly nods in what feels like understanding. She, too, knows the pain of losing a mate.

"We will help you learn how to breathe again." Her voice is tender and clear. "When the time comes, we will still be here."

She turns on her heel to leave, sniffing away the sadness welling in her eyes. Pausing beside me, she places her hand on my shoulder but keeps her head forward. "Time will heal."

I can't take my eyes off my best friend and my chest burns at seeing him so broken. When I lost my mate, there were no remains. She was simply gone. The last memory I have of her was her smiling before she went off to sea.

But Draven… He's going to have a hard time picturing her smile when he now knows what it looks like to see the light leave her eyes. The pale skin that remains cold. The pain of losing a mate already feels like an open wound that will never heal. But to have their corpse right before you must be torture. Yet, I can't make him let go, or give her a proper burial because if my mate was dead in my arms, I would do the same thing.

Slowly, I turn to look at the side of Queen Zoraida's face. "I think you and I both know time won't heal for him." Looking back, I watch Draven brush more of Emma's hair back behind her ear with quivering fingers. "My worry is that we will soon lose him, too."

Her head snaps to me and I can feel waves of emotions rolling off her, but I can't make them out. Her weak and trembling voice gives away her fear as she says, "Please keep an eye on him. Time *will* heal."

My brows automatically furrow when she says that again. When I meet her deep ocean eyes, they gaze into mine like she's trying to tell me something I don't understand. Begging me to figure out the reason behind her words.

But all I can say is, "I will watch over him."

She nods. With one final glance back at Draven, her chest deflates, and then she strides out of the room. Leaving me with a male who is shattered but can't find any of the pieces to put himself whole again. The worst part is, I don't think he wants to be put back together.

CHAPTER THIRTY-EIGHT

Emma

The last remaining bit of air leaves my lungs as everything becomes freezing and dark. But then, the world around me blurs and I feel like I'm floating. Drifting on a soundless current that's pulling me farther away from those I love.

I know this is the end. Death has finally caught up to me, and the music has stopped playing. A hollowness fills my chest as if I left my heart behind. And in a way, I did. I left *him.* Leaving me with an insistent ache that spreads through my veins as my blood calls for his.

But I will endure this pain for eternity. I'd die a thousand deaths if it means saving him. A small glimmer of peace settles inside me, knowing I got to see those beautiful blue eyes one last time. Something I will cherish until the stars choose for us to meet again. I just hope he knows that he has my love until the end of time.

Coldness bites at my skin, and my body feels weightless as I continue to float towards a small opening that shimmers with light, looking like the end of a blackened tunnel. When I near it, the air mists around me in a gentle blanket of fractured rays, tingling against my skin before clearing away when my feet touch solid ground. With widening eyes, I scan my surroundings, unable to stop my mouth from falling open in awe.

Two suns fill the sky, warming my skin in a comforting heat. But this place... It looks so similar to Deyadrum. As if every court was combined into one: snowy peaked mountains in the distance; lush green hills that roll for miles; towering trees that sway to a gentle breeze; a waterfall rushing over a small cliff into an iridescent pond; and flowers in full bloom. Everything is more vibrant here, saturated with colors that seem impossible to the naked eye.

A freshness fills the air with a sweetness I can't describe, but it makes me inhale deeply, wanting to soak myself in it. Oranges? Vanilla, maybe? I can't pinpoint it, yet it's such a calming scent.

It brings back memories of a time when I was a child, a time when I was once free. Back when I used to run through the morning dew, clinging to the field on a spring day in the Mortal Lands of Helestria.

This has to be the afterlife, yet I'm not sure where I'm supposed to go. Am I here in this place all alone? Is there an afterlife for each of us, or one that is shared? Because I don't see another soul in sight.

Slowly, my feet walk over the blades of grass, feeling them tickle against my bare feet. Only now do I look down to notice I'm wearing a soft ivory dress that sweeps around my ankles. The linen is light against my skin, with short, flowy sleeves, a scooped neck, and two buttons donning the top.

I head over to the pond and crouch down to dip my hand in the water, feeling the cool kiss of it against my fingers. When I scoop some out, my reflection ripples before me, making my lips part on a silent gasp. The hue of my skin shimmers as if stars dance beneath it. My eyes are their normal silvery grey, but there's a brightness to them. As if they, too, have stolen a star from the sky.

Gingerly, I touch a hand to my cheek in disbelief before a shadow casts over me, blocking the light of the sun. And when I look above my reflection, it's only then that I realize who the shadow belongs to.

"Hello, Princess."

I'm frozen in shock for a moment. My eyes and ears not believing who is right behind me, even though I know the deep richness of that voice as clear as day, and the endearing nickname that will forever be tied to him. The organ in my chest beats wildly, my lungs struggling to keep up with my shallow breathing.

Crying out, I spin around and throw my arms around Kye. Burying my face into his neck as his arms haul me up, causing my feet to hover above the ground. Tears spring to my eyes, absorbing into his white shirt as his sweet, musky scent I've known most of my life swarms around me.

I hold tight for a long moment, never wanting to let go. Eventually, I loosen my arms so he can set me down. It takes him just as long to let go of me.

"I'm so sorry," I rush out. "You being here is all my fault."

"Shhh." He pulls me back into his chest. "Never blame yourself. I willingly stepped between you and Whiro's power, and I would do it over and over again. There was nothing you could have done to stop me." His hands soothingly rub circles over my back, and my eyes close briefly as my breath feathers against his sturdy chest.

My mind races, on the verge of spinning out of control. He risked his life to save me, and yet, here I am, fucking dead.

Tipping my head back, I stare into his blazing amber eyes that are glowing brighter than I have ever seen them. "But you should be raging at me, yelling at me, or something. You sacrificed yourself, and I still ended up dying with you in the end." A single, lonely drop falls down my cheek, but he catches it with his thumb.

I don't find any regret or displeasure creasing his face as I scan him over. His skin is smooth, his mouth curved in a gentle smile, and adoration swims in his gaze "There will never be a day where I could be mad at you." His thumb catches another lone tear. "But there is something you need to know, Princess."

"What is it?"

His eyes soften. "You're not dead. Not fully."

All the air rushes out of my lungs as I stumble backward. "How–how is that possible? I'm here. My body *died*. I *felt* it." My hands shake, gesturing down my glowing frame, and to the colorful world around me.

Understanding glimmers beneath his gaze as he holds his arm out for me. "Come, let me show you instead."

Without hesitation, I snake my arm through his, latching on. Because it seems like the whole world is about to be ripped from beneath my feet and I need something to hold onto to keep from falling.

Kye guides me through a waterfall that parts when we step through, with not one drop of water landing on us. On the other side, a small, cave-like tunnel opens up to a forest that beams majestically. The leaves seem to twinkle, the flowers blush warm with richness, and every step I take on the forest floor leaves behind a glowing footprint. I watch as my golden imprint shimmers before fading away, as if it never was.

"I never imagined this," I breathe out as we step over a glittering, moss-covered root.

A low chuckle vibrates his chest. "I didn't either, but I never truly took time to imagine what the afterlife would be like." His head dips down to regard me with a raised brow. "What did you expect?"

"Fire? Maybe a deep pit of darkness that isolates you with madness or somewhere that makes you rip the pages out of a book, one by one, for the rest of your days. Both are equally horrifying," I ramble until I find Kye looking down at me with both eyebrows raised in amusement. Just imagining those fates has chills erupting over my skin, making me shiver.

"Maybe for the true sinners. The ones that act on pure evil with no good intentions and only for selfish reasons. And that's not you, Princess." His words twist something in my stomach. So, I avoid his gaze and look ahead, following the path that looks walked on many times before.

Softly, though, I let my thoughts tumble out. "But you said I'm not dead yet. How do you know?"

A hand grasps my shoulder, pulling me back only to find Kye stopped in his tracks. "Because I only am loyal to those who are worthy. And you

—" The tip of his knuckle taps the point of my nose with a small curve of his lips, the scar lining his face stretching. "You have the biggest heart I have ever known. Not even this place is good enough for you."

"And what about you?" I ask, because if he believes I have the biggest heart, then he hasn't taken a step back to look at himself. He's the one who helped me survive in such a cold, cruel world. The one who showed me how to be strong when everyone else wanted to see me break.

This time, his eyes light up like never before. Small creases form at the corners of his eyes, mouth widening as his cheeks lift with a full smile. "I'm happy here." He pauses. "You don't have to worry. This was always meant to be my time, and I know that now." I tilt my head in a silent question, waiting for him to answer as his eyes seem to get lost in a dreamy memory. "My mate is here. She's been waiting for me."

Burning builds behind my eyes as they well with tears, my mouth trembling with a smile. "Can I meet her?"

"You don't even have to ask, Princess. But first, someone else is waiting to see you."

Kye continues to follow the path beneath the trees, moving a branch out of my way as we step into a clearing. He stops when we reach an archway of stones, covered in an array of purple and white flowers. Green vines intertwine themselves around the perfectly bloomed flowers, hugging the stone while five pillars create a circle just beyond it.

"What is this place?" I step through the archway, waiting for Kye to answer me, but a familiar voice that I haven't heard since I was a child fills the silence instead.

"It's the heart of the afterlife, my sweet Emma."

With my hair whipping through the air, I spin around on my heels and coming face-to-face with Aunt Lydia. I cry out, the tears that were already welling at the surface spill free as I close the distance to hug her before she can even open her arms. Burying my face in her shoulder, I breathe her in. She looks just like she used to when I was little. The memory of her, the sound of her voice, all of it was starting to fade when I was desperately trying to hold onto her.

"My brave girl," she whispers. "You aren't so little anymore." Her nimble fingers play with my hair.

I pull back and take in her fiery hair, the light dusting of freckles and hazel eyes that I used to stare at every night when she would tuck me in. And I'm drawn back to a time of sweet lullabies and dresses dusted with dirt from playing outside.

"You look exactly how I remember." My voice is full of awe as my eyes take in every inch of her face.

A light laugh follows her soft smile. "That is a blessing here; we simply stop aging." She winks before her eyes cast over my shoulder. "Someone else has been waiting to see you."

Her hands lightly grip my shoulders, turning me around, and I slam my hand to my chest. Urging my heart to calm when my eyes stumble on ones that match mine.

"Mother," I croak out. My heart doubles over itself, refusing to slow down. The muscles in my legs threaten to give out with seeing her again.

Her arms spread wide, and I welcome myself into her embrace without a moment of hesitation. Sniffling, I whisper, "You weren't supposed to leave me again."

"Shh." She nuzzles her head against mine. "It's a mother's job to protect her children, and your life is just beginning."

"Everyone who protects me dies," I mumble, sniffing away the tears threatening to fall. My cheek rests on her shoulder as my gaze connects with Kye's.

Her eyes must follow where I'm looking because she says, "Kye told us what happened, but you must know… Nothing could have changed his fate. It was his time."

A choked sob rips from my chest, shaking my head against her because I don't want to believe it.

She grabs my face between both of her warm hands. "And if I remember correctly, you have someone who would walk through fire to protect you, laying his heart on the line. A heart that is beating and still very much alive."

"But Kye—" I turn to face him again, the one who put himself in harm's way, only to find him now smiling with a female under his arm. She's looking up at him with doe eyes that hold so much love.

"It was my time, Princess," he speaks so calmly. So at peace. "I knew what would happen, and I did it anyway. My vow was to protect you." The muscles in his jaw tense, his eyes growing dark. "I messed up before. When you were consumed by the darkness and left, I should have stopped you. I should have done everything I could to help you fight the demons that were trying to take you away from me."

He pulls who I assume is his mate closer to his side. The tension leaves his body, his shoulders relaxing as he beams at her. "But the stars knew you would need me." He turns those now-gentle eyes to connect with mine. They glimmer like a male in love. "And I swear on the stars Princess, I'm happy."

My mother releases me as Kye steps forward, bringing his mate closer. Her auburn hair shines brightly, waving down to the dip of her waist, with small pieces braided throughout. She's about my height, curvy, and the most stunning female I have ever seen. Her golden skin radiates brightly from the small rays of light streaking through the branches, and her eyes… They are the deepest green I have ever seen, reminding me of the pines in Asiza when they get caught by a fragment of light.

She holds a delicate hand out to me. "I'm Elira." I try to stop my hand from shaking as I take her hand in mine, only for her to pull me in for a friendly hug. "Thank you for bringing light and meaning to my mate's life when I couldn't. I will forever be thankful."

My muscles loosen as I hug her back. "It is I who should forever be thanking him. And now, you, because I know he won't be alone. That he has someone who will take care of him."

Elira lets go, snuggling back into Kye's side. "He may be a big brute, but deep down, he wears his heart on his sleeve," she responds as she rests her hand on his chest, and he holds it there.

Kye looks down at her, and all I see is contentment. An ease in his body that was never there before. My heart feels like it's ready to burst out of my chest. He is truly where he wishes to be… He's more than happy.

Rustling draws my attention away from Kye and Elira. Twigs snapping, the ground vibrating from what seems like an army marching against the forest floor.

"Emma, there is much you need to know." My mother's voice reaches my ears above the hundreds of footsteps growing closer and the drum of my heart pounding louder in my ear.

Before I can ask her what it is that I need to know, bodies of males and females step from between the trees surrounding us. Hundreds of them circle us, and they are all looking at *me*.

CHAPTER THIRTY-NINE

Emma

*R*emaining steady, I stare back, my gaze roaming over them carefully. As I scan each one, watching them pause their movements, their shoulders lower in what seems like relief... I don't find an enemy looking at me. Only warmth and kindness.

My mother comes to stand beside me, her arm brushing mine, as my eyes connect with one person after another. Slowly, my breathing evens out, and my feet loosen. "They are stuck in the in-between, just like you."

"What do you mean?" So many of them border the clearing of the woods, making it impossible to truly see how many are here. Shock still mutes my mind from comprehending what is being told to me.

"You are not dead, nor are you alive." Snapping my head to hers, I hold my breath. "The Sea of Souls makes your body appear dead—like a deep sleep—while keeping it preserved. But it does not kill your soul. It traps it, holding onto your power and storing it."

My face blanches as the air being held tight in my lungs rushes out. "Trapped?" I bring my gaze to the surrounding Fae watching us.

Then, suddenly, my psyche flashes to when Whiro had me throw a Fae male into the Sea of Souls as a demonstration. And I won't ever forget his face or his name—Vincent.

I had asked where his soul went, and with stark clarity, the whole memory comes flooding back.

"They have all been trapped here…" Remembering all the bodies floating in the Sea of Souls. Lifeless, but in perfect condition. There were…so many of them.

In my peripheral, I see her nod. "It is also the reason your father wants your mate."

My head jerks swiftly to my mother, eyes widening as they connect with hers. My heart weighs heavily, feeling it sink to the bottom of my stomach, twisting roughly as bile burns up my throat. "How do you know—"

"I've been watching over you. From here, there are no limits to what I can see. I was the Goddess of Light after all." She gives a playful smirk after that before taking my hand in hers, brushing her thumb over my knuckles. "Without even knowing it, you saved the world by sacrificing yourself for love. Your prince is the final piece Whiro needed. He's the last one remaining from his bloodline."

My brows crease together, and a ball of worry lodges itself in the base of my throat. I'm not there to protect him now. I left him alone and he doesn't know. He has no idea why my father wanted him. I swallow down the lump of worry and fear, hating that I'm not beside him.

Her hand gestures to all the Fae lining the woods. "They are all wyverns in one way or another. Whether a full shifter or half, all of them were once the chosen one from their bloodline."

"Wyverns… Not dragons?" I ask because both terms are used in Deyadrum, and the iron used against them is widely known as Wyvern.

She only shakes her head. "The use of dragon became well-known from the people's fear, not quite understanding the difference. They only know that the beasts from their bedtime stories look similar to the Wyvern shifters who used to thrive in Deyadrum. And so, it stuck with each story-teller and townsfolk as the dragon bloodline."

I can see how that could become altered over time because I've never seen a fully shifted dragon or wyvern to tell the difference.

She turns back to the Fae bordering us. "But since the beginning, Whiro has been hunting them down to trap them in the Sea of Souls and collect his power they carry. I've tried to stop him many times." Her chest deflates before dragging those mirror-like eyes to lock on mine. "When a chosen one passes, another is born."

"So, every time my father forced one into the Sea of Souls…it kept their power locked away with their body, while their soul came to the in-between? Even though they aren't fully dead?"

Solemnly, she nods. "The Sea of Souls acts as a semblance of death, holding a well of power that grows stronger with each soul." Her hand finds mine at my side, squeezing it. "Your mate is the last one to live since he has not born any heirs, holding the fate to his bloodline."

The organ in my chest stutters, struggling to push blood through my veins as I take in her words. But all I can focus on are the countless eyes that remain fixated on me. I repeat her words. "They were all…the chosen one at some point in life."

"Yes." Her voice is strained, mixed with an undertone of sorrow. "Many of their kind were killed, out of fear or aggression. But the chosen were taken, once your father was able to find them."

I fist my chest, clutching the material of my dress there. What is the point of becoming so consumed with power that you plan to wipe out an entire race? To kill off innocents to appease your own thirst for selfishness?

A twisted part of me wants to laugh about how fate could be so vile for giving me two fathers in my life who share a similar mind. Two males that would destroy the world if it meant being the most powerful. It's a sick joke.

Crunching registers from my left, to find some of the Fae splitting, revealing a single male walking through. He's tall, and though still youth-ful, the air about him makes me think he's been alive for centuries. His footsteps are assertive, and his striking face remains composed.

As he approaches, my lips part with a sharp inhale. Those eyes… they are calculating, fierce, and shine a crystal blue just like a piece of glass lost beneath the sea. They lift on the corners with a welcoming look, making me take in his other features. Sharp jaw, raven hair, and…

Everything comes to a halt. Bringing my hand to cover my mouth as I bite my bottom lip to stop it from trembling.

Standing a foot away, he smiles softly, and the aroma swirling around him reminds me of…*home*. Of a Dark Prince who smells of cedar and maple and a place where a dense fog hugs the trees with safety.

"Are you Prince Draven's—"

"Father?" he finishes for me, but then he nods with a small chuckle. "The one and only." Something in his eyes twinkles as he observes me. "My son seems to have finally opened his heart." Though his voice is rich and low-pitched, each word is pronounced crisply and clearly.

Speechless. My hand falls away and my mouth opens to speak, but no words come out.

"You can call me Irad." I swear his white teeth sparkle when his smile stretches.

"Are you trapped here, too?" Out of everything I wish to say, that is the question that comes tumbling out of my mouth.

He hangs his head with a slight shake. "Sadly, no. I went searching for a peace offering in the Court of Ashes but ended up caught in the wrath of the God of Darkness instead. And though I may have Wyvern blood in me to partially shift, I wasn't born a chosen with the power to command shadows. So, there was no need to keep my soul captive. In the end, he managed to trick me, driving a sword made of shadows straight through my heart."

Wetness stains my cheeks and I wipe it away with the back of my hand.

He looks far off into the distance, a deep crease furrowing his brows. "There are so many things I wish I would have said to my family before that trip. If I'd known…"

"You didn't," I hurry to add.

His tight smile tells me he understands, but I know it doesn't change the regret of how his death came so suddenly.

Turning to connect his gaze back with mine, he speaks hesitantly, "But you… You can offer them some peace by telling them the words that they never got to hear."

"H–how? I'm *here*, not there."

The comforting sweet scent of my mother pulls my eyes to her. "You hold the light to break through the darkness that is blocking the path back to the living." My mother's hands cup my face gently, a warmth of pride shining in her eyes. "You, my dear daughter, are the soul of salvation. Only you are able to free the souls trapped here."

With a racing heart, I twist out of her hands and scan all the Fae shifters closing in, until my eyes lock on one who has haunted my dreams. His face is one I've grieved every night, knowing nothing I can do will earn his forgiveness. Because I–I killed him. It was my bare hands that sent him here, to be trapped in a prison that balances between life and death. Even though he's not a chosen, maybe…maybe he, too, can be saved.

Vincent. The one I stole from his mate. The one Draven saved, and I destroyed. I let the tears fall, keeping my gaze on his as I silently mouth, *I'm sorry*.

Something I never thought I would see flickers behind his eyes, as he brings his one hand to his chest, dipping his head with a single blink. One whispered word leaves his lips loudly enough for my ears to catch it: "Forgiven."

Before I realize it, my knees slam into the soil and I shatter. Everything inside me rips open, freeing a demon that has been suffocating me every time I close my eyes. It feels like something in my chest cracks, so painfully loud, and I wonder if anyone can hear it. If the world quaked from the force of it.

But finally… Finally, my chest is lighter, and I can breathe a little bit easier.

The tips of my fingers dig into the dirt, hanging my head forward as I slowly pull myself together. Steady breaths flow in and out of my lungs, determination steeling my spine.

With one final exhale, I rise to my feet, looking directly at my mother. "Tell me what I need to do."

CHAPTER FORTY

Emma

A kernel of light floats above my mother's palm as her grey eyes meet mine. "I've managed to save the last shred of power I can hold to give you the extra boost you will need. Because this could drain all your power…"

"Which would permanently keep me here?" I finish what she couldn't seem to say.

"Yes," she chokes out. "You only have one chance to break through the seal."

We stand in the center of pillars that circle around us. The chosen wait right beyond the stones, full of hope. I can sense the eagerness drifting from them, to go back to their lives and welcome their souls home. It's the subtle shift of their feet, inching closer, with widened eyes.

Swinging my gaze back to my mother, a seriousness hardens her face. "Light may clear the darkness, it can even restrain it if bright enough, but only his own power will be his undoing." I tuck that information away as her hand waves to the waiting souls, who are paces closer than mere moments ago, ready for their freedom. They are souls of the chosen who are ready to seek vengeance. An eye for an eye. Blood for blood.

Suddenly, a flash of understanding slams into my mind. I snap my eyes back to my mother's already-waiting gaze. She seems to know her words finally clicked into place as she silently nods her head with a smile.

"They *all* hold the power of his shadows." She cups my cheek with a gentle touch. "You were always meant to be great. I knew it from the first moment you were born, when those big grey eyes latched onto mine. No matter what you might think for everything you have done, I am beyond proud of you."

"Mother…" A sob works itself free as I realize this is it. This is the goodbye I never got to have. My feet move before I realize it and I crush myself into her arms. "I would be nothing without you."

Her chest shakes against my cheek. "You are everything and more. I told you once that no matter in this world or the one beyond it, we will be together again. But now is not your time." She tucks a strand of my hair behind my ear. "My heart is always with you. I love you, my beautiful daughter."

"And I love you," I force through the lump of emotions in my throat.

Her eyes glisten with tears as she turns me to Aunt Lyd, who already has streaks of wetness coating her cheeks. She pulls me in, her hand rubbing my back. "I knew the day I lost you that you were brave, but seeing you now…" She looks over my face, swiping the crystal drops away that fall in an endless flow.

"I've never been so blessed to know what it felt like to have a daughter of my own. My only wish was that I could have protected you when you needed me, to watch you grow, but it seems now you are strong enough to hold your own. Embrace who you are, Emma."

Sniffling, I huff a watery, "I love you, Aunt Lyd."

A quivering smile as she answers back, "I've never stopped loving you, sweet girl."

A throat clearing has me turning to find Kye waiting, with Elira standing close behind him. "Princess."

I run, diving into his arms and cementing myself to his chest. "I wish I could bring you with me."

His hand gently brushes over my hair. "I know." He holds me tighter. "But don't worry about me. Live the life you were always destined to live."

"And what's that?" I ask, tipping my head back to look up at him.

His eyes soften, a watery sheen making the amber hue flare bright. "One where you are shown love every day. A life where your smile is permanent, and your laugh fills the halls. The life you deserve to enjoy beside your mate."

On a shaky breath, I suck back the tears. "Life won't feel the same without you."

"I'm still here, Princess, and I'll be waiting." My eyes follow the tear that's slowing trailing down his cheek, but he never wipes it away. Never takes his gaze off me.

"Promise?" I ask with a small huff of amusement, trying to see him smile again.

And the moment he does makes my heart somersault in my chest. "I promise," he says roughly, but still holds his smile.

I look to Elira, the organ in my chest softening at the warmth in her gaze, before locking on his again. "You deserve a new beginning that's full of love," I say softly with all the adoration I feel for him.

A harsh exhale deflates his chest, and more tears brim the corner of his amber eyes as he slams me back into his chest. Each ragged breath of his brushes the top of my head. "Stay safe, Princess. And always remember how much I love you."

"I will never forget as long as you don't forget how much love I hold for you." My tears soak into his linen shirt that the afterlife dressed him in, and I clutch him tighter, hating that this is goodbye. But he said he'd be here when it was my time. He promised it. So, I suppose this is more of a 'see you later.'

Stepping back, I look to Elira, gently reaching for her hand. "Thank you. I know you will take care of him now."

Her smile is radiant and the amount of love she holds for Kye is evident, making my heart surge for them. "I'll never stop."

With a final nod of farewell, I turn to walk back to my mother, but a strong hand curls softly around my wrist. My eyes land at the point of contact before dragging up to find Draven's father.

Crystal blue eyes hold mine.

He leans in, whispering into my ear, and his words cause waves of emotions to lodge in my throat. I swallow them down as I focus on listening, hanging onto his every word. His final wishes and last chance to ease the ache in his family's hearts.

When he's done, he cups my hand in his and brings it to his lips to press a tender kiss to the top. "I am so blessed to have had a chance to meet the love of my son's life." Turning my hand over, he looks longingly at the markings of our mate bond. Though faded, the design is clear.

"Stars above," he whispers, letting his fingers trace the crescent moon. "It was always you his dreams were leading him to without him ever knowing." A small laugh of disbelief shines in his eyes. "Night after night he would tell me about them on the roof. Talking about how his heart felt pulled to this mark, but he didn't understand why. Only that it felt *right*." Smiling up at me, he squeezes my hand. "His other half of the moon, his heart."

Heat rises to my cheeks from his words because I now see where Draven gets his poetic confessions from. My heart squeezes at seeing how much they are alike, and wishing I could bring him back with me so he can hold his family again. So that Draven could fill the hole in his heart that will always be missing. I know that pain well, though Draven had a lifetime of memories with his father.

Curling my fingers around his, I hold tightly. "He told me about those dreams," I say, softly. "We didn't know then what we were to each other, but...our souls kept drawing us together." Releasing his hand, I pull him in for a hug that he willingly accepts. "You have my promise that they will know every word you wish to tell them."

"Thank you." The strain in his voice is loaded with emotion. Breaking apart, those icy eyes stare deeply into mine. "And I'm glad my son found someone to keep him on his toes."

"Wha—"

He chuckles deeply with a playful shake of his head. "I always knew my son's mate would be one who challenges him, which is what he always needed. A fighter."

Grinning, I start walking backwards. "It pissed him off at first." I laugh as his roars to life, placing a hand over his heart. The look in his eye constricts mine, knowing I'm able to give him some peace and a bit of joy to hold onto. But to do that, I need to make sure I can get us all free.

Turning on my heel, with my heart feeling lighter after seeing the look on Irad's face, I step back in the center of the pillars. The air thickens, weighted with a hum of power that threatens to buckle my knees.

"Come, my sweet daughter. Your destiny awaits." My mother's hands grow brighter, holding them out at her sides.

With a final look around me, stealing one more glance at all those I love, a tear streaks down my cheek. One that will soak into the soil and remain with them until we meet again.

Inhaling slowly, my eyes fall shut as I scratch the surface of my power. I call the light to me until I feel it rush through my veins and crackle against my waiting hands. The bloom of warmth that races beneath my skin builds and builds, forcing my glowing white eyes to flare open and meet hers.

Like two stars shining against the night, my mother steps closer. The ends of our hair pick up, whipping around on a current of otherworldly energy. The beats of my heart pick up speed, desperate to return to Draven. To feel the heat of his skin against mine, to hear the sound of his voice, and look into eyes that have snared me in their magnetic pull from the first time I saw them.

Our forever isn't over, because the stars are finally aligning for our lives to begin as one.

My breath hitches when my mother places her hands on the center of my back, her magical voice singing into my ear. "Think of breaking a shield, one created solely by darkness, because that's what it will feel like."

The air grows denser, cementing my feet more firmly into the ground.

"Even when it feels too much, don't stop. You must not pull back. There is only one chance to free yourself and all those with you. Only you can do this." My mother's voice is strong, holding the strength of a Goddess.

Pressure builds in my chest, tightening as my breaths become labored. Every ounce of my power hums beneath my skin, heavy and buzzing, wanting to explode free. Gritting my teeth, I draw in one final lungful of air until it stings, before letting the light blast out of me. The force of it slides my feet backward on the soil, but my mother's hold steadies me, offering her strength.

Blinding light is all I can see. My molars grind together, and my skin feels like it's melting off my body. As if flames are licking just beneath the surface and searing through bone. The pain is agonizing, like I'm being burned alive.

A guttural scream tears through my throat when my power slams into the wall of darkness trapping us here. It's solid, unfazed by the first touch of my power.

"Fight it, Emma!" My mother's voice echoes faintly in the back of my mind.

Tears bleed from my eyes, and something wet drips from my nose as I push past the ripples of pain. But I won't stop. I will fucking fight to make my way back to him. Even if this kills me, at least the chosen will be free and won't be forgotten anymore. Draven will have his people back, never to feel like an outcast again. He will be able to fly with his kind.

Waves and waves of light penetrate the wall, pounding relentlessly. Another searing scream shreds the insides of my throat. Chest heaving, muscles strained tight. The earth beneath my feet struggling against the weight, my feet digging further into the soil.

But then the shield starts to crack. A fissure spreading from its center, weakening as I target more power to that spot. Shadows begin to creep around the edges of my vision, and white spots start to float around me. Everything doubles.

My blood burns me up from within like every nerve in my body is being torn apart, piece by piece. More wetness trickles from my nose as I exert more power. Crying out, my knees slamming into the hard ground.

"Keep going! You're almost there!" My mother's voice sounds far away, barely audible as the world around me grows hazy.

Right when my body feels like it will give out, a burst of energy courses through me, causing my spine to arch as an earth-shattering scream expels deeply within my chest.

My mother's power she's been holding flares to life inside me, giving the extra boost my body needs. It streams through me, flowing through every vein, before exploding free, combining with my light, and detonating the remaining strength of the wall.

In the next heartbeat, it shatters. Falling away as my palms hit the ground in front of me. My muscles are heavy, weighing me down as my mind tries to come back into focus. But then, shrieks and roars fill the air.

In what seems like slow motion, I lift my head to see hundreds of wyverns flying above me. Ones that look just like Draven in the way he shifts into his wings and others… The ones who must be from the very beginning of the bloodline have shifted into full-blown wyverns. Their massive, scaled bodies soar above me as shadows dance around them, all heading towards the opening that leads back to the living. The path to return their souls to their waiting bodies.

I watch in awe as they all peer down at me with slitted eyes when they pass, bowing their heads. Suddenly, my head feels too heavy, but hands cup my cheeks, catching me before my skull hits the ground.

Gently, those hands turn my head, only to find grey eyes that match mine glistening back at me. "It's time for you to go home, my sweet girl."

My mother wipes away some of the blood staining beneath my nose, her fingers coming away red, before pressing a loving kiss to my forehead. Everything hurts. It's hard to breathe as my limbs shake beneath me, unsure if I can stand.

With a wave of my mother's hand, one of the fully shifted wyverns swoops down, landing before us, and my jaw goes slack. Its giant claw digs into the earth, its wings spread out, before dipping down to the ground. Am I supposed to ride it?

The answer to my question is given when Kye scoops his arms beneath me, curling me to his chest. My arms barely have the strength to cling onto his broad neck as he takes long strides to the wyvern. A slitted eye watches me as we approach, before Kye gently lifts me, setting me at the base of the wyvern's neck.

Kye gives me a final peck on the cheek before backing away. He must notice my shallow breathing and the slight tremble taking over my limbs because he says, "You saved them all, Princess. Now save yourself."

My mother gives a soft pat to the wyvern's thick neck. "Do not be afraid, my daughter. It is a sign of respect and honor for one to allow someone to ride on its back."

Steadying myself, I study the beast beneath me. The scales are woven together to create a smooth but thick layer of skin. A shield of its own. Spikes penetrate from the head that follow the length of the spine as I settle between them, curling my fingers around two for support.

A gasp leaves me when a band of shadows secures me against the Wyvern, holding me against its body, and I couldn't be more thankful.

A barbed tail swishes through the air before it pushes off the ground with two powerful legs and its wings slam down in one mighty stroke. A throaty growl vibrates its body, building up for a roar that ricochets through the air. It sounds like hope for life. A cry of freedom.

As we ascend, I never take my eyes off my mother's. She rests her palm on her chest, right above her heart, mouthing *until we meet again*. I silently mouth *I love you* as I stretch my hand out.

But now, her frame starts to become smaller the farther we fly.

This should hurt, but instead, my heart feels light. I got to see them all one last time, and that is a gift I will cherish forever. One that will always bring me peace.

The wind whips through my hair, the wyvern's wings beating in a steady rhythm as we fly to the shimming opening. No darkness to be seen, just light as we break through it. The entrance back to the living tingles over my skin, and in the next moment, everything blurs. The beast beneath me is no more as my body begins to free fall.

With a pounding chest, I hurdle towards a blinding light, and when I reach it, my lungs sharply inhale life once more.

CHAPTER FORTY-ONE

Draven

*E*verything is dark and I've lost track of the days because I don't fucking care. Nothing in this life matters without her. And I can't get myself to let go, no matter how many pitiful looks I can feel burning into my back when someone steps in the room.

She's dead. There is no mistaking how her pallid body wars against the black satin sheets beneath her. The way her face would crease while smiling and laughing, or when her feistiness took hold has faded. Nothing but smooth skin that is missing its rosy spark.

Clutching her hand in mine—refusing to let go and break our connection—I drop my head and press my cheek to her frozen palm before holding my lips on our mark. The one that still remains. Though faint, it's there.

I refuse to let our love ever die with her. She still holds power over me, and always will. My eyes never stray from her as they plead for the stars to breathe air into her lungs, to take it from my lungs instead.

For centuries, I was lost until I found myself in her. Her soul forced me to face the part of me I ran from. She saved me without ever knowing. And she is the reason my head remained above water.

Without a chance to fight it, my eyes fall shut. A sign of my body wanting to force itself to shut down. I know when Cora visits, she pushes some of her power into me to heal the energy draining from my body. And I let her, not bothering to push her away because my mind can't stray from Emma. I don't have the strength to fight her, to tell her to stop so I can join my mate.

I can't seem to break out of this dark hole I'm endlessly falling down. There is only one person who can stop the madness catching fire in my mind and solidify the ground beneath my feet. My chest tightens, forever aching as I press my lips harder against her palm.

But my head jerks back when something twitches in my hand. Holding my breath, I stare at where my fingers interlock with hers, hoping it wasn't a figment of my imagination. Minutes pass, but it feels like forever until two fingers quickly spasm against mine. So fast and featherlight that if I wasn't looking, I would have missed it.

Leaning forward, I kiss her fingers repeatedly with whispered pleas spilling from my lips. "Please. Please. Please, come back to me." Another rain of kisses. "I'm right here, always have been."

Rocking back and forth, I hold onto her hand so tightly that my heat warms her skin as if I can pump life back into her. My heart squeezes painfully in my chest as I struggle to breathe. Everything drowns out around me, getting consumed with the rush of blood pounding in my head, drumming loudly in my ears until a scratchy voice I never thought I'd hear again cuts through my torment.

"Draven."

Everything stops. Time ceases to exist as the bond in my chest comes flaring to life. My heart stutters as I snap my head up to her.

My mate.

Finding grey eyes bright and full of life. Bringing the storm of who she was back to life and once again snaring me in the tempest of her chaos. Tears track down my cheeks as I blink, disbelief still clinging to my eyes. But every time they land back on her, her smile grows.

The tightness in my chest fades and I carefully flatten my hand over her heart, needing to feel it beat against my palm. A desperate need to feel her chest rise with proof she's come back to me. It's only then that I take my first breath with her.

The legs of my chair scrape against the floor as I push to stand and lie on the edge of the mattress, resisting to pull her into me. She looks so fragile, so breakable. More so than when her heart wasn't beating, as if it took all her strength to come back to me.

Leaning down, my head drops to her chest as every emotion rolls through me, and broken tears soak her shirt I'm clutching onto. Every piece of shrapnel my heart shattered into slowly works its way back together…because of her.

Fingers brush through my hair, smoothing the tension berating beneath my scalp. Burying my face into her, I breathe her in. Rose and honey fills my soul, calming the beast inside. Her heart beats strong beneath my cheek and my breathing syncs with the rise and fall of her chest.

"I'm so sor—"

"Don't," I cut her off, lifting my head to find her eyes closed tightly, but the wet streams falling down her cheeks can't be missed. And the ache in her heart pierces mine deeply, slicing through the bond. Her sorrows are buried and rooted with mine. Deep and grounded, but never alone. Not anymore. "Look at me, Emma."

Every time she gives me those stormy eyes, my breath catches, and I swear the world tilts on its axis. Making me want to fall to my knees, submitting myself to her. Only for her. My eyes penetrate hers, finding a well of remorse swimming in the depth of her soul. Everything she is feeling brushes through the bond, and I know it has to be because she left me. Because she sacrificed herself in my stead knowing she would die.

But the stars listened, knowing I was nearing the end, and that my beast was moments away from breaking through fucking fate itself to get to her.

She watches me, patient and waiting.

Dipping my head, my lips press a soft kiss on her stomach before looking deep into her eyes. "You have nothing to apologize for. So, I don't want to hear it fall from those perfectly pink lips." I can't stop my eyes from dropping down to them when they part. The blue tint of them is long-gone, blooming with life now. And I have to force my gaze back to her wide eyes as she chews on that bottom lip, holding her breath for me to continue.

"But don't ever fucking think that my life is worth saving over yours." Cupping her face, I pull myself up to rest my forehead against hers. "Promise me, little demon."

"Promise what?" she sniffles.

"That you won't ever leave me again," I rasp, deep and low.

She's quiet for a moment before soft lips brush over mine, and I groan. Pressing harder into the kiss, desperate to feel her. But she pulls away, breaking the connection too soon.

"I can't promise that." The muscles in my jaw jump, but she sweeps the tips of her fingers over them to smooth them out. "Because if your life was on the line, I won't hesitate to save you. Ever."

Inhaling deeply, I blow out a harsh breath. "Little demon," I growl low from in my chest, letting my lips trail over the shell of her ear. "Always finding a way to push back, making the beast in me want to punish you." I nip at her earlobe before trailing down her neck.

A sharp sting spreads through my scalp as she grabs at my hair to pull my head back, her nose touching mine and our mouths only a hair's breadth away. "This goes both ways. The way I am yours, is the same as how *you* are *mine*." Her teeth scrape over my bottom lip, pulling. "So, get it through that handsome head of yours that your life will always be worth saving."

A shudder tracks down my spine, my heart pounding harder in my chest. Her words do something to my soul, seeming to heal a piece of me that I didn't know was bleeding. I've always felt like I had to step up and protect everyone who needed it when my father passed. But it was always a one-sided task.

"Say that again," I choke out, closing the distance and taking her lips with mine.

She whimpers before breaking away to catch her breath. "You are mine," she says possessively, and *fuck* does that do things to me. She pulls me back down to her, opening for our teeth to clash and tongues to battle with each other. A frenzy of love, lust, and our souls desperately needing the connection.

"You." She kisses me again. "Are." Another searing press of her lips. "Worth." She bites my lip and sucks. "Saving." And then she moans, arching beneath me as I lean over her. Her arousal causing my mind to blank on nothing but her and her needs.

My hands gently trail down her sides, my thumbs brushing just beneath the swells of her breasts. I just got her back, needing to be gentle, but she seems to think otherwise because she grabs my hand, forcing it up to her breast. Wrapping her palm over the top of my hand, she squeezes hard. Silently telling me what she needs. So, I roughly grab her breast, earning the gift of a moan to tear from her throat.

Fuck.

My control is snapping. The beast in me breaking through the surface of my resolve. I need her. I need to feel her squirming and writhing underneath me. To feel her body alive and screaming my name. My cock is painfully hard, begging to sink deep into her soaking core and how she sucks me in, squeezing. The image has my balls tightening as I kiss her deeply. Tasting her, stealing every whimper that tries to escape. I swallow them all, needing her like a male starving and she is the only way to cure this hunger.

Pinching her nipple, she arches her back and I drop my mouth to suck the rosy bud through her shirt. A shiver of goosebumps raises along her skin as she grabs hold of my hair at the root. Pulling tightly while pressing me harder into her chest.

This need is uncontrollable. Both of us are consumed by the bond flaring back to life. Possessive of the other. Desperate to connect in every way possible.

Right when I go to rip her clothes off and lose myself in her, scuffing sounds behind the door, followed by a loud knock.

Turning, I block Emma's view from the door, shielding her body as the handle turns. My shoulders sag with a deep exhale when Fynn's blonde hair comes into view, Cora following behind him. The rest of my body is still tense, with a buzzing suddenly filling my mind. Shadows whip out around me and Emma in a chaotic storm, making both of them freeze and stare at me with furrowed brows.

"Draven?" Cora's eyes squint through the tendrils of shadow, while trying to peer behind me. She must find a breathing Emma because her eyes widen as her mouth falls open. She goes to sprint to Emma's side, uncaring of the beast tracking her movements before her, but Fynn blocks her with a stretch of his arm.

"Hold on, love," he says softly next to her ear. His eyes are on mine, searching as I protectively stand in front of my mate.

I don't know what's happening. I can't think straight. The only focus is to protect my mate. My beast surges in its wild possessiveness with a small snarl. She was dead, but the stars have deemed us worthy for a second chance. I just got her back, and nothing can harm her again.

Fynn takes a small step forward, my eyes hard and unyielding as a low growl unintentionally vibrates from deep in my chest. With raised palms, Fynn takes another step closer. "Drav, you know she's safe with us."

Cora hesitantly watches me as she speaks to Fynn, "What's going on?"

My chest coils tighter, the beast in me stealing my grip on reality and rearing its feral head.

Fynn refuses to take his eyes off mine as he responds. "The sealing of their mate bond is still fresh. Many who complete the bond spend months at their mate's side—consumed by love and lust—never losing sight of the other. But they didn't." Fynn wearily attempts to look at Emma before I block his line of sight, teeth grinding together with a heaving chest.

"And then, she died, gutting him on the inside. Only to somehow come back to life." The V between his brows creases deeper.

"What does that mean, then?" Cora asks.

"It seems the primal side of Draven, his beast, is reacting on natural instincts. To protect his mate because everyone is a threat. Only it's worse now that he has felt the loss of her."

Blood boils beneath the surface of my skin as Fynn inches towards me. Red blurs my vision with a haze of warning. Even though I try to clear it. But I can't lose her. She's *my* fucking mate.

"Draven," a soft whisper of a voice distantly catches behind me over the pressure rushing in my skull. But my attention snaps back to Fynn when he speaks.

"If we rush to her, he will try to kill us no matter who we are to him. He can't think straight at the moment, which is why we need to move slow and show him we're friends. Going to him first, not her."

Another step. Hands reach. My fists clench, nostrils flaring.

The muscles along my back bunch until his hand rests gently on my shoulder, his head bowed forward. Showing submission to my beast. "Come back, Drav. Clear the haze, it's just us."

"Draven, please. I'm safe with them and by your side." That sweet voice again, twisting my neck to peer down at Emma, my little demon, who is sitting up with worry in her eyes. Her hand gently rests on my forearm, and her touch takes away the red haze blanketing my mind.

Everything still vibrates inside of me, but no longer threatening to snap. Lifting my head again, I find familiar hazel eyes connect with mine, and my lungs slowly deflate. Fynn. The longest friend I've ever had, who is like a brother to me. The one who has been with me at my worst, and I, him.

He smiles. "There you are." Raising to full height, he places his free hand on my other shoulder, squeezing. "Lost ya there for a sec."

I grunt. "You're going to hold this over my head." The fog clears away and my shadows dissolve, even though my hand still twitches to take Emma somewhere that is away from everyone.

A bolt of laughter spills from him as he winks. "Even when we're both dead. Because for a minute there, you looked like you wanted to snap my neck."

"I still do, you insufferable bastard," I mumble.

Patting my shoulder, he holds his hand out for Cora. "May we see her?"

Stepping aside, but not far, I let them go to Emma. Cora doesn't rush. She slowly approaches, sits on the edge of the mattress with a watery sheen in her blue eyes, and grabs Emma's hand.

"Hey Cor," Emma says, gripping Cora's hand tightly back.

Ugly sobbing, she throws herself over Emma, hugging her as her back shakes with every cry. "I couldn't save you. You died, Em. I tried and tried, but my power failed me."

Emma just holds her, tears springing to her eyes as she listens while Cora struggles to speak through broken sobs. "K—Kye died, and I couldn't save him, and then you…"

Emma's hand pauses, the soft rubbing on Cora's back. "Kye is happy, Cor."

Her head jerks up at that, roughly wiping the tears away with quick swipes of the back of her hand. "What? How do you—"

"I saw him."

Shock ripples through me as I stare at my mate. We all do. Only silence fills the room as we hold our breath.

"There is much I have to tell you." Emma's eyes find mine then, and what I see there has my heart tripling its pace.

Suddenly, light pulses from Cora's hands, spreading into Emma's body. Thankful is all I feel that she has a friend who will walk alongside the demons wanting to hunt her. And thankful she is healing her body back to full health because I have a gut feeling a darker storm is coming for us.

CHAPTER FORTY-TWO

Emma

*C*ora's power has cleared the exhaustion that was burrowing in my bones. And I'm thankful for her, all of them. Before I can explain what happened, they go to bring me food while I clean up. My clothes from the night I...*died*...have been washed, and the night I was brought back, Draven cleaned me and placed me in one of his oversized shirts.

But I want to freshen up now that Cora helped give me some energy back. The hot water immediately soothes any leftover aches in my muscles as I scrub myself raw, then dry off and toss on my all-black attire. It has straps wrapped around my body with placeholders for various weapons, the pants fitting snugly over my hips.

I can't help the tug of my lips knowing Draven is right outside the door. An overprotective brute of a mate, but the thought warms me on the inside. Having him stand outside while I bathed was a task in itself because when I walked in here, he was stalking right behind me, hot on my heels. It's not that I didn't want him in here, but more so that I didn't trust myself. My traitorous body would have jumped on him, wanting to ease the ache that still lingers, pulsing in my clit.

I couldn't understand it when I woke, but a deep, soul-clenching hunger for him overcame me, to the point of pain if I didn't have him. It still lingers, but the others are waiting, and even though they would understand, what needs to be discussed is too important. We all need to be ready for the repercussions that may follow.

When I finish getting ready, I open the door connected to Draven's room, but my feet freeze when I'm met with his deliciously muscled back blocking my path. Draven's large frame leans on the doorframe like an unmovable boulder.

Biting my lip, I trail a single finger down his spine, watching his muscles tense where I make contact. A shot of arousal hits me hard down the bond. A faint whimper slips free unbiddenly, causing him to spin around, grabbing my neck and roughly guiding me back into the bathroom. The door slams as he kicks it shut, and then suddenly, strong hands grip beneath my thighs, hoisting me up until I'm set on the counter.

Before I can speak a word, his mouth is on mine, hot and heady. Taking what he wants, what he *needs*. I don't protest, opening willingly because this need heating under my skin is making me go crazy with lust. He doesn't just kiss me though. He's savage. Feral in needing to taste me.

I kiss him back with just as much fervor. He rips his mouth off mine with a low groan, my heavy eyes fluttering open, watching his flash between blue and silver, his pupil abruptly changing from a slit to its normal orb.

He's fighting himself. Restraining from the desire that is so thick we could choke on it. Swiping the pad of his thumb over my bottom lip, he dips down to press a soft kiss on the curve of my neck before inhaling deeply. As if he's breathing me into him, needing my scent to sate some of the lust that's pulsing in the air. To soothe his beast.

"*Mine*," he grinds out before flattening his tongue, trailing a wet path up my neck to the underside of my jaw.

I can't help the moan that rips from my chest, wanting more as heat pools in my core. I try to press myself to the hard ridge of his length that's bulging in his pants, greedy to stop this ache. I need friction, badly.

Without hesitating, I grind my hips forward, closing the space and rubbing against the seam of his pants. The delicious, hard feel of him causes my head to fall back.

He hisses. "Little demon, you need to eat first." A harsh exhale feathers my neck. "Plus, the others are waiting."

Before I know what's happening, I'm upside down, staring at the most toned ass I've ever seen. "I'm not hungry for food," I mumble.

Tossed over his shoulder, Draven almost rips the bathroom door off its hinges as he storms back into his bedroom, then drops me on his bed. He's the one who shoved me back in the bathroom with him, igniting every nerve ending in my body until I'm soaked, only to stop so quickly.

And yet, he is the one who seems frustrated with annoyance that he can't take me hard and deep, crossing his arms with a huff. He owes me for this—unleashing an ache that has yet to be sated, forcing me to squeeze my thighs together.

I right myself on the bed, quickly swiping my hair out of my face to find three sets of eyes on me. Fynn chuckles, kicking his feet up at the corner of the mattress before pulling Cora into his lap in the chair he's sitting in. And Draven's eyes darken, looking as if he's threatening to take me over his knee right here and now no matter the audience.

Cora's cheeks rise in color with a knowing smirk, nodding towards the food beside me. "We brought food for you."

Trays of food are scattered on the mattress, and the sight makes my stomach rumble loudly, causing Cora to bite her lips to stop from laughing. I narrow my eyes on her, but the laugh I was holding back slips free, and she joins in.

"Hurry and get some food in you before your stomach tries to eat itself," Fynn pipes up, and I do exactly that. Tearing into the steaming rolls and roasted chicken that bursts with flavor on my tongue.

They make small talk, but every glance I take towards Cora, I can see a heaviness shadowing beneath her eyes. Her blue irises that are always so bright and full of joy are now dim, and it makes me swallow the rest of the food down quickly so I can hopefully ease some of the weight on her heart.

Fynn is saying something about how he thinks some sort of dessert is being made in the kitchens because the aroma was so sweet it made him drool. I perk up at the mention of dessert, but when there is a pause in conversation, I use that as my cue. "I was in the afterlife."

All of their eyes widen, and the air shifts in the room, but they remain silent. No questions are asked because they want to hear what I have to say first. "When I was there, it was Kye who found me. He looked so at peace with a smile that I've never seen him wear before."

Sniffling comes from Cora, but she waves her hand in the air for me to continue.

I hold her eyes as I say this next part. "He found his mate." A gasp is all she gives me as I go on. "Her name is Elira, and she's been there, waiting for him."

A small, trembling smile lifts my lips. "It's not a goodbye because, one day, we will see him again, but he doesn't want us to grieve for him. He's truly happy even though he misses us." My smile is stronger now, remembering the sight of them together and the pure love that was shining in their eyes.

"How did you come back?" Draven cuts in, his icy blues probing mine.

"I never truly died. Not entirely." I inhale long and deep. "I was trapped, in-between life and death, along with hundreds of others." My brows knit together, wondering how long the rest have been stuck in limbo, never being able to be free in either world. But my heart constricts from Draven finally having people he can call his own. He won't be alone in who he is anymore, his beast can fly with the rest of the clan.

"Others?" Fynn asks with raised brows.

"Wyverns," I say softly, looking only at Draven. His body tenses and eyes go wide. A slight shake to his head gives away that he has a hard time believing the truth of my words. "And not just any wyvern shifters…" I pause, swallowing roughly as I admit the reason Whiro wants Draven. "They were all the chosen ones since the beginning of time."

Draven's muscles twitch in his jaw. Abruptly pushing himself up to stand, he paces with his hands in his hair.

But I don't stop, knowing he needs me to keep going. "You told me that Whiro's power slipped while creating the Fae, and that the outcome led to dragon shifters, but they are truly wyverns. You said that every generation a chosen was born, bearing the power of shadows. Honing the power of the God himself, just like you." My hands are shaking, disgusted by my true father, and how he's even more sinister than the man I believed was my father before him.

Cora and Fynn sit quietly. Both tense but hanging onto every single word as I go on. "He wants his power back, to store it or use it. So, he created the Sea of Souls to trap each chosen after he hunted them down. Keeping them from moving on in the afterlife, but also to stop them from living in *this* life. Containing their power for eternity." My face scrunches as I sneer in disgust thinking of how many lives he has stolen from this world.

"But…the wall that kept their souls from returning to their bodies was shrouded with darkness. The farthest point of where Whiro's power could extend before it touched the afterlife." I twist my fingers together, remembering the pain melting me from within to break through Whiro's shield. "Only light can cut through the dark."

A gasp comes from Cora as her eyes meet mine. "So, that's how," she says on a breath. "Only you hold the power of light."

Draven comes to sit down beside me, silently pulling me into him, and I let him, finding comfort in his warmth.

"And my mother," I add on. "I wouldn't have been able to survive it if she didn't save a kernel of her power to help boost mine." One single tear slips from the corner of my eye as my chest tightens from losing her once again. But this time, I at least got to tell her how much I love her. I at least got to say goodbye.

"So, you almost died on me…*twice*," Draven rasps out, holding me tighter into his chest with his finger stroking my hair.

"It was the only way back to you. The only way for them to finally be free. For you to have *your* people back and not feel so alone."

"And I'm so fucking grateful, little demon. But let's get one thing straight." He pulls my head back by my hair, forcing my gaze to lock on his. "As long as you are with me, I will never be alone. You are all I need."

A throat clearing makes us snap our heads to find Fynn staring with an expectant look, both eyebrows raised. "I'm hurt. I thought I was all you need." He delicately places a hand over his chest with a dramatic gasp. Cora giggles into his shoulder.

"What you are is a thorn in my ass," Draven growls out.

Fynn's lips tip up with a jolt of laughter. "But it's a big thorn, right?" He raises both eyebrows up and down seductively.

Draven mumbles under his breath, "Insufferable bastard."

Once the silence falls back over the room and the laughter tumbling from my lips fades, a weight starts to pull in my chest. Something heavy that burrows deep, like guilt.

Tipping my head back, I wait for Draven to look back down at me. "I'm sorry. It's my fault Whiro was hunting you down." His head tilts to the side with a crease in the center. "He never would have known of you being a chosen if you weren't with me in the forbidden library or needing to save me from his cell. Because only his power could undo those locks. Nothing else."

Draven seems to ponder that for a moment, but then his lips curve upward. "Then it's fate I was there or else who knows what he would have done to you and your mother if I couldn't free you." The soft plush of his lips press against my forehead. "You seem to forget that I will do anything to keep you safe. Fuck the consequences. You are all that matters to me."

"He's right," Fynn chips in with a bright smile. "You could have even tried to bind Drav up to a chair before we left for the forbidden library, but he'd still have found a way to be there for you. Even if that meant flying with a chair strapped to his ass." Fynn's chest shakes. Draven gives him a sharp look, which causes Fynn to burst into a fit of laughter, with Cora following suit.

I bite my bottom lip back as a silent laugh rattles through my body at Fynn knowing about that, but the reminder of that night causes my cheeks to heat, knowing they are blooming to a bright pink. Turning my head, I stare at the very spot where I bound him as I took my pleasure, the feel of his shadows filling my—

I shake my head to clear it. This is not the time.

But when I look to Draven, I find his eyes already on me, darkening every passing second with a knowing look. *"It's my turn next, little demon."*

His voice fills my mind, traveling through our bond. *"You are going to look so pretty tied up,"* he smirks.

My mouth parts from the image he's creating in my head, and suddenly, I can't breathe, my pulse quickening.

Before I can think of a reply, the door creaks, ripping me away from my lust-filled haze I was starting to get sucked into. Queen Zoraida waltzes gracefully in with Emil on her heels. It looks like she's floating, the way the hem of her navy dress sweeps the floor.

She passes Fynn with a wink and says, "Time has healed." I watch as his mouth falls open before it's replaced with a smile as he shakes his head.

She reaches Draven, pulling him in for a hug.

"I'm sorry I yelled," he says softly.

"Shh. Nonsense." She pats his head before pulling back to look at him with a wide smile. "I'm your mother; I expected it. You were suffering from immense pain." Her smile softens and then turns, those deep ocean eyes locking onto me. "Welcome home, my dear."

Home.

My eyes begin to well as I stand, needing to feel the warmth of her motherly touch as she opens her arms for me. "I know, dear. I know." Her voice brushes over my hair. I drag in a long, slow breath to try and steady myself. As if everything I just went through hasn't fully hit me until now.

Emil crushes into Draven's chest, holding the Dark Prince tightly to him and it swells something in my heart. To see how much his little brother looks up to him and how Draven helped take care of him when their father passed.

In that moment I remember Irad's final words for them. With soothing strokes, Queen Zoraida drags her fingers through my hair, my heart thumping wildly in my chest at what I need to tell them. "I have a message for all of—"

"We have a visitor," she cuts me off as she turns quickly to face the door. In the span of a full breath, chills lick down my spine and the hair on the back of my neck rises. The door opens and that's when I realize my body was trying to warn me of who was lurking within the castle.

CHAPTER FORTY-THREE

Emma

A guard with broad shoulders and covered in armor steps over the threshold. He claps the heels of his boots together with his arms pinned to his side. "My apologies, but Prince Aiden is here and has requested your presence."

A grunt with a nod is all Draven offers, along with a twitch of his veins in his neck.

As we all take a moment to process why Aiden might show up, Queen Zoraida grasps my elbow and leans towards me. Her whispered words skate over my ear: "Sometimes, pretty hearts filled with lies need to be crushed."

Confusion etches my features as I stare at her with a pinched face. "What does that mean?"

A humming grows in my skull as I wonder if she knows of the guilt I carry from the hearts I have already crushed. How the pulse of their life still lingers on my hands… But the gentle tone of her voice makes it sound as if she's reassuring me, letting me know that even fate believes death is deserving to some who have run out of chances.

"That you do not need to bear the weight of one's life when it's the right thing to do." And with that, she kisses my cheek before doing the same with Draven. She then takes Emil's hand to escort themselves out of the room. "Sorry to cut our visit short, but we will take our leave so you can attend to your…other matters."

Right before she goes to leave, she pauses in the doorway, turning her head to look back at us from over her shoulder. "Tell the new Prince Aiden to send a letter of some sort first to let us know of his visit before showing up on our doorstep. Remind him it's the princely thing to do."

When the door clicks shut behind her, the air in the room becomes eerily cold. It has the hair on the back of my neck rising.

Draven clears his throat, placing his hand on my lower back. "Let's go see why the bastard is here."

He applies a little pressure on my back as he goes to take a step but stops when I don't budge, my feet rooted in place.

"Should I stay back? We don't know the reason behind his visit." I release an uneven breath.

Those striking blue eyes probe directly into mine. He turns his body to face me, covering me in the shadow of his tall frame. "I am done hiding us." His large palm that bears our mark cups my cheek. "And I can't bear to have you out of my sight right now," he rasps, a vulnerable catch in his throat.

His eyes stay steady on mine with such raw emotions swimming in them. An icy sliver of fear inches down the bond, as if the thought of being separated from me for only a moment will haunt him.

"Okay," I whisper, tucking my hand into his. "Lead the way."

He never lets go, keeping our fingers intertwined as we make our way to the main doors with Fynn and Cora following suit. Each step I take, I am more thankful for Cora healing the exhaustion from my body or else this trek would have my lungs wheezing and my legs threatening to buckle.

The moment we step off the final stair, the sight of Aiden standing inside near the doors elicits a warning growl from Draven. His grip tightens on my hand, keeping his body in front of me like a shield. But those familiar green eyes have already found mine.

Before Aiden can utter a word, Fynn steps beside Draven, crossing his arms over his chest and speaks. "The Queen wanted us to relay the message to send a letter before visiting. It's the princely thing to do."

Aiden sputters before collecting himself, patting the nonexistent wrinkles out of the lapels of his tunic. "Do you know who I am?"

Cora lazily drags her eyes down to his feet and back up. "Someone who's unwelcome."

Draven jerks his head to the two guards standing on each side of Aiden. "You may go."

They dip at the waist before exiting the main entryway, leaving Aiden standing there with all of us watching him closely. I track every twitch of his muscles.

"Why are you here?" Draven's own muscles are tense beneath his shirt. His hands are strained and his voice terrifyingly low.

Aiden drags a hand through his hair, softening the hardness that was sharpening his face. "I came to see with my own eyes if it was true." He leans to peer around Draven, green eyes locking on me. "I had to know. My father, as you know, is a Seer. He *saw* you die, and Whiro confirmed it a day ago when my father wished to know the truth."

Aiden goes to instinctively take a step towards me, but Draven mirrors him, causing Aiden to retreat.

Blowing out a deep sigh, Aiden lets his arms limply fall to his sides. "I came to the one place I knew I would get an answer, much to my disgust." His eyes dart to Draven on the last word, before flitting back to mine. "But…you're alive," he whispers in disbelief.

Wait. Aiden's words rushing replay in my mind, making it a little harder to breathe.

Shooting my hand out, I latch onto Draven's arm, making him look down at me with a frown. "I was only gone an hour, or so it seemed. How long was I…" Do I say dead? Asleep? I don't even know, but I don't have to because Draven understands.

"Almost a full week," he says, softly, and sends a comforting warmth down the bond.

I still can't hide the shock splaying over my face, or how it suddenly hurts to breathe as my lungs constrict. Grabbing my stomach, I hunch over to help draw in more air, breathing through my nose and out my mouth.

"Time moves differently there," I whisper. "I never knew because I couldn't keep track of time when I was there." My next words I go to speak through the bond, *"I'm sorry—"*

"Don't," Draven rushes out. *"No more apologizing, little demon. All that matters is that you are here now."*

All I can do is nod and clutch his arm a little tighter, needing to feel his strength. But then, a throat clears, and my focus is back on our visitor.

"I traveled all this way." Aiden's hands curl and uncurl. "I can't believe you are alive and well. That everything I've done wasn't for nothing." A smile graces his face, but my eyes narrow, not understanding what he means.

Ignoring Draven's growling protest, I move to stand beside him. "Why does it matter to you?" My heart thunders in a maddening pace. "Trying to see if you can claim your prize for the deal you struck with Whiro?" Rage boils my blood as I once again find betrayal flashing in his eyes, like a bad habit he refuses to learn from.

His eyes widen a fraction before he pulls his face back to neutral. "Please," his voice breaks. "Let me explain." I stand there, waiting with my arms crossed over my chest, and he sighs. "Can we talk privately outside and out of…*here?*" His arms gesture to the door behind him as his eyes scan the room with disgust. As if being in Draven's castle is revolting for him.

"I think you're in no place to ask anything from her unless it's mercy for a slow death," Fynn snipes.

The knot in Aiden's jaw ticks until he closes his eyes, clenching his jaw. When he opens them again, you would never have guessed Fynn's words irritated him. "Just one last time, Emma. Please. I want to apologize, and then I promise to let you go."

"She's not leaving my side," Draven's voice holds no warning, just a promising threat.

Aiden's eyes look like they flicker with something dark, and I would have missed it if I wasn't watching his every move. "Then join us, if you must." Dragging his gaze back to me, he says, "I just hope you'll allow me one last conversation before I let you be."

There's an odd desperation clinging to his eyes as he waits for me. If he thinks he's walking out of here with his hair perfectly intact and not a single mark of revenge, then he's delusional. I never claimed to be the one who always forgives, because there are some things that are unforgivable. And there are times when it feels good to become the fear in another's eyes.

My mind is stuck on how many ways I can cause Aiden as much grief as he has caused me. To make him know the torment of my heart being shredded apart, and to understand that his selfish actions only lead to the pain of others.

"One last conversation," I find myself saying, making Aiden's eyes widen with a single drop of hope.

"Thank you," Aiden responds.

I only have to look at my mate to know that he understands. That I mean one last conversation in a literal sense because I need Aiden's betrayal to be paid with flesh and bone. Even fate deems it okay if what Queen Zoraida said pertained to Aiden. With a smirk, I dip my head for Draven to voice what I heard him mumble in his mind.

"You misunderstand," Draven chuffs. "One last conversation here, in this fucking room, with *all* of us. I don't trust you."

Aiden audibly gulps before you can practically hear his teeth grind to dust. "*Fine*," he forces out. "Is that all?"

"For now," is all Draven responds with, as a feather of amusement tickles me through the bond.

A shiver works its way through my body as I peer out the windows arched beside the double doors, looking at the expanse of the forest. It all seems so tranquil, how the grey fog rests itself between the branches without a worry in the world, sedately clinging to the towering pines. Yet something prickles the back of my neck, setting me on edge.

Chewing on my cheek, a sense of urgency twists my stomach, making my fingers twitch with the need to act even though nothing is amiss. But the one thing I have a gut feeling about is Whiro. If my soul has made it back to my body, then so have the others', alerting him to the lack of power in the Sea of Souls.

A throat clearing pulls me out of my daze, only to find Aiden's gaze zeroed in on me. Wiping my hands down the front of my tunic in hopes of getting rid of any lingering nerves, I let out a deep sigh as I wait and watch him carefully.

"I went about it all wrong, and I'm sorry," Aiden rushes out. "I have no excuse for what I have done. I just wanted you to want me back because all I have ever dreamed of was for us to finally be together." His chin drops to his chest as he breathes deeply.

A snort snaps my neck to the side, the noise quickly covered by coughing as Fynn brings his arm up to his mouth. Cora gently pats his back with her head turned the opposite way. A light bubble of amusement once again seeps through the bond. I have to inhale fully, and then hold my breath to fight off the laugh threatening to slip because of them.

Aiden's feet shift. His nostrils flare slightly with a quick darting glare towards Fynn before it all wipes away, as if nothing had bothered him.

When those familiar eyes connect back with mine, he inches closer. "I know now that dream will never come true." He quickly glances at Draven standing tall and menacing beside me. If it were possible, I have a feeling smoke would be pluming out of his nose.

Aiden's hand disappears, digging into his pocket. "I brought you something."

Draven shifts closer, but I already know what Aiden brought. It's what he always brings me. White shells. As if it will remind my heart of a time when we were close, and when he used to offer me some semblance of comfort.

The beautiful shell looks out of place in the hands of someone so warped that not even finery threaded with gold can hide his true nature. No care what is right and wrong. He hides his own demons behind his polished mask, but I've seen them, and they aren't pretty. They are ugly and vicious with sharp teeth, never walking beside Aiden but instead dragging him with them. It's the same reason why the food in my stomach sours as I stare at the shell being held out to me. A pretty distraction.

"A peace offering," Aiden says, rolling the shell over in his hand as he continues to hold it out to me. "To have a clean slate and start over."

I eye him warily, wanting to hear the nonsense he's conjured for everything he has done. But the moment my eyes laid upon him, I had already planned on not letting him leave.

Shaking my head, I drag my gaze away from the shell and back up to Aiden. "Our time has already ended, burning to ash only to be lost in the wind." My brows furrow as I steel my spine. "My new beginning is not with you." I tilt my head to peer up at Draven, curling my pinky around his at our sides. "It's with my mate."

Pride swells down the bond, but a harsh gasp has me finding Aiden stumbling back a step. His eyes are wide and locked on my hand. My *left* hand.

"No…" Aiden says on a strained breath, his whole body shaking as something in him seems to snap. His cool exterior now contorts into something menacing. "It doesn't matter. You are *mine*. He said you would be."

Draven growls so deep it vibrates in my bones.

That only irritates Aiden further as he throws the shell to the ground, making it shatter between us. "You lied to me!" His eyes are wild as his chest races. "I heard you that night, with *him* in your room before everything was silenced. The night you claimed exhaustion. You said you were done with him." His emerald glare pierces Draven before sliding back to me.

I don't let any shock display on my face. I had an inkling before, when we had lunch on the shore, because the things he said… Whiro already confirmed this knowledge, but it seems Aiden needs to get it off his chest.

"This is all your fault," he seethes, specks of spit spraying from the harshness of his words. "And everything I've done and what's to come is because of you."

"Seems like you need to stop pointing blame where it doesn't belong and learn when to stop talking," Fynn chides, squaring his shoulders as he stands.

Draven steps in front of me. His whole body is rigid, and the air around him seems to grow darker, heavier. "You dare to speak to my mate that way?" His tone is calm. Too calm. It's calculating and promises punishment.

Aiden senses the danger drifting from Draven. In the next breath, his body blurs and then vanishes, only to appear behind me. He wraps his arm around my neck, while pressing a gilded dagger to the dip of my throat under my jaw. It cuts just past the first layer of skin as warmth trickles down the curve of my neck. The sting is a reprieve almost. It cements the truth I've always known about Aiden, though I kept letting him spew charming lies.

Draven's roar rips from him, but he was already on the move. Spinning around to catch Aiden mid-phasing, he holds his own sword out to rest the blade on the side of Aiden's jugular.

I can feel Aiden's smile stretch over his face as he presses his cheek roughly against mine. "When will you learn, Emma? I will never let you go," his harsh whisper slithers over my ear, and bile rises up my throat.

But Queen Zoraida's words come tumbling forward in my mind, and understanding sinks in. "Sometimes, pretty hearts filled with lies need to be crushed," I whisper, making Aiden tighten his hold, but I can feel his muscles trembling against my body.

"What?" Aiden sneers, but I don't respond.

Fynn and Cora are tense, flanking Draven on both sides a foot behind him as my eyes stay trained on crystal blues that keep flashing to silver. My power stirs inside me, waking to expose the fake prince that lies through his teeth, the one who wants everyone to believe his heart is made of gold.

My eyes slide to Draven's sword. The sharpened steel that always brought me comfort. Its silver can slice through every lie. My tongue rolls in my mouth, ready for a fight.

"One move and she is gone for good," Aiden says, and I know Draven presses the blade harder into his skin when Aiden hisses. But my mate won't go further because he and I don't need shiny weapons to kill. We only need the shadows that bind us.

Fear never comes, knowing I can crush Aiden's heart without him ever seeing it coming. So, I ask, "Why?" Curious to know a true villain's intent before he dies.

A dark laugh from his chest vibrates against my back. "Because, if I can't have you, then nobody else can. You must know, I really don't wish to kill you. I'd rather take you home and lock you away so we can have a life together." Knots twist in my stomach at how much he sounds like his father and King Oren. "But that's a broken dream now. I've done my job, and my prize is your pretty little head. Though, it's much more rewarding since you are alive and well."

"What job?" I grind out harshly, gnashing my teeth tighter until it hurts as I pretend to strain against his hold.

"What did you do?" Draven seethes.

A devious chuckle grates in my ear, sending chills over my skin. "I thought Emma was dead. So, I was only a distraction for him to end you. Revenge for not staying away from her. But she's not dead like I thought. So, the deal I struck with Whiro can still hold true. You in exchange for her." A vile chuckle grates up Aiden's throat. "I'm simply the lure to hook the bait."

Shadows lash out from Draven like a raging storm. The room grows dark, and the air is weighted with power. He knocks Aiden's dagger to the ground with one strong tendril of shadows before grabbing hold of his neck. I take a deep breath when Aiden's dagger clatters to the floor, and watch his feet now dangle above the ground as Draven holds him in the air.

"I've been wanting to do this for a long time." Draven's low voice holds a dangerous threat, one that I know he will fulfill. Even though his eyes stay glued to Aiden, he speaks through the bond, "*May I?*"

I don't hide the smile that overcomes me. "*Yes, but leave the final blow to me.*"

"*Was already planning on it, little demon.*"

A huff comes from him before he winds his hand back, tightening his fist and slamming it straight into Aiden's nose. A crack splinters the air, followed by a yell as Aiden's face gets thrown back.

His head limply falls forward, trying to right himself in Draven's hold. His nose is bent unnaturally, blood dripping down from it, and his eyes are unfocused. Draven drops Aiden's body like a sack of potatoes, towering over him, and waits.

"Get up," Draven orders, roughly.

Aiden sneers as he spits blood on the ground, with his lip split. He pushes himself up, stumbling sideways as he raises his fists in front of his face. "That all you got?"

Draven laughs, low and deep. He doesn't bother responding as he stands with his arms crossed over his chest, showing how unthreatened he is.

That pisses Aiden off more because he throws his whole body at Draven. But Draven is ready, moving faster than Aiden as he spins around him and plants his boot in Aiden's back to knock him forward.

Grunts thunder from him as Aiden tries again with all his strength, his feet trying to kick Draven to the floor. Then, he lunges toward Draven with his shoulder to try and shove him with his body weight. Every attempt Aiden makes to land a blow gets blocked. His movements are uncoordinated with no thought behind them; he's just swinging blindly.

Draven could pulverize him, but he's only landing single blows to make a point: that Aiden will always be beneath him. When Aiden screams with another futile punch, Draven ducks and swings his foot out, causing Aiden to fall to the floor.

Draven's breathing calms. The red haze hiding behind his movements fades away as he towers over Aiden, who still has the nerve to bare his teeth. Teeth that are now coated in crimson.

A metallic scent fills the air, but something else has my nose scrunching up in disgust. It's foul and hangs in the space around us with no reprieve. Only then do I notice the dark stain that has spread on Aiden's pants, right in the center. He pissed himself.

His arms tremble as he struggles to push himself off the floor, and his head is swaying.

"You drew blood from her. Dared to fucking touch her." Draven's voice is eerily quiet. "It's taking all of my control to not break every single bone in your body. To not kill you myself." The truth of his words cut sharper than his blade. "You are like a plague, infecting anyone in your path without knowing who is already suffering."

A whistle expels from Aiden's lips when he wheezes in air. Opening his mouth to speak, no words come out as he starts coughing.

I step forward, gently placing a hand on Draven's chest to offer some comfort, and nod to Fynn and Cora who still stand behind him with stern expressions. Fynn grasps Draven's shoulder to help pull his anger back before it ignites again. I stare down at the male before my feet, who is wincing in pain.

"You are clueless. Seeking vengeance on those who are not the enemy, all for selfish acts. Do you even care how I died or why?!" My voice raises with all of the emotions charging me at once. "You chose your side, and it was the wrong one. Whiro doesn't give a damn about you or what you want. He only seeks power for himself." My hands ball up at my sides, and the tips of my nails bite into my palms from the force. "You mean nothing to him. Nobody does."

Grunting through his teeth, Aiden sits partially up, staying slightly hunched. "Of course, I did! That's why I sailed here as fast as I could!" His voice is raspy and strained as he takes another wheezing breath in. "You died because of this bastard!"

He jerks his head to Draven before sliding his gaze back to me. I can feel a renewed anger rolling in waves through the bond. It's so strong that I fear I will choke on it and Draven will snap from Aiden placing blame for my so-called death on him when he already feels so guilty.

Aiden's head drops, fingers curling into the hard ground beneath him. "Whiro said he would help me, because the two of us have the same goal. To rid the world of one single soul."

The blood in my veins chills, growing colder by the minute, while my darkness rises to the surface. My teeth grind together, hard exhales huffing out of my nose.

Crouching down, I grip Aiden's chin roughly between my fingers and force him to stare into my eyes as I let them darken, becoming a little fucking demon.

"Except, Whiro wants to rid the world of every soul," I say with a tone that holds no emotion.

Aiden's face blanches, looking strange with the contrast against the blood still coating his skin. "W–what?"

"That's right. You didn't care to know the bigger picture. But I suppose you might be right about something…" I trail off.

He holds his breath, waiting.

I grip his chin harder, jerking his face closer. "To rid the world of one single soul will be beneficial."

The harsh inhale gets caught in his throat as my shadows trickle out, dancing around me. Ripping his chin from my grasp, he falls back on his elbows. A blubbering mess trying to speak.

He coughs, and the blood in his throat makes it sound wet. "You won't kill me," he says when he finds his voice. He's trying to sound confident, but I can hear the faint tremor behind each syllable. "It will eat away at you if you do."

Cocking my head to the side, I watch him carefully. Taking note of every twitch his body makes, the way his eyes gloss over, and the hitch in his chest. It's his *fear* of me at this moment.

Shaking my head, I sigh. "I hold a lot of guilt for many of those who have died by my hands, but you won't be one of them."

His jaw falls open, and before a plea or a protest to give him another chance can spill past his lips, I let my power whip out. One arrow-pointed shadow pierces into this chest, constricting around his heart and squeezing. The swell of the beating organ before it bursts is the same as the others. Except, this one was deserving and one that won't keep me up all hours of the night.

Aiden's eyes remain open, frozen in shock as his body falls limply to the side, internally bleeding in his chest. I draw my shadows back while keeping my eyes on his lifeless body, waiting for the grief of a friend's loss to sneak up on me. But he stopped being a friend to me a long time ago, even when I didn't want to admit it.

Strong hands grip my shoulders, spinning me to tuck me in his chest. Just the smell of his cedar and maple scent has my darkness receding faster. My eyes fall shut, soaking into his haven and breathing in his strength.

At that moment, the entire earth beneath our feet rattles.

The castle walls tremble and the ground quakes as if the world is being ripped in half.

The snapping of my neck sets my gaze towards the doors rattling with force. To the windows offering sight to the way the trees bend, almost snapping. The once-calm fog now swirls in chaos. A thunder of power surges in the air, silencing the outside world. It's heavy and suffocating. And the darkening sky steals the sun's final descent—an omen of what's to come.

I know this power just as well as my own.

Whiro is here.

CHAPTER FORTY-FOUR

Emma

*A*ll four of us race to the heavy double doors, opening them and peering out into the trembling forest. The harsh pounding of footsteps rages across the ground as soldiers race around the perimeter of the castle, readying their weapons.

"Fuck," Fynn breathes out, watching a wisp of shadow spiral in the sky, tunneling down towards the ground.

The silence is heavy as we all hold our breaths, watching the top of the funnel kiss the soil. The moment it hits, darkness explodes in a wave, rolling with a strength that sends the waiting soldiers hurtling backward. In the blink of an eye, Whiro steps through a portal of his shadows, bringing a deadly chill to hang in the air.

We rush back in and slam the door. My thunderous heart steals my breath as I move to peer out the window. Draven shadows us all from prying eyes as we watch from a distance.

My father's hands raise in the air, wide and taunting as he slowly walks in a circle. "I know you're here, *Emmerelda!*" he bellows maddeningly.

"That you are *alive*." His fists clench and snakes of shadows lash out around him.

"Are you hiding from me, Daughter? Knowing you stole from me by setting free all the souls that are rightfully mine?!" His feet root themselves into the ground, facing the castle. "Come out and face me. Have a little chat with your father."

Draven's solid form tenses beside me, with an all-consuming warmth of protectiveness unfurling in the bond. It makes my heart swell, but I can't hide. This is our last chance to end this once and for all. To save the world from his fury.

My mind races with a million thoughts on what to do to not go down there blind. And right then, one memory becomes clearer than all the rest. Something my mother said: *Light may clear the darkness, and can even restrain it if bright enough, but only his own power will be his undoing."*

An idea sparks along with that fickle thing called hope.

As I twist my head to look at Fynn, Cora, and Draven, my heart thumps with love for them. They have proven that I don't need to fight any battles alone, that we can all sharpen our swords together. And now... we have a greater power on our side. Hundreds of those who wish to see Whiro destroyed.

Stepping closer to the door again, I pull it slight ajar and harden my spine with determination. The frigid kiss of the wind seeps through the crack, wishing me good luck as I breathe it in deeply, burning my lungs from the chill as I do.

"I have a plan." Peering over my shoulder, I smirk. "Are you with me?" I know I don't have to ask. Especially given how both Draven and Fynn huff, and the way Cora rolls her eyes. They all smile while doing so, nonetheless.

"We are with you always, Em," Cora says with a wink, and seeing her next to Fynn, it's so easy to see how perfect they are for each other.

Draven grips Fynn by the nape of his neck, getting his full attention, the shift in the room growing heavier. "Find my mother and brother... please," he strains out. "Put them somewhere safe, and with guards."

Fynn's brows lower as he dips his head in acknowledgment. "I will ensure they are safe before I find you again."

"I will join you," Cora adds. "In case someone gets hurt if there are any surprises."

Draven looks at her then, a grateful smile on his face. "Thank you," he says softly, the emotion he's feeling from that small offering clinging to every word. His mother and brother are everything to him.

Before we part ways, I quickly tell them my plan, hoping that it will work. *Needing* it to work. For one wrong move will determine the fate of the world.

I open the door fully, so Draven and I can walk out to where Whiro waits. The sound of scraping steel is faint in the background as soldiers right themselves back into position after the blast of darkness. The force of Whiro's power humming in the air is suffocating, making it feel as if I have an anchor tied to each of my ankles that's weighing me down.

I can feel Draven's beast surge forward, tearing through him with a primal force as his wings snap out and eyes melt to a molten silver. Fury consumes him as he looks at the threat looming before us, the muscles in his jaw pulling taut. Whiro is standing in a vortex of shadows, clashing against one another as he pins his deadly eyes on me.

"I should have killed you when I first had the chance. For centuries, I've been reclaiming my power, and one worthless girl thinks she can destroy it all," Whiro spits, fists shaking with crazed energy crackling around his fingers. "You have no idea what you have done," he seethes, his eye twitching as the strength of his power causes the wind to pick up speed.

My eyes remain firm and steady on Whiro, never wavering. I dig my heels deeper into the soil as I let my power thrash within my veins. "Oh, but that's the thing, *Father*. I do."

In the blink of an eye, that funnel of power grows. Lashing out to slam into the ground, cracking it with a booming thunder that feels as if it's drumming in my own chest, banging against the cage of my ribs. Draven moves, putting himself between me and Whiro.

A crippling dose of fear penetrates my chest with a brief flash of memories from the night I died. I stare at Draven's back with his wings flared out, muscles bulging and strained. But looking closer, I don't miss the slight tremble to his fingers, and the racing pulse in his neck. He looks tragically beautiful.

"I won't lose you again," his deep voice rasps down the bond.

Before I can respond, Whiro's hands swiftly raise as small pods of shadows scatter the ground, and with them emerge the Corrupted. They stand there motionless as they wait for their command. And when a row of Scavengers materializes in front of Whiro, I get déjà vu.

Which only intensifies when Fynn and Cora portal in nearby, giving Draven a quick nod to let him know they took his mother and Emil to safety. Both of their eyes widen when they take in Whiro's army, yet they withdraw their weapons anyway.

"Oh, Emmerelda, you can't save your friends now." Whiro's chuckle sounds uneven and wrong as it slithers over my skin, leaving a vile sensation clinging to me. "How does it feel to know you are the reason this whole world will be wiped away?"

My molars gnash together so tightly I feel like they might shatter. But I don't give him a response because he knows he's holding my biggest worry, aside from Draven, and threatening to sever it. To be the reason so many innocents will suffer.

"You won't get the chance if I can help it," Draven seethes. His words a barely restrained simmer compared to the fury wrestling to spill over within him.

The wind billows around us, growing more frenzied, and I watch the others drag their gazes to each threat. Their grips tighten on the hilt of their weapons, readying for what we all know will come.

Before Whiro can set his army on us, the sound of a stampede descends, revealing another mass of soldiers charging down the path. This must be the second part of Asiza's army, the ones that watch over the remaining lands outside of the castle.

Whiro doesn't hesitate, unleashing the Corrupted and Scavengers on the warriors closing in. Shrieks, snarls, and yells blend together in the air like a roughened symphony, mingled with steel cutting through bone.

The fight turns to havoc. My pulse races, watching a soldier get shredded limb from limb by a Scavenger. Draven and I share one soul-searching look, causing my insides to flutter, before tossing ourselves into

326

the chaos. The darkness of my power lurks right at the surface, but it's my light that I call upon. Hunting down the Corrupted and filling them with light until the curse is extinguished from their bodies.

A shriek pierces my ear from behind, making me spin on my heel to find a Corrupted sinking its talons into the leg of a soldier. He rears his sword back with both hands, aiming for the Corrupted's chest, and my heart freezes.

"Stop!" I yell, his head snapping to me with wide eyes and a deep V creasing his brows.

The male watches me with pained confusion as I place my palms on the Corrupted's back before it notices, letting light flow from me. Its shoulders fall, the talons receding. And then the female is no longer cursed as her body drops limply.

I gently lay her on the undergrowth, bringing my gaze back up when the male speaks.

"Y–you… She's *cured*," he says in astonishment, like he can't believe his eyes. But I don't blame him. I didn't quite believe what I did when I saved that little girl.

I smile softly with a dip of my head, right as Cora skids to a stop on her knee next to us. She holds her palms over the male's leg, and the wound immediately starts stitching itself back together, faster than a Fae could heal on their own. All that remains is the red stain that saturates the material on his thigh.

Jumping to my feet, I go to hunt down another Corrupted but pause when the soldier speaks again.

"Thank you. I am forever in your debt."

Shaking my head, I smile down at him. "The only thing I wish is for you to stay alive." And with another dip of my head, my feet push off the ground, and I charge into the middle of carnage, needing to put the rest of my strength into fighting Whiro.

Piles of ash dust the ground and the sight twists knots in my stomach, knowing those are lives I could have saved. But I can't save them fast enough—not when the head of the snake poisoning them is still alive. So, I pump my arms harder and strain the muscles in my legs to move faster, relishing in the burn.

But then, my breath catches, a burning sensation slashing along my arm. The soles of my boots quickly lock into place, halting my movements. I scan every inch of my arms, but find nothing. That's when my heart sinks, causing my eyes to snap towards my mate.

He's mid-air, sending tendril after tendril of shadows whipping towards Whiro. The dark gleam in his eyes holds a deadly promise, and for the smallest moment, those maddening silver irises find mine, conveying a plethora of emotions. One sticks out sharply against the rest: Determination.

He swerves around Whiro, dodging the bolts of shadows targeting him as the sky continues to grow darker. I go to race towards them again, but before my feet can launch me forward, the earth shakes beneath the soles of my boots and my knees buckle, slamming into the ground. Pain radiates along my spine, and a splintering ache flares to life in my head.

Draven.

Shoving myself up, I race towards him, my breathing harsh and strained. Immediately, my eyes snag on him lying flat on the ground, with cracks fracturing around him from the force of impact. My heart surges into my throat when I see him roll over with a grunt to pull himself up. His legs shake with a grimace on his face when he straightens his spine. Thin trails of blood cascade down his face from the top of his head, his hair wet and matted in red.

Whiro's hand snaps up, preparing to crush Draven, but I shoot out a stream of light to wipe away the dark orb swirling in his palm. His hand rears back, shaking as if it was burned. But then, those ominous eyes find me, leaving Draven forgotten.

Before I can blink, Whiro disappears and shadows himself to stand right in front of me. Too quick to see, his strong hand grabs hold of my throat, stalling any air from leaving or entering my lungs.

"You will never win against me, just like your mother couldn't."

Something snaps inside my head, cracking so loudly I think I hear it. Because this is not just to save the world or seek payback for myself. This is to avenge my mother.

Light blinds behind my eyelids as it streams up in a single beam in the sky, burrowing a hole through the dark veil of Whiro's shadows. It contrasts against his darkness, like yin and yang, gleaming bright enough to penetrate through his power.

The fingers wrapped around my throat tighten, bruising with pain, and my lungs begin to burn as they seize in protest. Whiro pulls me closer, keeping my feet dangling off the ground as he brings us nose to nose.

"A little light show won't save you," he seethes through his teeth.

Right as the last word falls from his lips, a thunderous roar ruptures from above. And even though dots start to dance around my vision and my head grows light, I don't hold back the smirk gracing my face when Whiro's deadly eyes finally hold a semblance of fear.

Because this is a dangerous game we are playing, and the biggest mistake Whiro could have done is underestimate his opponent.

CHAPTER FORTY-FIVE

Draven

*W*hen my vision comes back into focus, I find Cora beside me, pouring her power into me. I push away the unforgiving pain that remains, throbbing in my head as I stand. I hurry a quick thank you to Cora, who is already on the move, before I search for Whiro.

When my eyes land on him, everything turns fucking red. His hand is wrapped about Emma's throat with her chest hitching in short bursts, struggling to breathe. But she smirks, not caring that she's in the hand of Death.

I whip out a stream of shadows towards him when his head snaps up to the sky, following Emma's light. The distraction lets me hit my mark, forcing his hand to release her. I launch myself with a sharp gust of my wings, tucking them in for speed, and kicking up dirt and leaves as I do.

Before her body can crumple to the ground, I'm there, catching her and pulling her into my chest. With another hard thrust of my wings, I fly us higher, letting us hover above.

Emma greedily draws in air, coughing every time she sucks in too much. It's colder up here, her skin freezing to the touch as a shiver skates over her body. I press her closer, offering her my warmth. Once her pulse steadies and her chest rises and falls in a calm rhythm, she places her hand on my face. Instinctively, I lean into her palm, closing my eyes, the roars of battle drowning out down below. But her raw voice makes me open them, looking deeply into her eyes.

"You don't have to hide anymore."

With furrowed brows, I open my mouth to speak, but then what sounds like a million wings beating against the wind draws my head to look in the same direction as Whiro. My heart thumps almost painfully in my chest when I see a mix of fully shifted wyverns and half shifted like... me. The glow emitting from Emma's light contrasts their sharp features, reflecting off the spikes and talons on those who possess them. It's astonishing. A magical vision of finally returning home.

The backs of my eyes start to burn, clinging onto the sight with every powerful beat of their wings as they soar closer, leaving a dark fog of shadows in their wake.

"Are they..."

Emma finishes what I still can't seem to believe, but what my heart knows is true. "All of the chosen."

So many... And they were all trapped until *she* freed them. Something constricts inside me, zeroing in on their eyes. They glint silver, but underneath, they carry a loaded promise for revenge with the hardness of their gazes. To take back the lives that were stolen from them. But what they all have in common is who is locked in as their target.

My eyes follow to where Whiro stands as his scream thunders through the air, almost splintering the particles in it. His hands thrash around wildly, trying to slam a tornado of shadows at them. It grows in size, whipping through the air. His movements are rushed and unsteady, never tearing his gaze from all the wyverns that sync up.

The half-shifters use their hands to flood out shadows, and the fully shifted open their jaws as wide as they will go, releasing fiery shadows with a collective roar. They all share the same dark power, aiming into the swirling vortex and disintegrating it before it could get close enough to touch them.

The sight gives me hope because just the two of us wielding his power is no match to take him down. It will only put a dent in his armor, but hundreds of us combining our range of shadows could destroy him, could finally rid the world of his curse. Whiro thought to take us chosen one by one until no more existed, an easy task because a single person doesn't stand a chance. But a powerful army…? That would get a different answer.

I know my theory is right when Whiro takes a step back, never straying his eyes from the wyverns racing towards him.

"It's time," Emma says on a breath.

Those two words bring me back to the risk hanging before us, but I trust her with all that I am. Without a thought, I press her closer into me because we need to finish this once and for all. Emma deserves a life without someone trying to take control of her. To fucking have freedom to breathe and end this game of survival she's been tossed into.

The battle still rages below as I narrow my wings, letting us fall, fast and straight like a shooting arrow. The distance between us and Whiro closes quickly, but before we are near, I yell, "Fynn!"

His head briefly snaps up, right when his elbow rears back to connect with a Corrupted that tries to attack from behind while his focus remains on the one in front of him. His blade burrows deep within the Corrupted before him, all while he's splattered in blood, one sleeve of his tunic torn and hanging off his shoulder.

Even with his chest heaving, the bastard smirks, and is ready for his time to shine. He yanks his blade free in one hard pull, portaling himself behind Whiro, and steadies his hand on the ground before his feet. A gold ring sizzles to life, the shimmery blackness of the portal opens and starts to spread wider. The force of Fynn's power makes his boots slide back in the dirt, but he manages to dig his heels into the soil, holding open the portal as we barrel closer and closer.

Whiro is still focused on the wyverns, attempting to knock them from the sky, unaware of the two of us spearing straight towards him. We cut through the air, Emma's hair whipping behind us over my shoulder. The wind bites at our skin, making my eyes burn, but I force them to stay open. We slice through the darkness like a sharpened blade, and the shadows fogging the forest swirl around us in our wake.

Once we are close enough, Emma releases a deep sigh before she stretches her arms out, beaming a rope of light to snag around her father's leg. The moment her power touches him, he throws his head back, roaring in pain as if the light is burning through his clothes and branding his skin.

It all happens in a blur, us hurtling through the portal, the chain of her power dragging him with us. With one quick glance over my shoulder, the mass of wyverns follows behind. They all stay in perfect alignment when they dive down in a wave.

A single roar rips through the sky from the fully shifted wyvern front and center, while the rest mimic it. Their shrieks bounce off one another as they tuck their wings in. The wyvern in the front breathes out a flame of shadows, but I don't get to see what happens when the air turns to ice, and my muscles tense from the stark difference, straining for warmth.

The floral scent of jasmine burns my nose and stings my lungs when I breathe in as we continue our descent. From entering through a portal at the top of the mountain, I am truly able to realize how massive this cave is. The towering heights of the hollowed stone walls, and the pillars that help hold it together on the wide stairwell that spirals the perimeter to the top.

"Wow," Emma whispers, the air from her lungs pluming in front of her. "They are expanding on the portal with their shadows, creating one of their own. Just like what I do, but…bigger."

So, that must be why the wyverns fired darkness from their mouths. But my focus is too concentrated on the Sea of Souls looming before us, and the stone crumbling from the power vibrating off Whiro. Even the specks of ashes floating in the air seem to tremble.

"Hurry—" Emma rushes out as her arms start to shake with the weight of restraining Whiro, but before she can say anything more, she gasps.

Whiro manages to blast her tendril of light off himself, shadowing away and appearing on the ground. He's standing in the same spot where I pulled a lifeless Emma into my arms. The spot near the Sea of Souls that still haunts me. And the memory makes me hold her tighter, needing to feel her heartbeat against my chest as my throat dries, making it hard to swallow.

Shaking my head to clear the image away, I focus on the ground as I stretch my wings out, letting the air catch in the curve of them to slow us down. When my eyes drag back up, I find the spot Whiro was just at, empty, causing my heart to race from not seeing him move.

Not even a half a breath later, I see him hovering above the water, shielding himself in shadows. They swarm around him like the evening tide, growing darker and concealing anything within.

Then, the gust of powerful wings ripple the air as the wyvern shifters join us. One by one they position themselves to form a circle around Whiro in the air, banding around the stream of water that seems to fall from nowhere at the top of the mountain. About thirty shifters have taken position in the circle, while the remaining wyverns steadily flap their wings to hover above us like a cloud.

They crane their heads, eliciting threatening growls as they all pin their gazes to the one who was leading them.

My eyes follow suit, taking in his body and how massive it is in size with his wingspan on full display, with a leathery black hide that looks impenetrable.

Emma shifts in my arms, noticing who everyone is looking at, and gasps. "He's the one who carried my soul back to you," she whispers. Her words make my heart thump painfully against her, and it's shocking enough to steal the air straight from my lungs. I'm thankful for the wyvern before us, but the image of her soul lost to her body has my insides trembling.

At the sound of her voice, the wyvern's head snaps towards us. Those slitted silver eyes like mine pin on Emma, roaring loud enough to send ripples over the top of the Sea of Souls beneath us. The beast in me seems to know what he's asking, knowing he means no harm, and that I can trust him.

I nod, giving a single thrust of my wings to make my way to him. Emma's hands give a reassuring squeeze and the other wyvern shifters part to let us through.

When we near, he dips his head low, and waits until she reaches for him.

"It's okay," Emma whispers.

"I know." I give a reassuring kiss on her temple before stretching my arms out for her to climb onto his back. She situates herself between the spikes at the base of his neck.

I wait for the part of me to drag her back into my arms, to show my claim on her. But my inner beast seems to not feel threatened by one of my own, and all I can feel is relief when my mind remains sane. My vision stays clear.

The wyvern dips his head to me, and a tingle of familiarity brushes over my skin. His eyes cut to Whiro—still swarming in shadows—and I know that look well. It's one that says, *It's time to finish this.*

The wyvern's chest pulls up tightly, and with one drawn-in breath, unleashes a torrent of dark power. A roar rumbles deep from his belly, the mountain around us quakes, and the other wyverns release thunderous war cries. The wyvern's own shadows strike into Whiro's power that still rages, signaling for the rest to follow suit. Emma and I share one final look before adding our own, hurling currents of energy into the same spot.

With my arms free from holding Emma, I can grasp better control of my aim, making sure to hit my mark. All of our powers blend together, becoming one as they slam against Whiro's. Even the petals on the jasmine flowers hugging the splintered pillars wilt, cowering away from the intensity.

The wyvern's collective attack sounds like the rush of a waterfall, slowly drowning Whiro's energy underneath ours.

But then a loud clicking echoes, cutting through the whirling stream of our power. My gaze snaps down, finding ghouls beginning to trickle out from the opening on the ground below, and some even work their way up the winding steps that wrap around the Sea of Souls, hugging the side of the cave. Their pointed teeth are bared, and their skeletal bodies crouch and sway with hisses as they spit towards us. They've come for their master, to protect him, but I have no doubt that Whiro would throw them in front of him like a shield if it meant he'd save himself.

A splintering crack ricochets in the air, and I snap my head back to Whiro, whose shield starts to rupture. Suddenly, he disappears, only to slam power into us from below. I manage to duck and dive out of his path, snapping my wings out to catch myself and halt my movements. My eyes hurry to find Emma, and I breathe out a sigh of relief when I spy her, and that the wyvern also dodged the sudden attack. But I can't say the same for others as they are thrown into the stone of the mountain, imprinting their bodies into it as it fractures around them.

I launch myself to Emma's side, and she is already twisted on the back of the wyvern. Grunting, she blocks Whiro's next attack, almost as if she can sense his next move. She has a mix of her light and dark power, both weaving together in perfect harmony as she dispels his shadows from reaching us.

She holds that flow of her power, letting it flood the surrounding air around Whiro that allows us time to dive down, landing on the other side of the stone floor. Emma shifts, righting her body to straddle the wyvern to face forward again, and pulls her power back to find Whiro standing among his vile creatures that have begun to crowd behind him. Before she can fully seat herself, she throws her darkness out in a steady stream when Whiro tries to lash out again at her.

His fingers are straining from the force, his veins are bulging in his neck, and spit is flying from between his bared teeth, practically foaming at the mouth. The rushing of power hums throughout the cave as Emma puts more force into it, her nostrils flaring from the exertion as their shadows clash against one another.

The rest of the wyvern form behind us, many staying airborne. And in the span of half a breath, the rest of us join in to combine our power to blend with Emma's, forcing Whiro to stumble back a few steps and growl in frustration.

I grit my teeth, feeling my body start to shake with the rush of energy flooding out of me. Beads of sweat form on my forehead, immediately cooling with the temperature of the realm.

"*Don't stop. I can sense him weakening,*" Emma links into my mind, though even her voice in my head sounds rough and breathy. The toll of using so much of her energy is becoming a burden on her body.

"*Never. I won't ever stop, little demon,*" I say back, earning a smirk from her when she briefly cuts her eyes to me, and I swear my cock pulses from that one look. *Fuck.* I'm so gone for her if she can get me hard in the middle of a fucking battle.

I force the raging need for her into my power, letting it course through my veins wildly. Growling through clenched teeth, my tendril of shadows grows and strengthens. The flow of it pours from my fingers unforgivingly and my vision starts to blur around the edges.

It feels like hours pass, but it's only been minutes when Whiro's band of power explodes. Leaving him open for our wrath, and revealing a God who, for the first time, is understanding what losing feels like. To know he can't escape this fate as all of us constrict our shadows around his body before he can retaliate. And for him to finally come face to face with death.

CHAPTER FORTY-SIX

Emma

With a twist of my hand, I alter my shadows to coil around Whiro like a rope, feeling his body tense the moment I trickle in a small thread of light. He tries to break free from the restraint, but it's no use when all the shifters do the same, binding him in darkness. The black veins that web around his eyes swell and pulse. His grunts and snarls echo in the cave as he continues to protest against our hold.

The ghouls creep closer, shrieking and scraping their claws on the weathered stone floor. One tries to help Whiro, but the force of our power consuming its master throws it backward, fast and hard. It smacks into the spiraling stairs, falling limply to the ground.

I shift my weight on the back of the wyvern, clenching my thighs tighter against his hide to keep from sliding. The drumming in my ears intensifies when those black orbs lock on mine. "You can't kill me," Whiro seethes, and I feel a growl vibrate from the wyvern beneath me. "I will make the world fall apart and take every soul with me."

Clicking my tongue, I cock my head slowly to the side as I study him for a moment. Much like how I would to those Fae I was seconds away from killing when I lived here.

"You seem to forget." Narrowing my gaze, I watch his face morph into confusion. "That was you, *Father*, who killed my mother, a goddess of this world. For even a god can't escape death. But you also seem to misunderstand." Leaning forward on the wyvern, I pause to reign in the current of rage filling my veins.

Gnashing my teeth together, I swallow the ball of anger down roughly. "I've had time to think about this, and how you bring nothing to this world. Only pain and heartbreak, while leaving the dust of bones in your wake. Your death would be inconsequential to the world."

I catch the way his eyes widen for a split second, his nostrils flaring as he jerks against our power binding him.

Even though the pressure of my power is weighing down on me, I huff with a slight smirk. "But who said anything about wanting to kill you?"

That gets a true reaction from him. His head rears back, shaking while trying to muster up enough power to fight off the energy of hundreds.

"Death would be a mercy and not nearly deserving enough for what you have done." My lips stretch, a bitter smile curving my lips as I watch Whiro continue to struggle.

I can tell he still doesn't know what his fate will be as those black pools bore into mine. His entire body stops fighting for a moment, his gaze narrowing, thinking, assessing. But then he freezes. Understanding igniting in his deadly eyes, until it wipes away with a smirk of his own.

"Impossible," he spits. "There is no way you can trap me in something from my own making."

Looking over to the Sea of Souls, the water reflecting back, eerily still, I find myself shifting another piece ahead in this deadly game. A silent move that he never saw coming.

I tsk. "You forget that I'm more than a weapon you tried to wield."

"Instead, you became a deceitful little monster. Thinking you could go against me without realizing your place," he seethes. "And assuming you can take me on with an army that has been dead longer than they have been alive. You forget I have my own." His ghouls shift on their taloned feet, readying for a command to strike.

I relinquish my power binding him, letting the shifters' darkness take control and keep him imprisoned in their grasp. With a deep breath, I move my left hand to rest behind my thigh that hangs off the side of the wyvern, keeping my shadows subtly trickling from my fingers, while pushing against the fatigue my body is starting to feel.

Then, I hold my right hand out in front of me. A blinding crackle of light comes to life in that hand, glinting in Whiro's dark pools. The power kisses against my fingertips, ready to silence the world from Whiro's darkness.

"*Father*, you should be proud. I might be a monster, but I'm one that you created, for my heart was never born black." I have been burned too much in this life. King Oren physically played his part in breaking my body, but Whiro… he likes to torment my mind. Sinking his claws in my psyche while fusing his venom into my veins. A toxin so potent and dark, it forever will stain the organ beating in my chest. "How does it feel to have your own power take you hostage?"

He bares his teeth, snarling as he loses control of his indifference. "All of you only have this power because of *me*! You should all be bowing at my feet!"

The wyvern beneath me beats its powerful wings in what seems like a display of anger holding a threat. He keeps his talons secure by scraping them and gouging holes in the rocky ground. The powerful muscles beneath me shift when he beats his wings again, and my hair flies up off my shoulders.

Playing with the light, I let it dance over my fingers and swirl around my hand. "Hmm. If it was truly your power to wield, then why do the shadows betray you and serve us?"

Draven inches closer to the wyvern's side I sit on, but slowly, I push up, rooting my feet between the wyvern's spikes to stand.

"And how does it feel to have your creatures turn on you?" I taunt with a wicked tilt of my lips.

Whiro starts to strangle out a laugh, but it dies the moment my smile falls away, letting an unsettling calm overcome my face. I never tear my eyes away from his as I finish targeting each ghoul, infusing my will into them. During our conversation, I began snaking minuscule trails of shadows along the ground without being noticed. Traveling them down from behind my leg, along the side of the wyvern, and to the ground where my shadows seeped into the fractured crevices. Making my way to the other side, I filter my darkness into each ghoul to claim them as mine.

He finally notices his army of ghouls that once faced us to prepare to strike are now all turned toward him. Slowly surrounding him in a trap of his own making.

Whiro goes to speak, but I beat him to it. "They wait for my command now." I prove it by making the closest one to him slice its arm through the air, eliciting a hiss from Whiro as the ghoul's talons leave behind a slender cut.

I wait for my father's eyes to lock on mine, relishing in the shock that is showing through his hard mask. "But it's not the darkness you should fear... It's the light that will smother it."

Before Whiro can come up with a vicious retort, all of our shadows drown away his words. Draven's tendril of power pries its way past Whiro's lips, snaking down his throat to keep him silent. We hold him hostage as I stretch my mind to each ghoul, letting my darkness manipulate their control. A pinching pain spreads beneath my skull when I collectively order the ghouls to lift up their previous master, carrying him over to the Sea of Souls.

I try to ignore the uncomfortable ache, while keeping a hold on my power. My gaze stays secure on Whiro. He jerks and bucks against his creatures' hold on him while trying to release his hands to break through our shadows, but it's no use.

With every scraping step, the ghouls shift closer to the still water, the wyverns hovering above and growing restless as they sway, following right above Whiro. I hold my breath the moment the ghouls shriek, tossing my father into the Sea of Souls. The water splashes when he goes under, but we don't relinquish our hold in fear of him shadowing out. He sinks beneath until the surface of the silver water settles as if nothing happened.

In unison, the shifters tighten their darkness, roaring loud enough to shake the mountain.

Without a second thought, I close my eyes, grabbing hold of the light flaming inside me. Letting it spark beneath my skin, I steady my balance on the back of the wyvern and inhale deeply. Then I count to three.

One. I let the light strengthen.

Two. My power begins to rush fiercely through my veins.

Three. A single tear slips free as I finally exhale.

My arms snap out, but my power doesn't trickle, it overflows in a torrent as it floods all around us. I guide it to the Sea of Souls, wielding it to blanket over the surface. It skims the water, and I grunt as I push more energy out, layering itself to create a shield, to become dense enough to be impenetrable. Layers of skin feel like they are being singed from my body, causing my teeth to grind together to fight against the force of power propelling from me.

But a silent gasp escapes me when a black orb releases from the water, floating higher towards the opening at the top of the cave.

"*What is that?*" Draven asks through the bond.

"Whiro's soul," I say out loud, stunned by the sight.

It doesn't surprise me that it's not a spark of light because what dwells within him is evil and poisonous. A stain that is finally removed.

When his soul disappears, I gently nudge the wyvern, dipping my head closer to his. "I believe we are safe to drop the shadows."

A jerk of his head is all I get before he bellows out a roar and the rest mimic it. Suddenly, all the shadows disappear as the others reign their power in, but I don't stop. With trembling hands, I keep flooding the Sea of Souls with enough light to seal away Whiro for eternity. He can't break free from a place where it's too bright for shadows to exist.

It's in this moment that I know my mother was right. His power being used against him will become his undoing, but a bright enough light will restrain the darkness of his soul.

Now, he is simply a ghost with a wicked heart that is trapped in the in-between.

My shoulders drop, exhaustion pulling at me as I crouch down. My hands fall when I let my light die away, and I stare with half-lidded eyes at the Sea of Souls. The silence in the cave is almost deafening, all of us in disbelief at how the water now shimmers like a white veil, which looks wrong in the blackened cave. Even the flowers that were once decorating the pillars have fallen ill, drooping with withered petals, as if their job to conceal death is finally over and they can rest.

A warm, gentle touch brushes my shoulder and I turn to find Draven scanning my face. He must feel the fatigue that is burrowing in the marrow of my bones and see the way my eyes feel heavy. I carefully let myself lower all the way onto the wyvern's back, once again sitting because the muscles in my legs have started to feel weak.

My eyes fall back to the water below, and even though we've won...I don't feel the revelry I thought I would have. But there is a peace that is warming my heart and a weight that lifts from my shoulders. It seems strange for this to be the end without spilling his blood or making him scream out in pain like I always imagined. Then again, it doesn't need to be anything else. It only needs to be over so everyone can freely live their lives again. And for the wyvern shifters... For them to start life again.

A new beginning.

The whisper of wings multiplies as the wyverns begin to fly upward. Their shadows cascade around them before they disappear, portaling back to our realm. Strong arms slide underneath my body as Draven lifts me to hold me once more. The scent of him helps soothe the throbbing that lingers behind my eyes and in the front of my skull. I rest my cheek on his chest, letting my body release all the tension that it's been holding onto.

"No more monsters, little demon," he whispers, his breath fanning my hair.

"There is one more," I say softly, but he's one that I already have plans for.

Draven's brows furrow, but my eyes drift to the wyvern who carried me. He huffs through his nostrils with a powerful thrust of his wings before shadows consume him and he vanishes from sight. He was the last shifter to leave Gehendra.

The ghouls stand aimlessly around us, and seeing them brings back everything I suffered through here. Suddenly, I become angry, my breaths turning shallow. This place has been a hell that kept me from everyone I love. That has stolen a piece of my heart by taking away Kye. A place that now holds the monster that tried to ruin us all.

"I need to do one more thing," I quietly say to Draven, and all he does is nod. I know he can feel the rage that is simmering beneath the surface.

Guiding him to fly me out of the mountain and back to the open expanse of Gehendra, we hover in the air with Whiro's castle staring back at me.

"Don't drop me," I tease, before I unleash every torrent of emotion Whiro inflicted on me.

I raise my hands and slam both light and dark into the castle. Rumbling echoes throughout the realm as I aim into the tower that held my room, never wanting to see it again. It crumbles, taking the spire with it and knocking into the base of the castle, making huge chunks fall down the mountainside before disappearing in the endless drop.

Stone crashing against stone cleaves through the air as I destroy everything Whiro created here. Leaving behind nothing but rubble, dust, and a soul that will never be free. I will make sure of it, because no one will enter Gehendra again.

It doesn't take long for the destruction to sizzle away my rage now that nothing remains standing. I finally feel like I can breathe again now that the lives of others aren't threatened. That the world is safe, and I'm no longer trapped in this life.

Through the rubble, I can see the Sea of Souls peeking back at me, still glistening against the dark, with stones piled on top of my power holding Whiro as its captive.

Once I finish, I wrap us both in my shadows, snuggling into Draven's embrace, and take us back to Deyadrum, not bothering with a farewell to Gehendra. The moment we touch Fae lands, I ignore the white spots dancing in my vision as I spin, using my light to seal the perimeter of Gehendra so no one can portal in or out again. If someone tried, all they would be met with is a blinding light that will burn them the moment it touches their skin.

CHAPTER FORTY-SEVEN

Emma

The land of Asiza comes into focus. The shrieks of battle aren't bleeding into the air, but a litter of carnage is painting the ground. Draven sets me down on my feet as I frantically search the area, spotting Fynn, whose hand falls to his side, his sword clattering to the ground.

My heart stills when I drop my gaze to his feet. Cora. She's alive but curling in on herself as she holds her hands to her shoulder.

Fynn drops to his knees as he pulls her into his lap, brushing her matted hair out of her face. I don't think. I take off, my boots pounding into the sodden ground, with Draven right on my tail.

Fynn grunts and it sounds strained, dirt and blood staining his skin with beads of sweat trailing down his face. "She was bitten," he grinds out.

My own knees slam to the ground as I try to catch my breath. Gently moving Cora's hand, I look at the wound and there are black veins

345

tracking to her heart. My eyes start to well as I shake my head, the world doubling as I do. But I notice it's not spreading, and the blue hue of her eyes start to brighten.

"Em—" Her voice is raw as it scratches up her throat.

"Shh. You're going to be okay." I wipe the lone tear tracking down her cheek as a small smile pulls at my lips. She was hurt last time for my sake, and I could do nothing to help. I sniffle, knowing this time she is going to be okay. She won't suffer by turning into a vessel of darkness.

"She's healing," Fynn says in a hushed tone.

The tip of my finger traces the black veins that are receding, dying away as if they never existed. I wasn't sure what would happen to the Corrupted by trapping Whiro, but it seems his curse cannot surpass the light that conceals him.

I smile wide then, my lips trembling. I unsteadily stand, my legs shaking, but I have to see. I have to see it with my own eyes, because I didn't pay attention before, not truly. My main focus was making sure my friends were okay.

Numerous Fae stand in torn clothing, frozen still as they watch us while looking back down at their bodies. Their *cured* bodies. Every single one of them. Draven's warmth brushes my side, his hand stroking my back as I look around in awe.

Such a warring feeling, the ripples of pain that grow and the swell of my heart from knowing so many lives were saved this day.

Draven's hand stops rubbing my back, his voice sounding faint to the fog filling my head. "Emma, what's wrong?"

Darkness creeps on the edge of my vision as I go to open my mouth to speak. But my body suddenly becomes weightless, feeling as if I'm floating. The next thing I feel is strong arms wrapping around me as my body collapses and everything goes black.

"Emma," a faint, soft voice calls to me in this dark void I'm sucked into, and I follow it. "Emma, please wake up." This time, the voice sounds shaky, but awareness finally reaches my mind as I let myself come back into the present.

Slowly, my eyes flutter open, feeling heavy with the effort.

Bright blue eyes look down at me, wide and hopeful. And as soon as my eyes fully open, a toothy smile stretches on Cora's face as she drops herself on top of me and hugs me tightly.

"Stop scaring me, Em," she cries happily into my neck.

"What happened?" I croak out, my voice sounding rough to my own ears.

"You fainted from using too much power, draining your energy," Fynn adds from the foot of the bed.

"Is everyone—"

"All are saved, little demon." My head turns sharply at the sound of Draven's voice, letting my eye scan every inch of him to make sure he's not injured. But he looks freshly washed, as if we didn't just come out of a gruesome battle and destroy an entire realm.

"Even me," Cora's voice pulls me back to her and it's then I notice she, too, looks clean and rested. Confusion furrows my brows as I look to Fynn, knowing he was covered in filth from battle the last time I saw him. But I don't find a speck of dirt or blood on his skin.

"How long have I been out?"

"Two days," Draven says gently.

I stare off in shock, trying to wrap my head around the fact I've been asleep for a solid two days. Immediately, my breathing becomes shallow as I fist the sheets. My gaze locks on Draven again as a million questions fly through my mind.

"Where are all those who were Corrupted?" I rasp, desperate to know what I missed.

The mattress dips and Draven presses those lush lips of his to my forehead before breathing in deeply. "Home." Pulling back, his crystal eyes probe mine. "They all went back home, little demon."

I close my gaping mouth as I ask, "What about the Scavengers? They can create more—"

"They are gone." He tucks a loose strand of hair behind the shell of my ear. "Their bodies disintegrated into thin air." Grabbing both my cheeks in the palms of his hands, he presses his nose to mine, looking deeply into my eyes. "We won because of you. It's all over."

Reaching up to press my hands to his cheeks, I hold him to me, giving my head a small shake. "Not because of me. We won because of all of us."

Warmth swells through the bond as he kisses the side of my mouth, only to pull back, his eyes roaming over every inch of my face.

The way he looks at me makes my heart flutter even though my mind is still in shock, unable to truly grasp what he said.

A knock sounds on the door and Fynn jumps up to open it, revealing a male I've never seen before. He has long black hair that is pulled back into a messy bun. Muscles stretch against his clothing, and he has the palest skin I've ever seen. Draven walks over to him before I can ask him who it is, and they grasp hands, pulling the other in and patting each other's backs.

"I see she's awake," the male says. His voice is smoky and deep.

Draven nods, letting the male walk over to me as I push myself up to sit, resting my back against the headboard. "Have we met before?"

A humorous smile touches his lips. "You can say that, but I looked a little different."

His eyes are a deep brown, almost black in the way the light hits his face. As he steps closer, I notice specks of green are mingled in the color. Then, the pupils of his eyes shift to a slit, changing to a glowing silver, much like Draven's when he changes his form.

When they return to normal, my hands fist the sheets and I stare unblinkingly at the male before me. "You're the one who carried me."

The corners of his eyes crinkle with his smile as he nods. "And you're the one who saved us all." Before I know what he's doing, he drops to one knee and bows his head. "My name is Ragon."

My heart stalls in my chest at his name, one I've only heard once before. He's Mauve's mate.

"And I speak for the rest of my people that we are yours to command." He pivots on his knee, facing Draven. "As well as yours. You are the true chosen one that we will follow."

Draven looks to me with a silent question he doesn't need to voice through the bond because I already can sense what he's thinking. So, I nod. Draven never wants to be above anyone; he only has ever wished for peace and to live as equals. But the one wish that he never thought the stars would answer would be to have his people back.

Draven rests his hand on Ragon's shoulder, pulling him up to stand. "We will never command you. We only wish you to live freely and for us to share the sky as one."

Ragon stands, following the movement and placing his hand on Draven's shoulder. "We must fly together soon then."

"It would be an honor," Draven says, before Ragon turns back to me, engulfing my hands with his.

"You freed us all, and the tethers between our bodies and souls were able to come to life again. We didn't hesitate to shadow out of Gehendra, even if it meant using what little power we had." He squeezes my hands more firmly. "I am forever in your debt." He dips his head again before gently releasing my hands. "I apologize for needing to leave so quickly, but it's been too long without my mate, and I don't want to miss another moment with her. I only wanted to wait until you woke so I could speak with you and formally introduce myself."

Placing my hand over my heart, I feel the back of my eyes burn. "Mauve has missed you terribly, and she has been blaming herself for your death."

He shakes his head with a sigh. "It was never her fault. There was nothing she could have done back then. But I plan to make it up to her for all the days I've missed."

I offer a wobbly smile as my eyes glisten with unshed tears, and his do the same. Then he sniffs roughly and pulls back to stand at full height. "Thank you, my Goddess. I'll take my leave."

Something tightens in my chest from his words as my eyes are glued to his retreating back. A different weight has settled on my shoulders, that I am now the sole blood of the Gods that exists. But the weight doesn't feel like it will drown me. Instead, it feels like it will make me stronger.

The door clicks shut behind him and Cora races back to my side, brushing her fingers through my tangled hair. "Come, let's get you washed up."

In that moment, I couldn't be more thankful for her. Because though they have made sure I'm clean while I rested, this will feel like a different kind of cleanse. One where I will be scrubbing the grime of Whiro's deeds and Aiden's deceit from my body. A finality. The ending of this fatal game.

CHAPTER FORTY-EIGHT

Draven

*A*fter Emma freshened up and ate, she said she still felt a little tired and wanted to lie back down for a little while. It has been an hour since I tucked the blanket over her and came down to the library. I've been sitting by the fire, mesmerized by the flames that sensually dance together, getting lost in thought.

Until I sense her.

Her rose and honey scent blend into the air around me, causing me to close my eyes and inhale deeply. "Little demon," I growl low and deep because she is supposed to be resting.

When she doesn't respond, I peel my eyes open only to find smooth legs on display from the short hem of her nightgown. I'm momentarily mesmerized until I notice the piece of paper dangling between her fingers as it hovers in front of my face. "What is this?"

Shifting around my chair, she drops down to her knees, resting her arms on my thighs while chewing on her bottom lip. And because I can't resist, I cup her jaw and pull her lip free from her teeth with the pad of

351

my thumb. She looks at me hungrily, like whatever she came down here to give me is long gone and replaced by the lust radiating from her pupils.

She shakes her head as if to clear it before placing the paper in my hand. "I didn't get a chance to tell you before since Aiden showed up." My jaw ticks roughly at the reminder of him, but this time I don't feel the burning rage to kill him. The bastard is already dead. She won't see the reminder because I got rid of his body while she was out cold for those two days.

She clears her throat. "When I was in the afterlife, I met your father."

Every muscle in my body tenses, my fingers creasing the suddenly heavy paper in my hand. My chest feels tight as I stare at her unblinkingly, waiting.

She peers up at me, and those big, swirling grey eyes draw me in, slowly loosening whatever is fucking constricting my heart. "He had a message for each of you and asked me to tell you, but I thought it would be best if I wrote them down. A keepsake for his final words he wished he could have spoken, and this way you all can have privacy to hopefully get some closure."

Swallowing roughly, my eyes zero in on the paper as if it will come to life and bite me. "This letter is for all of us?" I manage to rasp out, unable to tear my eyes away.

In my peripheral I can see her head shake. "No, this one is yours. I have already delivered your mother's and brother's letters to them."

When the danger had passed, Fynn left to bring Emil and my mother back home, telling them the good news. But the best news was knowing they were safe.

Suddenly, my heart starts to race as it drums frantically in my ears. How many times have I wished that I could hear his voice again now that it's started to fade these last five years? To have one more conversation or the chance to say goodbye?

My eyes are still locked on the parchment as Emma stands. "I'll let you be alone to read it."

As soon as the words leave her mouth, my heart sinks, and it's hard to breathe. I can feel the blood drain from my face at the thought of her not being here. She's the oxygen to keep me alive and the beat of my heart to keep it calm and steady.

Whipping my hand out, my fingers grasp her wrist, forcing her to stop her retreat as panic starts to creep in. "Please." My broken whisper is barely audible over the crackling fire. When I finally manage to shift my gaze, I look up at her. "Stay."

Wordlessly, she nods with a soft smile and climbs into my lap, wrapping her arms around my neck. The weight of her body against mine is comforting and I breathe in deeply through my nose and exhale out my mouth.

My grip shakes as I hold the letter up to her. "Will you read to me?"

Because I don't trust my eyes to read the words he wishes to convey. I can't. Already, my vision blurs. I blink it away and reach to grab my drink on the table beside me, tipping the rim to my lips. The bourbon burns down my throat, but it warms as it settles in my system.

Emma doesn't say a word as the paper crinkles when she starts to unravel it, and I don't dare to fucking look. I keep my eyes fixated on the flames feathering over the slabs of wood.

"Draven, my dear boy," she quietly says as she shifts her hips to sit up a little higher on my lap. "I'm sorry I left you and never came back like I always promised I would." My eyes squeeze tightly shut as she continues. "That has been my biggest regret, and I know there is no way for me to make that up to you now, but I hope you will forgive me."

Bringing the glass to my lips, I struggle to swallow it down as my heart thumps unevenly.

Emma's fingers softly play with my hair in a soothing way as she reads the next line. "There is not a day that goes by where you don't make me proud." Her voice wavers, making her draw in a shaky breath. "One day, we will be together again, but for now—"

A small sniffle from her sounds near my ear as a lone tear trails down my cheek.

"I will cherish the memories of our nights on the roof with all the stars in the sky above and the cool breeze that embraced us. Now, you have someone special to sit silently in the dark with. And boy—"

She pauses again, and when I turn my tear-soaked face to hers, I can't help but wipe the wetness on her own cheeks away with my thumb.

Her breath hitches when she looks back down at the paper. "This girl loves you with every part of her soul. I can see it in her eyes, and it gives me peace to know your heart is protected and in good hands. And always remember that I love you with all my heart."

Scrubbing a hand down my face, I try to pull in the overflow of tears prickling at my eyes. But I fail. They fall on their own and all I can manage to say is a choked, "Thank you."

I set my glass down the moment Emma pulls my head into her chest, holding me like the world is erupting and she can shield me from the pieces falling. And I fucking let her. His words have torn fresh wounds into my heart, all the while stitching them back together. It was the closure I needed and never thought I would get. And I think my father knew that.

Words can't express how thankful I am. What had been the kind of grief that kept me submerged beneath the surface is now a sorrow that pulls me back up to keep my head above water. His words are healing and so is my mate being here in my arms. She has no idea how much I fucking love her. And how every day we have together will be me cherishing her mind, body, and soul.

We sit silently in each other's embrace while the orange glow of the fire basks us with its warmth. No words are needed as the night ticks by, and slowly, my heart mends.

CHAPTER FORTY-NINE

Emma

*W*e ended up falling asleep in the chair and woke to a dark fireplace that long since died away. I wake before him and can't help but drink in every inch of his face. His hair is ruffled from my fingers sifting through it, his dark lashes that curl so beautifully frame his resting eyes. Stubble dusts his jaw and I just barely let my fingertips trace the sharp edge of it.

When I reach his lips, my fingers hover above a hairbreadth away. He is absolutely breathtaking. And *mine*.

My eyes drag up his face to look at the piercing glinting in his brow and how all the harsh creases fade away when he sleeps, looking so peaceful.

"See something you like?"

I startle at the sound of his voice, jumping in his lap, but his hands shoot out to pull me harder against him. His eyes crack open, and I swear I melt as everything inside me warms at the way he looks at me.

Leaning down, I smile against his neck before placing a lingering kiss there. "No," I respond as I inch up to his jaw, pressing another kiss to his skin. "I see something I love."

His growl vibrates from his chest and along my body, sending goose-bumps to raise along my skin. He reaches up, grabbing the nape of my neck and slamming my lips to his in a searing kiss. Nipping and sucking the air straight from my lungs.

I feel him harden beneath me and it rips a moan from my lungs, making me push down and grind against him. Shoving his tongue in my mouth, I suck on it before catching it between my teeth with a smirk.

"You are such a little fucking demon," he growls, and the way he says it causes heat to pool in my core, feeling myself become slick between my thighs.

I go to take his lips in mine again, but he's hooked his fingers around the strands of my hair, pulling my head back. The slight sting makes my pussy clench and I have to squeeze my thighs together. Eyes locked on the other, our chests move together in a harsh rhythm.

"I want nothing more than to fucking strip you bare and bend you over this chair, burying my cock so deep inside of you and never leave." His eyes darken as he stares at my swollen lips. "But if we go any further, I won't stop. It's taking all my strength to restrain myself right now with your tight, little body pressed against me, wet and ready."

His jaw tightens as he swallows roughly, then tucks his head into the crook of my neck, breathing in deeply. "The things I plan to do to you will take days. The need to fill you with my come over and over again will be all I can think about."

His teeth scrape against my throat before licking away the stinging pain. "But you fell asleep right before I did and I heard a mumbled promise fall from your lips. A death you wish to take. So, the first thing we are going to do is pay someone a visit."

Draven pulls back to look into my eyes. I don't have to ask whose death I seek to claim because I've been planning this for weeks now. He's already suspected as much when he followed me that night I met with those who are part of the rebellion.

It's still daytime as Draven flies us to Asov. Though I could have shadowed us, he said he enjoys the part where he gets to hold me.

We're currently standing outside, staring up at the pristine double doors. Two white pillars stand tall on each side at the top of the steps as I make my way up with Draven right behind me. He keeps his wings out, full shifted form on display, and the freedom of him not hiding makes my heart swell.

Instead of storming inside, I take my time. Every step is sure and steady because Calloway will never run away. He's too greedy for power, and too arrogant to fear me if he senses my presence. Unknowingly letting death walk through the front door.

The moment my boot steps over the threshold, I let my darkness invade. It veils over the ivory stone floors in a swirling mist, spreading in every direction as it climbs up the walls and blocks the light from the windows.

The guards finally panic when they realize I'm not here as an ally or for a friendly visit. But their warning cries get silenced when Draven chokes them with his shadows. Not enough to kill them, but enough to make them pass out and drop like a sack of rocks to the floor. I'm sure they will feel that in the morning.

One of the guards accidentally falls on top of another, his face landing on the other's backside, right between the legs. I hear Draven snicker behind me, and I turn around quickly to smack him in the chest before ascending the flight of winding steps.

When I reach the wide hallway, I turn left and head straight to where I know Calloway will be. It's where he always hides out.

Our boots are silent on the polished floor as we reach the menacing door that always led to such horror. But this time, I have the control. Draven kisses my cheek, giving me a wink, and then strides back the way we came down the hallway, going to do what I asked of him while he flew us here.

Straightening my spine, I turn back to twist both handles without knocking and push the double doors wide, making them slam and bounce back against the walls.

Calloway is hunched over his desk, but his head snaps up at my intrusion. His shirt is untucked, hair frazzled, and papers are strewn about all over the top of his desk and floor.

Blood rushes to his face as he storms around his desk towards me. "I saw my son with you last in my vision, and now I can't *see* him at all!"

Before he can take another step, I throw my shadows at him, grabbing him by the throat. I squeeze tight enough to hold him in my grip while allowing him enough air to breathe.

"D–did you kill my son?!" Spit flies from his mouth as he jerks against my power.

Tilting my head slowly to the side, I purse my lips. "Seems like he did that all on his own."

If I thought Calloway's face was red before, then the shade it is now is darker than the blood running through his veins.

"Y–you monster!" he blubbers. "I should have killed you the first chance I got."

My face scrunches from the scent of stale booze reeking on his breath.

I tsk, shaking my head as I circle around him. "Think what you like, but you are mistaken about one thing." He tries to twist his head to look at me, but I command my shadows to grip him harder to keep him from interrupting. "You never had a chance. You are *weak*." I round his side before stopping right in front of him. Face-to-face. "A *coward*, and undeserving of the throne, let alone being able to breathe a moment longer."

"They are ready," Draven's voice travels from the doorway, causing Calloway's eyes to widen as he looks over my shoulder.

"A–A–Drag—" He can't finish his words as I choke him tighter, causing him to cough, and the redness in his face tints to a deep shade of purple.

"You fear him and yet you will wish he was the one killing you." Turning on my heel, I ease the shadows enough to allow air to fill his lungs as I drag him down the halls and outside in front of the palace.

A sea of people waits at the bottom of the steps, surrounding dual wooden posts I had them keep on hand to stake into the ground. Multiple Fae reach for the chains and cuff them to Calloway's wrists before latching them to the hooks embedded in the top of the posts.

I draw my shadows away now that he's restrained, but his eyes dart around frantically. "Who are these people?"

A full-toothed smile spreads on my face as I lean my shoulder against one of the posts, crossing my legs at the ankle. "You don't recognize them?" Clicking my tongue, I take a few steps in front of him. "Some of them are the people you rule, but better yet…" Spreading my arms out wide, I watch as each person pulls a whip from their satchels. "They are the rebellion."

Calloway's mouth gapes open until pure fury distorts his face. "Why are they listening to you?!" he accuses, and I can't help but laugh.

"Because I'm their leader." Turning my back to him, I peer over my shoulder with a smirk. "You didn't think the moment I set foot back into this palace that I was just going to keep my head down, did you?" I scoff.

"You helped King Oren chain me and laughed as he whipped me. I've been plotting and waiting for this moment." My gaze shifts to behind Calloway, meeting icy blue eyes that are locked on me. "And let me tell you, revenge tastes sweet."

I look out to the crowd as more approach. "And it's not only me who wishes to know what retribution tastes like." My hand gestures out to the growing audience. "You have ignored them, refusing the help they sought in order to simply live."

Cheers of agreement ring out around me.

"Many have had to relocate their families to have enough food for each meal. To live a life where they aren't forced to pay double the price of their homes just so their coin can mend your ships." More yells of rage in the air. "Face it. You were never fit to be a king."

Turning on my heel, I look to Draven with a nod. His steps eat up the distance between us, scooping me up in his arms. "He's all yours," he tells the people whose faces are now blistering red, their eyes zeroed in on Calloway before Draven launches off the ground.

I wrap my arms around his neck as we cut through the wind. His wings beat to propel us higher while his arms pull me closer into his body. I look over his shoulder for one final glance to see whips slicing through the air, landing their strikes on Calloway. His cries stretch for miles, but eventually those piercing screams grow faint and get lost in the wind as we soar across the sun-kissed sky.

CHAPTER FIFTY

Emma

A day has passed since we left Calloway to his much-awaited death. It's fitting, really, for me to help secure him in the same fashion he did for me. Delivering him to the horror of how the end of a leather whip feels when it slices through skin.

Earlier, a letter from one of the rebels arrived saying it didn't take long for Calloway to fall limp and for his heart to cease its beating. After reading the note, I tossed it in the flames, watching it shrivel and burn, much like my sympathy for him. From the moment he spoke ill towards me, I knew I would never feel anything but hatred for him.

I leave the library and walk outside through the forest, following the path towards the shore. The pines stand protectively tall as the fog weaves around their branches in a sheltering embrace. The hard soil crunches beneath my boots and the wind gently picks up strands of my hair.

I scan the area as I walk, taking notice of how there were bodies littered about and blood staining the land, but now all that exists is a clear forest with no streaks of red in sight. The two days my body fell into a deep, replenishing sleep, everyone had worked diligently. Now looking at it, you would think there was never a battle here in the first place.

Inhaling deeply, the fresh air fills my lungs and settles my soul, a smile settling over my face. For once, nothing is threatening to take my life and use it against me. The invisible chains have finally been cut from me, and it's an unfamiliar feeling… To simply walk without looking over my shoulder. To not fear for my life or others, with the weight of death anchored to my ankles.

Leisurely, I continue my way down the path until the sound of waves lapping at the shore reaches me. A tingling sensation tugs me forward, my steps quickening, until I reach the end and look out to the sea.

My breath catches as two golden eyes connect with mine, hovering just above the surface. A wide grin stretches across my face as I take a subtle step forward, the water kissing the tip of my foot as the Masiren watches me.

Its tale flicks out of the sea, cutting through a wave. *"You found your light."* My lungs momentarily stall as its voice penetrates through my mind. Slowly, it lifts its head above the surface. *"You have grown stronger, and so has our bond."*

I take another step closer, letting the water lap at my ankles. *"It's not just me who has become stronger."* A small jolt of warmth rushes into me from our connection, and I cross my arms around the front of my stomach.

"So, it seems." The Masiren's eyes flare brighter before it dives under the water. *"Your mother was right about you."*

My muscles tense as I stare at the empty sea, knowing the Masiren is still lurking close by. This time I don't take another step closer. I stay rooted in place. *"Right about what?"* I'm sure my voice in its head gives away the desperate need for an answer.

The Masiren's body pops out of the water, only to curve and duck back in with one swift movement. Its tail grazes the surface, leaving behind ripples as it swims away, leading towards the horizon. *"That you are worth everything. That you will truly make the world shine once more."*

A hiccuped cry escapes me as I cover my mouth with my hand.

Another wave of comforting warmth seeping through the connection, my eyes track the Masiren drifting farther away, until its voice enters my head once more. *"I'm here for whenever you need me, Goddess."*

This time, I sniffle a small cry, chewing on my lip as I stare at the line in the distance that separates the sea from the sky. My heart feels full, more than I ever thought it could. With a deep inhale, I prepare myself to turn around and head back to the castle.

But I sense him before I hear him. "Are you ready, little demon?"

Strong arms wrap around my shoulders, and I twist my head back to peer up at him. "More than ready."

Snatching me up in his arms, he flies us back to the castle where everyone waits. They stand around, talking among themselves in the main room when we enter through the double doors. All eyes land on us when Draven sets me back on my feet.

Cora rushes to me, throwing her arms around me. "Are you sure?"

With a wide smile, I nod against her shoulder. She asked me this the first time I had brought it up to her.

"There is no one else I'd want more to take the throne of Asov. Plus, I think it's time for a queen to reign." She is perfect for the role. I trust her with my life, and so do the people of Asov. They know her like a friend from when she would go through the village and help heal them, only to then check up on how they are doing. She's earned their respect and kindness all on her own. And most of the people still view me as their princess, standing with me for my decision.

I hear her sniffle before she hugs me tighter. "But only until you come back, okay? When you are ready, it is yours. It always has been, but I'll just warm your seat until then."

My eyes find Fynn over her shoulder, arms crossed and smiling. His hazel eyes glisten, gaze fixated on Cora, until he raises them to meet mine. "I'll be by her side the whole time. She won't be alone." He winks. This time it doesn't feel like it's a wink for amusement, but instead a promise that she will be cared for.

I see Emil go to his brother and I watch them say their "see you later" with a long hug.

When Cora steps away, Queen Zoraida is there, pulling me in. "Do you have another book with a cryptic message in it for me?" I ask.

Her singsong laughter fills the air. "No, my dear, I'm afraid not." When she lets go, she brushes both of her hands down the side of my head, smoothing my hair in a motherly gesture. "Cherish every second and don't let my son get away with stuff too easily."

A giggle leaves my lips, followed by heat rising to my cheeks. The thought of his mother knowing what will happen once we leave has me feeling the need to hide behind a curtain of my hair. But she is still stroking my head with a gentle smile, and I swallow down the lump of embarrassment.

"I won't," I choke out as Draven snakes one of his arms around my waist and pulls me away, my back crushing into his chest.

"Now, if you will excuse us, it's time for me to steal my mate away so I can have her all to myself."

His mother steps forward to smack him on the shoulder. I have to stifle a laugh because it's so unqueen-like and it makes my heart warm in my chest.

"Go, go, go." She throws her hands up with an amused huff. "Maybe you will even bless me with a grandchild when you come back." She looks at us from the side of her eyes, with both eyebrows raised.

"And that's our cue," Fynn cuts in with a wave of his hand. Gold shimmers beside him and Cora, opening a portal to the palace of Asov, where they will rule. He quickly walks over, wrapping both arms around me and Draven, squashing me in the process as I get sandwiched between them. "Don't be good," he whispers to us before spinning around, grabbing Cora's hand, and walking through the portal with a final wave.

The gold power falls to the floor like dust when it seals shut and then suddenly, I'm hauled up in Draven's arms. "I can just shadow portal us there," I say into his neck as I snuggle in closer to him.

His response is to hold me tighter. "But this way allows me to have my hands on you for longer, so we will be flying."

I don't argue because I prefer this way of travel, too. There is a whole world to explore, and flying with the clouds lets you see everything some can only dream about. Just like I used to.

With a final farewell, Draven has us air-bound, slowing his speed as we glide under the dying sun.

"I've changed a few things for us," Draven says almost hesitantly as we land in the Caves of Tsisana. I step farther into our temporary home, and where there once was a couch is now a four-poster bed with lanterns lit on each side.

"I've stocked all the food we will need and brought all our other necessities. There is a wardrobe full of clothes for you in the back room, but I don't think you will be needing those much."

Biting my lip, I dip my head to hold back my smile, but I can't stop my eyes from taking it all in. It's beautiful, and he really did think of everything and more. With all that we have been through, some time away together is desperately needed. He wants me to experience freedom without being tied down to anything or having anyone try to harm me. To see what it feels like to truly live without worries as we start our forever together.

Turning around to face him, my heart thuds wildly in my chest at the sight. Just like the first time he brought me here, he stands tall and is covered in dark shadows. Small flakes of snow drift behind him outside, with a bluish-purple twilight sky as his backdrop.

The orange glow from the lanterns contour over the sharp angles of his face. My eyes drop to his lips that are parted, almost begging to be kissed.

Slowly, I walk to him, and when my hardened nipples press against his chest, I push up on my toes and softly touch my lips to his. The muscles in his chest expand with a growl and he wraps his arms roughly around me. One grips the nape of my neck and the other presses hard into my lower back before sliding down and palming my backside with a stinging squeeze.

His mouth devours mine, guiding me backward until the back of my knees hit the bed and shoves me on it. My body jumps when I hit the mattress, but then he's there, aligning his hard frame to mine. I spread my legs wide, allowing him room to shift his hips, pressing the hard ridge of his cock right where I need him most.

With a nip of my lip, he rears back to look down at me with a smirk. "Do you trust me?"

I lift my head enough to grab his bottom lip with my teeth and pull. "With my whole life."

In the next breath, he's tearing at my clothing, ripping it clean off my body before dropping to his knees to yank off my boots. His clothes fall to the ground next, and I push up on my elbows to watch with half-lidded eyes as he grabs my ankle and starts trailing kisses up my calf, licking and sucking as he inches closer to my center.

His eyes lock on me when he reaches my inner thigh, biting the skin there. His wings wrap over us, those silver eyes darkening with a rough swallow, making his throat move in a way that makes me want to lick it. "I can't restrain myself from you any longer," he grinds out between his teeth before nipping at my skin.

"I don't want you to," I breathe out.

"*Fuck.*"

A scream rips from my throat when he crashes his mouth to my pulsing clit, sucking it between his teeth and lapping his tongue over my slit before pushing it inside. My head falls back, hitting the mattress as I grind against his mouth greedily.

His breathy laugh fans over my pussy but I'm so crazed for him that it only makes me wetter. I reach forward, grabbing the strands of his hair by the root and pulling him up to me. The amusement glinting in his eyes vanishes when he sees the raw desire swirling in mine.

"Fill me," I rush out.

His response gets stolen when I claim his lips with mine, shoving my tongue into his mouth as he kisses me back with the same intensity. My hips arch off the bed, seeking him. Needing him.

The bond in my chest heats, and the mark on my palm starts to tingle, my blood humming through my veins. His must feel the same because he tears his mouth off me, shoving his fingers between my lips. I eagerly suck on them, swirling my tongue around his digits. But then he pulls them out, shoving that hand between us and rubbing those fingers over my clit. And with no warning, he inches them down and thrusts them hard into my core.

My eyes roll back at the intrusion, and immediately my inner walls clench as he tauntingly moves them in and out of me.

"Just making sure this pussy is ready for me, but you're already dripping." He leaves me feeling empty when he brings those fingers up to his mouth, sucking my essence off them. "So fucking responsive for me, soaking the sheets before I can bury my cock inside of you."

His words send another wave of lust to roll through me, feeling more wetness pool between my thighs. I watch his nostrils flare and his pupils blow out wide. Before I can blink, he's gripping my legs, shoving my knees to my chest, and lining his swollen tip to my entrance. I catch a quick glance to see a bead of pre-cum drip down his tip, and it has me licking my lips.

But then it's gone when he thrusts his thick cock all the way inside me, stretching me wide as he fills every inch. I clench tightly around him, my legs trying to do the same, but he holds them hostage. His hips pull back, slowly dragging himself out until just the tip is in me, only to slam back in.

This position has him hitting that spot inside me that makes my toes curl and my vision blur. I try to grind my hips to seek more friction, but my attempt fails when he begins to drive into me. Hard and fast. Whimpers fly from my lips and my breathing grows harsh.

"That's it," he growls huskily. "Fucking take it."

Our moans and grunts echo as they bounce off the cave walls, but I couldn't care less. I can't think straight; all I know is that I need to come as I feel my orgasm rise.

"Draven," I breathe out.

A protest is on my lips when he yanks himself out of me, but then he flips me over on my knees. Wrapping his hand around my throat, he hauls me up so my back presses into his chest.

His fingers slightly squeeze my neck when he realigns himself and plunges back up into me, my moan silenced by his hold. His free hand snakes down, pinching my nipple before sliding lower and brushing over my clit. My hips punch forward in a silent plea, which makes him bite down on the side of my neck, sucking the pain away.

366

Two fingers press down hard on my aching bud, rubbing quick circles over it. Sparks shoot behind my eyes, and my hands fly up to hold onto his forearm that chains me to his body.

The ache deep in my belly grows, his breathing becomes ragged behind me. "You're going to take everything I have to give you," he forces out.

Straining my neck up, his fingers loosen just enough for me to speak. "I want every last drop."

"*Fuck*, little demon. It's yours. It's all fucking yours."

His pace picks up, thrusting into me savagely, putting more pressure on my clit as the tip of his cock hits that spot deep within.

My breath hitches, getting lodged in my throat, the muscles in my stomach tighten, and tingles lick down my spine as my orgasm crests.

"Draven!" I scream.

I fall, thrown over into a sea of ecstasy. My pussy grips him so tightly I lose my breath, sucking him deeper inside before I start to pulse around him. He groans, biting into my shoulder with stinging pleasure as he finds his release. His hips jerk behind me as warmth fills my core. I feel him swell and pump his orgasm inside me and that almost sends me into a second one myself.

The air pulses around us as our chests rise and fall in sync, both slowly coming down from the blinding high. He lowers his hand from my throat, resting both hands on my hips, keeping me tightly pressed to him as he remains buried inside.

I slightly shift and the movement has me immediately clenching around him again with a whimper.

He groans, his body tensing behind me, but I can't help myself. I rotate my hips in a rhythm, feeling my body tighten and a new ache building in response. His nose trails up the curve of my neck, breathing me in. He's still hard inside me, and he slowly starts to move his hips with mine.

"I need—" I start to say before he cuts me off.

"You need me to pleasure your body over and over again. This is just the beginning, little demon, and I don't plan to waste a second of it where you aren't screaming my name."

Flipping us so he's on his back and I'm on top, he guides my hips to sink down on him. "Take your pleasure, Emma," he says in a softer tone. "I'm not going anywhere."

And I do. I scream his name repeatedly, even after the sun wakes along the horizon.

EPILOGUE

Emma

One Year Later

*W*armth blankets my body as I wake to Draven's arms and legs curled over me, his entire front pressed into my back. This past year has been deliciously addicting and the hardness of him poking into my backside is proof of that.

The snowfall outside the mountains is light this morning. The sun shining against them looks like glitter falling from the sky. Very slowly, I untangle myself from Draven's sleepy embrace, taking the sheet with me to wrap around my bare body, and pad toward the cave's opening.

In a couple days, this cave will be a place where Draven and I sneak off to and visit from time to time. But it's time I take the throne as queen, with Cora as my right hand. Draven said he will rule by my side, passing down his crown of Asiza to Emil.

Together we will be king and queen, and the thought makes my heart swell with everything we can change to make the world better. And those haunted palace walls will be painted with new memories, layered with strokes of love and family.

Already, the chosen wyverns have found their loved ones that have been grieving them, starting life anew. And for those that came back to empty homes, we welcomed them into ours. The palace always had so many empty rooms, but now they can be filled with a new kind of family.

The people of Deyadrum have been welcoming to the shifters living among them again, bowing in respect when they pass one another for the way they fought to protect them. It's easy to see they mean no harm when there aren't any vile lies being spread about them from those whose only love is power.

There has also been a lightness to Draven since being reunited with his people. The first couple months we came to this cave was us being solely consumed with desire for each other. We still are, but the desperate need started to fade long enough for us to leave the bed, and we began adventuring. Whether flying just the two of us, or alongside fellow wyverns, Draven took me to every court. He let me freely explore each shop and every inch of land, while showing me all the things I've never been able to see.

As I stare off at the snow-capped mountaintops, strong arms wrap around my waist. I turn my head to nuzzle against Draven's cheek, loving the slight scrape of his beard that dusts his jaw. When I peer up at him, his smile stuns me to the spot, his dimple on full display and I smile back, still not believing that this is my life now. That *he* is my life.

He grabs hold of my left hand, the one with our mate mark that now carries a ring he had made for us. His is a circle that represents the full moon and mine is a crescent, and when you put our rings together, they fit perfectly in place to one another. I had cried when he surprised me with them during a small celebration with our closest friends and family.

He twists the ring around my finger, always playing with it because he says he loves the sight of it decorating my hand. Which is good, because I'm never taking it off.

His lips brush the curve of my neck, sliding his hands down to palm over my stomach, causing my heart to flutter. "Our little angel," he says softly.

I lace my fingers over his, looking down to where a second heartbeat lives inside me. "Our little angel," I repeat on a single breath.

Looking back out to the frozen sea, I can't hold back the single tear that slips free. Because as I stand in the arms of my home, with our future growing inside me, I realize for the first time in my life, I'm finally free and I have my very own family.

THE END

BONUS EPILOGUE

Kye

One moment, Emma's tear-streaked face is looking down at me, and the next, I'm sucked into utter darkness before waking up to twin suns shining down at me. This must be where a soul goes after death.

Everything is too…perfect. Vibrant in color with a light shimmering over every inch. With unsure steps, I start walking through the lush, grassy field, making my way towards the trees in the distance. As I near the border of the forest, a figure stands between two oaks. Her hair is streaked with russet red strands, and two skinny braids catch on the breeze. Her golden skin shimmers even beneath the covering of the trees.

She slowly takes a single step toward me, causing my feet to root to the spot. An ivory dress dances over her curves, the hem getting picked up by the wind, showing me a peek of the skin above her knees. Another step toward me, and I suddenly find myself closing the distance.

Green flecks glimmer in her eyes, deep and radiant.

My lips part as I become entranced by her, watching the way her lips move and how her delicate hand is held out in front of her.

She laughs, and the sound brings me back into focus as I shake my head to clear the spell I must have been lost in. It's only then that I realize her lips were moving, speaking to me, and her hand is between us so I can shake it.

"I–I'm sorry," I say, quickly and with a furrow of my brows. What the ever-loving fuck is wrong with me? I haven't been dead for more than a few minutes and I'm already becoming a stammering, frozen mess in front of a female.

"I'm Elira." She nudges her hand higher between us and instead of shaking it, I pull her hand up so I can press my lips to the top. A spark flares against my lips, causing my eyes to widen and my heart to hammer in my chest. Her cheeks tint a light shade of pink when I hold my lips against her skin, looking down at her.

I pull away from her hand, take a step closer, and pick up one of her braids between my fingers, twisting it. "You're my mate," I say it so softly, I'm afraid she won't hear. Afraid I could be wrong, even though I can feel it in the marrow of my bones.

But she does hear because that smile fades and instead, a longing fills her eyes as she glances up at me, biting her lip. "Some find it harder to recognize their fated mate in the afterlife if they never met when they were alive," she trails off, tilting her head as her eyes take in every inch of my face.

"I've stood here every day, waiting for my mate to join me." She twists her head to look out to the field as if she's ashamed she's been waiting for her mate to die. "So many have entered the afterlife, and I've felt…nothing." Those green eyes snap up to mine again. "Until you."

Smiling, I let her braid fall as I brush the tips of my fingers over the delicate skin of her face. "I'm Kye."

She bites her lip to hold back a laugh and I do the same. I'm not going to shame her for hoping her mate dies so she can be with him, because right now, I'm feeling fucking lucky that it was me.

Darting my eyes back and forth between hers, I let the silence settle between us. The way I feel more alive while dead is just pure fucking irony. The way the blood in my veins hums as if I was still alive at just the touch of her, and how hard my pulse is racing.

"All my life I have never felt what I'm feeling at this moment." I accidentally let my thought slip free and speak it, but I'm glad I did because her smile is radiant.

"And what was your life like?" she asks.

I look off into the distance for a moment as I settle on the truth. "My life was worse than a death sentence." I sigh and go on, wanting to explain my past to her. "My parents were accused of rebelling many years ago, and to save their heads, I offered up my life to serve the king that was ruling. Every day, I had to fight my instincts to slit his throat with every order he gave that I disagreed with. But my parents' lives were on the line."

I think back to every command I had to follow, and some were so bad that I couldn't sleep for days. Only one thing helped make living as someone's puppet more bearable. "But the daughter of that same king became a lifeline. The first person to make living in that hellhole not as bad. She became someone I truly cared for, as if she was a sister I never had."

I glance back down at Elira, and she's watching me with interest, hanging onto every word as I spill more than she asked for. I smile at her, loving that she wants to know about me.

With a shrug, I continue. "After that, life became better, and I got to feel what it was like to be a free male again and have friends who mean the world to me. But there was still something missing, I just couldn't put my finger on it."

She tilts her head, smiling softly. "Maybe that something was a someone?"

Swallowing roughly, I clench my jaw and nod. "I believe so."

A comfortable silence settles between us, but then I ask, "What was your life like?"

She inhales nice and slow, quirking her lips to the side. "My life…" she trails off, seeming to get lost in memories for a moment before looking up into my eyes. "My life ended a long time ago," she says softly.

I brush a loose strand of hair behind her ear as I wait for her to continue.

"My family died while I was young when our small village was raided. I hid, trying to hold my little brother back with me as our parents fought, but he ran out to them with arms wide open for a hug." She swallows roughly. "He didn't understand the danger, and it all happened so fast."

She sighs, shaking her head. "So, my life has been…lonely. I lived secluded from any village, in fear of another raid, and just let the days pass as I learned how to take care of myself."

She cups her small hand to my jaw, letting her fingers dig into my beard. "That's why I've been waiting and standing out here alone; it is not new to me. But the hope of meeting my mate, knowing I will never be alone again, and having someone I can care for wholeheartedly, makes it all worth it."

Her eyes bounce back and forth between mine, her chest rising and falling faster.

On pure instinct, I dip my head, lightly pressing my lips to hers. She won't ever be alone, not with me. She sucks in a gasp before pushing up on her toes to press her mouth firmer against mine.

That alone has me growling and swiping my tongue over the seam of her lips, asking for her to let me in. But I don't need to ask, because with one swipe, she's already willingly opening for me. Tangling her tongue with mine, deepening the kiss as we become more desperate for the other.

I'm lost in her.

Our hands pull on each other's clothes, as this bond grows stronger. Somehow, I have her back pinned up to a tree and I'm so far gone I don't know how we ended up here. My hand grabs the back of her knee, pulling it up as the hem of her dress lifts, too, and I press the ridge of my hard cock to her center. And fuck, she is wet. The only barrier is my pants and the thin scrap of lace covering her.

She rocks over my length as I swell against the seams, and our teeth clash as I devour her. But I pull back, keeping my lips barely touching hers as we share the same breath. "Not here," I rush out. "I need you spread out, wet, and ready on a bed for me for our first time. Where no one can see what's mine, and what I plan to do to you."

My fingers grip her thigh possessively, loving the feeling of having her silky skin clutched in my hand.

She leans forward, pressing her lips to my chest. "Then later, you will have your way with me, and after…" The tip of her index finger swirls playfully over my shirt. "I get to have my way with you."

A deep groan falls from my lips on a drawn-out breath. "You will be the death of me."

"Then good thing you are already dead."

Fuck. In that case, she can kill me over and over again for eternity.

His secrets were unknown,
While the shadows remained his home.
Left alone in a concave of his own making.
The truth of his words I started craving.
Deception always danced with me in the dark,
Until he swooped in and left his mark.

- Ali Stuebbe

ACKNOWLEDGMENTS

Wow. I believe I am still in shock that this book is complete. To be honest, I didn't know where this book was going to go, but I knew how I wanted it to end. To say this was a challenging journey is putting it lightly. This book put me on a flimsy boat in a rough sea. Many times, I began to drift off course. There was no sympathy in the waves. No reprieve. I learned to push back a little harder, to not give up so my characters can have the ending they have been waiting for. The ending that their hearts deserve. Towards the end, I found my writing to slow. Not because I didn't know what to write or what my characters would say… It was my heart refusing to let them go. This duology is bittersweet. My characters get to live together forever, and although they have unknowingly healed me, I will only be a blip in their life. My chapter in their life ends the moment I close the book. But their happily ever after wasn't achieved from me alone. I had an incredible group of people who helped.

To Chris, Melanie, and Anthony— you are all my biggest supporters and number one fans. My life would be colorless without you three. Chris, you are a true book husband, the way you tell everyone about the stories I wrote as if you were on top of a mountain screaming how proud you are of me. And I love this beautiful, adventurous life we have created.

To my family, thank you for checking in on me when I go silent. My hermit instincts kick in when I become overwhelmed, and your phones calls helped me crawl back out of the hole I burrowed into.

To Stevi, my incredible editor. Thank you for putting up with all my chaos and having to reread Aiden's death scene three times because I kept rewriting it. That is true love. I am so appreciative of all the wisdom you share and how you help me brainstorm if I become stuck. You always offer the most encouraging words, and I can never say thank you enough to truly encompass what that means to me. Vous méritez que tous vos souhaits se réalisent. Merci, Stevi.

To Fay, my best friend. Thank you. For all that you do. For laughing with me, crying with me, the late-night video chats, and everything in-between. You have been with me every step of the way for this duology. You are the one I can count on no matter what, and you have a permanent place in my life. Even when we are old and grey, I know you will be by my side while we continue to read spicy books and laugh through the bullshit life throws our way. As Kevin Hart says: "The day that we sign up and say that we best friends, that means that my bullshit is your bullshit. And your bullshit is my bullshit." Forever.

To my alpha readers, Shannon, and Shaunna. You read this book when it was in its roughest form and words can't express the gratitude I have for that because I *know* there were crazy errors and that the story needed a lot more detail. Alpha reading is not for the faint of heart since you are the first set of eyes to look at the manuscript, which is why I cherish you both so much and all your feedback. You both are so kind and wonderful. Thank you, loves.

To my beta readers, Antonia, Christin, Courtney, and Dallas. You powered through the manuscript, and I loved reading all your comments and suggestions. You four are amazing and I'm grateful for the way you helped shape this book for its final stage. Thank you so, so, sooo much.

To Callie, my proofreader. You are so sweet and kind. I appreciate you working with me to polish this book so it's perfect for release day. Thank you so much for making this part of editing a smooth process and stress free. You are beyond amazing.

To Jaqueline, my cover designer. Once again, you nailed it. The talent you have and the way you listen to any changes I ask. It's amazing to work with you, and you created the most beautiful masterpiece to reflect this the story told in this book. Thank you so much, and I am so in awe of you.

To Zoe and Meri, you both are amazing artists. The pieces you drew for this book still have me bowing down on my knees. I'm so insanely obsessed, and I know readers will be as well. You both took the idea I asked and brought it to life to the point that it gave me chills. I am in love. Thank you both for working with me again.

To my readers, you are my light. My reason for writing. And why I won't ever stop. The fact that you took a chance on me and immersed yourself in my story means everything. I am forever grateful, and I finished this book for you. You have cheered me on for this duology and waited patiently for this second book. It makes my heart flutter with affection for all the messages, posts, reels, and reviews you have created. Thank you from the bottom of my heart, and I will continue to write so many new stories for you.

ABOUT THE AUTHOR

Ali Stuebbe grew up in the state of Ohio, near the city of Cleveland. At the age of 21, she married, becoming a military spouse, and has called three other states home. She studied English Literature at Cleveland State University and American Public University. She began writing her debut novel when she grew confident in her writing and felt ready to bring this story to life. When she's not writing, she can be found at the gym or sitting on the couch with her nose in a book and a large coffee in her hand. Ali is the author of Blood of Desiderium, and currently lives in Texas with her loving husband and two beautiful children.

To get updates on future books, follow me!

    Website: www.alimariestuebbe.co

    Instagram: @bookedbyali

    TikTok: @bookedbyali

    You can also find me on Goodreads!

THANK YOU

I cannot express the gratitude I have for you joining me on this journey and reading The Divide duology. I'm only here because of you.

Be ready, because I have more book ideas in my head that are desperate to be written and read by you.

As always, it would mean the world to me if you could leave a rating/review on Goodreads or Amazon because that helps tremendously for new authors.

Thank again for reading not only my story, but Emma and Draven's.

Made in the USA
Columbia, SC
02 January 2025